TENDER TEMPTATION

Elizabeth looked into his eyes. Their mysterious depths fascinated her. Again she felt that awareness. That inexorable pull. The very air seemed to vibrate with a seductive insistence.

She sensed where it all was leading. She could not deny her attraction to this man. She thought of how her past had held so little happiness; how her future was so uncertain. Why not live for the moment? Why should she not have some happiness to remember?

In one swift motion she was in his arms, so close to his hard chest that she could feel the beat of his heart echoing the urgent pounding of her own. A new warmth began to flow through her, a warmth like that of the brandy and wine, yet infinitely more pleasurable. Why not? Why not? cried her heart.

She swayed in his arms as the room began to revolve around her and made a grasp at his shoulders to steady herself. The room stopped spinning.

"Simon," she murmured, and he could read the passionate invitation in her eyes, "will you take me to bed?"

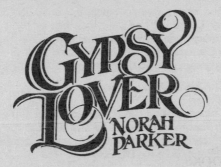

GYPSY LOVER

NORAH PARKER

ZEBRA BOOKS
KENSINGTON PUBLISHING CORP.

ZEBRA BOOKS

are published by

Kensington Publishing Corp.
475 Park Avenue South
New York, NY 10016

First printing: August 1987

Printed in the United States of America

Prologue 1645

She was so tired. The labor had gone on now for fifteen hours. Shuddering from another ravaging pain, Sarah's slim fingers tightened on the gnarled hand on her old nurse. Throughout the long night, Nana had been crooning reassuringly to her, "Not much longer, love. Not much longer."

Did all women suffer such pain? Sarah wondered. If so, why did they continue to bear children? What a terrible price to pay for a few moments of pleasure.

Oh, Thomas, my love ... Thomas ... Thomas ...

In the dimly lit bedchamber, with its dark Tudor paneling, all the heavy old furniture had been pushed back from the big canopied bed. Sarah's eyes softened as she recalled the sweet bliss of an afternoon when she and Thomas had made love in this same bed, the deep rose hangings made aglow by the afternoon sunshine. He had been so gentle . . . so adoring . . . She could almost hear his warm voice softly quoting:

"Shall I compare thee to a summer's day?

Thou art more lovely and more temperate."

What a sweet difference his lovemaking had been from Ralph's quick and rough coupling. Tears of sorrow stung Sarah's tired eyes. She remembered Thomas murmuring. "We must put a lifetime of loving into these few weeks." It was almost as if he had known.

The news had come the day before of the king's defeat at Naseby. Both Thomas and Ralph had fought in the battle, but only Ralph had remained alive afterwards. Thomas had died from a deep chest wound. When word had reached Sarah, she had wanted to die, too, but instead this premature labor had begun.

Sarah's whole body convulsed from a new wave of pain. Her knuckles turned white as she clung even harder to Nana's hand. Perspiration sprang out on her small, contorted face. Taking a damp cloth in her free hand, the old nurse gently wiped Sarah's forehead. She ached for this child she had raised from infancy, who had been forced into a loveless marriage with a man twice her age. When, the previous autumn, a handsome young man had arrived at Neville Hall to join his lordship's hunting party, was it any wonder Sarah had fallen in love with him? Was it any wonder he stayed on, when his lordship had been called away to join his king? It had not seemed unreasonable at the time, but now Nana cursed herself for not realizing what was bound to happen.

From her stool below the bed, Mistress Bedloe, the midwife, spoke out. "Bear down, milady! Bear down hard!"

Another pain wracked Sarah's weary body as she crouched in the way she had been told, her knees up to her swollen belly. It was all so coarse and crude, she thought. She felt like a cow, as low, ugly grunts escaped her lips.

"More! Bear down more!"

"Dear God, I cannot . . ." Sarah groaned in agony. "Oh, Thomas! Thomas!" She screamed aloud, as the most excrutiating pain of all consumed her whole being and she felt something being torn from between her loins.

She was unaware that she had called out her lover's name but only her dear, trusted Nana was aware of it, the midwife being too busy with the birth to pay the slightest heed to her cries.

" 'Tis a daughter, ye have," Mistress Bedloe said now, as a wail went up from the newly born child she had slapped soundly on its tiny bottom. She held out the slippery infant to the nurse to bathe and swaddle and Nana gently released Sarah's hand to take the babe in her arms.

"A bonny child," she admired, but Sarah did not hear her. Another devastating pain had made her cry out again. What could be happening? Hadn't she suffered enough? She felt the midwife's hands kneading her belly.

7

"There be another," the woman announced, "and 'tis coming fast."

Hurrying with the babe she was bathing, Nana wrapped it quickly in a shawl and placed it in the old wooden cradle which stood waiting beside the bed. Despite Sarah's desire to have only Mistress Bedloe and herself present, Nana now wished she had had the foresight to have called in one of the maids to help them.

"Bare down again, milady."

"Oh, please . . . no!"

"Just once more for me, love," Nana's quiet voice soothed. "Once more now. Harder! That's it! That's it!"

Sarah caught the words . . . "Another daughter. Why they be identical!" . . . before completely exhausted by her efforts, she fell back against the soft feathery pillows and drifted off into merciful oblivion.

When she opened her eyes, it was to see her old nurse smiling down at her as she slipped an arm beneath her shoulders and lifting her up, pressed the rim of a goblet to her lips. The contents tasted cool and sweet and Sarah swallowed the liquid gratefully.

" 'Tis all over, child," Nana told her. "Ye have given birth to two lovely daughters."

"May I see them?" Sarah whispered.

"In a moment. First, let me wash thee and change thy night dress. We managed to give thee fresh sheets while ye slept."

"I feel so weak," Sarah murmured as Nana bathed her and dressed her in a clean gown.

"Ye have been through a long labor, child, but ye be young and will soon regain thy strength." She began to brush Sarah's long fair hair, but the young woman impatiently pushed the brush away.

"Please, Nana, my babies ... I want to see them."

The nurse nodded, but before she turned away from the bed, Sarah saw the light leave her eyes. Immediately sensing something was the matter, Sarah was filled with sudden fear and struggled to sit up.

"What is it, Nana? What is wrong with my babies?"

"Nothing is wrong, child. They be small, but they be strong and healthy."

"Still, there *is* something, isn't there? Sarah insisted. "Nana, please tell me!"

She saw the look that passed between the nurse and the midwife who was busy gathering up her belongings.

"Perhaps 'tis best that ye know right away," Nana sighed. Reaching into the cradle beside the bed, she picked up one of the bundles and placed the sleeping babe in Sarah's arms. Gently, the young woman pulled back the shawl which covered the little form.

"Why, she is fair ... like me," Sarah smiled down at the soft, pale fuzz on the top of the baby's head. Slowly, she began to examine her daughter all over. She seemed so tiny and yet so perfect. And then Sarah's eyes fell upon the child's left hand. She opened it slowly. It was obvious, even in one so small. The baby bore a vivid birthmark on her tiny palm!

Sarah let out a muffled gasp. "Oh, God in Heaven! The mark of Thynne!"

"Aye, love," Nana murmured, " 'tis said to have gone down in that family for generations."

"Thomas had the mark." Sarah had turned quite pale. "Do both the babes possess them?"

"No. Only this one."

"Oh, Nana, if His Lordship sees it, he will know he was not the father," Sarah moaned.

"Aye," the old nurse nodded. "It could not be hid from him for long."

"But what can we do?" Sarah despaired, her eyes filling with tears.

"Hush now," Nana murmured, lowering her voice. "While ye slept, I took Mistress Bedloe into our confidence."

Sarah glanced at her in alarm. "Was that wise? Can she be trusted to hold her tongue?"

"I believe the promise of a pension will insure her silence."

"A pension? Yes ... Yes, of course," Sarah's brows furrowed. "I could sell some of my jewelry..."

"I can have that arranged," Nana said, looking hard at her young mistress, "but ye must realize there be only one way to solve this dilemma." An expression of sadness crossed her wrinkled face. " 'Twill not be easy for thee, child."

Sarah stared wordlessly at her old nurse. She was struggling to make her weary brain grasp the full implications of the situation.

"Ye must part with the babe ye hold in thy arms."

Fiercely Sarah drew the child closer to her. "I cannot let her go," she cried. "There *must* be another way."

"Nay, love, there be none. Ye must give up the babe," Nana said sorrowfully. "No one outside this room knows of her existence. They will think only one child was born to thee."

"But —"

"Mistress Bedloe knows of a childless noble-woman in the next county who has tried time and again to carry a babe to full term. Yesterday, she was present when the lady lost yet another one. Stillborn it was. Mistress Bedloe feels confident the lady will receive thy child joyously into her home and raise her as she would her own. The lady and gentleman are good and kind. Thy child will be well looked after and dearly loved."

Not looking at the babe, Sarah suddenly thrust the child into her nurse's arms. "Then, take her," she choked. "Take her away quickly, but never speak to me of her again. I could not bear it. I will try my best to forget she ever existed."

Chapter One

The annual St. Margaret's Fair, outlawed during the time of the Puritans, had been revived by King Charles II. In September of 1663, the weather was warm and pleasant and crowds had gathered long before the Lord Mayor, with great pomp and ceremony, officially opened the fair.

Tents and booths had been set up all around the fair grounds and their owners loudly hawked their wares over the noise of blaring drums, flutes, and screeching fiddles striving mightily to drown each other out.

The noisy, jostling throng made the rounds from booth to booth, exclaiming over the juggler and the contortionist, the tumbler, and the magician.

"This way! I pray thee, worthy sirs!" a hoarse voice bawled. "See a sword of steel swallowed before thy very eyes!"

"This way!" another shouted. "This way to see

the two-headed calf!"

The Punch and Judy show drew the children, while the womenfolk flocked to the booths offering ribbons and laces, colorful embroidery and sweet-smelling sachets and pomanders. Appetites were whetted by the food stalls where minced pies and meat pasties, still warm from the oven were sold, honey and cinnamon cakes, sugar plums and gingerbread. A wild boar was being roasted over a large spit and over smaller fires pigeons and capons were turning a golden brown. There were steamed oysters and clams, lobster and stewed crabs. Large barrels of ale, cider, and wine were being readily tapped to ease the parched throats of the noisy, merry crowd.

What a motley mixture they were. Soberly dressed merchants and bankers with gold chains, mingled with farmers and servants in serviceable homespun, with here and there the silks and velvets and plumed hats of ladies and gentlemen of rank and fashion, masked to hide their identities.

It was a paradise for every rogue and criminal. Mountebanks flourished amongst those offering games of chance and skill. Pickpockets found easy pickings in the crushing throng which swarmed around the cockfights and bearbaiting.

Flocks of Londoners were ferried across the Thames to partake of the many pleasures too long denied by the long faced Cromwellites who had favored abstinence and piety. Restraint had been gladly thrown off. The social pattern had made an about face in England. Eager to follow their new king's example, old virtues and conventions were abandoned and wanton pleasure-seeking had become the vogue.

As evening approached, more ribald entertainments were offered to the crowds that swarmed to St. Margaret's Fair. The music became louder and the dancing wilder. Prostitutes tantalized and often openly displayed their charms. Thieves and pimps and cutthroats plied their dishonest trade more easily amongst the growing shadows.

In twilight, the black tent that stood off by itself at the edge of the fairground seemed even more menacing. Covered with mystical markings and signs of the stars and moon, it belonged to a gypsy fortune teller who, it was rumored, could tell at a glance all about a person and what his future held. There was talk that she was *chovihani* — a gypsy witch — for when she had appeared at Bartholemew Fair a young gallant who had laughed at her warnings had died in a duel the very next day!

Outside the dark tent, a skinny young lad, wearing a long black cloak and a conical hat, patterned with glittering astrological signs, called out. "This way, noble lords and ladies! Let Marta the Soothsayer evoke the spirits and read thy future!"

Two hooded and masked figures glanced furtively at the tent as they moved nearer. The

15

silken hems of their gowns could be seen beneath their cloaks, as well as their dainty embroidered slippers. Two young gentlewomen bent on adventure, the young lad thought, and beckoned to them.

They were now only a few yards from the ominous-looking tent, but suddenly the taller one stopped, grasping the other's arm.

"I've changed my mind, Frances," she said, her voice trembling a little. "Pray let us return to our friends."

"And not have our fortunes read? Why, 'tis the very reason we came to the fair."

"But the hour is growing late and the play will have started."

"Pooh! There are many acts to it." Frances leaned closer to her friend. "You're not afraid are you, Angela?" she taunted.

"Of course not, but if we aren't back within the hour, we will be found out."

"We won't be found out, I promise you," she was assured. "Even if we were, I'm certain 'twould be worth it."

Still her friend hesitated.

"Do you not wish to know whom you will marry?" Frances prodded.

"I already know that. I was promised to His Grace, the Duke of Claridge when I was a child."

"But you know little about him."

"I know he has finally returned to England and will be arriving at Court very soon."

" 'Twas not what I meant," Frances gave an exasperated sigh. "Aren't you the least bit curious to learn if he is handsome and if he will fall in love with you?"

Angela considered. "Well, I — "

"Of course you are and the gypsy is supposed to be uncannily accurate," Frances urged.

"There are some who say she is a witch," the girl whispered, shivering slightly at the thought.

"Oh, Angela, do you really believe in witches?" the other teased. "Have you ever seen one riding on a broomstick?"

"I believe in evil," Angela said solemnly, "and witchcraft is evil. We are not supposed to see into our future."

"But what fun to try," Frances laughed. "Oh, come on now, don't be such a little goose." She grasped her friend's hand and dragged her toward the tent.

Clad in a bright purplish-red costume, only the gypsy's eyes were visible between a veil which fell from the bridge of her nose to her shoulders and a black linen coif, which covered her forehead and hair. She sat behind a small ebony table, on which stood a single candle. The gypsy's bangles and long golden earrings flashed in its dim light. The air was smokey with incense.

"Come in, pretty ones, let Marta foretell thy future," the gypsy crooned in a low, husky voice.

Having lifted the tent flap, the two wavered in indecision, their hearts beating wildly.

17

"Come forward. Don't be shy."

Frances was the first to move, although her urge to bolt was now almost as strong as her friend's. Apprehensively, she entered and seated herself on a low stool before the table.

"Thy hand, child," said the hoarse voice.

Frances held out a trembling white hand and the gypsy grasped it firmly with a dark skinned one that was almost covered by the long sleeve of her bright costume.

"Ah," the gypsy whispered, looking at the palm before her, "I see ye are inclined to be impetuous, child. Even reckless."

Frances gave a little embarrassed nod of her head.

"Ye must be more careful in the ways of the heart. Do not rush into marriage. Ye have yet to meet one who is worthy of thee."

"Oh, but I have," Frances cried out impulsively, and then she blushed, for she had not even told her friend about the gentleman who had lately singled her out.

The gypsy shook her head. "He is not for thee. He can be faithful to no woman. Ye must wait, child. Wait and the right one will come."

"But how long will that take?" Frances pouted. She hated to wait for anything.

"Weeks ... months ..." the gypsy shrugged. "Who can say?"

Frances's face fell. This was not what she had come to hear.

18

"Ye must be patient. Ye enjoy pleasures, child and thy head is easily turned. This ardent gentleman whose eye ye have caught. He will offer thee jewels and riches . . . but never his name. Ye must refuse him, though ye be sorely tempted."

"And if I fall in love with him? What then?"

"Ye fall in and out of love easily, child."

"You think me fickle?" Frances was clearly piqued.

"Nay, only young and impulsive. Thy true love will come if only ye will be patient," the gypsy repeated her message.

She was silent then and Frances had the temerity to ask, "Is that all?"

The gypsy put the tips of her fingers to her temples, and closed her eyes. She appeared to be almost in a trance. Frances decided she did not wish to hear any more and rose quickly to her feet, opening her small embroidered purse to lay some shillings on the table.

" 'Tis your turn now," she turned to whisper to Angela, but her friend had vanished from the tent.

Taking to her heels, so as to put as much distance as she could between herself and the unnerving gypsy, Angela rejoined her friends who were watching a performance of Shakespeare's "A Midsummer Night's Dream" in another tent. Several minutes later, Frances slipped into the empty seat beside her, casting a disdainful glance in Angela's direction.

Angela did not care. There had been something about the gypsy which had disturbed her greatly. She had felt herself being drawn in some inexplicable way toward the woman. It frightened and upset her. Even worse, there was a feeling of familiarity, as if she knew the gypsy; as if there were an amity between them. It made no sense at all, but Angela had known, instinctively, that she must never let that gypsy tell her fortune.

Chapter Two

His Grace, the Duke of Claridge, was over six feet tall, with broad shoulders and the muscular body of an athlete. Although his gray eyes often had an amused twinkle in them, his usual expression was slightly cynical. He wore no periwig. Curling, dark hair fell thickly to his formidable shoulders and a dark mustache covered his upper lip. Women thought him wickedly handsome. Especially when his white teeth flashed into an insolent grin.

Tonight, his large frame was wrapped in a long, charcoal gray cloak and his face was masked, as were those of his boisterous, Cavalier friends. They had been celebrating his return to London and were, for the most part, well into their cups when they decided to partake of the entertainment of St. Margaret's Fair.

Making the rounds of the booths, the group became more raucous and noisy as the evening

21

wore on. Ribald jests were made, followed by great bursts of laughter, as they approached the dirt circle set up for the cockfights.

Only two men in the merry group appeared to be still halfway sober. Because of his size, Claridge's capacity for drink was larger than most, and his friend, Lord Musgrove, had been warned by his physician to cut down on his intake of rich food and drink or develop the incapacitating gout that greatly plagued his father.

Waiting now for the cockfighting to commence, Musgrove clapped Claridge on the shoulder.

"Ah, Simon, 'tis good to have you home."

" 'Tis good to be home," Claridge smiled, "and to see old friends again. Still," he lowered his voice, "I must confess to you, John, that I've actually been in the country these four months past, straightening out my estates. I put off coming back to court."

His friend stared at him. "Put off . . . but why?"

"Marriage," Claridge chuckled. " 'Twas my father's wish before he died. Pledged me to a young chit and I know well that our king will make me honor that pledge. Charles reminded me of it, in fact, while we were with him in France."

"Devil take it! Have you ever seen the girl?"

"Never."

"Is she at Whitehall?"

"Aye, she was presented at Hampton Court this summer. The Queen has even made her one of her

22

ladies in waiting."

"Then surely I have made her acquaintance. What is the lady's name?"

"Lady Angela Neville. the Earl of Westbury's daughter."

"Good God!" Musgrove slapped his thigh. "The Snow Maid!"

"The Snow Maid?"

"That's what we've nicknamed her. Pure as the driven snow, she be. A real beauty, Simon. Fair hair, blue eyes, and well formed, but cold enough to freeze your very blood." Musgrove gave an expressive shiver.

"You realize you're offering me a challenge, friend," Claridge grinned at him. "Think you I cannot melt that coldness?"

"If anyone could . . ." Musgrove laughed, "but I thought you preferred females with more experience."

"That I do, old friend. That I do. Virgins have never appealed to me."

"Then I suggest you come with me," Musgrove urged. "Forget the cockfight. You've won more than your share of wagers tonight. There is a little gypsy dancer in a tent across the way who—"

"Perhaps later, John. Right now I mean to consult the famous witch. Are you with me?"

"Not me," Musgrove shook his head. "The last time I consulted a soothsayer I was told I'd have a dozen children. 'Tis why I've remained a bachelor."

"You remain a bachelor solely because you hate responsibility of any kind," Claridge laughed. "Why, your by blows have probably reached that number long since."

Musgrove's reply was lost as a loud roar went up from ringside. Two already bloodied cocks had been released and pushed into the center of the torch-illumined ring.

The big man seated before her seemed to fill the whole of the little tent and yet there was nothing heavy about him. He had, in fact, seemed as lithe and graceful as a cat when he had ducked beneath the flap and strolled into the tent, sweeping off his large, plumed hat. Now the soft candlelight caught the gleam of his thick, dark hair. His cloak had parted enough for her to see the burgundy velvet doublet beneath and the glint of his sword. The gypsy stared at him long and hard, finding herself wishing he would remove his mask so she could see his whole face.

"Are you going to tell my fortune or not?" he drawled.

"Of course," she said hastily, forgetting for a moment to speak in the low, hoarse voice she normally used. She reached for his hand, noticing as she turned it over that it was not as smooth as most of the gallants who came to see her. Nor did he seem to possess their foppish manners. Instead, he appeared cool and hard and perhaps even a little dangerous.

She examined the lines of his palm and her voice took on its usual rasp. "Ye are a soldier, sir, or have been until recently."

He lifted a cynical brow. "An easy thing to guess with peace only a few years old."

"Still, ye have fought longer than most."

He affirmed this with a slight nod of his head.

"In France, I believe." She had recognized the intricate French lace at his throat.

He made no acknowledgement.

"And now ye have returned to reclaim your estates and," she peered closer to his palm, "to marry."

She caught his low intake of breath and knew she had guessed correctly.

"The lady is very beautiful, but she is not easily won." She paused and looked at him wonderingly.

"Go on," he urged. Although he would never admit it, he was finding this little gypsy very intriguing.

"There is another lady," she murmured, while the small hand that held his large one trembled a little. Why was this man's nearness disturbing her so? "She is also very beautiful and ye have known her for some time." Looking up at him, she saw him staring at her intently. Their eyes met and something odd happened in her chest. A brief catch, a tightening that caused her to drop her gaze and try to steady her breath. "Intimately," she finished, her cheeks growing hot beneath her veil.

He grinned. "I know well of whom you speak."

"Ye must beware of her!" the gypsy's voice rose in warning. "Beware, sir! She is a very jealous woman and could do thee much harm."

He burst out laughing. It was a deep, full-bodied sound. "Do you expect a soldier who has faced death a hundred times to be frightened of one lone female?"

"I only tell thee what I see, sir," she said tersely.

"Aye, and what you have already seen has been quite uncanny," he admitted. "So uncanny, in fact, that I wonder if one of my friends has not told you of me."

"You doubt my powers?"

He watched her eyes flare slightly. "You can persuade me otherwise if you can tell me something known only to me," he smiled with lazy good humor.

She shrugged and again examined his palm. "I will tell thee that ye are happiest when in the country." (Those rough hands speak for themselves.) "Court life bores thee. Ye hate the affectation and the present foppish fashions." (No periwig, no painted beauty marks, or ribbon-bedecked clothes.) "Ye are inclined to be tena-

26

cious when ye want something." (A stubborn jaw.) "And a little cynical." (That sardonic smile.) "Especially of women." (A mere guess.)

"Really? Well, I am no longer cynical of you," he shook his head in disbelief. "In fact, I apologize for mocking you. You possess much knowledge." He rose from the stool and reaching into a pocket, dropped several gold coins onto the table before him. "I only wonder how one so young obtained such wisdom?"

"S—so young?"

"I, too, am observant," he grinned, but before she could reply, he had raised the tent flap and disappeared into the darkness outside the tent.

The gypsy sat staring after him. It was her voice, she chastened herself. She should have been more careful. For surely it was the only way he could have known she was not the old gypsy soothsayer she pretended to be.

Getting to her feet, she stretched her cramped muscles. Sitting hunched over the little table all day, although profitable, was most uncomfortable. She was tired. Despite their fear of her, many had come to have their futures foretold that day. The intent concentration took a great deal from her and the last one had quite unnerved her. She would tell no more fortunes tonight.

Lifting the tent flap, she informed the young lad who hawked for her that she was finished for the day. Catching the gold coin she tossed him, he grinned and handing the cloak and hat to her, set off eagerly in the direction of the refreshment booths.

She returned to where the big man had sat on the low stool before the table. Who was he? she wondered. Why had his presence upset her? She could still feel the warmth of his hand, the intensity of the gray eyes behind the mask staring directly into hers. She remembered the gleam of his strong, white teeth as they flashed in a smile, the sound of his rich, deep voice. She had caught the aroma of spirits about him, but he had not been the worse for drink. The faint smell had not been offensive to her after the sweaty odor of many of her rural customers or the heavy musk perfume of some of the gallants. She now burned incense to help mask these unpleasant emanations.

Approaching her own stool at the table, she lifted the cushion that covered it and extracted the coins she had slipped beneath. She did not count them, but dropped them into a large red kerchief and tied the ends together. Extinguishing the incense and candle, she left the tent.

A gaudy gypsy caravan was set up just behind the black tent and she climbed the steps to it and opened the red-painted door.

Inside all was neat and tidy. There was a table and chairs and a cabinet that held dishes and cooking utensils at the front of the caravan. At the back, separated by a curtain, was a bed, a small clothes chest and a washstand.

She carried the coin-filled kerchief to the back of the caravan and bending down beside the bed, extracted a metal box from underneath. Using a key she wore about her neck, she turned the lock and opened it. The coins were duly counted and added to the amount in the box, which she again locked and returned beneath the bed.

Rising to her feet, she sighed deeply. It would probably take several more months before the amount she needed was accumulated.

She removed the veil that covered the lower part of her face and the black coif that concealed her forehead and long hair. For a moment she studied her reflection in a small mirror that hung from the wall above the washstand.

A pair of deep blue eyes looked back at her. They were eyes that had seen much for one so young, for the tall, dark stranger had been right. She was much younger than she appeared — barely eighteen, in fact. She knew that she was pretty. What she didn't know was that she was gloriously beautiful. Her features were delicate, her abundant hair, almost silver in its fairness, and the skin of her face and her body, flawless and white. Only her hands appeared incongruous to the rest of her person. She smiled as she gazed down at them, for they were dyed nut-brown with the juice of berries, so that they would more easily resemble those of a gypsy.

She was about to remove the bright purplish-red costume she wore when something stopped her. It was foolish. She should wash herself and head straight to bed. Tomorrow would be another busy day and she needed a clear head for her observant readings. Still, her thoughts returned to the dark-haired giant who had challenged her powers. She remembered the recurring dream she had had in the past few weeks and she shuddered at the memory.

She had dreamed that she was being pursued by a wild-eyed, angry mob who screamed accusingly at her, paralyzing her with fear. Everything inside her told her to run, but her legs couldn't seem to move! The terrifying hoard pressed closer and closer! Panic filled her as they bore down on her and she was unable to flee.

With all her might she willed her legs to move and suddenly she began to shuffle forward, slowly at first, and then more easily. Just when she felt she might get away in time, she stumbled and fell. And then it happened. Strong arms scooped her effortlessly up and she looked into the face of a tall, dark man dressed all in white. He had saved her, she was sure, from certain death! He said nothing, but carried her to his waiting white horse and before she knew what was happening they were galloping off into the moonlight.

Every time she had this dream, she woke up wondering about the white-clad knight. She knew so little of men. How did it feel to fall in love? Especially with a man who resembled her "Moonlight Cavalier"?

Now, tonight, she was struck by an overpowering feeling that she had just come face to face with that man in the flesh!

Chapter Three

It did not make sense, this compelling need to see the tall, dark stranger again. Yet, even sensing something inherently dangerous about the man, she still felt drawn to him. He was worldly; he had lived; yet, he was different from any man she had ever encountered before. He fascinated her. She knew she would not be content unless she had one more glimpse of him before he left the fair.

She took down a dark blue cloak from a peg on the wall by the caravan door and wrapping herself in it, pulled the hood carefully over her head to cover her pale hair.

A mask! She would need a mask. A frantic search began of her clothes closet. The black domino she discovered concealed only three quarters of her face, leaving her mouth and chin visable, but it would have to do. She hadn't much time. He might already be starting back to the barge.

The moon was nearly full and riding high above the fairground when she emerged from her caravan. The noise and merriment had not lessened, despite the late hour. Normally, she would never have ventured out alone into such a crowd. A lone woman placed herself in a precarious position when she mingled with these drunken revellers. Still, something spurred her on.

Quickly descending the steps of the caravan, she rounded the corner of it so precipitously that she collided head on with large form that loomed out of the darkness at her!

Claridge had stood in the shadows outside the gypsy tent for some time after his visit. He had felt puzzled and much intrigued by the gypsy fortune teller. She had seemed to know so much about him and his life.

He had observed the departure of the lad who hawked for her and the darkening of the tent. Still watching, he had seen her leave and hurry over to the caravan. Not until the door closed had Claridge begun to walk away. Then, something had stopped him and made him turn about and return. It was when he reached the caravan that she had come hurtling around the corner at him. Now she was staring up at him, the fear leaving the luminous eyes behind the mask as she recognized him.

He had caught her with strong, yet gentle

hands and stood looking down at her, not releasing his hold. Feeling masculine hands upon her brought back a painful memory of a time when she had been held against her will. But this was different. There was something reassuringly protective about the way he held her. In fact, when he finally released her, she felt a strange longing to feel those strong arms about her again.

He smiled and she caught the sparkle of his dark eyes behind the mask. "Off to an assignation, little gypsy?" he drawled, and then his smile faded and he reached to cup her chin and tilt her face up so that the moonlight clearly illuminated the lower portion of it.

"Devil take it!" he whistled. "You're no gypsy at all!"

The pale color of her skin had given her away, but he was admiring the delicately proportioned, yet generous mouth, and the firm little chin. "Why the masquerade?" he asked.

"I—I found it necessary," she stammered, moving her head quickly to free her chin.

He nodded. "I understand. You must disguise yourself in order to protect your beauty."

"My beauty?" Her mouth suddenly quirked in amusement. "How can you know my visage? Perhaps I'm hiding a disfigurement."

He shook his head slowly as she went on.

"I may be as ugly as a toad—crosseyed and pock-marked."

"No," his voice was sure. "While seated across

34

from you in the tent I saw those lovely eyes above your veil, as deep a blue as the sky at twilight. They are most certainly not cross-eyed and the complexion I view now is as smooth and soft as velvet."

"Still," she insisted, a little breathlessly, "I could be fat and—"

Again he shook his head. The eyes behind the mask were dancing now. "After holding you in my arms, I am assured that your figure is as beautiful as your face."

"You flatter me." The moonlight caught the blush that becomingly darkened what could be seen of her face.

"I think not. I also deem it criminal that you have hidden that low, melodious voice behind an old crone's whine." He leaned closer to whisper, "Are others aware of this?"

She was suddenly wary. "No! I beg of you, sir, please tell no one about me."

"And if I should keep your dark secret . . . ?" He moved forward and placed his hands on either side of her against the caravan.

His arms made an effective cage and she felt a little uneasy. He was so close . . . too close. And she was very much aware of his nearness.

"I will be grateful," she said in a small voice.

"Really?" he grinned, and at the faint edge of laughter in his voice she knew he had taken a different meaning from her words.

"There are, of course, limitations to my gratitude," she said hastily.

He leaned back. "You do not trust me?"

"I trust no man," she said crisply. "They flatter a lady for only one reason."

"Oh ho!" he chuckled. "You admit, then, to being a lady."

She smiled an enigmatic smile. "We are both in masquerade, sir, and therefore not supposed to know anything about the other."

"Not true! Having read my palm you have me at a distinct disadvantage."

"But you have found me out to be a charlatan."

"As a gypsy, perhaps, but not as a fortune teller. Much you told me was true."

She smiled, despite herself. "At times," she admitted, "I do seem to possess what they call 'second sight,' but with you I merely guessed, based on close observation and selection of evidence."

He lifted an amused brow. "What evidence did you gather from me?"

"I noticed that the palm of your hand was calloused and your clothing, although well made and elegant, not as effeminate as some of the other gallants who have visited me. You wear no wig, sir, and your only jewelry is a signet ring with your family crest. The faint lines that etch your mouth indicate the fact that you have become a trifle cynical about life for one so young, but your laugh and the warmth I have glimpsed in your eyes show me that you normally possess a pleasant disposition."

"Quite astute, aren't you?" he grinned.

"I have to be. 'Tis how I make my living."

"An odd way for a lady, I would think." He regarded her for a moment, rubbing his chin with his thumb and index finger. That she was a lady he now had no doubt – the proud carriage, the lack of servility. "Masquerading as a gypsy would be an excellent way to hide from someone," he said unexpectedly.

She started at his words. So he had guessed correctly, he thought. She had run away from someone to hide here at the fair. This knowledge made him even more intrigued to learn the identity of this beautiful, mysterious creature.

"Tell me," he said, "when it does not relate to their personal appearance, how can you be so accurate in what you tell people? Word of your amazing powers is spreading about London. 'Twas what prompted me to seek you out."

Glad that he had not continued in his former line of questioning, she smiled. " 'Tis simply the law of averages. Nearly everyone falls in love, has quarrels and reconciliations, receives money at sometime and meets attractive strangers. There is often someone of whom one should beware and there are always dangers about in one form or another."

"You are disillusioning me," he gave a wry smile.

"I think not. A gentleman as worldly and as

handsome as you is rarely taken in."

The smile widened. "Handsome? Behind this mask I may be as ugly as a toad," he quoted her.

She laughed then. A delightful, throaty sound. "No," she shook her head. "You have a presence about you that only comes with self-assurance. An older man, if ugly, could have gained self assurance by what he has accomplished. A younger man, like you, has to be handsome to possess it. Since you also possess rank and wealth, it is a wonder you are not unbearably conceited."

He burst into his deep, rich laugh. "But you do not think I am?"

"No. I think those years in the army did much to develop your character."

"But make me cynical." He laughed again. "You're quite delightful, do you know that? Will you tell me your first name, at least?"

"I am called Marta."

"I wish your real name."

"No names, sir. It is better."

"I swear I will find it out," he said resolutely.

"Pray do not try," she said a little anxiously.

"But I must see you again. I have never met anyone like you before."

Without warning, his arms drew her to him. She put her hands to his chest to push him away, but before she could, he was kissing her. No one had ever kissed her in such a way. Certainly not the insistent Ramsden with his thick, wet lips. This man's kiss was warm and gentle so that she felt no fear, but slowly succumbed to the tender sweetness of it. As he felt her gentle response, the pressure of his mouth deepened. His arms pulled her closer and she relaxed, letting her body mold to his, letting him lead her forward into the kiss.

A quivering sensation shot through her. His kiss was awakening unknown senses, making them come frightening alive. Never had she experienced such pleasure! She wanted the kiss to go on and on, but he drew back his head and whispered, "So very sweet. I've never tasted sweeter lips."

She pulled away from him, trembling, trying to regain control of herself. "This is wrong. I must go in."

"Don't go yet."

"I must."

"And I must see you again."

"No."

"You cannot enter my life, steal my heart, and then disappear."

"Do not say such things."

"I would like to say more. Tomorrow night. I will come again tomorrow night."

He tried to draw her again into his arms, but she broke away and quickly fled around the corner of the caravan. He heard her run up the steps and the portal open and close.

She bolted the door behind her and stood leaning back against it, her heart beating wildly. She closed her eyes to shut out the vision of him laughing down at her, holding her, kissing her. It had all been like a dream, she thought. A wonderful, incredible dream.

She had never felt desire before. Until now it had been an unknown emotion to her. Now she was experiencing a newfound awareness of her body and how it could be stirred to respond. His kiss had not frightened or disgusted her the way Ramsden's had. Instead, it had thrilled her to the very depths of her being. She knew, without conceit, that he had also felt an attraction. Something had sparked between them from the moment they had laid eyes on one another. She felt it, yet. The awareness. The pull. The insistence. She had not known before of this deep sensuality in her nature, but now she was sure that if she had allowed him to kiss her again, all reason would have been swept away.

Left alone, Claridge stood for a moment, frozen in place. His pulses still raced. Perhaps the girl really was a witch, he thought, as he started slowly back to the fairground to join his friends. There was certainly something different about her, something that drew him like metal to a lodestone. She had captivated him from the first moment he had gazed into her dark eyes across the table from him in the gypsy tent. Had she cast a spell over him?

He frowned. Who the devil was she? She had

seemed so innocent when he had kissed her. As if she had never been kissed before. He gave a self-deprecating laugh. She really *has* bewitched you, you fool. She all but admitted running away from one man, and no wench who lives amongst this fairground rabble could remain innocent for long. Why it was more than likely she had been on her way to meet a lover when he had intercepted her.

Yet, he shook his head, she had blushed so easily and there was something so fresh and ingenuous about her. He would indeed return to the fair again on the morrow, if only to settle the issue for himself.

Chapter Four

Later that night, as he lay in the big four-poster bed in his apartments at Whitehall, Claridge found sleep elusive. When it finally did claim him, he slept restlessly, with troubled dreams of a bright-eyed gypsy girl who beckoned to him, only to disappear into a swirling fog whenever he got close to her.

When he awoke, he chided himself for a fool, to be so captivated by a wench he had never really seen. Yet, the memory of her remained with him as he began his day.

Claridge dressed carefully, for he had been sent an early morning summons to attend the king in his chambers. His doublet was of plain, French, gray velvet and the matching thigh-length cloak was lined in the same shade of burgundy as the feather which swooped down from his large-brimmed gray hat. He wore his grandfather's ornate-hilted sword at his hip.

* * *

Despite the early hour, the anteroom was already crowded. Men stood about dressed as gay as maypoles in the very latest of fashion which, at this time, featured ribbons and bows on everything from hats to boots. Several hundred yards of ribbon might be used to decorate one suit, and all in the brightest colors imaginable. This extensive use of decoration was thought to be a reaction from the sterner days England had lived through under the Puritans and exemplified the extravagance of a king who had suffered the indignity of poverty and exile.

Claridge was looked at rather askance by some as he entered in his subdued clothing and murmurings of "Puritan sympathizer" were made by a few. But he was instantly recognized and enthusiastically greeted by most of the gentlemen of the court.

His Grace the Duke of Claridge. The name was well known. The big man had attended his monarch during his years of exile on the Continent, as had many who stood about the anteroom. Claridge, however, had not returned with Charles to England when he had claimed the throne, three years before, but instead had remained to do service in the army of France in the wars of the Continent. He was surrounded by many now and welcomed heartily back home.

Claridge caught sight of his friend Musgrove

through the crowd and winked at him. Only *he* knew the truth – that Claridge had actually been home since the spring.

Musgrove stifled a yawn. How could Claridge manage to look so wide awake, he wondered, when their celebrating hadn't ended until the sun was coming up?

Suddenly, the door to the king's private chambers opened, and the elderly Clarendon, the king's chancellor, hurried out, a worried scowl on his face.

"His Majesty has obviously been overspending again," someone said jokingly.

A page appeared at Claridge's elbow. "The King will see you now, Your Grace," he said, bowing.

"I've been waiting a full hour," one gentleman objected. "Why should he . . ."

Claridge was ushered into the royal bedchamber and gave a low bow to his monarch who had risen to greet him.

Charles was freshly shaved and dressed for his early morning walk with his dogs in St. James Park.

"Delighted to see you, Simon," he said, grasping the big man's shoulder.

"And I to see you, Sire."

"An honest face is always welcome at court," the king smiled sardonically. "I encounter so few."

He strode across the sumptuously furnished room, and took a chair by a broad mullioned window that gave a panoramic view of the

Thames. His spaniels arranged themselves around him. At a wave from his monarch's hand, His Grace seated himself across from him, stretching out his long legs before him. Being fond of Claridge, Charles permitted him more familiarity than most.

For a moment his dark hooded eyes regarded Claridge's plain and unadorned clothing. "You've been in the army too long, Simon, you must brighten up your wardrobe. You are quite out of style."

"I enjoy my own style, Sire," Claridge drawled. "I wear what is comfortable to me."

"Always so damned sure of yourself, aren't you?" Charles smiled. "What if I ordered you to dress the dandy?"

"I think my king far too clever to play childish games with me."

Charles's smile broadened. "He also values your friendship too much." He paused, his face growing serious. "But enough of this. I have been asked to speak with you on behalf of the Earl of Westbury. I understand he and your late father arranged a marriage between you and his only daughter, the Lady Angela."

"That is correct."

"The young lady is now at court, Simon. She is a maid-of-honor to the queen." His sensuous lips twitched. "I might also add that she is beautiful and will make you a very suitable wife."

Claridge appeared indifferent to his words. "I

45

have not met her, Sire," he said succinctly.

"That can be easily arranged."

Claridge sighed. "Will you not give me a little time, Sire, to savor my recent freedom from the restrictions of army life?"

"You have already had four months, Simon," Charles said, in a dangerously quiet tone.

Claridge turned his head sharply to look at his king, but Charles was bending over stroking one of the spaniels that had curled up at his feet.

"I beg Your Majesty's pardon," Claridge said, suddenly contrite.

"So you should. There is little that doesn't reach my ears. How, pray, did you find your estates?"

"I was among the fortunate, Sire. Claridge House had been confiscated, of course, and occupied by the Roundheads, and my lands stolen, but with the help of relatives and faithful friends, most have been reclaimed," Claridge told him. "There is much to restore of the house, but at least everything is intact."

"You are indeed fortunate," Charles sighed. "I still receive petitions. Hundreds, all over the country lost their land and want it back. Many of their fathers, their brothers, and their sons died for our cause, as did your own father, Simon. I am not forgetful of this, but all the land that has changed hands cannot be given back. Some of it was purchased in good faith at public sales. How can I confiscate the land now without committing grave injustices? In some cases the land has changed hands many times and has been broken up into parcels and the boundaries altered. The confusion would be too chaotic. There is no entirely right or wrong answer to the problem, I'm afraid." He made an impatient gesture with his hand. "But I am digressing from the point of this meeting. We are here to discuss your betrothal."

"I am yours to command, Sire, where my service, my sword, and my fortune are concerned," Claridge declared. "But I beg the right to choose my own bride."

The king shook his head. "Your father relinquished your right, not I." He sighed deeply. "Take my advice, Simon. Do not look for the impossible in marriage. I can assure you that one rarely finds delight and duty in the same bed."

Claridge caught a brief wistfulness in the king's dark eyes. Charles's arranged marriage with Catherine of Braganza, the Portuguese princess, had taken place only a year before and he and the country had gained materially by it, but it was clearly a loveless match on the king's part. Nevertheless, Charles had the beautiful Barbara Castlemaine to console him.

"And duty and honor must come before love," Claridge murmured.

"Do not look so gloomy, my friend," Charles consoled him. "Who is to say you will not fall in love with the lovely Angela? Besides," he smiled, "there are many at court who would welcome your

47

attentions. I hear Lady Quillby is returning to Whitehall." He rose to his feet. "I will give you a week to declare yourself, Simon. Now, will you join me for a turn around the park?"

Claridge had risen with him. "I would be delighted, Sire."

"I cannot bear to face that mob this morning," Charles said, pulling on his gloves. "All waiting to beg favors or to make me listen to some petition or other. Let us escape down the Privy Stairs."

When the Lady Angela learned that His Grace, the Duke of Claridge had arrived at Whitehall, she grew very anxious. She had no desire to marry a man she had never met, yet she was not the sort to disobey her father's wishes, or refuse to honor the pledge he had made.

With her moon-pale hair and wide, innocent blue eyes, the Lady Angela seemed pure and fresh and ingenuous to the jaded court. Convent raised, she was still unused to the ways of the outside world—especially the wild and decadent mode of life she encountered at court. Soft spoken and gentle, Angela saw everything black and white, good and bad and in Whitehall she saw what she considered to be the embodiment of all wickedness. She could not help, therefore, but wonder if her husband-to-be enjoyed all the depravities of court life—the gambling and wenching and debauchery. She shuddered at the thought of being married to such a man.

As the days passed and Claridge still had not sought her out, Angela felt not only relief, but a faint hope that perhaps he, also, had no wish for their union.

Did he care for another? Was that the reason he did not press his suit? If that were the case, she could well understand. Didn't she, despite the many weeks they'd been apart, still think constantly of Gerald Waybridge?

It seemed odd to remember now that while she lived at the convent she had thought never to care for any man; that men would never be necessary for her happiness; that she could live very well without them. She had almost decided to take the vows, when her father had come for her . . .

Ralph Neville, the Earl of Westbury, was still a fine figure of a man when he returned with the triumphant new king from the Continent. After the coronation, he had travelled north to the convent on the Scottish border and brought his daughter home with him to Kent and Neville Hall. He had been a fearless soldier and was still an unexcelled sportsman, but a rough, bear of a man who even at sixty loved nothing better than to bed a lusty wench.

Sarah, his refined and delicate wife, had died of a summer fever when he had been away fighting for his king at Worcester in 1651. Angela had been only six when she had been placed in the convent and was sixteen when she returned to her almost forgotten home.

Having lived so simply, she had not been prepared for life outside the convent walls. She found little in common with the Kentish neighbors and friends whose kind invitations the Earl accepted on her behalf. The young people she encountered seemed purposeless and shallow, only bent upon enjoying what they called 'the good things of life'. The girls her own age spoke of nothing but their foppish suitors, the latest fashions and the next party or ball. Angela considered them to be frivolous featherbrains and found she much preferred her own company to theirs.

Upon arriving back at Neville Hall, Angela had inquired about her Nana, who had nursed her and her mother before her. She learned that the old woman lived in a small cottage in the next village and was not well. Angela began to visit her several times a week, taking her food and medicine and whatever else she required. She found a widow in the village who was having a hard time making ends meet, and hired her to live with and care for her old nurse.

To everyone who came to call, Nana would declare, "there be no one in the whole wide world as sweet and caring as my little angel." This only embarrassed Angela who was happy to be of help to others.

Yet Nana was not the only one to sing her praises. She had hardly been back home a week before she had most of the household adoring her. She made up a toothache remedy for one of the footmen when she saw his swollen jaw. She gave food and clothing to a young housemaid whose mother had just given birth to her eleventh child. She defended a young gardener on the estate who had engaged the Earl's wrath by digging up the wrong flower bed, by claiming she had wanted it for a herb garden.

Horseback riding was something Angela had never learned before entering the convent, and although her father now instructed his head groom to teach her, she trembled every time she was helped up onto the back of the gentlest animal. Instead, she preferred to ride about in a dog cart which was pulled by a fat, piebald pony. Always obeying her father, she took either Jenny, her maid, with her on these rides, or was accompanied by a groom on horseback.

The spring day Angela met Gerald Waybridge, therefore, had been unusual, for she had been completely alone.

Not being able to locate Jenny that morning, and feeling, instinctively, that she must hurry down to the village and see her Nana, she had rushed to the stables, found a young stableboy to hitch the pony to the dog cart and after waiting a half hour for her groom to appear, had finally decided she could wait no longer and so had set off by herself.

When she arrived at Nana's cottage, it was to

51

find that the old woman had taken a turn for the worse. She seemed unaware of anything or anyone around her. Angela remained with her all day, holding her hand, until Nana passed away late in the afternoon.

Just before she died, she opened her eyes and looked at Angela quite lucidly.

"You must find her," she said.

"Find whom?" Angela asked, but the old woman closed her eyes again and began to ramble.

"Twins . . ." she murmured. "Identical twins . . . Had to send one poor wee thing away . . . birthmark . . . he would have known."

Her words made no sense at all to Angela and yet they struck an odd chord within her. She had often felt a strange sense of loneliness. It had come over her many times during the years, even before her mother had died, even before she had been left at the convent. It was an uncomprehensible feeling and yet one that returned to her again and again.

Sadly, Angela had given the widow final instructions and left the little cottage. Realizing that those at home might be worried about her absence, she hurried toward the village green where she had left the dog cart, so that the pony could nibble away at the grass while he waited for her.

There were wooden stocks at the edge of the green and on the other side a duck pond in which legend had it more than a dozen witches had met their death in the last century. The spot always made Angela shudder.

The afternoon shadows were growing larger as she unhitched the reins and climbed into the dog cart. Leaving the village behind, the pony jogged along the road back to Neville Hall at a brisk pace. A few miles on, at a crossroads, Angela decided to take the short cut that led over the hill so she would be sure of arriving home before dusk.

The pony was making good time, visualizing his comfortable stall and fresh hay waiting at home, when, rounding a corner of the road, something small suddenly dashed out in front of him.

Angela immediately pulled back on the reins, but not before she heard a cry, followed by a thud. Bounding from the cart, she was soon leaning over a small crumpled heap on the road. Under a mop of tousled curls, lay a sweet-faced little boy of about three, Angela judged, as she examined him carefully. There did not seem to be any blood and she was about to pick him up when she heard a voice say, "Don't touch him."

Startled, Angela looked up to see a tall, sandy-haired young man approaching. A second later he was crouching beside her, inspecting the child.

"Is he alive?" Angela's voice shook. "He—he just darted out in front of me."

"I saw it happen," he replied. "Yes, he's alive, but I'm not sure if any bones are broken." Very gently he picked up the child in his strong arms.

"Do you know who the poor little mite is? Is there anything I can do?"

"His name is Willie. He's from the orphan's home up on the hill. We'll take him back to Auntie Maude."

"Auntie Maude?"

"The woman in charge of the children."

He instructed Angela to get into the cart and then gently placed the child on the seat beside her, with his curly head in her lap. Angela stroked Willie's forehead as the man took the reins and led the pony and cart along the road to where a driveway intercepted it. He turned off onto it and they made their way up the winding overgrown trail until they stopped before an Elizabethan Manor House.

Angela noticed that the gardens before it were overgrown and untended, and yet she could see where there had once been a symmetry to them.

The young man carried Willie up the steps and into the mansion, with Angela following behind. Just inside the large banqueting hall, they were met by a plump little woman whose gray hair, although pinned into a knot on top of her head, had stray tendrils escaping from it around her kindly, anxious face.

"Not Willie again?" she said to the young man.

"I'm afraid so. This time he dashed out in front of this lady's pony cart."

The woman was too concerned with the child to

pay any attention to Angela.

"In here, please sir," she said to the young man, indicating a room off the hall which appeared to be an office of some kind. He followed her into it, still carrying the child.

When he returned, a few minutes later, Angela was still standing in the doorway to the hall.

"Would you care to wait until Auntie Maude determines Willie's injuries?" he asked. "She knows as much or more than any physician."

"I would, indeed."

He lead her over to a wooden settle before the enormous fireplace. It was covered with heraldic devices, shields and crests carved from stone and painted in heraldic colors. Still Angela could not help but notice that the carpet before it was almost threadbare.

"I am afraid I have neglected to introduce myself. Gerald Waybridge at your service," he gave Angela a little bow.

"Angela Neville," she smiled, "from Neville Hall."

"His Lordship's daughter?"

"Yes," she said shyly.

"I have heard tell of you."

"You have?"

"Word has spread of your kindness to many in the district."

Angela looked surprised. " 'Tis strange, but I have never heard of this orphan's home or of Auntie Maude."

"Or of me, I imagine," he smiled. "May I?" he indicated a chair opposite her.

"Pray do."

He began to tell her about the orphan's home and himself.

His uncle, it seemed, had been the last squire of the Manor House. He had died during the war, but it wasn't until after the present king's triumphant return to England, that Gerald had learned he was his uncle's heir and had come to claim the house and land.

He was surprised to discover that a woman, whom everyone called Auntie Maude, had set up an orphan's home in the deserted house, having gained permission from the Countess of Westbury, Angela's mother, the Earl being away from Neville Hall at the time.

The war had orphaned many children and others had been abandoned and Gerald was loathe to turn them out into the cold. He decided the Manor House was big enough for all of them, and had simply chosen to live in one of the unoccupied wings.

As Angela listened to his warm voice, she could not help but wonder if he were living there alone. Did he have a wife looking after him? His clothing was well worn and rather out of fashion from the young men's apparel she had seen at the parties she had attended.

Gerald Waybridge appeared to her to be in his late twenties, with serious blue eyes set in a pleasant looking, if not handsome face. He was quiet-spoken and thoughtful with a sad look in his eyes which made him seem older than he probably was. It was romantic, Angela thought, and intriguing.

Little Willie, as they soon learned from Auntie Maude, was fortunately only bruised and shaken up. It was not the first time, apparently, he had run away from the girl who was supposed to be looking after him.

"Perhaps she needs more help," Angela suggested.

Auntie Maude gave her a weary smile. "We have not the funds," she said simply. "We just do as best we can. There be twenty five children here and only three of us to care for them. The two who help me are orphans themselves, only twelve and fourteen years old."

As he accompanied Angela to the dog cart, Gerald Waybridge answered her unspoken question.

"I am trying to find a woman to help them, my lady. I contribute as much as I can, but my expenses have been great since taking over the estate. The tenants and their farms had long been neglected."

"I understand," she nodded, smiling shyly at him. "I will speak with my father. After all, 'tis in his district, too."

"No," he said and she caught the proud lift of his head. "I feel it is *my* responsibility. Though the Manor House borders your father's estate, it belongs to me. I will find a way to help the children."

The dying sun made a last effort and a ray of sunlight shone on Angela's face as he was about to assist her up into the dog cart. For a long moment they stood staring at one another before Gerald spoke.

"We must hurry if we hope to have you home before dark," he said huskily.

His man was holding the reins to his horse, which he must have ordered saddled, and Gerald quickly took them from him and mounted the animal.

On the ride back to Neville Hall, Angela told him the reason she had come out without someone to accompany her and of her Nana's death.

"You have had a difficult day," he said, offering his sympathy. Yet he cautioned her never to ride out alone in future.

When they came within sight of Neville Hall, Angela insisted she could go the rest of the way on her own, so he lifted his broad brimmed hat and bid her farewell.

She looked back once over her shoulder, only to see that he was doing the same. He waved to her and disappeared around a bend in the driveway.

Upon her arrival home, Angela apologized for giving them any worry, but explained that she had stayed with her Nana until she died. Even her father was solicitous when he learned what had happened and said he would attend to a service in the Hall's little chapel.

Angela told no one about the accident with Willie, the orphan's home, or about Gerald Waybridge. She kept her thoughts of the latter deep within her, quietly reliving her meeting with him again and again in the days that followed.

Chapter Five

It was barely light when the gypsy fastened the brass-studded harness about the old horse and hitched the animal to the gaudy caravan. She sighed as she climbed aboard and snapped the reins. She had lain awake for a long time the night before, finally realizing there was only one way to resolve the problem. She must leave the fair immediately. The big nobleman had said he would return the next night to see her and she simply did not trust herself as far as he was concerned. Besides, he knew her secret and it put her at his mercy.

She did not want to be at any man's mercy. Not ever again. Even if this man did not seem the type who would force himself upon her.

Yet, she had to admit, he *had* taken advantage of the moment, the night before, to kiss her. How could she have allowed it to happen? How could she have actually felt a strange, sweet pleasure racing through her when he had held her so close against him? Was that not the real reason she was fleeing now? Was she not afraid of her feelings for this stranger?

It was better to go away; better to put as much distance as she could between herself and St. Margaret's Fair. She would travel northeast. The country villages held fairs at this time of year where she might tell her fortunes, although they were never as profitable as the fairs close to London. Still, she would manage. Hadn't she managed quite well on her own so far? Fairclough Manor and her life there now seemed a very long time ago.

Yet, as she travelled along, memories returned to her. She had had a happy childhood growing up as Elizabeth Fairclough, the only daughter of Sir George and Lady Mary. They had adored her and each other and theirs had been a truly happy home.

That had all changed one rainy evening when Elizabeth had been twelve. On their way back to the Manor House after visiting friends, her parent's coach had plunged down a hillside, overturning and squarely hitting a large oak tree at the bottom. Sir George had been killed instantly. Lady Mary had never regained consciousness and had died the next day.

Arriving from London to attend the funeral, Elizabeth's Uncle Matthew had promptly moved into Fairclough Manor, bag and baggage, having been declared to be her guardian in her father's will.

A bachelor, who had no use for children, he took no interest in the grieving girl, preferring to let others care for her needs. Accustomed to a close family life, Elizabeth felt bereft and alone, despite the kindness and affection shown to her by her governess and the servants.

Sir George had not seen his only brother for several years prior to his death, or he would never have made him the guardian of his daughter. It soon became apparent to those employed at Fairclough Manor, that Sir Matthew was a dissolute gambler and a drunkard. Fortunately, he found the country life far too dull and spent little time at the estate, preferring his apartments in London. However, when he did journey to Fairclough Manor, it was usually to bring with him a group of his disreputable friends, who spent their days and nights gambling, drinking, and carousing at the local taverns.

As the years went by and Elizabeth developed into an exquisitely beautiful young lady, her governess took it upon herself to hide her away from the lascivious eyes of Sir Matthew's cronies when they made their visits. This worked very well until Elizabeth reached her sixteenth birthday. On that day her Uncle Matthew had made a surprise visit and coming upon her in the library, had been greatly impressed by her beauty. From that day on, he had started to bring suitors down regularly with him from London. Most, unfortunately, were older gentlemen who were cut from the same cloth as himself.

Elizabeth politely refused them all, stating quietly to her uncle each time that she wished to make her own choice of a husband.

As the months passed, Elizabeth began finding it more and more difficult to sidestep her uncle's matrimonial plots. His manner toward her was becoming, not only short, but almost threatening. She would never forget the February evening six months before when she had dashed into the manor house late from her afternoon horseback ride and had encountered her uncle and another gentleman in the front hall, newly arrived from London.

With her cloud of moon-pale hair escaping from the ribbon that tied it back from her delicate face, her cheeks flushed, her wide blue eyes sparkling from the wild gallop home, Elizabeth had never looked more beautiful.

"You remember Lord Ramsden, don't you, Elizabeth?" Matthew Fairclough drawled by way of introduction.

The other man stepped forward and made an elegant leg to her.

The brightness in Elizabeth's eyes faded in dismay as she viewed the man before her. Yes, she certainly did remember him. He had come to Fairclough Manor before with a party of her uncle's friends and had tried to waylay her in a dark corner. Fortunately Simmons, the butler, had appeared at that moment on his way to the wine cellar, and Elizabeth had been able to make her escape.

Lord Ramsden was a heavyset man in his late forties. The years of loose living had taken their toll with him. His coarse features were thickening, two heavy lines etched the corners of his thick lips and there were dark pouches beneath his eyes. There was something disturbing about those eyes as they raked over her. Elizabeth felt a sudden apprehension and could not help but shudder.

" 'Tis a great pleasure to see you again, Elizabeth," Lord Ramsden was saying and aside to Sir Matthew, "You were right, my friend. She's grown into a fine little filly."

With avidity those dark, glittering eyes were completely divesting Elizabeth of her clothing, making her feel naked and so repelled she made as if to dash toward the staircase.

"Where are your manners, girl?" There was a decided edge to Sir Matthew's voice.

"Lord Ramsden," she dropped a little curtsy of recognition before she sped across the hall toward the stairs.

Sir Matthews glared after her retreating form. "You will dine with us this evening, Elizabeth," he called after her. "I will brook no excuses!"

She wore her plainest gown. Dark blue, with a high neckline, it nevertheless managed to define

64

the perfection of her figure and to highlight the fairness of her skin. Her maid had pulled her fair hair primly back from her face, at her governess's request, but it only seemed to emphasize her high cheekbones and wide-set blue eyes.

Her uncle frowned at her appearance. His wig was even now askew and his face flushed by the spirits he had already consumed.

Elizabeth said little throughout the many elaborate courses of the supper her uncle had ordered, but barely touched. Lord Ramsden indeed did most of the talking, directing his conversation almost exclusively to her.

He told her how he occupied a high place at court and was one of the king's most valued confidants. He spoke of his vast estates and his considerable wealth and at the same time he devoured his food he devoured her with his dark eyes.

Elizabeth gave a sigh of relief when the supper ended and she was able to rise to her feet and prepare to withdraw.

"We'll join you presently," her uncle announced, as Simmons brought the brandy to the gentlemen. Elizabeth knew he was warning her not to escape upstairs.

It was less than an hour later when the two gentlemen appeared in the open doorway of the drawing room where Elizabeth waited. It seemed as if they had come to some agreement in her absence. Elizabeth felt instantly wary of what was to follow. She rose to her feet, dropping the embroidery she had been working on.

"I've a happy s'prise for you 'lizabeth," Sir Matthew slurred. He carried a full snifter of brandy into the room with him. "Lor' Ramsden has done you the honor of asking for your han' in marriage and I've given my consent."

She gazed at him in horror. "But how could you —"

He interrupted. "As you know, my girl, you have no say in the matter. I am your guardian.

Ignoring the satisfied smile on Lord Ramsden's face, she defiantly addressed her uncle. "I will not . . . marry him!" she said, lifting her chin. "You had no right to promise me to anyone without my consent."

Sir Matthew's face darkened to a mottled shade of purple. "How dare you question my jug'ment, chit! I say you *will* marry his Lor'ship, and the sooner it can be 'rranged the better." He turned to his friend. "I 'pologize for my niece's wilfush- willfullness. She is in need of a firmer hand than mine."

"Not at all," Lord Ramsden said silkily. "I can fully understand why such a lovely young girl would not care to be thrown at a man old enough to be her father."

He looked at Elizabeth sympathetically and for a moment her heart leaped at the hope that he might release her from her uncle's promise.

"But you see, my dear," he went on, smiling

sadly at her, "your uncle must honor his gambling debts and as he has, unfortunately, lost your entire inheritance, he had nothing left to wager last night but this estate. I'm afraid, Elizabeth, that Fairclough Manor now belongs to me."

"No!" Elizabeth couldn't believe her ears. "How could you?" she accused her uncle. "My father put his trust in you. You had no right to gamble away my inheritance. No right at all!"

Sir Matthew wouldn't meet her eyes as he downed the last of his snifter of brandy.

"I agree with you, my dear," Ramsden went on smoothly. "The man is an incorrigible gambler. But you see, you are now without a dowry. Despite your considerable beauty, there are few wealthy enough to ask for your hand. I will provide for you and your uncle's future." He gave a triumphant smile. "So you see, Elizabeth, 'tis very simple. Accept my proposal of marriage, or find yourself and your uncle turned out in the cold without a farthing."

He moved closer to where she stood, looking at her in a manner which made her feel as if she were already imprisoned in his arms.

"Shall we seal our coming nuptials with a kiss?"

"No!" She took a step backwards from him, feeling a shiver of revulsion run through her as her eyes fastened on those thick, expectant lips.

"I will leave you two . . ." Sir Matthew belched loudly. ". . . to get better 'quainted," he finished, and stumbled toward the door.

"Uncle, I pray you, don't leave . . ." but the door closed firmly behind him.

Lord Ramsden moved quickly to her side and before she could protest, he drew her roughly into his arms.

"I've wanted you, girl, since the first time I laid eyes on you."

His wet lips pressed greedily down on hers, forcing them open to this thick, exploring tongue. Almost gagging, Elizabeth tired desperately to turn her head away. Waves of nausea washed over her as she struggled to get free.

"Let me go!" she cried, managing to bump against a spindly table, hoping Simmons would hear it as it crashed to the floor.

Ramsden only laughed at her. "Come, come, Elizabeth, we are to be man and wife. You must get used to my kisses."

"Never!" She kicked him smartly on the shins.

"Little bitch!" he growled, jerking her hands behind her back and thrusting her before him toward the low sofa that stood before the hearth.

Tears of fear and rage filled Elizabeth's eyes as she struggled against his superior strength. He forced her roughly down onto the sofa, the fingers of one hand fastening in the neckline of her gown and ripping it savagely from one shoulder.

Then he was upon her, imprisoning her beneath the weight of his heavy body, his hands all over her, tearing at her chemise, finding the warm softness of one breast, kneeding it so roughly she cried out in pain.

Elizabeth tried to push his hands away, biting and scratching at him, but he only laughed at her, the hard mound of his arousal thrusting at her as he fumbled with her skirts. Her hands found his chest and with a sudden burst of renewed strength, she pushed at him so hard that he toppled over sideways and rolled with her off the sofa and onto the floor. His head snapped back to crack sharply against the heavy brass fender of the hearth. Momentarily dazed, he released his hold on her and she jerked herself free of him, scrambling to her feet.

Picking up her skirts, Elizabeth raced for the door. She ran as fast as she could out of the room and across the great hall, down a corridor that led to the rear of the mansion and to a back hallway that led off the kitchen.

There she saw cook's heavy wool cloak hanging on a wooden rack by the door. Pulling it down, she snatched open the door and ran out into the cool, frosty air.

She never returned to Fairclough Manor.

Chapter Six

As he had promised, the Duke of Claridge returned to St. Margaret's Fair the next evening, only to find the gypsy tent and caravan gone. He spent the rest of the evening trying to discover when she had left and where she had been headed. No one seemed to know. Even the lad who had hawked for her had no idea. He had been just as surprised as the others that morning to find she had gone.

Claridge questioned him, nonetheless, about the gypsy, but all he could get out of the lad was that she had been kind to him and paid him after every performance. This was far better treatment, he said, than the other hawkers received. He had gladly worked for her both at Bartholemew and St. Margaret's Fairs and was sorry to see her gone. No one else Claridge asked that evening seemed to know or care what had happened to the gypsy. "She kept to herself", was what they all told him. Leaving the fairgrounds, he felt at a loss as to where to begin to look for her.

He paced his apartments that night, finally making the decision to hire couriers to spread out and comb the surrounding countryside in the hope of finding a certain gaudy caravan. Surely, covering every possible road, it would not take them long to locate her. Yet why, he kept wondering, did he feel so compelled to pursue the chit? Why did he feel that at all costs he must find her again and uncover the truth about her?

Was it because, for the first time, he felt he had met someone completely different from any woman he had every known before?

She had quite enchanted him. Although apparently born of gentle blood, she had had the strength of will and courage to strike out on her own, relying on no one but herself. The girl was a delightful mystery and besides she had the sweetest lips he had ever kissed.

Claridge smiled to himself. She had told him he was tenacious. Well, she was right about that. Just as she had been right about so many things. If he wanted something, particularly something not easily attained, he let no obstacle stand in his way.

Old Marta had told Elizabeth that it was the lot of the gypsy to be despised by gorgios (non-

71

gypsies). Never had she realized that more than in the days following her departure from St. Margaret's Fair.

As her caravan rumbled down the narrow country roads and through the small villages, people often shook their fists at her or crossed themselves and called her a daughter of the devil. She was even spat at once and accused of being a thief, when all she had done was to try and buy some food.

The first fair she happened onto refused to let her set up her tent and so she travelled on. The second day she reached a larger town and found a fair on the outskirts where a gypsy was, and although still treated with suspicion, at least she was not stopped from telling her fortunes.

That night, as every night since she had let the big nobleman kiss her, Elizabeth lay in bed thinking of him. With eyes closed she let the remembered feelings sweep through her vibrant young body. Would she ever see him again? No, she told herself. She would not return to London. It was best to forget him. Forget entirely that brief encounter.

The Duke of Buckingham was the host of a supper on a moored, floating house of entertainment on the Thames. To Claridge, it was no different than the other private parties he had attended that week in London, whether held in a mansion, gambling house or brothel. So why, he wondered, had he bothered to attend? The evening's antics were only boring him and consequently he sat in brooding silence, a cynical smile on his lips, consuming far more brandy than he wanted.

The couriers he had hired had not been able to find his mysterious little gypsy and he was beginning to wonder if the meeting had all been just a dream. What was the sense of finding her anyway. The king's week of grace was nearly up and soon the Lady Angela would be presented to him and their betrothal announced.

His boisterous Cavalier friends had reproached Claridge this evening for not joining in their merrymaking, but finally they had thrown up their hands and left him alone. He wished the opposite sex would do the same. There were no ladies present tonight, but several of the young trollops, in varying degrees of undress, had made it blatantly apparent that they were eager for the attentions of such a handsome gentleman. He had ignored their seductive smiles, their ample display of bosom as they leaned over him to refill his goblet, or rub against his firmly muscled thigh. Barely a week, and he was already tired of the excesses and orgies that the king and his friends found so entertaining. Having seen it all before, he longed for something more meaningful.

The sumptuous supper, with its many over-rich courses and too much wine had been followed by more drink—flowing so freely that the company had become louder and noisier in their drunken revelry. Lewd jests filled the hot, smokey air and bursts of raucous laughter. Some had adjourned to the gaming tables where trente-et-quarante and embre were being played with reckless disregard to the stakes. Couples who had been embracing and already disrobing one another at the tables, rose and pushed their way toward the soft couches in the darkened alcoves beyond.

Claridge's cynical gaze swept down the length of the heavy oak table to where the king lounged in his chair. At that moment, Charles rose, sending a spaniel scurrying from his lap onto the floor. With a smiling beauty clinging to his arm, the king headed for the gaming tables.

It was a mistake, Claridge knew, for Charles to gamble. He was already heavily in debt, despite Parliament supplementing his regular income with a hearth tax the year before. Yet, Charles heeded no one's advice on the subject of his finances.

As Claridge sat on alone, drinking, a dusky gypsy dancer appeared, casting her eyes acquisitively about the room. At the sight of him sitting back in his chair with such careless ease, she slipped through the crowd and headed in his direction.

Appearing at Claridge's elbow, Lord Musgrove winked at him. "You wouldn't go to see her at the fair, so I brought her to you," he said, helping to hoist the dancer onto the heavy table before them. "Maybe she will make you forget your other little gypsy."

The girl's dark eyes met Claridge's and her lips curved in an inviting smile as she began to dance, the tiny brass cymbals on her fingers providing her only accompaniment as she twirled about on the polished oak surface, her high heels tapping in constant rhythm.

As those around the table began to clap, the tempo of her dance increased and she danced nearer and nearer to Claridge, her supple body swaying with an undulating movement, luring, teasing. The sparkling eyes taunted him as she twirled above him, her brightly colored skirt flying wide above her bare legs, clearly displaying to him alone what lay beneath. The heaving young breasts strained against the thin, damp blouse as she leaned towards him, her eyes growing even darker with passion as they locked with his amused, lazy stare. Claridge caught the heavy breathing of someone behind him and suddenly there was a drunken roar and a pair of powerful hands reached above him and grabbed the girl about the thighs, pulling her roughly off the table.

It was the giant Scot, Lauderman, Claridge saw, who had captured her. He made no protest, although he caught the flash of disappointment in the gypsy's eyes as she was swept up into the Scot's big arms and carried off, accompanied by much ribaldry from the cheering crowd.

Claridge could not deny that the rhythm and passion of the gypsy's dance had not fired up the blood in his veins, erasing his lethargy. He was young and he was human and he remembered that Hester Quillby, who had once been his mistress, was said to have returned to court that day. Why not pay her an unexpected visit? He was confident enough to know that he would not be turned away. To hell with gypsies, he thought. They always seemed to elude him. Shoving back his chair, he got to his feet, not waiting to kiss the king's hand, as was the custom, before heading, with only a slight sway in his walk, across the room to the door. A flunky standing there was quickly dispatched to call his coach and Claridge followed him outside into the coolness of the autumn evening.

He took a deep breath of the damp air outside. A vaporous mist was rising from the Thames. There was a faint, decaying smell about it. Suddenly, he stiffened. With a soldier's instinct, he sensed someone behind him and spun around, a hand at his sword hilt.

" 'Tis only me, Your Grace," said a solid, well-built man stepping out of the shadows. "Told I could find thee here."

"Giles," Claridge relaxed, recognizing one of the men who had served under him in the king's army and whom he had hired to search for the gypsy fortune-teller.

76

"Aye, Your Grace. I thought ye would like to know that I have found the gypsy ye sought."

"You have!" Claridge grasped the man's shoulder. "Tell me then where she is?"

"A full day's ride from here in Essex, at the Danbury Fair."

"Good man!" Claridge praised him and reaching into the pocket of his doublet extracted some gold coins and pressed them into the man's hand.

Light gray was streaking the sky to the east as Claridge headed out of London on the Great North Road. The air smelled fresh and good and the cool breeze soon cleared his head of the night's indulgences.

When his coach had deposited him back at his apartments in Whitehall, Claridge had stopped only long enough to collect a warm cloak, and without changing from his elegant clothing had called for his best mount.

Having grown up in the country, he was enjoying the ride. He was smiling as the sun rose in the September sky, reveling in the golden beauty all about him in the fields, and wondering how people could stay in the smokey, dirty city with its narrow streets and filthy, open sewers.

Whitehall was not for him. Day after day wasted on self-gratification and pleasure that came and went with little effort on his part and accomplished absolutely nothing. He longed to

77

return to his estates. To Claridge House.

It had been spring when he had arrived back in England and had journeyed to Essex to see his old home. He had ridden slowly up the weed-filled drive between the ravaged gates, and rounding a curve had had his first sight of the formerly splendid residence which had been captured and partly destroyed by the Parliamentary forces. He had resolved then and there to restore it to all its former beauty.

During the first few months, he had overseen the building of new stables and when he arrived in London he had contacted architects to journey to Claridge House and survey the damage. Among them had been the nephew of the original designer, Inigo Jones. The beautiful state rooms had all been destroyed so new ones must be added.

However, foremost in his mind, at the time of his return, had been to make agricultural improvements to his fertile lands. Claridge had learned new methods while in Holland, and that spring he had slowly begun putting some of them into use. He had not wished to leave Essex until he could see some of the results.

When, reluctantly, he felt he must go to London, he had been able to view the first yields from his fields and they were highly encouraging, being nearly twice that of the previous year.

The concerns of his tenant farmers had become his own concerns and he had enjoyed nothing more than riding about the fields and supervising the work, talking to the farmers and examining the crops.

A peer of the realm he might be, with efficient bailiffs and stewards, but Claridge saw nothing wrong in dirtying his hands in the good black earth of his land. He had fought many years for the return of his estates and every acre was precious to him, besides the hard working people who tended them.

War and soldiering were behind him now. His purpose was building instead of destroying. He was sure his grandfather would have approved.

The old Duke, a widower, had been the only father Claridge could remember, his own, having never been a strong man, had died of pneumonia when Claridge was only a toddler. Therefore, he had grown up under the guidance of his grandfather, whom he resembled both in appearance and disposition, and his mother, who, despite her gentle ways, directed an enormous household with ease and proficiency.

The original Claridge House had been Elizabethan in design, but it had been partially burned during the time of the second Duke. Claridge's grandfather had been one of the first to recognize the talents of Inigo Jones as an architect, and when he assumed the title, he commissioned Jones to design the present house. It was one of the earliest examples of the baroque style Jones favored.

His grandfather, Claridge knew, had built up his estates enormously during his lifetime, buying more land, making improvements, diversifying the farming. And then there had been his passion for good horseflesh. His breeding stables had been unsurpassed, even by the king's.

The old Duke had been a wonderful example of enthusiasm and industry to his grandson and Claridge regretted that he had been in France when he had died. With his mother gone in the same year, he had found no reason to hurry home after the king's restoration.

When he at last did return to Claridge House, he found the memories to be only good. He could almost sense the old Duke's encouragement as he took up the reins of duty he had long abandoned and set about the tremendous task of bringing the estates back to not only what they once had been, but also improving them as well.

Claridge hoped never again in his lifetime to take up the sword against any man again.

The sweeping meadows around him and the softly rolling hills, made Claridge's ride pleasurable, yet it was all he could do to keep from urging his stallion into a gallop.

Although she had been sighted at the Danbury Fair, he was not sure how long his illusive gypsy-lady might choose to remain there. Her ways, it seemed, were unpredictable, and he was afraid she might, like a will-o'-the-wisp, slip away from him again.

Nevertheless, as an ex-soldier, he rode his horse wisely, pacing him properly, neither too fast nor too slow. Despite his care, the stallion went lame early in the afternoon and dismounting, Claridge discovered that it had cast a shoe. The next town was several miles away and he was forced to walk the distance, leading his mount. The blacksmith was nowhere about and he finally located him in the local tavern. With an offer of extra money if he would do the job quickly, the man still seemed reluctant to hurry as he reshod the horse, trying Claridge's patience to the limit. Thus, it was that he arrived in Danbury later than he had intended and not in the best of tempers.

Chapter Seven

Angela left the queen, who was suffering from another one of her headaches, and returning to her own rooms discovered her father waiting to see her.

He rose from the armchair where he was sitting by the window and scowled at her. He was such a big man he could intimidate her just by his size.

"No doubt you have heard the news," he growled.

She shook her head as she approached him, wondering what had happened to displease him this time. Catching sight of her maid waiting in the doorway behind him, she waved her away. She did not wish to prolong her father's visit by offering him refreshment.

When the girl had departed, closing the door behind her, Angela seated herself, folding her hands primly in her lap like a little girl. The Earl sprang to his feet and began pacing up and down before her.

"His Grace has left the court," he thundered. "Took off in the middle of the night with no word to anyone."

"Perhaps he was called home," Angela said quietly.

Her father ignored this. "It's unforgivable! He was here over a week and never *once* did he call to see me. Must have had spies out to tell him of my whereabouts, so he could be sure to avoid me. It's worse than humiliating, it's downright dishonorable! I have half a mind to call the man out!"

"But you don't know where he is."

"And neither does the king. I managed an audience with him this morning. Claridge had the gall to leave Whitehall without so much as a by your leave to His Majesty."

"Emergencies do occur, Papa."

"Humph! The man's been procrastinating ever since he arrived at court. This is probably just another excuse."

"Has it not occurred to you that perhaps he does not wish to marry me? Remember this marriage was arranged by you and his father without his consent."

"Nonsense." Her father threw himself back into the chair he had vacated. "His Grace has known about the pledge for years. Known it was his duty."

"Duty," she murmured, "such a romantic reason to wed someone."

"What was that?"

"Nothing, Papa."

"I mean to do something about this, Angela. I won't stand by and—"

"Pray do not," Angela interrupted him, clearly agitated. " 'Twould only cause me embarrassment. I'm sure there is an explanation for His Grace's absence. You told me yourself he was an honorable man of good character."

"That remains to be seen. However, His Majesty is the only one to whom I have vented my feelings. 'Twill go no further, but I will give His Grace but a few days more. I have been far too magnanimous about this matter as it is."

After the Earl had departed, Angela gave a long sigh. It was in her nature to want to please people, to do the right thing. If only she had been able to talk with her father, to say to him, "I don't wish to marry His Grace of Claridge. I care for someone else." But she was all too conscious of her duty and her father's honor to break the pledge he had made. If it was to be broken, it would have to be Claridge who broke it off. She prayed again that he would do just that, although she was not blind to the fact that her father would never consent to her marrying Gerald Waybridge. Not that Gerald had asked her. He knew she was promised to another.

After her accident with the child, Angela, in order to make inquiries as to the health of little Willie, was forced to take another into her confidence. She therefore enlisted the help of a young groom whom she knew she could trust. He had accompanied her on many of her rides to the village to see her Nana, and she had talked with him and learned of his longing to read and write. She had made arrangements with a priest in the village to teach him on any evening when he was not required at the stables, and he was adoringly grateful.

Rising before the servants on the day after the accident, Angela had made her way down to the kitchens and before the sun burst over the horizon had packed a basket of pastries and sweetmeats, for the groom to take to Willie. She had also unearthed a small wooden rocking horse from the nursery which she sent with the message to Auntie Maude that Willie might rid himself of some of his excess energy on it.

The young groom reported back to her later that the child was his old self again and none the worse for the accident and her gifts had been greatly appreciated.

Angela did not stop there. She loved children dearly and after seeing Willie and the orphan's home, she thought of them constantly. In the latter years she had spent at the convent, she had begun to help the sisters with the younger children. She understood their fears and homesickness, their need for love, and had comforted many a child who was sick or unhappy. It had made her feel needed and she had started to think that this was to be her calling in life, when her father had come to take her home.

Now she wanted desperately to be of help to the orphan's home, but knowing it would be impossible for her to go there herself without her father's consent, she did the best she could. She sent the widow who had cared for Nana to Auntie Maude, to help with the children.

It was almost a week later when Angela again laid eyes upon Gerald Waybridge. She was out riding in the dog cart with Jenny, her maid beside her, enjoying the afternoon sunshine as they jogged along the river road. A horseman came into view approaching from the opposite direction and Angela recognized Gerald Waybridge.

It was a lovely spring afternoon. The silver birch that lined the road were now all in leaf and sunshine filtered through their branches to shine down on Angela, dressed in a white gown sprigged with pink rosebuds. A wide-brimmed white hat with pink ribbons topped her fair hair.

As Gerald Waybridge drew up alongside the dog cart, he thought to himself that he had never seen anyone more breathtakingly beautiful. There was something ethereal about her face, almost a spiritual look. Her eyes, he realized, were not the pale blue that one might expect to go with such light-colored hair, but a much darker shade. These eyes seemed to hold him spellbound for a moment before he was able to manage to speak.

"Good afternoon, my lady." He doffed his hat to

her. "A beautiful day, is it not?"

"Very beautiful, sir," she said, a little shyly.

"Auntie Maude has told me how kind you have been to the home. The gifts, the food, and now that hard working, cheery-faced woman."

"I was glad to be of help. I felt responsible for the accident. I might have been more alert that day if my mind had not been on my old Nana."

"Which, under the circumstances, was understandable. Still, it was totally Willie's fault. He ran out before you. Fortunately, the wheel merely grazed him."

His open admiration was beginning to embarrass her. She gave a quick glance in Jenny's direction, but the maid was staring off towards the river. Following her gaze, Angela exclaimed, "Oh look!" She pointed to where a mother duck could be seen with a sizable brood of ducklings. "What a big family she has." She began to count them.

"Nineteen," Waybridge said. "Sometimes one female will look after other ducklings as well as her own."

Wanting a closer look, Angela quickly tied off the reins and began to climb down from the cart. Gerald Waybridge immediately dismounted and put out a hand to assist her. After seeing to his own horse, he followed her down the grassy bank to the river's edge.

The ducks were waddling along the bank in single file and the two of them watched as one by

87

one the ducks reached a low spot and entered the water. They swam out into the river and continued downstream where rounding a wooded point of land they were soon out of sight.

Angela looked around her. It was such a peaceful, tranquil scene. Wild flowers were growing in the grass at their feet. Bullrushes edged the river bank, and on the opposite side, several willows dipped their branches into the clear water.

" 'Tis lovely here," she whispered, opening her arms wide like a child. "So quiet and away from everything."

Gerald looked back toward the road, but the dog cart and horse were hidden from them by a small copse of trees. Without a word, he led Angela back from the river to a spreading beech tree, hung with drooping clusters of purple blossoms. Removing his riding cloak, he placed it on the ground beneath the tree.

"Would you not care to sit down for a little while and admire the view?"

"I truely would," she said, "but . . . well, just for a moment." A little warily she lowered herself to the ground.

At first Gerald spoke to her of the orphan's home and then he found himself opening up to her, telling her of his own hopes and dreams for his land.

She sat as if enraptured as he told her of his farms, of the crops and cattle he hoped to raise. How good the earth was hereabouts, how gentle the weather, compared to his old home up north. He told her stories, some amusing, some sad, of the farmers on his land. He seemed to know each family well, to want to do the best he could for them. He really cares about people, she thought, and her eyes shone up at him as he talked.

"You love this country, too, don't you, my lady?" he said, his eyes never leaving her face.

"I never wish to leave it and yet . . . , my father says . . ." She stopped.

"You must go out into the world," he finished.

"Yes," she turned to him, a look of acute unhappiness on her face. "Eventually I must go to court and be presented to their majesties."

"You are very beautiful," he said a sadness returning to his eyes. "The court loves beautiful women, I hear."

"I know I will hate that world," she said passiontely. "I have no desire to go to masques and balls or be dressed up like . . . like my father wants me to be."

He smiled at her. "It may not be as terrible as you imagine. You are very young. You may enjoy the glitter and excitement."

She shook her lovely head. "Never," she said dully.

"Have you told your father this."

"He would not listen to me. Oh," she sighed, "if only I could sit here forever beneath this tree and never go back."

"Surely 'tis not as bad as all that," he smiled

gently at her.

" 'Tis worse. Far worse. There is another involved, you see."

He frowned. "Is there some way I can help?"

"No. No one can help me. When I was but a babe, my father pledged my hand in marriage to a man I have never seen," Gerald saw the glint of tears in her eyes and reached out to take her hand. "I will meet him at court when the time comes, and then the arrangements will be made for our wedding."

"I see," he said quietly, an empty feeling stealing over him.

"I must . . . go," she said, beginning to scramble to her feet.

He rose beside her, but he did not let go of her hand. She looked down at it and then up into his face and as their eyes met, Gerald felt unable to move. It was as if a spell bound the two of them. Very slowly, as if compelled by something stronger than himself, he drew her into his arms.

He held her like a fluttering young bird, feeling her body quiver against his, feeling . . . sensing . . . her vulnerability. He held her close to comfort her, he thought, but his mouth could not help seeking hers and he found that her lips were as soft and sweet as the petals of a rose.

For only a moment they were joined together, until with a little sob, Angela broke free from his grasp and ran back up the riverbank towards the road.

He watched her as long as he could, until her light-colored gown vanished from view among the trees. Somehow he knew with a certainty he was the first man who had ever touched her.

Remembering this meeting, Angela sat gazing out the window of her sitting room at Whitehall Palace, tears clouding her lovely eyes.

Her father had sent for her shortly after her return to Neville Hall that afternoon. He had learned of what he called "her tryst" with Gerald Waybridge by the river. Never had she seen him so angry.

"Did you open your legs to him, girl?" he had crudely demanded.

It was obvious to Angela that he was well into his cups, and though accustomed to her father's vulgarity at such times, she was nevertheless appalled by his words.

"How can you even suggest such a thing?" she cried, trembling with indignation.

"Your popish prudery doesn't fool me. You females are all alike. Full of outrage one minute, panting for it the next. Well, if it didn't happen this time, it damned well will the next. You're pledged to another, girl, and don't you forget it. His Grace won't be wanting soiled goods."

He then made her promise that under no circumstances was she ever to meet with Gerald Waybridge again. The man was a ne'er-do-well

who was causing grave concern to the other landowners in the county. Apparently having little
knowledge of managing an estate—he had, after
all, come from the bleak and barren Border-
lands—he had raised his laborer's wages even
before the crops were harvested, claiming many in
the district were starving. The man lived like a
pauper himself, with only one man to attend him.
No family. Had lost his home in the war and a
wife and child somewhere.

Angela's eyes misted. Now she understood that
look of sadness in Gerald's face. Yet, she thought,
he had tried to comfort her. He, who had suffered
so much more than she could imagine. It made
her feel very small indeed.

The Earl was going on about Waybridge obviously not being used to his new status. He had
inherited his uncle's title, it seemed. Fancy a
baronet working as his own bailiff! It was unthinkable! Most distressing to the local gentry.

"I think it admirable of him, Papa," Angela had
the temerity to say. "His estates have long been
neglected and he is working very hard to bring
them back and—"

"So you think him admirable," the Earl snorted.
"No doubt his efforts would seem heroic to one as
green as you. It appears the sooner we remove
you from the country the better."

During all the lonely years she had spent at the
convent, Angela had developed an idea of what
the man she would marry would be like. That

was, of course, if she did not decide to renounce the world entirely and take her vows. The man she married must be a sensitive, gentle, dedicated man. A man, she realized now, not unlike Gerald Waybridge.

Lying in her bed that night she instinctively put her fingers to her lips, reliving Gerald's kiss. She could still feel his warm mouth on hers, hear the deep note in his voice, the pounding of her heart when he pressed her close to him.

He had been so sweet, so gentle. All those things she had hoped for in a man. Although she was but seventeen and quite innocent, she felt sure she would never feel quite the same about any other man.

Chapter Eight

Inside the black tent, Elizabeth was unaware of the group that was gathering a short distance away. She had not heard their low murmurings.

"The Scriptures say, 'Let no witch live'. Shall we allow it, brothers?" said a tall, gaunt man dressed in somber black. "The devil's handmaiden is in that tent!"

"But 'tis a full moon, tonight," said one. "Her powers will be their greatest."

"Then we must grasp her soon, before the sun sets."

"How can we be sure she be a witch?" another asked.

"Will Barlow saw the devil's mark on her."

"The devil's mark!"

"Aye, Satan has marked her as one of his. Should we allow his daughter to remain among us?"

A groan went up. "She'll poison our wells!"

"Bring the plague down upon us!"

"Aye, we must be rid of her," more than one confirmed.

"She must surely burn!" The gaunt man cried hoarsely.

"Aye, burning the witch will gain us salvation for our sins."

"Burn her!" the hue and cry was taken up. "Burn the witch!"

The group had grown ugly. Grasping sticks and whatever else they could use as weapons, they moved menacingly toward the tent.

"Out of the way!" they cried to the black-cloaked lad who had been proclaiming the gypsy's uncanny powers outside the tent. "Out of the way, or be burnt alongside the witch!"

"She be no witch," the lad had the temerity to declare. "She be but a poor gypsy woman."

A brutal clout to the side of his head silenced him and he fell heavily to the ground and lay quiet before the entrance to the tent. Several rushed past him, ripping open the flap and bursting inside.

"The witch! Get the witch!" yelled those left behind.

Hearing the commotion, Elizabeth had jumped up and now stood uncertainly in the center of the tent.

"What do you want with me?" she asked, striving to keep her voice level as the wild-eyed men lurched toward her.

They said nothing as they roughly seized her by the wrists and dragged her out of the tent.

A sizable crowd had now gathered and hoots and catcalls greeted her appearance.

"The witch! The witch! Death to the witch!" The cry was taken up by the gathering mob.

Terror filled Elizabeth as she viewed the unconscious body of the boy she had hired, and looking into the faces of those around her could see none that bore the slightest compassion for her plight. It was clear that she was on her own against this unruly bunch. No one would dare interfere on her behalf.

"I've done nothing to thee," she exclaimed, holding her head high. "I am no witch."

"Liar! the devil dwells in thy tent!"

"Aye, many saw his glowing eyes!"

" 'Tis false!"

"Nay! Thou hast brought Satan with thee," said the tall, gaunt man who had made himself their leader.

"Injuries have plagued our townsfolk since ye came to this fair!"

"My John fell from his horse and broke his arm."

"Aaron, the tinker, tumbled into the stream and nearly drowned."

Elizabeth spoke up at last. " 'Twas all the mead they consumed and not—" but she was instantly silenced.

"You lie! Both had just been to see thee and

ridiculed thy powers."

"Aye. Thee had Satan put a curse on them!"

"Witch! Ye be in league with the devil!"

"If that be so," Elizabeth's voice rose. "Then you'd best let me go." She stared at them intently. "I could put the evil eye on all of thee!"

Some of the crowd drew back in superstitious fear at her words, but the two who held her fast did not loosen their grip, as the leader produced a wooden cross from beneath his cloak and held it up before her.

"This symbol of our Lord will protect us!" he shouted. "Thy powers are useless against it."

With the tall man holding the cross in front of her, the men dragged Elizabeth away from the tent.

She now realized what a mistake it had been to pretend she possessed supernatural powers. They were all firmly convinced now that she was a witch. She knew it was useless to struggle. There were too many of them and even if she could manage to break free, other hands would grab her. She had never felt such abject terror! Still, she was determined that they would not see her reduced to fear and trembling. Elizabeth raised her head high and kept her eyes straight ahead.

Surrounded by the jostling, jeering crowd, she was pushed and shoved onward toward the center of the lea. She didn't doubt now that the mob was in deadly earnest and she tried to keep the panic from rising within her as she saw where they were headed. A flagstaff was set solidly in the ground in the center of the lea. It would make a perfect stake to which to tie her.

"Burn her! Burn Satan's handmaid!"

The crowd stormed onward, pushing the slim girl in the gaudy gypsy costume before them.

Elizabeth fell once under an onslought of acorns that some youths had gathered from the woods nearby, but she was yanked to her feet again and pulled on.

When the crowd reached the flagstaff, the somberly-clad man grabbed Elizabeth's left hand in his and held it up for all to see.

"Here be the proof of her guilt," he cried, showing them the vivid birthmark on her palm. "It be the shape of a cloven hoof! Satan's mark!"

Low, frightened murmurs went up from the superstitious rustics and they drew back in fear.

Elizabeth now remembered the fellow who had been slightly foxed and had stumbled getting up from the stool before her table. She had put out her left hand to keep him from falling and he must have seen her birthmark. That was how all this had started! The man had thought her marked by the devil!

"There be only one way to deal with a witch," the leader cried. "Burn her, I say! Burn her!"

The chant was taken up again by the mob and Elizabeth was roughly shoved against the flagstaff, her hands bound with rope behind her back, her ankles also secured.

A yell went up just then from the area where the gypsy's tent had stood. "They've fired her wagon!" someone shouted.

A cloud of smoke was rising in the autumn twilight.

"Burn all her tools of evil! Burn everything she has touched!"

The gaunt leader now began directing some of the men, making them spread out to gather dead branches and twigs from the woods behind the lea.

They had been afraid to remove Elizabeth's veil and her large, terrified eyes watched the men gathering the wood into bundles and throwing them at her feet. She longed to scream out against them but knew it would do no good and might even incite them further.

Would it have made a difference, she wondered if they had seen she was not a gypsy? If she had flung off her head covering? No. They would probably have accused her of using trickery, of calling on the devil to change her appearance.

Surely this would not be how her life would end? Perhaps she was dreaming. In that dream, there had been a mob at her heels but her 'Moonlight Cavalier' had rescued her in time, before they had reached her. Where was he now? Would no one save her in time? This was no dream. It was all too real! She should never have left St. Margaret's Fair! She should never . . . But what good did it do now to think of that? Her time was

99

growing short. All she could do was pray.

"Where is the resin?" someone asked.

"And the tinder. We need the tinder."

"Watch how the witch will burn!" The tall leader rubbed his hands together gleefully.

The crowd had moved back to better view the proceedings. They stood at the edge of the lea, gazing mockingly at the figure tied to the flag-staff.

"Hurry!" someone cried. " 'Twill be dark soon. We want to see the devil fly out of her."

The resin torch was ready. There was a flicker of the tinder and then a sudden shout of triumph. The torch was blazing.

"Burn the witch! Burn her!" The chant began again.

At the moment the gaunt man stepped forward with the torch, the dull thud of approaching hoofbeats could be heard over the hush of the crowd. Suddenly a horseman appeared, galloping hard up the lea, heading straight for the knot of people standing there.

Afraid of being trampled, they scattered before him as he reined in his coal-black stallion, bringing it to a nervous, snorting halt.

Elizabeth could only stare unbelievingly at the man who quickly dismounted and confronted the crowd.

The fading sunlight caught the white satin lining of his cape as he threw it back from his shoulders, the brocade of his silver-colored doublet, and flashing diamond in the frost-point lace at his throat, his proud, angry face, as he swept the large, white-plumed hat from his head.

"What deviltry is this?" he demanded in his deep, rich voice.

Being used to submitting to rank, the crowd stepped back for a moment in deference to such a splendid figure. But it was only for a moment. They were too fired up now to stop. They wanted only one thing. The witch's death!

" 'Tis no place for a fine gentleman," the leader sneered. "Take thy hand off thy elegant sword and let us do what we must do."

"Aye!" Let us burn the witch!" another shouted.

In answer, the newcomer drew his long pointed weapon.

"The first one who steps forward is a dead man!" he said quietly, although the clear resonance of his voice was heard by all.

"What right have you?" demanded the leader, his pale face contorting with anger.

"Every right," the voice above him bellowed. "I am the Duke of Claridge. This is *my* land you stand upon."

Chapter Nine

Learning the newcomer's identity, murmurs of fear echoed through the crowd. "His Grace . . ." "The Duke of Claridge himself . . ." "He'll have us all hanged!"

Hats were hastily removed, some even fell to their knees before him. The torch that had been held aloft, was tossed aside to roll unnoticed down the lea and flicker out in the damp grass below.

The crowd began a general movement of retreat, but Claridge stopped the leader with a steely glare.

"You there!" he cried. "You untie her and be quick about it." He turned back to the others. "Dastardly cowards! The whole lot of you! Tormenting a lone, defenseless woman. Be gone before I have you whipped!"

The crowd quickly took to their heels as Claridge stepped back to observe the somberly-clad man freeing the girl.

"I warrant you incited this riot. A Puritan malcontent, are you?"

"Nay, Your Grace," the man swiftly denied the allegation. "I am a loyal subject of His Majesty."

"Mmmm. I wonder. I believe I will inform the justice hereabouts to keep an eye on you."

Considerably agitated by now, the so-called leader hastened after the others, melting quickly into the crowd fleeing down the lea.

With one of his Spanish leather boots, Claridge kicked away the piles of wood that lay at Elizabeth's feet.

"It appears I arrived just in time," he said, his dark eyes flashing in anger.

Reaching Danbury in the late afternoon, Claridge had noticed the flags and brightly colored tents of the fair set up on the lea beyond the town. As he had ridden toward it, the shouts and clamor of an angry mob had met his ears and spurred him into action.

In the fast fading light, Elizabeth's luminous eyes appeared extraordinarily large above her veil. The hot tears hadn't even started before he had her in his arms and was hushing her deep sobs, as all she had experienced in the last terrifying hour came tumbling out.

He stroked her head and her quivering back with his strong, sure hands, whispering words of comfort. She made no effort to pull away from him or to push him from her. Instead, she leaned against him for strength as the sobs slowly subsided. Her heart stopped pounding in her ears and her body ceased its shaking from her close encounter with death. She could hardly believe it was all over; that she had been rescued in time by her Moonlight Cavalier.

The two of them stood silhouetted at the top of the lea. Elizabeth, although she was quite tall for a woman, hardly reached the top of Claridge's broad shoulders. He held her gently, quietly reassuring her, until, at last, she stopped trembling.

"Thank you," she whispered, stepping back, her eyes never leaving him.

What a commanding presence he possessed, she thought in admiration. He was not wearing a mask and for the first time she was able to observe his face. His features were strong, his nose almost aqualine, his jawline clean and firm. It was a face one would not forget, uncompromisingly masculine; yet, she knew, it could be lightened by those teasing, smokey eyes, that devastating smile. The sudden catch in her throat attested to the degree of its handsomeness. She had thought him to be a nobleman, but never had she thought him to be of such a high rank. His Grace, the Duke of Claridge!

"They didn't hurt you?" he was asking her, his face showing caring concern.

"No." She shook her head, although she was rubbing her wrists where they had been so tightly tied.

"I had a devil of a time finding you," he said almost angrily, taking her arm to lead her over to where his big horse waited, impatiently flicking its tail.

Suddenly Elizabeth stopped, staring at Claridge's mount. "But he's the wrong color," she said inexplicably.

"He's . . . what?" Claridge turned to look down at her, a puzzled frown creasing his brow. Then the humor of the situation struck him, and he broke into rich laughter.

"I rescue you from certain death and you are bothered by the color of my horse?"

"But, you see," she explained, quite reasonably, "he should have been white. The knight who rescues the damsel in distress always rides—"

"A white steed," he finished, his laugh deepening. "I'm sorry about his color, but his name may make up for it. In fact, I think it quite apropos under the circumstances."

"What is it?"

"Satan." His voice took on a sepulchral quality. "Satan arrives precipitately to carry off his witch into the darkness of the night."

She shivered. "Do not call me that, I pray you, even in jest. I am no witch."

"I'm not too sure of that. You've quite bewitched *me* Why else would I have sent couriers out in every direction in search of you?"

"You . . . you did that?"

"I did. I returned to the fair the next night, as I

105

said I would, and found you gone. "I'm not used to wenches running away from me."

She didn't doubt that in the least.

"A soldier I had known in the army finally located you." Claridge grasped Satan's reins and assisted Elizabeth up onto the front of the horse. Quickly mounting behind her, he said, "we must away from here to some place safer for you."

"Please," she begged, as they headed down the lea, "could we first go back to where my tent and caravan were standing? Someone struck down the young lad who worked for me and I wish to see if he is badly hurt."

So saying she placed a hand on his arm and looked up at him with such trust in her eyes, that it made him feel even more protective of her. What an amazing creature, he thought. In spite of her strength at standing up to those ruffians, there was such an air of vulnerability about her.

They found the lad standing by the smouldering ashes of the caravan. He looked frightened as the big horse approached and took to his heels, loping off toward the woods.

"Don't run, Tim," Elizabeth called after him, in her husky, gypsy voice.

At her words the lad stopped and turned around, watching as the big horse and its dual burden drew closer.

"They burned everything," he told Elizabeth, indicating the destruction with a sweep of his arm.

"I know, Tim," she said, "but I'm more concerned for you. Are you all right?" Slipping easily from the horse's back, she walked over to him, moving so lightly that to the watching Claridge she hardly seemed to touch the ground.

"There be a lump on the side of my head," the lad said, feeling it, "but 'tis not so bad," he added bravely.

"I'm glad of that," she said. "You must leave here, Tim. It isn't safe for you now."

He looked confused. "But ye know I'm homeless. Where can I go?"

"Chichfield," Claridge quietly suggested, overhearing their exchange. "Go to Chichfield and ask for Master Pottle at the "King's Head". Tell him I said he should give you work."

The youth looked up in awe at the big man sitting on the back of the most magnificent horse he had ever seen.

"But . . . but sir, I do not even know thy name, though I give thee thanks for saving us both."

"His Grace, the Duke of Claridge," Elizabeth told him. "Do as he says, Tim. You're welcome to keep old Rom and ride her there. I have no caravan now for her to pull."

"Thank 'ee," the lad said, clearly moved by the gesture. Turning to Claridge, he attempted a clumsy bow. "And thank 'ee, Your Grace."

"Get along with you, lad," Claridge said, not unkindly. "You'd best away from here in case those ruffians come back."

"Aye, I will do that," the boy gave a lopsided grin and started off to where the old horse could be seen, safely hobbled, at the edge of the woods.

"Come, we must be away as well," Claridge turned back to Elizabeth, but she had picked up a stick and moving over to where the caravan had stood, began to poke about in the ashes.

"There's nothing left, lass," he said sadly. "Let it be."

But she paid him no mind and continued her search. Suddenly, she gave an exultant cry. "Here it is!"

With the stick, she pushed something out of the ruins and onto the grass nearby.

Claridge dismounted and came over to her. "What have you found?"

"My metal cash box, but 'tis still too hot to touch."

She removed a key and cord from around her neck and handed it to him. Claridge knelt down before the box and attempted to open the lock. Even through his gauntlets, he could feel the heat as he struggled to raise the lid. At last, the key turned and he threw open the box. It was half filled with coins.

Claridge looked up at Elizabeth with a smile. "Your wealth is quite intact," he said.

She thanked him and he carried the box over to his horse where he opened a saddlebag and poured the contents into it.

" 'Twill be safe here," he said, throwing away the

box.

" 'Tis all I have in the world," she said softly. "And still 'tis not enough . . ."

"Enough for what?"

She did not answer him.

"Forever a mystery," he smiled, as he again assisted her up onto the back of his big stallion and mounted behind her. This time he kept one hand about her waist as he held the reins with the other. "You not only keep your face hidden from me, but your thoughts as well. Do you think that fair, after what I have done for you?"

"No," she admitted, "but for the present, I cannot reveal more."

"What an intriguing little minx you are." He didn't point out to her how easy it would be for him to pull the veil from her face. He let her keep her disguise, but he held her firmly against him as he guided his horse around to the south of the lea, circling the town. He would not take the chance of a sudden ambush by that Puritan malcontent and his friends.

It had grown dark, but the moon was rising, a huge harvest moon shining down on them as they crossed an open meadow. A full moon, in a clear, starlit sky. Claridge kept his horse at a steady pace as they rode along, angling back to the main road, just west of Danbury.

"We'll head for Bridgetown. Put up for the night at the inn there and start for London in the morning," he told her.

"As you wish," she said. She patted the horse's neck. "What a beautiful animal he is. He must be at least sixteen hands tall."

"Seventeen and a half, to be exact," Claridge smiled. "You know something of horses?"

He thus discovered her love for them and got her chatting pleasantly about horses in order to keep her mind from returning to her terrifying brush with death.

He told her how his grandfather had bred horses at Claridge House for speed and beauty. How as a lad he had been taken along to horse fairs and auctions, the Danbury Fair being one of them. His grandfather, he explained, had imported numerous oriental animals and the present king's father had obtained many of his breeding stock from the old Duke.

Many of his horses had raced and won at Newmarket before the war, but all the stables had been emptied to help the king's army. So, he would just have to start all over again as he had begun to do with his land.

"It must be very difficult," Elizabeth said.

Claridge nodded. "But I'm enjoying the challenge."

He would indeed, Elizabeth thought, looking up at him admiringly. There would be little that would defeat this man, despite the tremendous job of reconstruction she was sure he would have to do to make his estates productive again.

He was a man who inspired confidence and got

things done. The soldiers who had served under his leadership would probably have followed him unquestionably. He was that kind of man.

Feeling his strong arm protectively about her, Elizabeth felt safe and secure for the first time in many months. She was riding off down a moon-drenched road with her Moonlight Cavalier. It was all so like her dream and yet so very real.

As they travelled on she became more and more aware of the intimacy of their situation, of his nearness. He had an immense physical attraction for her which had overwhelmed her from the moment she had first seen him. She felt he must surely hear how fast her heart was beating when the road dipped suddenly and he was forced to tighten his hold on her. She had thought never to trust a man again, but somehow she had known from the start that she could trust this one.

She might have thought differently if she had been aware of the effect she was having on Claridge as he held her slim body so close against his own. Through the thin skirt of her gypsy costume, he felt one soft thigh pressed against him and he was stirred by a hungry ache of desire. This little gypsy lady had haunted his dreams all week long. Now he was holding her near. Disturbingly near. Lapsing into silence, he spurred his horse forward toward Bridgetown.

When they reached the stables of the inn, Claridge dismounted and reached up to lift Elizabeth down from the saddle. For a long moment he

111

held her, looking into the deep blue of her eyes. A current seemed to pass between them and she could not look away. She was so very close to him. So close she could smell the warm, masculine smells of leather and horses that clung to him. Her body trembled with a strange anticipation.

In slow motion, he lowered her to the ground, his hands sliding downward from her waist to the curve of her hips, crushing her against his hard chest. A desperate longing rose unbidden within her and when he released her she found she had been holding her breath.

From under his saddle he removed and unfolded his long cloak, placing it about her shoulders and pulling the hood up over her head.

"This will shield you from curious glances," he said, before they entered the building.

One look at His Grace and the innkeeper promptly instructed his servant to give them the best rooms in the inn. Claridge ordered brandy be sent up with them and then assisted Elizabeth up the dark staircase.

The room they entered was pleasant, its walls panelled, its windows leaded, and the ceiling beams of heavy oak. A table and two chairs had been placed before a blazing fire. Noticing the adjoining bedchamber, Elizabeth found herself blushing.

" 'Tis not right I share your rooms," she whispered to Claridge as the servant placed a tray on the oaken table.

Claridge closed the door after the man. "We could have been followed," he said, without looking at her. "I didn't want to leave you alone."

She realized then that she didn't want to be left alone—not after all she had been through. She was still not completely over the shock. She could still hear that wild, inflamed mob shouting, "Death to the witch! Burn the witch!" Even the thought made her shudder.

He saw her tremble and quickly sat her down near the fire, pouring out a goodly amount of brandy for her to drink.

"Drink it down," he instructed. "It will do you good."

Lifting the edge of her veil, Elizabeth held up the goblet and swallowed some of the fiery liquid. She promptly choked.

"Drink it more slowly," he smiled.

She did as she was told and life seemed to slowly return to her numb limbs.

"To your bravery, my mystery lady," Claridge announced, raising his glass to her as he sat down on the opposite side of the table. "Never once, during that whole monstrous travesty did you break down or cry out for help."

Feeling embarrassed by his praise, Elizabeth looked down at her goblet. There was only a little brandy left in it. She drank it down.

"I'm afraid if I had cried out, the crowd would have thought I was summoning Satan," she finally answered him. A glowing warmth had begun to spread through her.

"You're probably right." He looked at her approvingly as he rose and picking up the decanter came around the table to stand by her side as he refilled her glass. "But your cool behavior was nonetheless remarkable."

"For a woman, you mean," her eyes smiled up at him. It was a mistake. He returned their smile. Standing so close to her his nearness seemed to radiate a sensation that both thrilled and discomforted her.

"No," he said seriously, "I've seen men in battle show fear at much less than you were forced to experience this evening."

"My veil did much to hide my fear."

"Yet I saw it mirrored in your eyes."

"Our most revealing feature, I've discovered. In my profession I have read much in people's eyes — suspicion, assent and denial, concealment . . ."

They stared at one another. The silence stretching out for a long, eternal moment. Finally he cleared his throat. "Would you care for some supper?" he asked.

"Yes," she agreed, a little breathlessly, "I believe I would."

The meal they were served was excellent — mutton, sturgeon, and chicken, served with a good Malmsey wine. Elizabeth watched as Claridge consumed a large portion of chicken and vegetables and helped himself to more. He was so big and disturbingly handsome, sitting so close to her across the little table.

Elizabeth ate slowly, not really tasting the little she managed to swallow. She watched as Claridge picked up a chicken leg, tearing the flesh apart with his strong, white teeth and felt a tantalizing shiver go through her body. He licked his lips and she saw his long fingers curl about the goblet as he took a long sip of wine. She could not help but think that those same firm lips had once covered her own, those same strong hands had held her so tightly against him.

He was treating her with infinite courtesy, keeping her wine glass filled, entertaining her with amusing tales of Whitehall and his years on the Continent. She noticed, however, that he never mentioned the battles he had fought in or the bloodshed. No doubt he wished to forget that part of his life.

All the while he talked to her, Claridge watched her carefully. Her table manners, he noticed, despite the difficulty of maneuvering beneath her veil, were as correct as any lady of his acquaintance, and in this age when the fork was only beginning to make an appearance, much better than most. Her soft voice had the same pattern of speech as his own. The questions she put to him relayed her high degree of intelligence.

"Is debt the main reason our king doesn't pursue a more vigorous foreign policy?" she asked. And when he had confirmed this, "Last year he was forced to sell Dunkirk to France. Soon England will not be able to defend any of her overseas possessions."

"You would get along well with my lord Clarendon," he smiled, "he holds a like view." The smile left his face. "Charles, I'm afraid, though a charming rogue, has no interest in matters of finance, either abroad or domestic. The gifts and titles showered on his mistresses and illegitimate children are a constant drain on the royal coffers."

A small silence followed his words.

"I must apologize for that remark," he said.

"Everyone is aware of it." Her eyes swept over him. She was wondering if his own morals equalled those of his king.

"Have you, like him, had many mistresses?" she asked unexpectedly, totally surprising herself by speaking aloud what she was thinking. The brandy and the wine must be having their effect.

"I would not be a gentleman if I answered that," he said solemnly, though his mouth twitched at the corners.

Mortification filled the deep blue eyes and she stammered, "Di . . . did I really say that?"

He laughed then, the fine lines etched around his eyes crinkling with humor. There was no cynicism now in the smile that widened his mouth.

His laugh was infectious. A little chortle of joy left her throat and soon her laughter joined his.

"How appalled Miss Inglis would be at my impropriety," she choked.

"Miss Inglis?"

"My governess. She . . ." Elizabeth's laughter faded as her eyes met his and her feelings were stirred by the intentness of his gaze. Inadvertently, she realized, she had given him another clue to her past. Only a few noblewomen were tutored by governesses.

"I — I think I would like another glass of wine, Your Grace," she said quietly.

"Simon," he corrected her. He poured the wine, his hand brushing hers as she reached for the goblet.

Raising it to her lips, she looked into his eyes. The pupils seemed to have darkened. Their mysterious depths fascinated her. Again she felt that awareness. That inexorable pull. The very air seemed to vibrate with a seductive insistence.

She sensed where it all was leading. She could not deny her gratitude or her attraction to this man.

She thought of how her past had held so little happiness, how her future was so uncertain. Why not live for the moment? Why not let this happen? Why should she not have some happiness to remember? He was, after all, her Moonlight Cavalier and after tonight she might never see him again.

"Little witch," he whispered. His face was close to hers. Very close. She set down her glass, her heart pounding wildly. Simultaneously they both rose from the table.

117

In one swift motion she was in his arms, throbbing against his hard chest so close she could feel the beat of his heart, echoing the urgent pounding of her own. A new warmth began to flow through her, a warmth like that of the brandy and wine, yet infinitely more pleasurable.

She felt languid and sleepy, the memory of her terrible fright becoming more and more hazy in her mind. The fire, the strong liquor, Claridge's warm, reassuring presence, were all having their effect. Why not? Why not? cried her heart.

She swayed in his arms as the room began to revolve around her and made a grasp at his shoulders to steady herself. The room stopped spinning.

"Simon," she murmured, a little slurringly, and he could read the passionate invitation in her soft eyes, "Will you take me to bed?"

Chapter Ten

Smiling to himself over the extent of Elizabeth's disarmament, Claridge was nonetheless surprised by her words. Ever since he had held her so close against him on Satan's back, a plan of seduction had begun to take shape in his mind. He had purposely kept her glass filled all evening. He had hoped the wine, her gratitude, and their obvious attraction for one another would, in time, lead her to his bed.

Why then, at her words, did he feel a strange disillusionment? It was what he wanted, wasn't it? And yet, somewhere, in the deep recesses of his mind, he must have hoped she would not be so easy to bed.

Elizabeth had let go of his shoulders and was swaying slightly before him, uncomfortably aware of the closeness of his lean, hard body. To combat her nervousness, she lifted her chin and asked, "Well?"

A slight mocking smile curved his mouth. "Why not?" he murmured.

She turned away from him as if to make for the bedchamber, but he laid a hand on her arm and drew her back to him.

"Remove your veil," he commanded quickly, "or do you want me to do it for you?"

"No!" she cried with dismay. "You must not look on me."

"What's this? he exclaimed, clearly annoyed.

"The bedchamber must be in total darkness or I ... I will not ..."

He gave a harsh laugh. "Do you actually think you can stop me now?" With no effort he swept her up into his arms and carried her through to the room beyond. He kicked the door closed behind him and crossing to the big four-poster bed, dropped her unceremoniously onto it.

The heavy curtains at the window had already been drawn and the fire was only dim embers in the grate, so that the only light in the room was from a candle on the nightstand by the bed. Elizabeth quickly reached over and extinguished it.

"This is damn nonsense," Claridge snorted, banging a shin against the bedpost. "Why shouldn't I see you? I don't even know your name."

"Beth," she whispered. "You may call me Beth."

"Am I likely to recognize you, Beth, if I should see your face? Is that the reason for this idiocy?"

he growled, beginning to disrobe.

Elizabeth said nothing as with trembling hands she removed her veil and coif. She felt a queer sense of detachment, as if this were happening to someone else. Even when he lay down beside her and took her in his arms, the feeling persisted. It wasn't her he was kissing, his lips warm and gentle against hers, it was some other girl. It must be some other girl. Elizabeth Fairclough would never allow this. It was all part of some dreamlike trance.

She felt him begin to unfasten her clothing, to slip the gypsy costume down from her shoulders. For a moment she was left shivering in her thin chemise before the warmth of him was felt against her side. When his hand touched her bare shoulder, she started and tried to pull away, but he held her with one hand while the other slipped beneath her head, burying itself in her thick, sweet-smelling hair.

"So soft and silky," he murmured, thinking to himself that it surely must be fair in color to match the fair skin that blushed so easily.

He tilted her face upward and his questing lips came down again on hers. Softly they touched and moved and drank, savoring the sweetness of lips that trembled beneath his warm, passionate mouth.

How inexperienced she seemed! Was this mere pretense on her part? He wondered. Nevertheless, the desire that pounded through him became gentler. He felt again a sense of protectiveness toward the trembling girl in his arms. Slowly he attempted to kiss away her trepidation.

She submitted lifelessly at first, shaking, unsure of what she should be doing. But as Claridge's soft lips moved over hers, the knot of fear inside her began to dissolve, to be replaced by that same sweet longing she had always experienced in his arms.

He explored her lips slowly, holding her a little away from him until, with a small choke, she wound her arms about his neck and melted against him. Her mouth opened under his gentle teasing and as his tongue slid against hers, his kiss deepened, joining them together with the intimate contact.

He drew her closer to him and her breath drew short as she felt the hard power of him against her. One hand slipped under her chemise, caressing the warm, soft skin as it cupped a satin-smooth breast. Slowly, his thumb worked the nipple so that spasms of joy washed over her. Kiss after breathless kiss followed, her mouth opening wider to him, letting him explore more deeply.

Encouraged, his hands began to move over her, gently stroking her body through the thin chemise, slowly peeling the light undergarment from her, revealing to his sensitive fingertips the beauty beneath.

His lips moved to her eyelids, her cheeks, the

hollow of her throat, trailing downwards, following his caressing fingers to her breasts. He heard her gasp as his tongue circled one sensitive nipple and then the other. She began to moan softly and come alive beneath his attentions, the ache inside her almost unbearable under his slow, delicious torture.

One hand began drifting lower in a gentle, teasing path, leaving a trail of fire in its wake as it moved over the delicate curves of her slim body. Lovingly he stroked her thighs, pushing them gently apart, searching further.

As he found the softness between, her body responded and she arched against him. The wine and brandy she had consumed made the inhibitions and fear Ramsden had instilled in her evaporate under this new feeling of desire Claridge was producing.

A sob escaped her lips as he continued to gently and rhythmically probe the most intimate part of her body.

Her response was exciting him. What a marvellously beautiful creature she was. The firm, high breasts, the small waist and gently rounded hips, the soft flesh ... He had never felt such warm, silken skin. It fairly glowed beneath his touch.

Elizabeth was sure she was in a dream. Claridge had aroused her beyond anything she had believed possible, awakening every inch of her body, setting her aflame with his soft caresses. She exulted in the tumultuous sensations he was creating. Her mind ceased to function as the passion rose. All that mattered was him. She would let him do whatever he liked with her.

Claridge continued to prolong the pleasure, holding himself achingly in check, stroking her slowly, reverently, until she began to twist and thrust against the velvet touch that had begun to drive her wild.

Her heart raced as he rose over her, the warm pressure of his manhood seeking entry. His lips were on hers once more and he murmured soft endearments to her. Raising herself to welcome him, she pushed eagerly against him, longing for more of him.

As she felt the pain that she should have expected, but under such intense pleasure had forgotten, she gave a little cry.

At the knowledge that he was the first to possess this passionate little creature, Claridge was both incredulous and delighted. Was this her repayment to him for saving her life? Or did she share the attraction he felt for her?

Having paused, he now began whispering reassuringly to her, holding her close, giving her a moment to accept their joining before he began to move within her, rhythmically, luxuriously, until the pain melted for her into a new, hungry anguish.

She told herself, even as her senses swirled with incredible joy, that it was only because he was the Moonlight Cavalier of her dreams that this magic had come about. Yet, all the while the all-encompassing passion rose within, rolling over her in rising waves of trembling ecstasy.

When at last she bridged the crest of the highest wave and the pleasure burst over her, she cried aloud with the sheer joy of it and he covered her cries with kisses until the pleasurable agony subsided.

In warm, languid contentment, Elizabeth lay against his broad shoulder. One of his hands rested protectively about her while the other played with a soft curl of her long hair.

"Why didn't you tell me?" he asked.

She didn't answer him, although she knew what he meant.

"Did you give me your precious gift because I saved your life?"

She still didn't answer.

"I hope I didn't hurt you," he said anxiously.

She shook her head. "Oh, no. It was quite . . . wonderful."

He smiled at her words. "I find you quite wonderful, too, my sweet Beth. You've bewitched me, do you know that? Since the first time I saw you I haven't been able to get you out of my mind."

He bent to kiss her again and this time he didn't have to tease her lips to open. With an eagerness that both charmed and amused him she lifted her soft mouth to his.

Hot waves of emotion flared through her, arousing her, filling her again with an aching hunger to feel him become part of her again. This time there was no pain for her, only sweet, intense pleasure.

Elizabeth felt no shame for what she had done. She was a woman now. He had made her a woman—this big man who had stolen her heart. It was as if something truly magic had happened when they came together. It had been more than wonderful. It had been perfect.

"My lovely little Beth, he whispered. "None has ever been as warm and sweet as you."

"Do you mean that?" her voice trembled. "Or do you always say—"

"I never say anything I don't mean."

"Then will you tell me something?" she asked in so soft a voice he had to turn his ear to her. "Does it get better each time? If it does I don't believe I can bear it."

Claridge laughed aloud. "You will. There is much I would like to teach you."

Her heart soared at his words, for it surely meant he did not intend to part with her. He must care for her, too! He must!

Holding her tight against his side, Claridge began to tell her about his home, of Claridge House, which lay only another day's ride from Bridgetown. Would she like to see it before they returned to London?

He talked animatedly about the improvements he was already making and the ones he intended to make. She listened and was not afraid to make the occasional suggestion.

"We are so much alike, you and I," he murmured, burying his face in the softness of her hair. "Oh Beth, my love, we are going to be together from now on."

"You are sure you know what you are saying? I'm afraid . . ."

"Don't ever be afraid. You will never have to hide from anyone again. I will look after you always."

"Look after . . ." her voice drifted away.

"Yes. You are mine now in everything but name. I cannot give you that, as my marriage has been arranged for some time, but I will give you all else you might desire."

At his words, a sharp pain pierced Elizabeth's heart and she felt her senses reeling.

"You would marry someone else?" she asked in a strangled tone. "After—"

He sighed deeply. "I cannot break my pledge, Beth. 'Twas something decided by our fathers long ago. The king has given me a week to declare myself. I will meet her then."

"You have never met her?" Elizabeth asked incredulously.

"No. But does it matter? 'Twill only be a *mariage de convenance*, as the French say. What I feel for you, my sweet, will always be something quite apart from that which I might feel for her."

"But you hardly know me."

"I know you enough to know we belong together. Don't deny our minds are as in tune as our

127

bodies."

"Simon, I—"

"Say you'll come with me," he demanded. "Say it!"

Again he captured her lips, but before she could give an answer, sleep had carried him off in a sigh of satisfaction. He had not slept at all the night before and had ridden long and hard that day in pursuit of her.

Elizabeth, lying rigid beside him, listened to his deep, even breathing, shame beginning to rise within her for the first time. Shame for the way she had thrown herself at him this evening. Shame for the feelings she had let him awaken her. Shame for the wanton way she had responded.

She was Elizabeth Fairclough, a noblewoman with a family as old and as honorable as the Duke of Claridge's, yet he considered her in the same light as a doxy!

How could he know? A voice within her asked. She had not permitted him to see her or know anything about her. She felt herself blushing at the thought that she had allowed him with his lips and his fingers to become familiar with every part of her.

She would leave before he awoke, Elizabeth decided. It was the only way. And this time she would make sure he didn't follow her. She would never be any man's mistress! She was far too proud for that.

Quietly, she crawled from the bed and felt around on the cold floor for her discarded articles of clothing. She would like to have opened the curtains in order to see more clearly, but didn't dare for fear he might waken.

At last Elizabeth had recovered everything and began to quietly dress herself in the gypsy costume. She left only her veil behind because at the last moment she dropped it and couldn't find it. Snatching up the cloak Simon had lent her and the saddle bag with her coins, she crept to the door. Her heart hammered as she eased up the iron crossbar. Luck was with her. The old door opened without a squeak.

Hovering on the threshold, Elizabeth looked back toward the bed. She could barely see his dark head against the pillows.

"Goodbye, my love," she mouthed, "my Moonlight Cavalier."

Tears filled her eyes as she soundlessly pulled the door closed behind her. No one saw her descend the old stairway and slip out of the inn into the early morning mist.

Chapter Eleven

Ever since the afternoon when her father had learned of her meeting with Gerald Waybridge and forbidden her to see him again, Angela had been suspicious of Jenny, her maid.

Who else could have told her father? No other had been present or could have observed them, unless someone had passed along the road and had seen Jenny waiting in the dog cart and Gerald's horse tied nearby. It hurt Angela to think that someone so close to her would betray her; yet, she decided to keep an eye on Jenny.

In the next few days, much to her dismay, she twice caught the girl slipping into her father's library. She is either spying on me and reporting to him, Angela thought, or she is the latest one to grant him her favors.

Since returning to Neville Hall from the convent, Angela had seen a marked change come over her father. When he had first brought her home, they had constantly sought each other's company. They had taken all their meals together and often gone off on long walks about the estate.

Although she found his manner rough, he was always gentle with her. He had asked her about the convent and told her in turn about his years in France and Holland, sometimes in rather colorful language. Then, suddenly one day, everything had changed.

Angela found herself eating alone at the long, oaken dining room table. When she did see her father, which was seldom, he could not seem to bear looking at her. She knew she resembled her mother a good deal. She had only to gaze at the portrait of her above the fireplace in the library. She had her mother's fair hair, her porcelain complexion and her deep blue eyes, but the eyes in the portrait had almost a haunted look about them. Looking at them, Angela had long ago decided her mother had not been a happy woman.

Days now passed when she did not see her father at all. Once she overheard one servant telling another not to disturb his lordship as he'd locked himself up in the library again. She saw for herself that he was drinking heavily.

As the days turned into weeks, Angela was often shocked and revolted by her father's boorish manners and vulgar tongue, both of which she attributed to the fact that he was never completely sober. Several times she had unexpectedly come upon him giving vent to his lust in a vigorous rough and tumble with one of the servant girls.

She had almost decided that the steel-eyed Sister Dominica had been right when she condemned all men as lecherous beasts. Then she had met Gerald. Dear, gentle Gerald.

Angela thought of him a great deal in the fortnight that followed. In fact, waking or sleeping she could not get him out of her mind. She remembered everything they had said to one another. She remembered his voice and his smile and the kindness in his brown eyes.

On the eve of her eighteenth birthday, the Earl summoned Angela to the library.

Ushered into the spacious book-lined room, she discovered her father sprawled in a chair before the hearth, sound asleep and snoring. A half-empty decanter of brandy was on the table at his elbow.

Angela's eyes rose to the portrait of her mother above the fireplace. No wonder she looked unhappy being married to such a man. Her father's lack of sensitivity and coarseness must surely have abhorred such a delicate, refined person. She remembered her mother's soft hand stroking her forehead, her sweet smile. Tears filled Angela's eyes.

"I didn't hear you come in," her father's deep voice made her start. He was sitting up in his chair, hastily straightening his neckcloth. He did not meet her eyes as he said, "I have something to tell you, Angela. I received word from Hampton Court this morning. You are to be presented to their majesties at the summer solstice."

"But that is only . . . ten days away!" Angela cried, completely unsettled by the news.

"One does not ignore a Royal summons."

"But I haven't a suitable wardrobe for court, Papa, and —"

"Then send for seamstresses to make you one," he declared. "We must leave here within the week."

That afternoon, Angela, wishing to be alone with her thoughts, sent Jenny into the village on an errand for her. With the help of the young groom, she swallowed her fears and rode quietly off on the back of a docile old mare.

When she reached the spot on the river road where she had previously met Gerald, she dismounted and led the mare down the bank toward the river, where she tethered her to a nearby willow.

She had come to this place to think and to remember the sweet, breathless moments she had spent here with Gerald.

She gazed out at the river before her, so crystal clear she could see the rocks and pebbles that lined its bottom. Since she had been a child, she had always been able to draw immeasurable sustenance from nature.

The sounds of a horse's hooves interrupted her thoughts as they drew closer. She heard them stop and looked up to see Gerald leading his horse down the grassy bank towards her. He stopped to fasten the reins close to where her own mare grazed and then he approached her.

"You don't seem surprised to see me," she said, smiling at him, noticing how the wind had ruffled his sandy hair so that a lock fell over his forehead making him appear quite boyish.

Seeing her eyes light up at the sight of him, Gerald felt a long forgotten ache in his heart. He had not been able to forget how she had trembled in his arms. He wasn't exactly sure what he wanted to say to her, having once more found her alone. He only knew that she was constantly on his mind and that he felt completely absorbed and enthralled by her.

What's more, he was almost sure that she shared his attraction. She looked so pleased to see him. He had sensed her matching spirit when they had last been together. They were completely in tune about so many things.

"I've been coming here every afternoon," he admitted. "Hoping . . ."

"My father forbade me to ever see you again."

This did not surprise him, but something else did. "I would not think you the sort to disobey your father. Why did you come today?"

"I came because . . ." Tears filled her eyes and she turned her head away.

"Whatever is the matter?" Concerned, he reached out and gently touched her arm.

134

It all burst from her then. How Jenny had surely told her father of their meeting. How angry he had been. How he must have immediately written someone at court, for today he had told her that they had received a Royal summons and were to appear before their Majesties at Hampton Court in only ten days.

"You do not wish to go."

"You know I do not."

Without another word he led her over to the beech tree they had sat beneath before and again laid down his cloak for her to sit upon. The touch of his hand on her arm had stirred wild feelings within her. She longed to feel his arms about her again, his mouth on her own.

She sat down, wiping her wet cheeks with the back of her hand. He handed her his handkerchief, looking down at her tenderly as she blew her nose.

"I want you to know something about me," he said, his voice quiet and serious. "I have been married and it was a happy marriage although it only lasted two years. My wife died in childbirth and my son lived only a week after she had been laid to rest."

"I am so sorry," she said, her blue eyes full of sympathy.

"When I learned I was my uncle's heir, I was glad to come here and leave all the sad memories behind. I've worked hard, and it has helped me to forget." He looked into her eyes, the love shining

135

in his own. "I thought never to meet another woman with whom I would be content to spend the rest of my life. I was wrong."

"Gerald—"

"Let me finish. I have found someone with whom my heart and my mind are in tune," he said. "I think you know who she is."

"Oh, Gerald . . . ," she whispered, choking over the words.

He sat down beside her, ignoring the strong urge to take her in his arms.

"I wanted you to know this. I wanted you to know that if you had not been pledged to another, I would have asked your father for your hand."

Oh my dear, she thought. Even if I had been free he would never have consented to our union. He does not care for you. He does not understand the way you live, or what you are trying to accomplish.

"There would still have been obstacles," she said softly.

"None we could not have overcome. Together. From the very first I've felt we were meant for each other." He shook his head. "Together we might have done so much good."

"You can still do much good, Gerald. I have heard that the laborers and tenants on your estate work much harder for you than the other landowners. It is because you have been fair with them and assisted them in many ways. By your example, you may well influence others."

He put his hand over hers. A silence fell between them. A silence woven with the intimacy of their shared thoughts and the sweet, springlike scent of the air around them. After Gerald's revelation, Angela felt even more desolate. Her eyes again grew moist as she thought of what might have been.

"Why did God allow us to meet?" she suddenly cried, giving a heart-wrenching little sob.

Without thinking, Gerald pulled her close to him. "I only wanted you to know my feelings. I didn't mean to upset you."

"But don't you see that your feelings and mine are the same?" She burst into tears.

"Hush, Angela, hush," he soothed, using her name for the first time. "Don't cry. I'm here now. Don't think about tomorrow."

He held her more tightly, softly rocking her back and forth to comfort her.

"I'm so afraid," she murmured.

"Afraid?"

"I've never met the man I'm pledged to marry. What if he should be rough like my father? What if he should . . ."

"Not all men are as he, Angela," he said gently.

She looked up into his soft brown eyes. Eyes so deep with feeling.

"I love you," he whispered. "I'll always be here if you need me. Always." His hands reached up to cup her face, his thumbs brushing away the teardrops clinging to her lips.

"I love you, Gerald. 'Tis not fair! 'Tis not fair!"

"Hush, my sweet." He kissed her lips, the kiss deepening as he drew her even closer to himself.

Everything about her began to blur for Angela, everything but Gerald. She reached up to brush back the lock of hair from his brow and ended with her arms about his neck, eager to hold him.

Under her hands, she felt the muscular strength of his lean body and the warmth of it. His arms were holding her tight against him. Her soft, rounded breasts were pressed to his chest. She was filled with a glorious happiness.

His lips moved down over her silken cheek, down to find the wild pulsebeat in her throat.

Her breath was coming faster and she felt frightened, yet thrilled, as his lips moved with feather lightness over her skin. His hands went to the neck of her riding dress, his lips following his fingers as he slowly unbuttoned it, moving lower, touching, caressing. Her hands went wildly out to push him away, more frightened now, yet surprised at the warmth and heat she felt rising in her.

She gave a little moan of delight when his lips found hers again and she found herself responding, letting him gently press open her mouth and search its sweet depths.

Slowly he laid her back on his cloak and she saw that his expression was very tender, his eyes soft and dark as he bent over her. She felt his hand slip inside her gown, cupping one bare breast, fondling it gently.

"So soft . . . so beautiful," he whispered.

The other hand went under her body, holding her against him as he lay down beside her. She felt his thighs pressing closer, felt the hardness swell . . .

She drew a sharp breath, pushing hard at his chest, frightened by the sensations he was causing her to feel.

"No! You mustn't . . . I didn't mean . . ." she gasped.

His head lifted and he stared down at her, saw the frightened face, the tears glistening on the long, dark lashes.

"Dear God," he groaned, "what am I doing?"

Abruptly he rose from her, turning his back on her, walking a few steps away. When he returned to her again he was composed, but she saw that the sadness again filled his eyes.

"I'm so sorry, Angela," he said and his voice shook. "Did I frighten you?"

"Yes," she whispered, looking away from him. Her face was as burning hot as her body as she refastened her dress. "I never have . . . and I hope you don't think . . ."

"I think I have behaved reprehensibly and I hope you will forgive me."

"Forgive you? It was as much my—" she stopped, seeing him shake his head, his eyes caressing her.

"No. You are so very young. You did not know."

"I'm eighteen," she cried defensively.

"And innocent. I should not have allowed things to go that far. I'm not worthy of you, my sweet Angela, but I do love you so."

"Yes, Gerald, and I love you. I cannot bear to be parted from you."

He reached out his hands and gently pulled her to her feet. Slowly they began to walk, hand in hand, along the river bank to where their horses were tied.

Angela had never felt so warm and so loved. She knew she would never forget this afternoon as long as she lived. She had never known desire before, had never been overly curious about what went on between a man and a woman. But Gerald's soft lips, his gentle hands, his warm body had awakened a host of new sensations within her. She had wanted him so much. She knew if she had not stopped him at that moment, they both would have been swept away.

Would she spend the rest of her life wondering how it might have been?

Chapter Twelve

It was still dark when Elizabeth left the inn, although there was a shade of gray in the east to indicate that daylight was not far away. It was cool and damp with a light autumn mist covering the town and surrounding countryside.

Starting off down the cobbled street of Bridgetown, Elizabeth pulled Claridge's large cloak more tightly about her shoulders. She seemed to be always running away. She shuddered, remembering the first time.

Leaving a fallen Lord Ramsden lying before the hearth at Fairclough, she had gathered up her skirts and had raced through the house as fast as she could, across hallways and down corridors until she had reached the kitchen door.

The air outside held the nip of frost, but it was a clear, starlit night and she was able to see her

141

way along the gravel path that led to the woods behind the mansion. Elizabeth didn't dare risk a dash down the wide front driveway leading to the main road. She could so easily be seen and overtaken there.

The cold began to creep through her thin slippers and despite the warmth of cook's cloak, which she had managed to wrap around herself as she ran, Elizabeth, found herself shivering.

The silent wood she entered was cowled in shadow. Surrounding the narrow path were tall gray beech, their skeletal branches forming almost a canopy over her head. She ran on, taking deep breaths of the cold air into her lungs, feeling the pain of it, but not daring to slow her pace.

This narrow path, she knew, was used by the gamekeeper and led to a country road that would eventually take her out of the district. She would stay clear of the main road and any dwellings she might come upon. Elizabeth had no destination in mind. For the present, it was enough to put as much distance as she could between herself and all the shock and horror that lay behind.

The underbrush was thick and the path a narrow trail. A branch swung sharply back and whipped across her cheek, but she did not lessen her speed, despite the fact that her breath was now coming in painful gasps.

The winter wind moaned eerily among the trees and again Elizabeth shivered. A burning sensation had begun in her side and as she continued

142

to run, she found herself bending almost double with it. She slowed only a little, until finally her legs began to fail her and she knew she would have to stop.

Standing still, her chest heaving as she struggled to regain her breath, Elizabeth felt the woods begin to close in around her. She listened carefully to hear if someone had followed her. There was only the sigh of the wind in the bare boughs high above.

Relief filled her. The clear winter sky gave enough light so she could make out the threadlike pathway ahead. She started on again, but this time she walked at as fast a pace as she was able. And as she walked, anger began to replace the fear and terror that had filled her.

Fairclough had been a prosperous estate when her parents had died and left it to her. Yet, in five short years, the greedy, dissolute man who had been given the authority to manage it for her, had squandered everything away. Now she was a homeless, destitute orphan, forced to find her own way in the world.

What was she to do? She would never consider returning and marrying Lord Ramsden. She would rather die first! Anger seethed through her. She hoped her drunken uncle would get everything he deserved. She hoped Ramsden *would* throw him out into the cold. Hot tears filled her eyes. Fairclough. Beautiful Fairclough. The only home she had ever known was gone to her now, forever.

Lord Ramsden would never appreciate the beautiful old Tudor house that had been in her family for generations or the peace and serenity of its remote location, so far from the mainstream that it had never been threatened by the civil war. He would probably turn Fairclough into a gambling den or worse.

She knew that Lord Ramsden was a powerful man, he had told her as much, so his hand would be long reaching. He would never forgive her for the humiliation she had caused him this night. She must make sure she never encountered him again.

Elizabeth shuddered, remembering his lordship's wet lips on hers and again quickened her pace, moving even deeper into the woods. She was free of the man now, and never, she vowed, would he ever get his hands on her again. The elation she felt at the thought that she had outwitted him, kept her going, though her feet were almost numb and her slim body shook from the cold that seemed to penetrate right through the heavy cloak.

She was so tired. She longed to stop for awhile and sink to the ground and sleep, but she knew she might freeze to death if she did. She must keep moving. It would keep her warmer, she reasoned, concentrating wholly on the way ahead.

Keep going, she repeated to herself over and over as the hours passed. Cover as much distance as you can before it becomes light. But where are you going? A voice inside her questioned. What are you going to do? You have no money for food or lodging.

"I'll find a way," she told herself, squaring her slim shoulders. "I'll find a way to earn what I need and then I'll go so far away Ramsden will never find me." The colonies, perhaps. She had heard that Virginia was beautiful.

Elizabeth was so deeply immersed in her own thoughts that she did not realize that the thick foliage was finally thinning and she was gradually approaching the edge of the forest. Suddenly, she came out onto a narrow road that wound to her right down through the rolling countryside.

She started along it, stumbling a little as she made her way over the uneven ground, rutted by the wheels of carts and wagons. A fox ran out of the underbrush in front of her, startling her so that she tripped and turned her ankle.

Pain shot up through her leg and she bit her lip as she stopped to examine it. Despite the pain when she put any weight on her ankle, she knew she must ignore it and go on. She started out again, limping more and more as her ankle swelled, slowing her pace until, after another quarter mile, she knew she could go no further.

She sat down by the side of the road and with shaking hands tore a strip off the bottom of her petticoat. She bound this tightly around her ankle and searching in the ditch for a stout stick, finally located a straight enough branch that had fallen from a nearby oak tree. Using it to lean on, she struggled to her feet and hobbled pitifully off down the road.

It was dawn when she came upon the caravan pulled off to the side of the road. It was garishly painted red and gold and could belong to no one else, she thought, but a gypsy. Yet, she wondered, why was it here, off by itself, in this lonely part of the country? She looked around her but could see no signs of a gypsy encampment close by.

Just then she smelled something cooking and noticed a campfire on the far side of the caravan. A surge of hunger filled her stomach.

Go on by, she told herself. Gypsies aren't to be trusted. Her old nurse had told her when she was a child never to go near them. "They'll steal you away for ransom," she had been warned.

Old Marta looked up from roasting a rabbit, which she had managed to snare during the night, and saw what looked like an old woman wrapped in a cloak limping down the road towards her. Groaning a little from her rheumatism, she pushed herself up from her hunched position over the fire and called out to the stranger.

"You there! Come over here."

Pretending not to hear her, Elizabeth moved slowly on.

"I have enough food for two," the old woman coaxed.

146

Shaking her head, Elizabeth continued on, but could not help turning her head to look at the gypsy as she passed by.

The scrawny figure standing by the fire appeared to be ancient. Her wizened face was seamed like old parchment and gray hair struggled out from beneath a bright kerchief that was tied about her head. The garments she wore were in varying stages of age. A bright blue skirt protruded from beneath the gold-fringed black shawl that was pulled close about her gaunt shoulders.

Elizabeth was so busy staring at the gypsy that she missed her footing and went down, landing hard on her sprained ankle. She let out a low cry of pain and tears blinded her eyes.

In a short time, considering her age, the old gypsy woman was beside her, kneeling down to put an arm about her.

"Why ye be but a child," she muttered, peering into the tear-stained face beneath the hood. "And near frozen stiff."

She wasted no time in asking questions, but helped Elizabeth to hobble over to the fire.

"Let Marta see to that ankle," she demanded, indicating a stump nearby where Elizabeth could sit.

As she held up her leg, Elizabeth noticed that her ankle had already swollen to twice it's normal size.

"Ye should not have walked on it," the old

woman scolded her.

She picked up a wooden pail and crossing the road, disappeared down into the ditch on the other side. Moments later, she had returned with a pail of ice-cold water and wringing out a cloth in it, wrapped it around Elizabeth's ankle. A shiver went through the girl at the coldness of the cloth.

"The cold will take down the swelling," the gypsy told her, overturning the pail and propping the girl's foot up on it.

An hour later, after being wrapped in a large wool blanket and given a goodly portion of hot rabbit stew to eat and a cup of mulled wine to drink, Elizabeth felt the warmth beginning to return to her body.

"Thank you," she smiled, edging even closer to the fire. "I only wish I had something to give you for your kindness, but I haven't a single coin with me."

"I would not take payment from thee, child," the old woman said. She was busy binding Elizabeth's ankle with clean strips of cotton after applying an evil-smelling ointment to it. She leaned closer to the girl, squinting up at her. "But I *would* like to know where ye are going and what it is ye have run away from."

Elizabeth stared at her. With her injured ankle she knew she was at the gypsy's mercy. If she told her the truth, the old woman might take it into her head to return her to Fairclough and demand a reward.

"Ye can trust old Marta," the gypsy told her, as if reading her mind. "I'll not take ye back if it not be thy wish."

Sitting before the campfire, as the day lightened about them, Elizabeth found herself telling the old gypsy woman about her parents' death five years before and the uncle who had become her guardian. Marta listened quietly as Elizabeth went on to describe her uncle's obsession with gambling and the final tragedy when he had lost her home to Lord Ramsden.

"Ye be a brave child," old Marta said, patting Elizabeth's knee with a clawlike hand, "but ye be unused to fending for thyself. Have ye no other relatives or friends to turn to?"

"No one," Elizabeth said sadly.

The old gypsy shook her head. "Alone ye will starve to death in a week."

"I will find something to do," Elizabeth tried to assure her, although she had begun to feel dubious herself.

"For the price of those pretty violet earrings ye be wearing, I'll take care of thee," the gypsy gave a toothless grin. "I'll teach thee the secrets of the stars and to read fortunes from the lines that criss-cross the palm of a hand. Then, child, ye'll be able to earn thyself a living."

She reached out for Elizabeth's hand and turned it over. The girl expected her to recoil when she observed the vivid birthmark on the fleshy part of the palm, but she did not.

149

"One of the blessed," she murmured.

"Blessed!" Elizabeth exclaimed. "Someone told me it was the mark of Satan. I've always tried to hide it."

"Nay, it be a mystic marking given to those possessing the second sight."

Elizabeth stared at her. "My old nurse was a Scot and believed in such things."

"Ye do not believe?"

"It—it rather frightens me."

The woman took Elizabeth's other hand, regarding it closely with a hooded gaze.

"Ye do not control thy own destiny. It be too intertwined with another Gemini," she said, looking up questioningly at Elizabeth. "Gemini is a sign of the zodiac which represents 'the twins'. Are ye one of two?"

"No. I am an only child," Elizabeth assured her.

Yet, she remembered when she was little how she had imagined a make-believe playmate, exactly like herself, to whom she confided all her thoughts.

"Your destiny is also determined by a man of much prestige and wealth," the gypsy went on.

Elizabeth gasped. "Oh, no! Surely not Lord Ramsden!"

The gypsy shook her head. "Nay, child, ye have yet to meet this gentleman. One day, though, ye may hold his very life in thy hands."

She stopped and slowly closed Elizabeth's hand.

150

"What did you see?" the girl asked shakily.

"Only that ye must be very careful," the gypsy said, her eyes lifting to Elizabeth and yet seeming not to focus on her. "Others may wish to use thee for their own ends. There be the shadow of death there." Her voice trailed off and Elizabeth shivered, but the gypsy's gaze had returned to normal and soon she was reassuring her.

"Don't look so frightened, child. What do I know?" she shrugged. "Only enough to trick the gorgios into thinking I can see into the future. 'Tis all a sham."

Elizabeth accepted old Marta's proposal and remained with her. Although search parties were sent out from Fairclough to scour the surrounding countryside and Marta was stopped and questioned, the old gypsy woman never let on that she was hiding the girl they sought in her caravan.

In the weeks that followed, Marta taught Elizabeth much about her craft. Spring came and the old gypsy began the rounds of the village fairs, in order to tell her fortunes. Now, at last, Elizabeth was called upon to earn her keep. The gypsy dressed her as a lad in a tall conical hat, which concealed her cloud of fair hair, and a long black cloak to mask her feminine figure. Assuming a gruff voice, she hawked in front of the gypsy's black tent.

Elizabeth had once asked Marta why she didn't travel with one of the gypsy bands and the old woman's dark eyes had flashed at her.

"Because I be no thief. In the old country, where I was born, we Romanies were a proud and noble people. I will not align myself with thieves and pickpockets. I earn my living honestly."

Elizabeth dared not mention the fact that tricking the gorgios into believing she could read the future was hardly honest. But by then she was beginning to believe that old Marta did indeed possess some special powers. Twice she had insisted they depart from villages before the fairs were over and only later had Elizabeth learned that a murdering band of cutthroats had killed several people at one fair and the village magistrate had arrested every gypsy at the other.

As the months passed, Elizabeth found herself becoming more and more atuned to Marta's thoughts, often answering her questions before the old gypsy had even asked them.

"Ye *do* possess second sight," the woman nodded knowingly.

One night, toward the end of the summer, Elizabeth dreamed of Marta's death. For several nights in row she had the same dream, but she did not tell the gypsy of it.

A few days later she was crossing the fairground to obtain some water at a stream nearby, when she had a terrible premonition. Dropping the pail she carried, she ran back to the caravan. Marta was slumped over the table where she had been counting the coins they had earned the night before.

" 'Tis my heart, child," the old woman moaned, clutching her chest.

"I'll fetch a physician," Elizabeth turned quickly back to the door.

"No use," Marta gasped. " 'Tis thine now," she indicated the metal cash box before her on the table as she collapsed.

Thinking back on the old gypsy's death, tears filled Elizabeth's eyes as she trudged along a side road leading out of Bridgetown. The caravan and everything that had belonged to Marta was gone now. Everything but the coins and the pair of amythest earrings that the old woman had admired so much and kept in the metal box.

Elizabeth switched the saddlebag containing all she possessed to her other hand. London was a big city, she thought. She could easily get lost in the crowds there. Especially if she resumed her gypsy disguise. She had learned at St. Margaret's Fair that the nobility paid well for fortune telling. If all went well, it would not take her long before she had enough saved to carry out her plans.

She tried not to think of Simon as she walked along. She was determined that he would never find her again, that she would forget him and what had occurred between them. Yet, she was not blind to the fact that it would not be easy. His lovemaking had been so glorious. Never had she felt so alive before. In his arms she had become a woman — a warm, passionate woman. She blushed as she remembered how eagerly she had responded to his caresses.

Wanton. That was what she had been. No wonder he had asked her to be his doxy.

"Men will want to possess your beauty," old Marta had once warned her. "Don't give it away lightly."

She had done exactly that when she had brazenly offered herself to Simon. Her blush deepened as she remembered her words, "Please take me to bed," she had said as bold as you please.

How surprised he must have been when he discovered her to be a virgin. But he had been so gentle with her. It had been such a perfect night of love. She gave a little sob. How could she ever forget it? She knew she would never again know that ecstasy which he alone had given her. But their love wasn't meant to be. Another woman would be his bride, feel his firm lips, his strong body . . . She blinked back the tears. Oh, if only she hadn't fallen in love with him! If only her emotions were as uninvolved as his must be, then perhaps she could have become his mistress. But loving him as she did, she would not be able to bear being only a part of his life — the dark, hidden part.

It was as well she had run away. Better to never see him again than to live on the outskirts of his life and watch her love destroyed and her pride trampled into the dust. She drew a determined breath. She would forget him. She *must* forget him!

Claridge frowned when he awoke and found the bed empty beside him. He rose quickly and strode over to the window, roughly yanking back the curtains.

She was gone. The room was clear of all her clothing it seemed, until he caught sight of something under the corner of the bed. He bent down and picked up her dark colored veil. Lifting it to his nose, he caught the sweet scent of violets — her scent. The same light fragrance that eminated from her hair and skin. He felt a sudden sense of loss. She had run away from him again.

He dressed hurriedly, realizing that she must have taken the cloak he had lent her. His bleakness increased when upon consulting the innkeeper he learned that no one had seen her leave.

He ate a lonely breakfast, anger slowly growing inside him as he thought of her. How could she have left him after last night? He had made her his own and she had responded so willingly to his passionate lovemaking. Never before, with any other woman, had it been so right — so good. It did not occur to him that it might be because it was his first encounter with the emotion — love. Instead, he raged. Hadn't he asked her to become his mistress? How dare she run off and leave him!

155

It was unthinkable that the wench should do this to him again. Why, he was the Duke of Claridge, was he not? She should have been honored . . .

But that was not necessarily true, a voice inside reminded him. He knew she was of gentle birth, even if he knew little else about her. Perhaps she had been insulted by his proposition. Damn it! Why hadn't he tried harder to discover who she really was? Beth. That was the only name she had given him. There must be thousands of Beths in England!

Where would she go? With no caravan she couldn't take to the road again as a gypsy fortune teller. Still, she wasn't penniless. She had taken the bag of coins with her. Perhaps she had hired a coach to take her where she wished to go.

Well, he would find her again and this time he would wring her lovely neck if she refused to remain with him!

Claridge was in a black mood as he left the inn and started out on the main road to London. Leaving the town behind him, he spurred Satan into a gallop.

A farmer's son in an ox cart had come along the side road leading from Bridgetown and had given Elizabeth a bumpy ride to the next town. Although it grew warm as the day progressed, she did not remove Simon's long cloak. The hood hid her fair hair and kept her face in shadow. She was wise enough to know that once seen, her looks would be easily remembered.

It took Elizabeth two days to reach London, taking the back roads, managing rides with kindly country folks who were taking their fall produce to market. Fortunately, the autumn weather continued fair, for she chose not to stay in an inn at night, but crawled instead into a farmer's haystack.

She had never entered London before and was disappointed by her first glimpse of the city. Elizabeth had always imagined it to be a city of gilded coaches, beautiful buildings and richly dressed lords and ladies. Instead, she viewed a vast jumble of old timbered buildings, their over-hanging upper stories almost touching over the cobblestones of the narrow, winding streets.

She felt suddenly boxed in by this clamorous, bustling city where people were everywhere — jostling one another as they passed down the street, riding by on horseback or in coaches or sedan chairs. There was a continual raucous din from the street vendors and the smell . . .

Elizabeth pressed her handkerchief to her nose as she passed by the open sewers. Over all of London was polluted, smokey air. Even St. Paul's Cathedral, high on Ludgate Hill, was partially obscured by the gray pall. The old church's spire had fallen down, Elizabeth was aware, damaging part of the nave, but it had never been repaired. The splendid interior, her governess had told her about, had been ransacked in Cromwell's time.

Hurrying on, Elizabeth passed a noisy tavern, where she was forced to skirt about a drunken man lying on the street outside its door. Filthy, ragged children were running about, begging for money, yet Elizabeth dared not stop and open her saddlebag, for fear that one of the unsavory-looking characters lurking about would observe it and try to steal it. She moved quickly on, now passing shop after shop—confectioner, a tobacconist, an apothecary. She didn't stop to look in the windows. Soon, the dirty, run-down hovels gave way to houses more sturdy and prosperous looking. She slowed her pace a little, examined the dwellings and finally sighted one that advertised rooms for rent. Brushing at the dust on her cloak and gown, she approached the front door.

Chapter Thirteen

Angela sat, pale and silent, looking at herself in the mirror above her dressing table, as her young maid, Nan (for all her conniving to get in the Earl's good graces, Jenny, unversed in the current court styles, had been dismissed), worked with a curling iron and nimble fingers to arrange her soft, fair hair in the latest fashion. Plump, shining curls were beginning to frame the girl's delicate features, pulled up from her neck at the back and fastened with combs and bodkins.

Her already small waist had been laced even smaller by a short, boned corset that she wore over her lace and ribbon-trimmed chemise.

Bursting through the door of Angela's bedchamber, her friend, Frances Stewart, came to a stop in the middle of the room.

"Oh, Angela," she cried, "you look glorious!"

"Glorious!" her friend sniffed. "I can hardly breath with my waist cinched in so tight and my breasts forced up so they look grotesque."

Frances laughed. "But so alluring to the gentlemen if your gown be cut low."

"Which 'tis most certainly not," Angela declared. "What would His Grace think of me if I met him falling out of my gown?"

"He would probably be delighted," her friend giggled, eyeing Angela with a speculative eye. Was the girl not aware of her perfect figure or her lovely face with those wide, luminous blue eyes and long dark lashes? It hardly seemed possible, and yet, Frances knew, there wasn't a vain bone in Angela's body. That was one of the reasons she had welcomed her friendship. Another was that Angela was even more innocent about life than she was, which made Frances feel quite wise and worldly.

Arriving on the same day at Hampton Court, the two young beauties had been presented to their Majesties at the same time. When, after several weeks, the queen expressed her pleasure in them by asking them both to attend her, they had grown even better acquainted.

Frances was lighthearted and open and eager to explore all life had to offer. Angela, in contrast, was serious and quiet and inclined to hold herself aloof from the pleasure seeking young people around her. Despite the two girls having little in common, except for their duties to the queen, they became close companions. Frances was bound and determined to bring Angela out of her

160

reserved shell and Angela was equally as determined to keep her friend from succumbing to the court's decadent ways.

"Oh, Angela," Frances said now. "Aren't you the least bit excited about meeting His Grace at last?"

"Would *you* like to be trussed up like a chicken and offered to a man?"

"I would if that man were His Grace," Frances sighed.

Angela turned quickly to her. "You've seen him, haven't you?"

"I did, but just at a distance."

Angela closed her eyes. "Pray tell me what he is like?"

"He is tall and well built and devastatingly handsome, you lucky girl. I only wish *my* father had pledged me to him."

"And I wish mine had not."

"Oh Angela, he's bound to be more exciting than that do-good squire you're always talking about."

"Exciting! Handsome! Is that all that interests you in a man, Frances? Gerald is gentle and kind and compassionate of others. His Grace cannot possibly be as caring a person. He was soldier and planned battles that killed people. He is used to bloodshed and violence and cruelty."

Her friend looked at her. "But did you ever think that a man who has experienced such things is desperately in need of the solace of a woman? He only did his duty, Angela."

"And was it his duty to remain on the Continent and continue his soldiering? Why did he not come home with the king?"

Frances shook her head. "Do not be so quick to judge."

Watching in the looking glass as her maid put the finishing touches to her hair, Angela thought, was Sister Veronica right about me? Do I only see people as black and white – good and evil? The gentle nun had urged her young charge to be less harsh with the weaknesses of others. Sins, she had told Angela, could be the result of ignorance or hurt or hunger. She must concentrate on the goodness of people and not the bad, and yet, since becoming a member of the court, Angela had seen very little evidence of goodness and virtue. The men and women she encountered seemed to be selfish, greedy, and immoral, their only religion self-gratification. Children, she had decided, must be the only innocents left in the corrupt world. If only she had been allowed to remain at Neville Hall, perhaps she would have found some way to work with the orphans at the Manor House.

From the first, court life had shocked her. She had expected to find that the king and queen lived exemplary lives beyond reproach. Instead, she had found a profligate, womanizing king and a lonely, pious little queen who confounded Angela by obviously adoring her husband.

* * *

It was just as well Angela, being in the mood she was in at that moment, could not see her intended, His Grace of Claridge.

Claridge had spent the night before on a last wild round of drinking and entertainment with his friends and morning dawned too soon for him. Opening his eyes, he groaned and quickly closed them again. He had a splitting headache and a vile taste in his mouth. The bright sunlight, filtering through a crack in the heavy velvet window hangings, shone directly into his eyes.

He made a halfhearted movement to rise. Oddsfish, but his head was pounding! Never before in his life had he ever experienced such a . . . and then he remembered.

Hester Quillby had been at Asherton's party. When had he and Musgrove and the others arrived there? It did not matter. He remembered her approaching him, her full white breasts swelling above the low-cut crimson gown she wore. Her ruby and diamond necklace winking at him, reminding him of when she had wheedled it out of him and the time she had coaxed him for the matching bracelet.

"At last, Simon," she said throatily to him. "Where have you been?"

"You'll have to ask Musgrove," he drawled. "I know we started at his apartments."

"I don't mean tonight," she pouted. "I've been

back at court a full week and you have never called on me."

"A full week? How quickly time passes. I thought to give you time to get over old Sommerton's death — or was it Dockville you were last with?" He put a hand to his forehead. "You must excuse me, madam. There have been so many."

"Bastard!" she said beneath her breath. "Why did you not come back to England with me?"

"I had matters on the Continent to attend to."

"Have you missed me?" She brushed her hips against his with a suggestiveness that could not be misinterpreted.

"Sometimes," he grinned. He was not entirely sober.

"We cannot talk here." She nodded toward the door. "There is a room down the hall . . ."

"What we once shared is long over, madam. It will do no good to —"

"I only want to talk with you, Simon," she exhorted. " 'Tis been two years." Putting her arm through his, she slowly propelled him in the direction of the door.

The room was small and dimly lit. A jug of wine and two goblets sat on a table before a low, damask-covered sofa.

Hester sank down on the sofa, while Claridge gave a shrug and poured wine into the glasses, handing one to her. Swaying slightly, he lifted his goblet to her.

"To you, my dear. The consummate seductress."

She gave a husky little laugh and patted the sofa beside her.

He looked down at her with a grin. Hester Quillby, the young widow of old Sir Thomas who had lasted only four months after marrying her. Where had he found her? Somewhere in the bowels of London, no doubt. But she had learned fast. She appeared as much a lady as any at court.

He remembered the first time he had seen the green-eyed, red-haired, young widow with the hand spanning waist and those provocative breasts striving to escape from her low-bodiced gown. From the start, she had invited seduction. And he had stolen her out from under the noses of Buckingham and the others—perhaps even Charles himself.

"You are too damned successful with the fair sex, Simon," the king had laughed and Claridge had gallantly rejoined, "Only a poor imitation of yourself, Sire."

At the moment, Claridge wished his head were clearer and he had never allowed Hester to lure him here. The scent of her heavy, musky perfume seemed cloying and over-pungent as he sat down beside her. Another scent—the sweet scent of violets—came to him in comparison, making him think of Beth.

It seemed incredible that after nearly a week she should still be so vividly present in his mind that he found it difficult not to wonder at almost any moment of the day where she might be. Over the years, he had made love to many titled beauties, short liaisons that were enjoyed, but quickly forgotten. Yet, here was a female of no consequence in court circles, whom he couldn't get out of his mind.

There had been an attraction, an affinity, between them from the very first instant their eyes had met in that gypsy tent. Ever since, he found himself thinking of her day and night — her soft voice, the fear in her eyes that had turned to trust at the sight of him, her warm, silken body that had yielded so eagerly to his touch.

What is the matter with me? Claridge asked himself, not for the first time. He was exhausted from day after day spent in the saddle, following false leads in a fruitless search for the girl. No one had found the slightest trace of her and he had sent dozens out to scour the countryside.

The king had been angry with him for his further delay in meeting with his promised bride. Angry enough to summon Claridge the day before and announce that he had made arrangements with the Earl of Westbury and his daughter to meet him at twelve noon on the morrow in the queen's rose garden.

Was it any wonder, therefore, that he had become engaged in this last night of partying and tavern crawling?

"I missed you so," Hester was crooning, as her soft arms crept about his neck and her two lips pressed a kiss to his throat. "No one will disturb us here," she added in an undertone.

But as tantalizing as Hester might be, she could not exorcize the vision of one slender, blue-eyed girl in gypsy garb.

Hester's hot breath was on his cheek as her fingers gently trailed down his chest, unfastening buttons. Claridge found himself trying to shake free of her arms and was surprised to see a hint of tears in the worldly green eyes.

"Do you no longer love me, Simon?"

Claridge sighed. It was an old, tired theme between them. One she had repeated every time she wanted something from him. And he had, he was forced to admit, loved her in a way — at least he had loved to bed her.

" 'Tis the little gypsy, isn't it?" she suddenly cried. "I've heard of your search for her. Do you think yourself in love with *her?*"

" 'Tis none of your concern, madam."

"Gypsies I hear are like wild animals in bed. Is that why you still search for her? Was she so much better than I?"

The smokey eyes flashed as he struggled free of her at last and rose to his feet. "Stay out of my affairs," he growled.

" 'Tis only because I love you that I care," she pouted.

Claridge turned to look down at her, a long, searching look. Could Hester have possibly thwarted his search for Beth in some way?

Quillby had left her wealthy enough to do it.

Hester should have been stilled by the furious glint in his eyes, but she unwisely continued to pursue the subject.

"Don't expect you can thaw out that little snow maid you are pledged to marry. You'll come back to me soon enough when she freezes you out of her bed."

"And if I don't?" Claridge gave her a cynical smile.

Damn him! Hester thought. He looked so incredibly handsome standing there before her, broad chested, slim hipped. Her eyes swept to his well muscled thighs. No other man had ever ... Desire began to build up in her as her eyes lingered. She wanted him achingly and she could swear he knew it as his grin deepened and he headed for the door.

Turning his back on Hester was a mistake. No man had ever refused her charms before. She picked up the wine jug from the table and swung it against the back of his head.

He remembered nothing else until his friends found him lying in the doorway and helped him back to his own apartments.

Chapter Fourteen

Lord Musgrove made a late morning call at the Duke of Claridge's apartments and found him dressing for his noon meeting with his bride-to-be.

"You should be happy the king arranged this meeting, my friend," Musgrove told him. "The Earl has been getting impatient and I hear he is not a good man to anger."

"Happy? Happy that other people should guide my destiny for me? Happy that I must wed someone I have never met?"

"Arranged marriages sometimes work out better than those begun with romance, moonlight, and unrealistic dreams. You may not have met her, but the Lady Angela's beauty will not be difficult to look upon, I assure you."

Gazing at himself in the mirror as his servant straightened his doublet, Claridge laughed. " 'Tis too bad I cannot return the compliment. The

169

devil himself couldn't look worse than I do this morning. I've a lump the size of an egg on the back of my head."

"Hester said you fell and hit your head on the table."

"So that's her story."

"The smashed wine jug told us a different tale. Never scorn a woman, Simon."

"Women seem to have the habit of making a fool of me."

Musgrove regarded his friend. "Have you had no word of that gypsy wench you seek?"

"None. And as I explained before, John, she is no gypsy wench. She is a noblewoman, of that I am sure."

"You must put her from your mind, Simon. Angela must be the only one in your thoughts this day."

"Angela." Claridge shook his head. "Poor girl, she must hate the very thought of me. Thrown at me practically from birth. Bound by her father's promise to mine."

"As you, too, have been bound and yet you do not hate her. Only the thought of marriage," his friend smiled.

"What man likes to be chained for life. It is only endurable if love is involved."

"Love? Do I hear right? You, His Grace of Claridge, speaking of love, who have always been so cynical about it."

"Only because I did not believe it could ever

exist between a man and a woman."

"And now you do?"

"For one sweet night I believed it so."

"Only one night? An illusion, surely."

"Aye, an illusion, but one, I fear, I will never forget."

Lord Ramsden had again been refused an audience with the king and he was angry as he strode down the long gallery away from the king's privy apartments. He had never been close to Charles, despite his boastings, but he had thought that at last, with his new wealth behind him, his king might view him in a more favorable light.

Turning a corner, he came upon a small group approaching the stairway to the garden. He recognized the dowager Duchess of Benham and with her a young girl who . . .

He stopped in his tracks. Nay, it could not be! Were his eyes deceiving him? As he watched, the youthful figure obediently followed the haughty duchess down the stairs. Ramsden stood still, looking after them even after they had disappeared.

"Close your mouth, Ramsden," said a husky female voice. "You look like a fish." Lady Quillby smiled humorously as she drew abreast of him.

"But who is she?" he whispered hoarsely. "It surely cannot be who I think . . ."

"Lady Angela Neville, His Grace of Claridge's

intended bride," Lady Quillby's lip curled. "They are meeting for the first time this morning in the queen's rose garden."

"I see," he murmured. His eyes shot back to the staircase then again to Lady Quillby. "Would you know if there be some place where the garden can be viewed?"

"Only from the queen's apartments," Hester Quillby shrugged. Then, remembering something, she put up a finger. "Except . . ."

"Except where?" he spat impatiently.

"I believe there are tall windows on the staircase landing which lead out onto a small balcony." She gave a sly smile. "Your reaction to Lady Angela is most curious, your lordship. Perhaps you would care to join me there and tell me what has disturbed you."

Claridge was not yet resigned to his fate as he waited with the Earl of Westbury in the queen's rose garden. The usually garrulous Earl was strangely quiet and seemed to grow more ill at ease as the minutes passed. Although on the surface Claridge appeared calm and relaxed, inside he felt a hard knot of anger. He wanted nothing given to him like this. How could his father have made this match with the Earl simply because of a shared victory scored against Cromwell eighteen years before? Both gentlemen had probably been well into their cups when they had made the agreement. And now, this warm autumn morning, in a garden perfumed by the last roses of the season, two lives were about to be ruined by the loose tongues of two drunken soldiers celebrating a victory that, for one day, had created a comradeship between them.

The dowager Duchess of Benham gave Angela a comforting smile, noticing how pale she had become as they reached the bottom of the stone stairway.

"You look lovely, child," she said as the low door leading outside to the garden was opened for them. "All will go well, I'm sure."

Angela drew in her breath in an attempt to stop the frightened beating of her heart and stepped outside. As soon as she saw the two gentlemen standing waiting by the sundial, her heart almost stopped completely. She barely saw her father as he stepped forward and introduced her to His Grace, for she was staring so deeply at the man by his side.

He was tall, his shoulders broadly filling an elegant doublet of forest green velvet. Frothy-white lace spilled from his cuff and throat as he made a deep bow to her. His hair was his own, dark and waving to his shoulders in the Cavalier style and his features were strong and strikingly handsome. He seemed completely in command of the situation. She was immediately aware of something she could only call magnetism about this man. A little smile played about his mouth

173

and she lowered her gaze, her cheeks growing warm under his frank appraisal.

The noontime sunshine highlighted Angela's exquisite beauty, the silvery-blond curls, the flawless skin, the soft, full lips curled into a shy smile, the wide, luminous eyes . . .

A shock of recognition shot through Claridge's body as she raised those eyes to him again. It was she! He could not be mistaken! Those lovely eyes had haunted him for too many days and nights.

She heard him repeat her name and overwhelmed by the intensity of his deep voice and his towering presence, she fought to keep her poise and dignity.

"Your Grace," she said softly, in the voice he remembered, and curtsied deeply before him, her eyes lowering again.

"If you will permit me," Claridge nodded to the Earl, "I will escort Angela about the garden."

"By all means," Westbury said, feeling greatly relieved. Only an hour before his daughter had begged him to let her return to the convent and take her vows. Now, it seemed, all would be well after all. He took the dowager duchess's elbow to lead her over to a marble bench in the shade.

As the two started down the pathway that wound amongst the fragrant rose bushes, Claridge slowed his large pace to match that of the girl at his side. She looked very lovely, the delicate blush still staining her cheeks, her eyes veiled by the fringe of long lashes, so much darker than her fair hair. He sensed a sadness about her he had never felt before. He hoped he had not been the cause of it.

"You are even more beautiful than I imagined," he told her.

"Your Grace flatters me."

"Nay, I speak the truth. All at court must envy my good fortune."

The blush deepened. "I am not used to coquetry, Your Grace. I do not know the right things to say."

"Then say what you will. We had no trouble conversing before. By the by, I gather that your demure appraisal of me was for your father's benefit?"

"I—I don't understand you." She gave him a puzzled glance.

"I think you do. 'Tis not as if you have never seen me before."

"But I have not," she protested.

He stopped walking and stared down at her. "Are we then to play a game? To both pretend we have never met, that I have never held you in my arms, never kissed you; never made love—"

The pale cheeks had become crimson. "You would suggest ... You think I ..." her voice choked. "I thought You Grace to be an honorable man."

"I am," he assured her. "Only to you would I mention—"

"Pray say no more," she warned. "I deem it a

175

grave insult to accuse me of such things when I come to you a virtuous maid and pure as—"

"—the driven snow." He grinned. "Only your tense is wrong. Came, my girl. Not come. However, if that is the game you wish to play, I will be pleased to indulge you. Starting anew could prove to be quite delightful."

"I do not understand your riddles, Your Grace, nor do I find them amusing."

"I'm sorry. I had hoped we might share a sense of the ridiculous. I hear it does much to keep a marriage from growing mundane."

"Perhaps Your Grace thought to lighten the situation, but I can assure you—"

He held up his hands. "I'll say no more. I only thought, since we are to spend our lives together because of the pledge our fathers made, we could—"

"Are you then only honoring that pledge?" she broke in, filled with sudden hope. "You did not wish to marry me?"

"Not until I saw you," he said honestly. Then he smiled, his warm, disarming smile. "Now I intend to do my best to mitigate the situation for you."

"You guessed I had similar feelings about the marriage?"

"Of course," he said. "Wasn't that why you ran away?"

She gave him an incredulous look. "I ran away?"

"Yes, from your home. You'll have to tell me sometime how it was you came to tell fortunes."

"Fortunes?"

"When you first told mine," he went on, oblivious to her perplexity, "You were naturally unaware of my identity. Then, when I found you again and you learned my name, learned I was the very man your father wished you to marry, you . . ." He suddenly grinned as something occurred to him. "So that was why you let me . . . You're quite a little minx, aren't you?"

"I'm sorry, Your Grace," Angela looked even more confused, "but I have no knowledge at all of what you speak."

"My pardon," he said, his lips twitching, "I had forgotten. We have never met before." He reached down, plucking a tea rose from a bush beside the path and with a little bow handing it to her, as if offering an apology.

Accepting the rose, Angela stood a moment, breathing in its fragrance. "I believe you have just returned from France," she said at last. Perhaps, she thought, it was the habit of the French to speak in riddles.

"Yes," he answered. "I stayed to do service in the army of France in the wars of the Continent."

"Why did you do that?"

"To repay, in part, their hospitality."

"I see," she said, a small spark of admiration showing for the first time in her eyes. "Apparently our meeting today was at the suggestion of the king. You must be close to him, since he takes such an interest in your affairs."

"I was once close to him," Claridge sighed, "but I'm afraid I no longer find the court life diverting. There is too much intrigue and opportunism . . ." He gave a short grunt. "Too much of everything. After the army, it seems an empty life."

They were circling the lower part of the garden and now Claridge stopped and turned to face Angela.

"If the king permits it, I wish to leave White-hall and return to my country estates as soon as possible. I will come back to court from time to time, of course, but I hope to make my home in the country for most of the year. I wanted you to be aware of this before I asked you to marry me."

A shy smile lit up her lovely face. "That would suit me well, Your Grace," she said. "I love the country. I find the diversions of the court not only empty, but often quite abhorrent."

Could she know what that smile had just done to him? Claridge wondered. How beautiful she looked, standing there in her shimmering gown of pale yellow, the soft rays of the autumn sun making a nimbus around her fair head, turning her moonlight hair to gold.

He felt terrible longing to take her in his arms and rein kisses on those slightly parted lips, but he remembered the two who hovered like bees at the top of the garden. Instead, he gently took her left hand in his and raised it to his lips.

"Will you do me the honor of becoming my wife?" he asked.

She looked past him to where her father sat with the Duchess of Benham. He was gazing expectantly in her direction. She must do her duty.

"Aye," she whispered, lowering her eyes beneath Claridge's intent gaze.

As he bent to kiss her hand, he turned it over, pressing his lips against the soft pink palm. He had not had the opportunity of viewing Elizabeth's left hand with its vivid birthmark, or he would not have felt so happy and exultant as he led Angela to her father.

Lady Quillby stood on the tiny balcony above the garden watching the man who still was so dear to her. She had seen the smile that had crossed the proud, handsome face as he viewed his intended for the first time. The same smile that could always make her forget his careless treatment of her.

"You hoped to wed him yourself, didn't you?" Ramsden's voice was low and silky as the two stood side by side in the narrow space looking out over the rose garden. Due to two pillared balustrades, they were well hidden from the ground.

" 'Tis my own fault. I should have got him to marry me two years ago in France," Hester sighed.

"And now he has tired of you?"

She narrowed her eyes. "I was with him only last evening."

"Then give him time. He will return to you."

179

"I only wish I could be sure."

"I, too, wish I could be sure."

"Of what?" She glanced up at him, catching a look in his cold eyes that made her shiver.

"The identity of that little chit."

"Can there be any doubt? That is Westbury sitting on yonder bench with the Duchess of Benham. Do you not think he would know his own flesh and blood?"

"Aye, she must truly be the Lady Angela, still . . ." He shook his head. "What connection can she have with Elizabeth Fairclough?"

"Elizabeth . . . who?"

"It does not matter. Elizabeth is the niece of a former friend of mine. Poor Sir Matthew, found dead in an alley in Cheapside last winter." He clucked his tongue. "The girl was to wed me, but she – er – disappeared."

"Disappeared?" Lady Quillby lifted a well-shaped eyebrow. "Perhaps she got wind of your reputation, Ramsden."

"She is still promised to *me* and I will find her," he said through tight lips.

Unconsciously Hester Quillby moved a little further away from him. There was something quite menacing in his tone. She had heard some unpleasant rumors about this man's treatment of women.

Watching Claridge leading Angela back toward them, Ramsden murmured, "Astonishing. Simply astonishing."

"What do you mean?"

"The Lady Angela is the very image of Elizabeth."

Lady Quillby stared at him. "She has that same pale shade of hair?"

He nodded.

"The same features?"

"Identical."

"How intriguing. How *very* intriguing." Hester Quillby pursed her lips. Perhaps there was something here that she might be able to use to her own advantage.

Chapter Fifteen

Elizabeth had not been able to rent rooms for fortune telling in the more respectable part of the city. No one wanted to rent to a gypsy, and she felt she must continue to wear her disguise in order to protect herself from recognition by any of her uncle's friends.

Upon making her way through the older part of London, she had noticed several signs with the familiar symbols of astrologers—the moon, six stars, and a hand painted on them. Most of these had been located along dingy, narrow passageways off the main streets and were no better than filthy, little hovels. Elizabeth was determined to find a better and cleaner location.

After having several doors slammed in her face, she decided to give up her search for the day. She found lodging at a small inn, but only after she had paid the reluctant landlord more than twice what her small room was worth.

She must find the best site possible for her fortune telling, she knew, even if it took many days, for she wanted her clientele to be able to pay well for her services. The initial outlay, for furnishings, clothing, etc. would require her to dip into her savings, but the return should be greater. She thought all this through as she lay in her bed that night.

Her room at the inn overlooked the front street and she found the noise of London made it difficult for her to get to sleep. From below came a medley of horses' hooves and wheels on cobbles, the voice of a town crier, the barking of dogs, loud bursts of drunken laughter, and screaming profanities. At dawn, these noises grew with the cries of the street vendors who offered fresh milk, bread, and herrings and coal for the fire.

Sleep forgotten, Elizabeth dressed, and after breakfasting in a quiet corner of the tap room she rented a hackney coach and set out to look and inquire for rooms.

The coach rumbled off over the cobbles. Leaving Cheapside, it turned into Paternoster Row where there were row upon row of dingy booksellers. Elizabeth got her first good look at St. Paul's as they took the corner into Paternoster Lane. She had asked the coachman to take her to where the fashionable shops were located and he had suggested the New Exchange.

Passing out of London proper, they were soon

diving along Fleet Street, past the houses of the wealthy, past St. Dunstan's Church with its wooden figures that came out to strike the hour on a bell with wooden mallets, past St. Clement Dane Church, which stood in the center of the early morning traffic with vehicles moving all around it. They swung left and down the Strand where the great mansions of the nobility lined the route. Essex and Arundel, Somerset and York, Exeter and Bedford House, and the Savoy Palace. Surrounded by large grounds, these houses had long gardens backing onto the Thames.

Just beyond the Savoy Palace was the New Exchange, and with slow progress because of the dense traffic, they finally approached the entrance and Elizabeth was set down.

Built around an immense courtyard, the New Exchange had double galleries of black stone, lined with stalls. The purpose of visiting the galleries was not just to buy, but to stroll about and to gossip and be seen. It had become a social gathering spot with a moving parade of elegantly dressed men and women.

On either side of the walks the shops, or stalls, had on display beautiful and fashionable articles of clothing, ribbons and laces, jewellery and essences. The young women who attended these shops were chosen for their elegance and beauty and many were reputed to be the mistresses of some of the foremost men in the country.

After an hour of viewing the premises, Elizabeth left to explore up and down the streets close by. Not far from Treadneedle Street and the New Exchange, she discovered a small, but well kept house with rooms for rent on the ground floor.

Luck was with her for it was owned by a woman, newly widowed, who was anxious to return to her family in the country. She barely glanced at Elizabeth, asking her only for a month's rent in advance and when Elizabeth gladly produced it, told her she might move in at the end of the week.

Location being of such a great import to her, Elizabeth considered herself extremely fortunate.

In the days that followed, she supervised the cleaning, painting and decorating of her new rooms herself and purchased with artful bargaining the small amount of extra furniture she required.

Before her sign was put up, advertising her as DEVINA-THE-SOOTHSAYER, Elizabeth decided she needed someone to answer the door and show her customers into the small, private parlor where she would give her readings. At a coaching inn on the edge of town, she hired a young man who had just arrived from the country seeking work in London. Elizabeth felt he would likely be more honest than one of the city-bred youths she had seen lounging about the crowded streets.

The parlor where Elizabeth intended to tell her fortunes was decorated in midnight blue. Even the ceiling was painted this shade, although gilt stars and a moon were added for effect. The gypsy costume she had made for herself was more elaborate than the one she had worn at the fairs. It was bright scarlet in color, trimmed with gold, clearly making her the focus of attention in the flickering candlelight of the dark room.

From the first day Elizabeth opened for business, she was a success. She instructed Jimmy, the young man she had hired, to go to the New Exchange in the morning, proclaiming to all who would listen that there was a marvellous new soothsayer, located close by, who could accurately foretell their future. The result of this modest advertising had been overwhelming. There had even been a queue of vehicles lined up outside by the end of the afternoon.

When Jimmy had finally drawn the blinds and gone home to his cheap room down the street, Elizabeth sat alone in the parlor and counted the coins she had earned that day. It was far more than she had imagined in even her wildest dreams! More than she had made in nearly a week at Bartholemew Fair. She put the coins carefully away in Claridge's saddlebag, where she still kept her money. Looking at the crest tooled into the leather, all thoughts of her successful day left her head, and her mind went to Simon. Where was he now? she wondered. What was he doing? A whole week had passed since she had seen him. A week so busy for her that she had fallen into her bed every night totally exhausted. And yet, she had slept restlessly, often waking in the middle of the night to think of him.

She wondered if he had searched for her again. Probably not. He had got what he wanted from her and was doubtless pursuing some other young female by now.

Why, she wondered, did this thought upset her so, making her feel so miserable and humiliated. The man could never be anything to her. Why should it hurt her to think of him in someone else's arms? She had only herself to blame for what had happened. Had she actually expected him to swear his undying devotion to her after she had acted the harlot, inviting him to take her to bed? The man was far beyond her reach. Homeless orphans did not wed peers of the realm.

Yet, against her will, in the darkness of the long nights, Elizabeth relived the memory of their few hours together. She remembered the long, strong body stretched out next to her. She felt again his heart pounding against her breast, his gentle, caressing fingers, his lips, moist and firm covering hers, the fire of his kisses. She wanted him desperately, aching for his intimate touch, tormented by their shared passion. She

187

would hear his rich laugh, hear his urgent insistence when he said, "Say you'll come with me. Say it!" Oh, Simon, she would think in despair, what have you done to me?

The Earl of Westbury planned a betrothal party for his daughter, Angela, and His Grace, the Duke of Claridge, but due to the size of his London townhouse, only a small, select group were to be invited.

Lady Quillby knew she would not be included, and yet she wished to speak with Lady Angela before the event. On the morning of the party, she paid her a surprise visit.

Dressed in the height of fashion, Hester was resplendent in a jade green velvet gown, her red curls set off by a large matching hat, with a long plume that swept around one flawless, ivory cheek.

For the first few minutes, they talked of trivial things and then Hester Quillby brought the conversation around to her favorite subject, the current love affairs at court. Sitting across from Angela, daintily sipping hot chocolate, she went on and on about who was sleeping with whom and who had produced whose bastard, while Angela sat shocked by her revelations and wondered what the real purpose was behind the woman's visit.

She did not know Lady Quillby. She had briefly viewed her in the queen's chambers the day before and had heard her name mentioned, but that was all. When Frances had glanced at her and hushed the woman who had spoken Hester Quillby's name aloud, she had been frankly surprised.

Suddenly Angela realized that Lady Quillby had stopped talking and was now examining her closely over the rim of her cup. "You're very young, aren't you?"

"I'm eighteen," Angela smiled. "Older than many who come to court."

"But quite innocent in the ways of the world."

"I—I suppose so."

"I shouldn't have spoken as I have to you," Lady Quillby apologized, although the slightly mocking look in her green eyes belied her words.

"I am not unfamiliar with court gossip," Angela said, raising her chin a little.

"Really? Then perhaps you are already aware of the reason I have called upon you this morning," Hester's smile was supercilious.

Angela shook her head, blushing slightly.

"No. I am afraid I am not."

"Your father, I believe, is hosting a party this evening to announce your betrothal to Simon Blair, the Duke of Claridge?"

"Aye, he is." Did this woman want an invitation, she wondered.

"I think you should know, my dear, that I am Simon's mistress," Lady Quillby astonished Angela by saying. "We have been together for years—since our days on the Continent with the king."

Angela cried, "Oh!" and sat trembling, staring at her guest, her face suddenly drained of color. "I see," she said at last in a small voice.

Lady Quillby rose to her feet. "I hope you *do* see, my dear, for he has no intention of giving me up. You will bear his name, but never forget that I possess his heart."

Almost numb with shock, Angela nevertheless remembered her manners and stumbled to her feet to see Lady Quillby to the door.

When she was gone, Angela stared at the closed door disbelievingly. She wanted to burst into tears, but her anger was so great it prevented her. She seated herself again, her hands carefully folded in her lap and gazed at the chair where Lady Quillby had sat.

His Grace had deceived her. She had thought him to be like Gerald in preferring the simple life of the country. He had seemed kind and gentle, when they had met, even a little confused, which had made him appear less frightening and much more human to her. When he had told her he disliked the life at court, he had put her worst fears to rest. Perhaps it would not be so difficult, she had decided, to live with a gentleman who thought so like herself.

He had not appeared to be the type who would force himself on her or make excessive demands. She could still not bear the thought of getting into bed with him, of letting him . . . The thought had come to her that if she succeeded right away in giving Claridge an heir, perhaps he would leave her alone after that.

She would love to have a child. That was the one side of this marriage which she knew she would enjoy. But the other side . . . that duty of a wife to submit to her husband's needs . . . she knew she would never enjoy it with anyone but Gerald.

Still, she had been prepared to put up with it. It was her duty to marry His Grace, and as his duchess she was sure she would be able to do much good. But now, all she had felt was gone. She was mortified and shocked by what Hester Quillby had told her. Claridge was like all the other court gallants with their mistresses and casual liaisons. How she hated promiscuity! His Majesty's unfaithfulness to his dear queen sickened her. Would Claridge be like him after he married her? Assuaging himself with the servant girls the way her father had done? Laughing behind her back with Lady Quillby? Dear God, how could she put up with it?

* * *

The betrothal party appeared on the surface to be a brilliant success. His Majesty, Charles II, was in attendance, but his little queen had sent her regrets. Catherine never braved the world outside of Whitehall.

Angela was coolly beautiful in a pale blue silk gown trimmed with Brussels lace cascading down the skirt, a deep fall of matching lace trimming the sleeves. The low neckline was modestly raised by a frill of more lace, above which was Claridge's gift to her of a diamond and sapphire necklace that had been his mother's. Angela looked the perfect Snow Maid.

His Grace was magnificent beside her in a dove-gray moire doublet, trimmed with silver. After the Earl had announced the betrothal, many toasts were made to the handsome couple in French champagne which the Earl had especially ordered and to Angela's relief, appeared to be indulging in very little of himself.

Watching the couple carefully during the sumptuous supper that followed, Lord Musgrove decided in his own mind that his friend, Claridge, had a long way to go to melt the heart of the Snow Maid. Although he appeared most attentive to her, even showing more affection than was usually displayed at such times, the Lady Angela's behavior, although always correct, still remained cool and detached.

The salon was ablaze with candlelight and at

the far end of the room a score of fiddlers awaited the signal to begin the dancing.

The king led off with the bride-to-be and Claridge stood by, until the dance ended, his eyes never leaving Angela until he could claim her hand. As they took their places for the dance, he said quietly to her, "I sense a remoteness in you this evening, my dear. Have I done something to offend you?"

"Your mode of life offends me, Your Grace," she said tersely.

He frowned. "How so?"

"I have learned that you are a man whose tastes are opposed to everything I have been taught to hold in esteem."

"My dear Angela," he said, a little amused, "I don't know which of my great follies you've heard about, but believe me, I've long since outgrown most of them."

"But not all, Your Grace."

"Then pray tell me what has occurred to bring about this sudden lack of regard for me."

The musicians began to play the slow and stately pavane as Angela answered, "Lady Quillby paid me a visit this morning."

Claridge said something short under his breath which Angela did not catch.

"I beg your pardon?" she asked.

"That relationship is a thing of the past," he assured her.

"But it *did* occur?" Her soft eyes met his, pleading for denial.

"Aye, she was my mistress," he admitted. "I would not lie to you, Angela. I have never professed to be a saint. I've been with many women, if you must—"

"I do not wish to hear about your lusts," she said in a shaking voice.

"Thank God for that," he laughed. "Let us henceforth resolve only to speak of our own desire for one another."

Shocked, she drew back from him. "I have *never* felt desire for you," she cried, color staining her cheeks.

This was too much for Claridge. "Little liar!" he roared. "Do you deny the passion we once shared?"

"What are you saying?" She stared up at him in horror. "How can you imply—"

Suddenly Angela closed her mouth, realizing that they were gaining the attention of the other dancers. Fortunately, at that moment, the music came to an end.

"Come," he commanded, almost dragging her through the crowd and out of the room by way of the servant's door. There was no one in sight in the hallway on the other side, so he stopped and confronted her.

"Now," he said ominously, "we will settle this once and for all."

Before Angela knew what was happening, Claridge pulled her against himself and his mouth found hers. She remained still in his arms, her lips closed and unresponsive beneath his, as unyielding as stone.

He drew away. "What the devil has come over you?" he demanded.

"Your wrongful deception," she cried, close to tears now. "You told me you abhorred the life at court. You gave me to believe you were different."

"And now?"

"Now I find that you are as licentious as all the others."

He shook his head. "I cannot believe we are having this conversation. If I am not mistaken, it was you, my sweet, who suggested I bed *you*."

His quick reflexes made him catch her hand before it connected with his cheek.

"That was ungentlemanly of me, I admit," he apologized. "But I assure you, despite what you have heard, Hester Quillby means nothing to me." He grasped her shoulders, looking down into her eyes. He had once read warmth and humor and understanding there. Now there was only anger and fear in the deep blue depths.

"Don't you dare kiss me again," she choked.

His hands fell from her and he stood back. "Rest assured, madam," he said crisply, "it will not happen again."

Angrily he yanked open the door and let it slam

behind him. Angela was left standing alone in the deserted hallway.

Good, she thought. He has gone away. Perhaps he will seek out my father and break his vow. Fervently she hoped he would. Then perhaps she could return to Neville Hall and somehow, someway, she and Gerald might . . .

Dear, sweet Gerald, she thought wistfully, her eyes clouding. Gerald who had always been so kind and gentle with her — not fierce, abusive, and demanding like Claridge. The hunger she had seen in the Duke's dark eyes, the latent passion, had filled her with fear and apprehension.

The king threw down the dice box and rose to his feet.

"Thank you, gentlemen," he said, his lips twisting into a cynical smile. "My luck seems to have deserted me again."

He crossed the room which was one of several the Earl of Westbury had set up for gambling, but as he neared the door, he was stopped by the Duke of Claridge who had been standing lazily in the doorway, surveying the room.

"May I speak with you, Sire?" he asked, and at Charles' nod followed him out into the hallway. He indicated a shadowed alcove beneath the high stairway.

"I'm surprised you could bear to leave the beautiful Lady Angela even for a moment tonight, Simon," Charles gently chided him.

"She is dancing with your brother, the Duke of York."

"And a graceful little dancer she is, seemly and demure."

Claridge lifted an amused eyebrow. "I'm quite sure you are aware, Sire, that those at court call her the Snow Maid.

"She's young and green," Charles smiled. "You must handle her gently, Simon, and with patience. Gentleness and patience work best on that type. You may have noticed I have my eye on that sweeting, Frances Stewart. The lass keeps dancing beyond my reach. Patience, I tell myself. Do not frighten the chit. You'll see, Simon. It will all work out in the end."

"I hope so, Sire," Claridge muttered, as if he didn't believe it. He had a vision of Angela lying stiff and rigid in his arms on their wedding night, permitting him his conjugal rights, only because it was a wife's duty.

"I have offered the Chapel Royal to Westbury for the wedding. The Bishop of London will marry you," Charles was saying.

"Thank you, Sire, but my bride and my wedding were really not what I wished to discuss with you this evening. If I could have but another moment of your time . . ."

"Do hurry, Simon," Charles said a bit impatiently, "The dice are not with me tonight so I wish to try the card room."

"That is exactly what worries me, Sire," Claridge said quietly. "You gave me some advice not long ago. May I return the favor?"

Charles shook his head sadly. "*Et tu*, Simon?" He gave a wan smile.

"If I might be so bold, Sire," Claridge grinned. "You do far better in the bedchamber than at the gaming tables."

The king let out a roar of laughter that carried out to the hallway beyond. It was overheard by another who had just left the gambling room. The man glanced around to see if he were alone in the hallway and then moved a little closer to where the king and Claridge were secluded. He didn't have to see the two men to know who they were. He recognized their voices.

"So you would suggest I curtail my gambling?" the king was saying. "Have you been talking to my Lord Clarendon?"

"No, Sire. But I could not help but notice you were gambling with Lord Ramsden tonight."

"Not for the first time. I've lost a good deal to that man. He has uncanny luck."

"Perhaps," Claridge said carefully.

"Perhaps?" Charles's dark melancholy eyes surveyed his friend. "I don't think I like the way you said that. Are you implying that my lord cheats?"

"Some day I would like to prove it, but tonight

is hardly the time."

"Many's the man he's ruined at the tables . . ." Charles mused.

"I don't trust him. Never have. He's too oily. I wouldn't be surprised, Sire if he is trying his best to get you indebted to him. Indebted, so you will be forced to grant him favors."

"I hadn't thought of that."

"That is why I warned you. Be sure with whom you wager, Sire, I beg of you."

"Thank you for your advice, Simon," Charles regarded him for a moment. "You really do not find the life at court to your taste, do you? Don't look surprised. I have been watching you since your arrival at Whitehall. Your dislike of our revels has not been lost on me."

"I have nothing against drinking and gambling and women," Simon grinned, "but I find myself bored by the constant round of pleasure-seeking. I'm not used to being idle. I need something to do. That is why I wish, at your pleasure, of course, to return to my estates after my wedding. I have a fit steward who has taken charge in my absence, but there is still much I would like to do."

The king nodded. "I can understand your feelings, Simon, but I will hate to lose your honest face. I hope you and your future duchess do not intend to be strangers at court."

"No, Sire. We will return for some time each

winter."

"Good," the king said, clasping Claridge's shoulder. "Do you know you have made me lose all my desire to gamble this evening? I think I will take me home to a warm bed." He gave Simon a meaningful wink.

"Then I will bid you good evening, Sire."

The man who had stood listening moved off quickly and silently down the hallway.

Claridge again, Ramsden thought. Damn the man! Somehow he had begun popping up regularly these days to thwart his plans. He would have to find a way to deal with him.

Chapter Sixteen

More than a week had passed since she had had the set-to with Claridge, and Hester Quillby was worried. They had argued and fought in the past, for Hester was hot-tempered and Claridge used to command, but he had always returned to her bed.

She knew that making love was what she did best and she was confident that Claridge would find none other who could give him more pleasure. Certainly not that wide-eyed innocent to whom he had become betrothed. Lady Angela, she was sure, would remain the virgin until she was wedded and then only endure with stoicism Claridge's embraces because it was her duty.

Hester had heard of Devina, the new soothsayer, whose name was on many lips at court. She decided to seek her advice on recapturing the illusive Claridge.

Clothed in a black hooded cloak and with a black velvet vizard-masque over her face, Hester sat across the table from the fortune teller in the semidarkness of her parlor.

"There is something I must know," she told Elizabeth. "It is of the greatest importance to me."

"Of course, milady, but first will you tell me the date and hour of your birth and where you were born?"

Hester told her the details she had asked for and Elizabeth insisted she make herself comfortable as she consulted several charts of the stars and moon.

Hester removed her vizard and drew back her hood from her face. Unfastening her cloak, she let it fall carelessly from her shoulders over the back of her chair.

Elizabeth tried not to stare at the beautiful woman before her. Her hair appeared flame-red against the whiteness of her skin. Her green eyes were emphasized by dark kohl that was drawn around them. Jewels sparkled in her ears, on her fingers and a large jewelled pendant lay in the hollow between her full, lush breasts, the tips of which were barely covered by her low cut gown.

Whose mistress was this? Elizabeth wondered. In the ten days she had been in London, quite a few had sought her advice. This Lady Quillby looked a little older than some and perhaps that was the reason for her visit. Her protector might be growing tired of her.

Elizabeth took one of the soft white hands in her own and turned it palm side up.

"What is it you wish to know, milady?" she asked the woman, making her husky voice sympathetic. "Is something troubling you?"

"Something is, indeed," Hester said, trying to find the right words.

"The stars indicate that this is a difficult time for you. The decisions you make may well affect your whole life." Elizabeth looked deep into the green eyes. "You must be frank with me, milady. No word of what you speak will go beyond these walls."

Hester gazed at the gypsy closely, but all she could really see of her were the dark, penetrating eyes above her veil.

"All right," she sighed, settling back in her chair. "I wish to know if the man I love will return to me."

"Is he on a journey?"

"No. He has not come to me since be became betrothed to another. You understand," she hastened to add, " 'tis only an arranged marriage he is entering into. It should not affect our relationship."

Elizabeth nodded. "Jupiter brings jealousy," she said, looking carefully into the palm she held. "And you possess a jealous nature, milady. You are jealous of the one who is to marry your lover, but since she learned of your relationship with him, all is not well between them."

"Good." Hester's eyes glinted with satisfaction. "But what of Simon? What of him?"

Elizabeth felt a lurch to her heart at the sound of Claridge's first name. Could the arranged marriage of which this woman spoke, be his? She had to know.

"He is an important man," Elizabeth pointed to a line in Hester's hand. "An Earl, perhaps, or . . ."

"A Duke," Hester proudly interjected. "And incredibly handsome. I knew him in France, you see, where we became lovers." Her green eyes misted. "There is no one to equal him. No one at all, and I've had many lovers."

"I see," Elizabeth said quietly. She was sure now that it was Claridge of whom Lady Quillby spoke. She even felt a little sympathy for her, knowing well how she must feel.

"Can you answer my question?" Lady Quillby persisted. "Will he return to me?"

"What you ask me is very difficult, milady."

"Why is that?"

"The answer depends upon a number of things." Elizabeth paused a moment and then went on. "I see a great ball taking place shortly at the palace. All three of you will be attending." She knew of the ball from one of her other clients. It was to be held in honor of Prince Rupert, the king's cousin, who had recently returned to court from Holland.

"That is so. I came here directly from my courturière, Madame Belyea. Would you believe she is also creating Angela's gown? Angela is the Duke of Claridge's betrothed . . ."

Lady Quillby had let his name slip. So it was indeed her Simon, Elizabeth thought, an ache forming in her breast.

" . . . the court calls her the Snow Maid. Madame told me her gown is to be in a pale lilac shade—too modest for words. Of course I insisted that in comparison she make me the most outrageous creation she could conjure up. Something so daring, everyone will be absolutely stunned when I enter. She suggested something in a filmy peach," Lady Quillby chattered on, "with an absolutely transparent bodice. What do you think of that? Then Simon will clearly see the difference between a real woman and a mere child." She drew in her breath as if to emphasize her already apparent attributes.

Elizabeth slowly shook her head. "I do not see you wearing such a gown."

"What do you mean?" Lady Quillby's voice was sharp.

"I see you instead gowned in a cloth of gold, sweeping into the ball like a queen. Everyone present catching his breath at your elegance and regal bearing."

"A queen . . . ," Lady Quillby murmured. Then her green eyes lit up. "Why, of course. The very thing! How much better to awe people than to shock them. Madame Belyea's idea would only have humiliated me. How *could* she have suggested it?"

Elizabeth said nothing. It was not for her to mention that it had, after all, been *her* suggestion, not her couturiere's.

"Cloth of gold, you say? That *would* look regal and I must wear a tiara. I have a beautiful one that belonged to my husband's mother. Oh, this will surely raise me in Simon's eyes. He will not only admire me, he will worship me! I can just see him going down on his knees before me."

Elizabeth thought that was asking a bit much of the proud Claridge. She could not picture him going down on his knees before any woman. However, she assured Lady Quillby that she would indeed look like a queen on the night of the ball and her admirers would be many.

Lady Quillby was so delighted with her reading that she was overly generous with her payment.

"You may be sure I will recommend you to all my friends," she said, drawing the cloak about her shoulders and lifting the hood over her bright hair.

Elizabeth pulled a bell rope and the young man in black swung open the parlor door for Lady Quillby and made a small bow as he led her along the hallway to the outer door.

The footmen who were waiting outside, escorted Lady Quillby to her coach and she was about to ascend when she remembered that she had left her vizard behind. About to order one of her footmen to fetch it for her, she suddenly changed her mind and retraced her steps, reentering the rooms she had just left.

The young man, busy closing the blinds for the day, looked surprised as Lady Quillby sailed by him and without knocking, opened the door to the parlor.

She was not prepared for the sight that greeted her. Having concluded her last appointment for the day, Elizabeth had risen and had just removed the confining coif and veil.

When Lady Quillby burst into the room, her eyes were immediately drawn to the figure in red standing behind the table, the candlelight reflecting on her face. She let out a little scream.

Elizabeth was herself taken aback by the woman's entrance. For a moment they stood staring at one another before Elizabeth managed to regain her composure.

"I'm very sorry, milady. The gypsy, Devina, was ill today and so I took her place," was her quick fabrication. "If you are not pleased with me I will be glad to return your money."

"Do not toy with me Angela! You did this on purpose!" Lady Quillby shrieked. "I suppose you bribed the gypsy and—"

"I don't know what you mean, milady. My name is not Angela," Elizabeth explained, but Lady Quillby wasn't listening to her.

"I'll admit this is a clever way to get even with me, but," she gave a little laugh, "I hope you aren't stupid enough to believe all the things I said."

"I believe you are confusing me with someone else, milady. My name is Beth."

About to make a sharp retort, Lady Quillby suddenly stopped and peered closer at the girl.

Beth, she thought. It was a nickname for Elizabeth. She was remembering what Lord Ramsden had told her about a girl named Elizabeth Fairclough, who looked remarkably like Angela Neville. She had run away from Ramsden. Could she have come to London? Could this be she? The resemblance between this girl and Angela Neville was remarkable. No wonder Ramsden had been dumbfounded by it.

"You do not know Angela Neville?" she asked.

"No. I do not."

"You are very like her." Hester shook her head. "So like her, in fact, I would think you to be twins. She is ... 'tis she who is to wed my Simon."

Elizabeth's eyes widened. "She looks like me?"

Hester had moved closer to the table, her gaze never leaving the other's face. "The very image," she said. "It's quite uncanny. She bears the same face and figure."

"But how can that be?" Elizabeth looked bewildered.

"You are the soothsayer," Hester shrugged. "Perhaps you should read your own hand."

My own hand, Elizabeth thought, thinking back to when Marta had read her fortune, remembering the words, "Thy own destiny . . . intertwined with another Gemini. Gemini is a sign of the zodiac which represents the twins. Are you one of two?"

Hester bent to retrieve the vizard she had dropped beside her chair and as she did she sneezed. Groping in her reticule for a handkerchief, she felt something else she had placed in it and forgotten. A square piece of heavy paper. An invitation.

In a flash an idea came to her. It was wild, of course, and there was only a rare possibility that it might bear fruit, but it was worth taking the chance. Surreptitiously, Hester extracted the invitation from her reticule and let it fall to the floor beside her chair.

"If you cannot lace me tighter, you clumsy fingered wench, I will have you beaten," Lady Quillby said in a furious voice.

The new maid who was attending her was so nervous she immediately yanked too hard and broke one of the laces.

"There! Now you've done it!" Lady Quillby screamed at her.

Fortunately for the young girl there was a knock at the door, at that moment, and Lord Ramsden, not waiting for it to be answered, strode into the room.

"Really, Ramsden, you could have waited to be

209

announced," Lady Quillby said disagreeably. She tore off the offending corset and thrust it at the maid. "Get me another," she ordered, turning toward the man who had just entered. She made no attempt to cover her half-dressed state. Hester Quillby had greeted gentlemen clothed in a good deal less.

Ramsden settled himself in an armchair and carefully crossed his legs. "What did you wish to see me about, madam?" he asked her.

"Something happened this afternoon that I thought might interest you," she said. "I paid a visit to that gypsy fortune teller everyone is talking about. The woman was ill, and another read my palm in her place."

"Really? Was she as good?"

"That is of no consequence." Hester motioned to the maid who had found a new corset in the clothes chest and was timidly standing waiting beside her. "Get out of here!" she spat at the frightened girl. "I'll ring for you when I need you."

The maid, looking as if she might burst into tears at any moment, fled from the room.

"Now," Hester said, placing her two hands upon her slim hips, "here is the interesting part. After my reading was over this afternoon, I left the soothsayer's rooms, only to remember I had forgotten my vizard. It was when I returned that I discovered it wasn't the gypsy who had told my fortune, but a young girl. She had removed her trappings and I swear to you, Ramsden, she was

210

the very image of the Lady Angela."

"Angela Neville?"

"Aye," Hester smiled. "In fact, at first I was sure it *was* the chit playing a trick on me. But when I realized it was another girl, I immediately thought of you and your Elizabeth Fairclough. The girl even calls herself Beth."

Ramsden had risen from his chair at her words and now stood before her, his eyes very bright. "Will she still be there?" he asked eagerly.

"No. Mine was her last appointment of the day."

"I must see her for myself. I'll visit her first thing in the morning."

"No!" Hester shook her head emphatically. "If she is still there, you would only scare her away. I have already done something better," she said proudly. "My invitation to the ball was in my reticule. I left it behind, as if I had carelessly dropped it."

Ramsden sniffed disdainfully. "What good will that—"

"If I don't miss my guess, your lordship, she will make use of it and come to the ball. Think. If you heard that there was someone in London who was the very image of you, wouldn't you be curious to see him in person?" She gave a sly smile. "If all goes well, Ramsden, and that chit comes to the ball, she can be made to serve both our needs."

Hester felt sure of Ramsden's cooperation in a plan that was already forming and maturing in her mind. He desired the beautiful Elizabeth—the image of Angela—her rival for Claridge's affections. She wished to drive a permanent wedge between the betrothed couple. Working together, she and Ramsden might easily achieve both goals.

Chapter Seventeen

Elizabeth stood before the desk clutching the invitation in her hand. The gold lettered words announcing the Royal Ball in honor of Prince Rupert wavered before her eyes. There was no name on it, but she never doubted for a moment that it had belonged to the last person who had sat in that chair. Claridge's mistress, Lady Quillby.

Upon noticing her resemblance to the Duke's bethrothed, had Lady Quillby left it purposely? Had she wanted Elizabeth to make use of it and attend the ball? Wanted her to cause trouble between the Lady Angela and Simon? There seemed to be little doubt.

Elizabeth wondered if Claridge had noticed the resemblance between her and his betrothed. She shook her head. No. It was not possible. He had never seen her without some facial covering.

What a strange coincidence that a girl who

bore her likeness was to marry Simon — the man she loved. The fates must really be laughing at her.

Was she related to this girl in any way? Could they be cousins, perhaps, or had her mother and Angela's father ... No! It was impossible! Her parents had married when her mother was barely sixteen and there had never been another man in her life but George Fairclough. They had been so close ... so much in love with one another. How different her life would have been had they lived.

Rightfully she should throw the invitation away. Yet, Elizabeth's mind raced with the possibilities the invitation offered. With it, she would be admitted to Whitehall and given a chance to enjoy a way of life she might never experience again. But, most of all, she would see Simon, her Moonlight Cavalier again.

The yearning which had been her legacy since that night in Bridgetown, welled up inside her with fresh intensity. She could be strong, but this need within her — which she felt for Claridge — was something which, when it overcome her, obliterated everything.

With a vividness that made her ache with hunger, she remembered the gentle touch of his lips and fingers, his warm, hard body. When she closed her eyes at night, he was there and although she might weep in helpless frustration, she couldn't forget his thrilling kisses. She knew that to remember such things was more than foolish. It was insane! She should be trying her best to forget the man. Seeing him again would only make it harder for her to do that. Besides, she did not trust his mistress. She must have had some plan in mind when she left the invitation.

His mistress. What a beautiful woman Lady Quillby was. Elizabeth felt a sharp pang of jealousy at the thought of her in Claridge's arms. The woman loved him. That was obvious. And Claridge? He had probably never lost his heart to anyone. Still, Elizabeth thought none the less of him for having a mistress. Since she had begun to tell fortunes, she had learned much about men and their needs and desires. Judging from Lady Quillby, Claridge's preference ran to women of the world and not young innocents. Had he thought *her* to be experienced when he had met her? Considering the way she had behaved, it was entirely possible.

Perhaps that was why, after he had made love to her and discovered himself the first, he had offered her his protection. She wondered what would have happened had she accepted? Would he have still kept Lady Quillby? Or would he have tried to juggle them both? The king seemed to be able to manage more than one affair at once, but Elizabeth somehow did not think that would be Claridge's style. Since his betrothal, his mistress had said he had ignored her. Obviously, one woman at a time was enough for him.

Dear God, if she could only be that woman! If

she could only take the Lady Angela's place!

She shouldn't be thinking such thoughts, Elizabeth cautioned herself, as an image of herself dressed as Angela, took shape in her mind. And yet? It would only be for one night. One wonderful night. Was it so wrong to want to go to the ball? Was it so wrong to want to reenter a world she might never taken her place in again?

She could do it. She even knew the name of Lady Angela's French couturiere. It should not be difficult to pretend she was Simon's bethrothed.

For three days Elizabeth worked with lemon juice and pumice stone to remove the berry stains from her hands. On the morning of the following day, she cancelled her appointments and, clad in a large hat and gown of a becoming sea-green shade which had been one of several made for her by a young seamstress down the street, Elizabeth rented a sedan chair to take her to Madame Belyea's establishment.

Currently at the top of her popularity, Madame Belyea was a Parisian dressmaker who had come to London to take advantage of the aristocracy's penchant for anything French.

A footman ushered Elizabeth into the shop, giving the name of Lady Angela Neville to the flustered looking little woman who had appeared from behind a table stacked with bolts of cloth.

She quickly fetched a tiny dark woman from the back of the establishment. Her cheeks were

painted bright pink and she wore a pair of pe-
rukes of false hair on either side of her small
head. These tended to bounce when she walked.

"*Mais alors*, there was no need for you to come
yourself, milady. I would have brought your gown
to the Palace."

Elizabeth smiled with relief. With no hesitation
on the woman's part, she was being accepted as
Lady Angela.

"I was in the vicinity, Mme. Belyea," she said
offhandedly, "so I thought I would like to try it
on."

"Why, of course. One of my seamstresses is just
finishing the hem. Could you wait, *un instant*,
milady?"

"I am in no hurry."

"You would like to try on the matching slippers, *peut-être?* The shoemaker delivered them
yesterday."

She snapped her fingers and the little mouse of
a woman reappeared to be tersely ordered to fetch
milady's slippers.

The poise and dignity Elizabeth had shown up
to this point was immediately threatened by the
thought that she and Angela might not share the
same shoe size. Lady Quillby had assured Elizabeth that she and Angela were of the same build,
so she had no doubt the gown would fit her, but
she had not thought of slippers.

Mme. Belyea indicated a comfortable chair and
her assistant soon returned carrying a pair of soft

217

kid slippers in a pale lilac shade topped by matching silk rosettes. She knelt down at Elizabeth's feet to try them on. They fitted perfectly! Elizabeth realized she had been holding her breath and slowly released it.

"I'm pleased with them," she nodded, trying not to show her real delight.

"Bring *l'accessoires, tout de suite,*" Mme. Belyea demanded and Elizabeth was soon viewing a delicate lace fan and a pair of long, perfumed gloves in the same shade of lilac as the slippers.

"Perfect," she nodded with pleasure as a plainly dressed young seamstress appeared in the back doorway.

"The gown is ready, Madame," she said to the dressmaker.

"If you will kindly follow me, milady," Mme. Belyea said to Elizabeth.

A few minutes later she was staring at herself in the looking glass. The soft lilac silk enhanced the delicate coloring of her skin and made her deep blue eyes glow. The bodice of the gown was mounted directly onto a stiffly boned corset which came to a deep V at the front and made Elizabeth's small waist look even smaller. The sleeves were full, and trimmed with lilac satin ribbons. The same ribbons outlined the additional overskirt of the gown and the oval neckline. Just tipping the shoulders, it barely dipped in front. "Too modest for words," Lady Quillby had

218

said. Compared to the currently popular off-the shoulder styles which delighted in revealing a good deal of bosom, it was indeed discreet, Elizabeth thought. A perfect gown for the Snow Maid.

"Enchanting," Madame exclaimed. "May I suggest your hairdresser curl your hair about your face like this . . ." She tucked some beautifully made silk posies in lilac and pink into Elizabeth's hair. "*Voila!* Much softer, *n'est-ce pas?*"

Elizabeth smiled in agreement. She had purposely worn her hair in a very simple style that day, unaware of the way Angela normally wore hers.

"Fetch the cloak, Marie," Mme. Belyea turned impatiently to the young seamstress who stood anxiously beside her. Of lilac colored velvet, the cloak was lined in white satin, and the attached hood was bordered with soft white fur.

Elizabeth had never owned a cloak as lovely as this one, but was forced to contain her delight as it was fastened about her shoulders. The Lady Angela would surely be used to wearing such clothing. Nevertheless, she was tempted to cry out with pleasure at the vision of herself in the mirror, the soft fur perfectly framing her face. She was instantly transformed into a lady of quality. She had been disguising herself as a gypsy for so long, it brought tears to her eyes to remember what she had once been. She silently thanked the Lady Angela.

As Elizabeth was helped back into her own

clothing, her purchases were wrapped and sent out to the waiting footman.

"The bill, of course, will go to your father, the Earl of Westbury?" Mme. Belyea said as Elizabeth emerged from the dressing room.

"No," Elizabeth shook her head. "I would prefer to have it now, if that is possible."

Mme. Belyea gave her a strange look. "A moment, milady," she said and hurried from the room.

I've given myself away, Elizabeth thought, wondering if she should make a hurried exit, but almost immediately Mme. returned with the bill in hand which she presented to her. By now she was used to the eccentricities of the nobility, and very little surprised her.

Elizabeth didn't so much as glance at it, but tucked the bill into her reticule and with a smiling nod to the dressmaker, sailed out of the shop and was assisted into the waiting sedan chair.

Not having seen his friend since the night of the betrothal party, Lord Musgrove was delighted, later that week, to encounter him at a horse sale in Knightsbridge.

Claridge was observing a coal-black stallion, its magnificent coat gleaming like silk in the afternoon sunshine, as it trotted around the small track.

"He's almost perfect," Musgrove said in awe.

"Aye," Claridge murmured. "See that development of crest? It promises great strength when he comes to his full growth."

"I wonder why anyone would be selling him?"

"I believe his owner's pockets are to let," Claridge answered.

As the bidding started, he explained to his friend that the present king's father had kept his breeding stock at Tutbury in Staffordshire. After his death, there was a stud of 139 horses, with 37 brood mares. They were dispersed in a series of sales, but six of them were taken over by Cromwell himself. This stallion, he told Musgrove, was said to be the grandson of one of them.

"That explains his excellence," his friend said.

"Aye, the Duke of Buckingham as the master of the old king imported numerous oriental animals for breeding as did my grandfather. That mixture of native and oriental blood has produced some of the finest animals in England."

Claridge said nothing more as the bidding by now had been left to only three gentlemen.

Musgrove watched with interest as Claridge rapidly outbid the others and purchased the stallion. Seeing him standing there in the sunny yard with the smell of damp hay and horseflesh and manure all around him, Musgrove thought for the first time in a long while that his friend looked truly happy. He told him so and Claridge smiled.

"Horses and the land are what I know best, Musgrove. I am not at home at Whitehall."

"I am well aware of that, old friend, but what of the Lady Angela? Does she share your view?"

"I believe she loves horses. Come John, I want to show you something."

Claridge led his friend through the crowd and around behind the stables where there was a small fenced-off paddock. He nodded toward a horse that was all alone there.

"What do you think of her?"

Musgrove gazed at a beautiful chestnut filly who was viewing them as they approached, her ears pricked, her bright eyes alert with intelligence. She started toward them with a flowing grace that made it seem as if her hooves barely touched the ground. The only marking that broke her rich red-gold color was a white star in the center of her broad forehead. Her neck was finely arched, her shoulders sloped cleanly and her chest was deep.

"She's a real beauty," Musgrove said.

Claridge agreed and reached through the fence to stroke the horse's neck. She nuzzled him gently.

"The perfect gift, I thought, when I saw her."

"Gift? For whom?"

"Angela, of course."

"I see you are trying your best to please her."

"I'm trying to make amends."

"You quarreled?"

"You may say that."

"I thought all was not well between you the

222

night your bethrothal was announced."

"Come, Simon, there's a better place than this to talk. The White Horse Inn is just around the corner."

Claridge quickly arranged the details of delivery of his new acquisitions and strolled off with his friend.

Seated across from one another at a quiet table in the corner of the taproom, Musgrove spoke first.

"You've been ignoring your friends for days, Simon. Are you still brooding about your fate?"

"I'm not brooding, John. I'm simply trying my level best to probe the intricacies of the female mind."

"Good God, what a fatal exercise."

Claridge's mouth didn't so much as twitch at this remark and Musgrove frowned. "What is it, Simon? Will it help to confide in me?"

"And have you think me completely addle-pated?"

"Go on, old friend," Musgrove urged, reaching for his tankard of ale. "I have plenty of time to here you out."

Claridge shrugged. "You may be sorry." He settled back in his chair and cleared his throat.

"You, of all people, know how long and how hard I tried to find the young lady who disguised herself as a gypsy."

"You were clearly besotted with her."

"Yes, and unable to bear the thought of marrying another. I received a shock, however, the day I was finally presented to the Lady Angela. You see, John, I felt sure I had seen those lovely eyes before ... that soft mouth ..." He paused a moment, remembering. "They were identical to those of the lady I sought."

"What!"

"I had never viewed my gypsy lady's face without a masque or veil, but I was positive. I could not believe my luck! I had not only found her again, but she was the very one I was pledged to marry!"

Musgrove stared at him. "Now let me get this straight. You thought your gypsy and the Lady Angela were one and the same?" he asked incredulously.

"In appearance, yes. But from the first she seemed to be playing a game with me – denying we had ever met before. Supposing she had some reason to want our relationship to start afresh, I decided to follow her lead. Thought it might be a bit of a lark. I was dead wrong."

"But isn't it obvious you simply made a mistake? How could Lady Angela be dashing around the countryside as a gypsy, when she was here in London attending the queen?"

"I had no idea. I didn't think much about it. I only knew she looked the same and sounded the same. But I soon learned she did not act like the girl with whom I'd fallen in love. My little Beth was warm and loving and full of life. Angela, is just the opposite, cool and quiet and solemn. Can someone change so completely? She was willing to have me kiss those sweet lips before." He gave a harsh laugh. "Eager, in fact. Now, she seems not only to abhor my kiss, but to despise me."

"Despise *you?*" Musgrove looked amazed. "Surely not." He had never met a woman yet who Claridge couldn't charm.

"She demanded I never touch her again."

"Damn it, Simon, what did you do? Force yourself upon the chit? I thought of all men you would have the finesse to attempt a more subtle melting of the Snow Maid."

Claridge shook his head. "It was Hester, John, who actually upset her. Perhaps she did it out of spite, I don't know, but nevertheless she told Angela of our past relationship."

Musgrove shrugged. "Since it is past, why should that bother her?"

"She is repulsed by my 'mode of life,' as she put it."

Musgrove laughed aloud. "Did the girl think you a monk?"

"Apparently she hoped I was as celibate as one."

"Good lord! Spare me from innocents!"

"I simply cannot comprehend the girl I knew as Beth reacting in such a fashion. She was a past master at observing and understanding people. That was why her fortune telling was so uncannily accurate. Angela, in contrast, lives in her

225

own little dream world, not wanting reality to intrude."

"Could it be the girl has two sides to her personality?" Musgrove declared. "I once had an aunt, the very soul of propriety, who was caught sneaking out to meet a lover one night, dressed like a street tart."

"The girl I knew as Beth was no tart," Claridge corrected him. He rubbed a hand over his brow. "Perhaps 'tis all a trick of the mind. Perhaps I wanted so to find Beth again I imagined her visage on Angela." He looked over at his friend, meeting his gaze. "Could I be going mad, John?"

The other smiled. "Not you, Simon. Of all the men I know you're the most sane. There must be an answer for you somewhere." He thought for a moment. "Have you considered consulting Devina, the new soothsayer everyone is talking about?"

"Spare me from fortune tellers!" Claridge roared. " 'Tis how I got myself into his predicament in the first place."

"You're right." Musgrove opened his hands. "I don't know what to suggest."

"If only Angela would consent to see me alone. Talk with me. Is it so wrong to want what we once had, John?"

Unexpectedly Musgrove sat bolt upright in his chair and snapped his fingers. "I have it! Will you and she not be attending the ball tomorrow night?"

"Aye. I am to escort her."

"Then all you need do is wait for a suitable time, Simon. Catch Angela off guard with something of which only Beth could possibly be aware. Then, my friend, you will have your answer to the question of whether she be one and the same girl."

Claridge nodded slowly. "I'll think on that. If the opportunity arises, it might merit a try."

Chapter Eighteen

Elizabeth took no appointments to tell fortunes on the afternoon of the ball. Instead, she rested, so that she would be sure to look her best for the evening ahead.

She picked up the invitation card from the night table by her bed and examined it again. A mere piece of stiff paper, she thought, but to her it meant a brief taste of the life she might have led if her parents had only lived.

She refused to let the slightest doubt enter her mind as she leisurely bathed and washed her hair in lemon juice to highlight its fairness. When it was dry, she brushed and curled it softly about her face as Mme. Belyea had suggested and lifted and pinned the mass of it at the back, so that it fell like a silver waterfall from the crown of her head to just below her shoulders. In the curls, she carefully positioned the delicate lilac and pink posies.

Checking her appearance carefully in the mirror, Elizabeth noticed that her flushed cheeks would need no rouge. So many of the ladies she had seen, hid their beauty beneath layers of face paint.

Stepping into her gown, Elizabeth pictured the confrontation that must have occurred between Mme. Belyea and the Lady Angela over it. The dressmaker would have sworn milady had taken the gown home from her establishment and milady in return would have indignantly declared she had done no such thing.

Had Mme. Belyea and her seamstresses then been forced to remake the gown and cloak for Angela? She was sorry to have given them the extra work, but it was really what she was counting on. It would make her deception complete if she and Angela were gowned exactly alike tonight.

Elizabeth doubted Angela could have sought out another dressmaker at such short notice and surely there was not enough time for Mme. Belyea to fashion something completely different for her. Of course there was always the possibility that Angela would simply wear something else from her own wardrobe.

Being without a maid, Elizabeth was finding it difficult to lace up her gown, but by standing with her back to the cheval glass and looking over her shoulder, she was finally able to accomplish the task.

Her only jewellery was her pair of amethyst earrings, which complimented the pale lilac gown. She fastened them in her ears with trembling fingers. A dash of violet water to her pulse points and she was ready.

A number of the aristocrats, who were subsisting on very little while waiting for the king to return their estates to them, were only too glad, for a healthy fee, to rent out their crested coaches and liveried servants. Elizabeth had arranged for such a coach to carry her to Whitehall Palace.

While she waited for its arrival, she had time to ponder about the large amount of money she had spent in the last fortnight. Half of the coins in the saddle-bag were now gone. Spent on fixing up her establishment, her gypsy accoutrements and costume. But this money she would see a return on. Not so the exorbitant price of Mme. Belyea's beautiful creations and the expensive coach— money wasted on one night which might come to nothing.

The ball had been set for nine o'clock, but it was close to ten before a footman knocked at Elizabeth's door.

He solemnly arranged her cloak about her shoulders and pulling the hood gently up over her hair, she picked up her gloves and fan.

As she began her journey to Whitehall Palace,

Elizabeth sat quietly on the upholstered seat, looking out the window beside her at the brightly lit houses they passed along the Strand, before Whitehall itself came into view.

Whitehall Palace had grown haphazardly and was made up of an ill-sorted collection of buildings, constructed over many periods and in many styles. Charles I, the present king's father, had enlarged and beautified the palace, which sprawled for almost half a mile along the Thames.

There were homely exteriors of black and white, half-timbering acres of rosy Tudor brickwork and newer facades of smoothly dressed white stone. Consisting of two thousand rooms in all, the palace was a rambling warren of council chambers, galleries, tennis courts, gardens and private quarters not only for the royal family, but for the king's mistresses, his courtiers and his government ministers.

Elizabeth's coach worked its way down narrow King Street, the crowded thoroughfare which passed through the center of the royal precincts, passing beneath its two Tudor gatehouses.

Streams of lantern light gleamed from the palace's many entrances and by the gatehouses, coaches and sedan chairs waited while their masters and mistresses attended the ball.

As her coach drew closer, the prospect of entering the royal edifice filled Elizabeth with both excitement and fear. They were readily admitted by the yeoman at the gate, who did not ask to see her invitation, but remarked to the coachman, "Ye be late with your mistress."

Driving on through the beautiful park surrounding the palace they soon pulled up before an impressive entranceway, guarded by two halberdiers.

As a footman handed her down from the coach, Elizabeth took a deep breath. Would she be able to accomplish this deception? she wondered. Or would she soon be fleeing back to her coach in humiliation and disgrace?

Upon entering the Palace of Whitehall, only a cursory glance was made of the invitation she held in her hand before Elizabeth found herself following a gorgeously arrayed footman across a vast echoing hallway and up a graceful double staircase. She could see them both reflected in a large mirror as they ascended. Music and voices could be heard emanating from the Grand Salon above.

Elizabeth tried to appear cool and unconcerned as they reached the gallery above, but she was so nervous she was afraid she would give herself away.

Looking toward the massive open doors of the Salon, she saw that due to the lateness of the hour, the rest of the guests had all arrived and were no longer being presented to the guest of honor. She had timed her arrival well.

She handed her velvet cloak to an attendant, but instead of moving toward the Salon, she asked him quietly where she might find the ladies retiring room. She had become suddenly aware that the lacing of her gown, which she had thought she had managed to tie very well herself, were beginning to loosen.

Elizabeth was directed to a door a little way down a corridor that branched off the gallery where she stood. As she approached it, an apparently flustered maid dashed by her, almost colliding with a figure in lilac silk who had just emerged from the retiring room. Elizabeth's eyes widened and she quickly slipped into a darkened doorway in order to observe them.

Angela had been annoyed. The last young gallant who had led her out onto the dance floor had whirled her about so giddily in the coranto, that the string of pearls entwined in her curls had begun to come down over one ear. She had excused herself afterwards, and made her way to the ladies retiring room, sending word to her maid to attend her posthaste. The girl had never appeared and so Angela had struggled valiantly herself for nearly twenty minutes to rearrange her own curls in the elaborate hairdress, which had originally taken the hairdresser more than an hour to accomplish. She had little patience for such things, preferring a much simpler hair style, but Frances had insisted on sending her own French hairdresser to attend her. Now she was sorry. The pearls simply would not stay in place.

"Bother," she cried, pulling the string from her hair.

"May I help you, milady?" A maid whose own mistress had just left the room approached her.

"No. This will do," Angela said, tucking in a stray curl and checking to see if the remaining lilac and pink posies were secure.

It was as she left the room that she came into collision with her maid. It was the final straw.

"Pray forgive my tardiness, milady," the girl apologized. "I was stopped by Lady Quillby to help her hunt for a diamond she had lost from her ring."

That woman again! Angela's lips tightened and she nearly made a sharp retort until she saw the frightened look that had sprung to the maid's face. She forced herself to smile instead. 'Twas not the girl's fault and it was not her wont to take out her troubles on others. What was the matter with her these days?

" 'Tis quite all right, Nan," she assured the girl. "Pray return these to my apartments. They refuse to stay in place." She handed the maid the exquisite string of matching pearls she had pulled from her hair.

Elizabeth watched with unbelieving eyes as Angela walked towards her. It was as if she were staring into a looking glass! The girl who ap-

proached her was her exact image! Even to the
lilac gown and the posies in her hair. Her heart
began to pound in her chest as Angela drew
nearer and passed by so close, Elizabeth could
have reached out and touched her.

What trick of nature was this? Elizabeth
thought in amazement. The two of them had to
be related in some way. Cousins, perhaps? No.
The likeness was too exact. The relationship must
be closer. Sisters. Identical twin sisters! That was
the only answer and yet . . . , how could that be?
She was the acknowledged daughter of Sir
George and Lady Mary Fairclough and Angela's
father was the Earl of Westbury.

There was a mystery here. A mystery Elizabeth intended to unravel. The more she considered it, the more certain she was that Lady
Angela was her twin sister! Yet she knew nothing
about her. She was a stranger. A sad-eyed stranger. Why, she wondered, did Angela appear so
unhappy? Wasn't she betrothed to marry the
most wonderful man in the world? It made no
sense at all.

If only she did not have to return to the ball,
Angela was thinking as she made her reluctant
way, slowly and resignedly, back to the Grand
Salon. Could she feign a headache and escape?
She had managed to avoid Claridge most of the
evening, only granting him one dance with her

before sending him off in search of a glass of wine. Soon, however, she knew a midnight supper would be served and he would seek her out again.

Lord Ramsden, coming out of a card room that led onto the gallery, caught sight of Angela moving almost surreptitiously towards the entrance to the Salon.

His shrewd eyes brightened. Could this be Elizabeth Fairclough? He wondered, staring at her. Had she put to use the invitation Hester Quillby had left her?

He had never seen the Lady Angela that she wasn't walking with her back straight and her head held high, while this girl was moving almost stealthily toward the doorway, as if she were afraid of being seen.

He noticed that her hair appeared to be a little disheveled. The fair curls were no longer in the elaborate hairdress she had worn earlier in the evening when she had been presented to Prince Rupert. Ramsden distinctly remembered when she had curtsied before him and bent her head, a magnificent strand of pearls, entwined with some posies in her hair, had caught the light. This chit's hair bore only the posies! He smiled to himself. This girl *must* be Elizabeth Fairclough!

Yet, he shook his head, she was indeed the image of the Lady Angela, even to her gown. The girl was clever. She must have had the garment made up by the same dressmaker.

He stepped forward to detain her as she

reached the doorway.

"Good evening, my dear," he smiled.

Turning to face Ramsden, the color left Angela's face. Of all the courtiers at Whitehall, she had heard he was the most dissolute. "The man is fairly steeped in vice and degradation," Frances Stewart had told her. "Why Lord Beauford's daughter is supposed to have killed herself because of what Ramsden did to her."

"The queen has been asking for you," Ramsden said quietly. "She had a spell of faintness just now due to the heat and closeness of the room. Hurry, come with me."

He took Angela's elbow and rushed her off down the hallway in the opposite direction to the Grand Salon.

Elizabeth did not see Ramsden's face as he hurried Angela away, or she might have been too frightened to have gone on with her impersonation. Instead, after waiting for Angela's maid to depart and carry out her mistress's orders, Elizabeth entered the retiring room herself.

The maid who had originally offered to help Angela looked a little surprised to see who she thought to be the same lady, reenter the room.

"Will you help me?" Elizabeth asked her. "I fear the laces of my gown are loosening."

The maid nodded and went over to her, complimenting her on her tiny waist as she tightened the laces at Elizabeth's back and tied them firmly. She looked puzzled, though, as she regarded milady's hair. Somehow milady had managed to rearrange it more becomingly than it had been only moments before. Milady had seemed so clumsy dealing with it herself before the mirror. The maid could only shrug.

Elizabeth gave a cursory glance at herself in the looking glass, smiled gratefully at the maid and left the room.

Moving back down the corridor, she had just entered the gallery when she caught sight of a familiar figure emerging from the salon.

It was Lady Quillby, looking quite dazzling in an elaborate gown of cloth of gold, deeply décolleté. She fairly glittered with a parure of diamonds – a tiara, dangling earrings, a pair of bracelets, and an eye-catching broach which nestled between her breasts.

Staring at her, Elizabeth stiffled a smile. Lady Quillby had taken her advice about wearing a regal-looking gown, but she had not been able to resist having the neckline made so low that it almost entirely revealed her creamy breasts.

"Looking for His Grace, Angela?" Lady Quillby sneered as she stopped to regard Elizabeth with a disdainful glance. "He went glowering off when he couldn't find you."

"I didn't –"

"Have a care how you treat him," Lady Quillby's voice lowered, as her green eyes flashed. "He is a very verile man. If you aren't woman enough to give him what he desires, he will go elsewhere for it." With a curl of her lips, she hurried off across the gallery.

A charming woman, Elizabeth thought, glad to see her depart. She wondered where the lady was off to in such a hurry, but had no time to think about it, for she suddenly found herself standing before the entrance to the Grand Salon.

Slipping quickly through the doorway, she stationed herself in the shadows behind a pillar where she could survey the room. She drew in her breath, trying to encompass the glittering beauty of it all.

Massive crystal chandeliers sparkled above the heads of the dancers. The candles from these and the sconces on the walls, plus the heat of many bodies, was already making the room hot and stuffy.

Elizabeth glanced at the exquisite gilt plasterwork of the walls, the beautifully painted pastorial scene on the ceiling above the glittering chandeliers.

The people present were all lavishly and beautifully attired. Elizabeth had not dreamed that the whole world held so many jewels as now glistened in the candlelight. The musicians, barely visible in a far corner behind banks of flowers, played so gaily and sweetly for the merry, dancing couples. As Elizabeth watched, the dance ended and she saw a tall man lead a diminutive woman back to a dais at the opposite side of the room. Catherine had been described to her, and Elizabeth was sure this little figure in ivory satin, with the sad, sallow face, was the Portuguese queen.

She recognized the king immediately as he towered above most of the others in the room. He had bowed to the little brunette with whom he had been dancing and was now rejoining his wife on the dais. He was not a handsome man, his face, in fact, was heavy and dark and yet even at that distance, Elizabeth could sense his magnetic presence. Simon, she thought, possessed the same commanding bearing.

But where was he? Her eyes had slowly circled the room when she had entered, but there seemed to be no sign of him. Apparently he had indeed left the salon as Lady Quillby had intimated.

The tall, dark-haired man who had been dancing with the Queen, took his place on the dais beside Charles. Elizabeth recognized the guest of honor, Prince Rupert.

He was more handsome than his cousin, the king, his features being finer, but he had the same Stuart look about him. He was a great hero, Elizabeth knew, who had fought for the Martyr King, leading his dashing cavalry from one end of the country to the other.

The musicians started up again and Elizabeth saw the king rise and walk over to where a striking-looking beauty with auburn hair and a voluptuous figure stood waiting, her chin lifting proudly at his approach.

Charles took her hand and raised it to his lips and Elizabeth glancing back at the queen, saw the brief look of pain that crossed Catherine's face. The beauty must be Barbara Castlemaine, she surmised, the king's mistress. It was said that Catherine was finally with child and Charles was delighted, but apparently he had no intention of changing his errant ways.

Elizabeth decided it was time to move out of her secluded spot, and mingle with the elegant and bejewelled guests. Smiling graciously whenever a gallant bowed to her admiringly, she found even this simple pleasure enjoyable. She took a glass of white wine from a silver tray a footman held out to her, and sipped it while her eyes took in all that was happening about her.

Her ears soon began to ring from the noise and laughter of the courtiers and the scrape of the fiddles. The king and his mistress danced the branle, the two moving in perfect rhythm to the music.

The dance had barely ended when Elizabeth looked up to see a young gallant bowing before her, offering his arm.

"A dance, milady?" he asked.

She smiled at him. Why not? She thought, putting down her glass and resting her hand lightly on his sleeve.

It was fortunate that Elizabeth's uncle had sent a dancing master to Fairclough Manor a year before to teach her the latest steps. Although he had ulterior motives in doing it, she was glad she had not refused. The running, gliding steps of the corante would have been difficult to follow if she had been unfamiliar with them.

Elizabeth's velvet soft eyes sparkled with happiness as she became caught up in the lilting music. She was enjoying herself and was not unaware of the appreciative glances of many of the courtiers who stood looking on.

After the first dance, Elizabeth found herself whirling from partner to partner. She felt light-headed from the abundant compliments she was receiving. She laughed at the bon mots told her by some of the wittiest men at court. All the while the room grew warmer and the candles burned lower. Yet her eyes kept a constant lookout for Angela's return and never once did she stop searching the crowd for Simon's tall presence.

She feared that when she had seen Lady Quillby leaving the salon, that lady had been rushing to meet Simon somewhere. Perhaps even now she was in his arms, and he was making love to her. At the thought, the light left Elizabeth's eyes and she felt a sudden affinity with the poor little Portuguese queen who was forced to sit on her gilded chair and watch her unfaithful husband sharing dances with his seductive mistress and a new little court beauty, whose name, she now learned, was Frances Stewart.

Elizabeth's partner whispered to her, "The king is clearly infatuated with La Belle Stewart and his best friends are doing everything in their power to snare her. Buckingham and Henry Bennet even set up the 'Committee For Getting Mistress Stewart for the King'," he laughed.

Elizabeth thought to herself that a considerable part of king's attraction for the young lady was probably her unattainability.

There was something familiar about the girl, she thought, as she watched Frances draw closer in the dance and then as the girl came opposite Elizabeth, she gave her a broad wink.

Instantly, Elizabeth recognized her eyes and smile. Of course! She and Angela were friends. It had been the two of them who had come to see her at St. Margaret's Fair! She had read Frances's palm, but Angela had slipped away before hers could be read.

The dance ended and Elizabeth managed to escape through the crowd and head in Frances's direction. She watched as the king returned to the dais and then she circled around and approached the girl from behind.

"He is not for thee," she repeated the words she had once said to her in a gypsy tent. "He can be faithful to no woman. Ye must wait, child. Wait and the right one will come."

Startled, Frances swung around and then a smile dimpled the corners of her mouth.

"Wretch!" she whispered to Elizabeth. "How is it you remember those words so well?"

"That gypsy frightened me."

"I remember. You ran away. It seems to be a habit of yours. I also saw you run away from His Grace tonight." She shook her head. "I don't understand you, Angela."

Nor do I, Elizabeth thought, but instead she said, "Who is that gentleman who cannot take his eyes from you?" She nodded across the room to a smiling faced young courtier.

"The Duke of Richmond," Frances blushed. "I have already allowed him two dances."

"I do not think you will have to be patient much longer."

"What do you mean?" Frances looked puzzled.

"Don't you remember. 'Thy true love will come if only ye will be patient'?"

"I remember," Frances said. "Do you mean . . . You think His Grace of Richmond . . . ?"

Elizabeth nodded and with a smug little smile disappeared into the crowd.

In heady succession, Elizabeth found herself dancing the coranto, the galliard, the allemande and the branle, stopping only to pause and drink a sip or two of white wine before she was led out again.

As the music ended and her latest partner led her off the floor, he remarked, "His Grace of Claridge is a very fortunate man."

The smile Elizabeth bestowed on him was so

dazzling, that she soon found herself surrounded by a number of young men requesting dances with her, then staying by her side, vying for her attention. Suddenly she sensed the presence of another and her admirers deferentially drew back.

"I believe this is my dance," the Duke of Claridge announced.

Ever since he had returned to the salon and spotted her, he had been wondering what had come over his betrothed. What had changed the solemn, sad-eyed Angela into this vivacious, little charmer? He was truly puzzled by this new attitude of hers and by her appearance. She had never looked more beautiful. Why, she fairly sparkled!

He was feeling the full impact of her beauty now as she was standing under a glittering chandelier, the candlelight emphasizing the silver lights in her hair, revealing the milky whiteness of her skin.

Elizabeth felt her breath catch in her throat as she regarded Simon. He was dressed in midnight blue velvet. His coat expertly cut to accentuate his broad shoulders and narrow waist. One large perfect sapphire sparkled from the depths of the frothy white lace at his throat.

A wave of sensation passed through her as his fingers closed over hers and he drew her hand through his arm, leading her out onto the floor.

"I wondered where you were," she said, trying to keep her voice steady, as they waited for the musicians to begin their piece.

"You expect me to believe you cared," he said sardonically. "Sending me off to fetch you some wine so you could conveniently slip away."

"I – I felt unwell," Elizabeth lied.

"You seem to have made a remarkable recovery," he said dryly. "I don't believe I have ever seen you look as radiant." Or as lovely, he might have added.

"I was enjoying myself," she said, as they began to dance.

"I see. You don't enjoy yourself with me."

She looked up at him. "Do I detect a hint of jealousy, Your Grace?" She gave him a coquettish smile.

"Simon, Angela. Since we are now betrothed, I think we might use our given names, don't you?"

"As you wish ... Simon."

She frowned at his back as he turned from her in a step of the dance. It was apparent all was not well between him and Angela. She could not understand why this should be, for when he had first looked at her she had caught almost a hungry look in those dark, smokey eyes, which gave hint to her of his restrained emotions.

Then she remembered Lady Quillby's words, "The court calls her the Snow Maid." Apparently, Angela was acting the proper young maiden and keeping Claridge at a distance. Her twin must not share the deep sensual feelings she had for Simon, or was keeping them well hidden.

What new little game was she playing with him now, Claridge was thinking to himself. Flirting with every blessed man in the room but him. Teasing and tormenting him with her smiles. The sparkling chandelier above his head took that moment to drip wax onto his shoulder and he scowled up at it.

"Damn!" he growled, brushing irritably at it and missing the measure of the dance.

He expected Angela to glance at him disapprovingly, but instead she began to giggle. His anger disappeared and he found himself grinning back at her, suddenly cheered by the fact that this evening he was glimpsing a personality more like that of his Beth.

In that moment, he decided to carry out Musgrove's suggestion and make sure of her identity. He purposely stumbled and checked himself.

"Pray excuse my clumsiness, Angela," he said, "I've been up since before dawn. One of my favorite horses was taken ill."

He caught her instant concern. "Not Satan?" she asked, without thinking. Still, she reasoned, he probably has accompanied Angela riding in St. James Park, so she would know the name of his horse.

"No, a gray gelding that had served me well on the continent," he answered. He gazed down at her, her beauty filling him, lighting a fire in his blood, sending the cold chills of uncertainty away. It *was* she! His heart sang. Angela *was* his mystery lady. He had no doubt now. No other woman could possibly have known Satan's name.

"Is he recovering?"

"Yes, but it was nip and tuck for a while. By the by, I have a surprise for you," he said, thinking of the beautiful chestnut filly he had purchased for her the day before. "I will have it sent over in the morning."

"I do love surprises," she smiled at him.

Claridge's dark eyes met and locked with hers, burning with intensity, for a brief, unguarded moment, revealing more to him than she could possibly have realized. In that instant, her soul became his, the look in her eyes one of tender yearning, of warm desire.

As if taking part in a mating ritual, they advanced and retreated in the dance, each seeming wholly absorbed in the other.

Excitement whirled through Elizabeth's body as Simon murmured, " 'Tis been a lifetime since we've been alone."

"Two lifetimes," she whispered, taking his other hand as she moved to step in front of him.

Looking down at the soft nape of her neck, he was tempted to kiss that delicate spot, as the sweet scent of her drifted up to him. Violets. What sweet memories that scent brought back. It was odd, but he did not remember Angela wearing it recently.

When the dance ended, he bowed elegantly over Elizabeth's right hand, turning it over to press an ardent kiss against her palm. A quiver went through her, which was not lost on him.

The late supper was announced and people began to stir around them. The two standing looking at one another paid them no mind. Elizabeth suddenly felt very vulnerable before him, as if Simon could somehow sense what was in her heart. A foolish notion, she knew. He could not possibly know of her feelings for him.

"Are you hungry?" he asked, and she sensed he meant for something other than the midnight supper.

She met his eyes boldly and slowly nodded.

"I thought you despised me," she said wonderingly, as he took her hand and led her toward the doorway.

"Why would I do that?"

"My way of life—as you so clearly pointed out to me. My past relationship with Lady Quillby."

"*Past* relationship?" she inquired.

"I assured you of that once before."

"I suppose I found it hard to believe. She is very beautiful."

"If one likes obvious beauty. Your beauty, on the other hand, is delicate and exquisite."

His husky compliment brought a flush of color to her cheeks. He was leading her out of the Grand Salon now and across the gallery.

This was wrong, she told herself. She was not Angela. She was betraying her sister. This had not been part of her plan. Yet Simon's strong arm was about her waist, hugging her to his side, and as he whispered all manner of endearments to her, any thoughts of resistance faded completely away. Her love for him overwhelmed her.

Chapter Nineteen

The small privy chamber was deserted. When they entered, Claridge closed and bolted the door behind them, securing their privacy. Without saying a word, he pulled Elizabeth close and they kissed, her lips as hungry as his. They clung to each other for a long time and then he kissed her again with a kind of desperation, covering her face with kisses.

"My God," he whispered, holding her tight, "how I've longed for you. Did you know you stole my heart that night in Bridgetown? Did you know I searched for you until I recognized your eyes, your sweet mouth, and realized that you and my Beth were one and the same?" He pushed her away from him for a moment. "But why have you been so strange and aloof with me? Why, Angela, why?"

"I—I was jealous," she stammered. "Lady Quillby—"

"The devil with her! You must know you're the

only one I love."

Elizabeth let out a little cry, pressing her face so hard against his chest that she could hear the pounding of his heart. If only he knew how he was torturing her by saying such things.

He kissed her on the lips in anguished passion, his few words those of love, pledges of commitment, confessions of need.

They touched each other almost reverently, tracing the sweet lips, cupping the beloved face. Neither spoke now, each revelling in the delicious torment of anticipation, savoring the sensations building, mounting inside.

It was wrong, terribly wrong, Elizabeth thought. Not here. Not now. And yet, when she felt Simon's nearness, his warmth, and saw those smokey eyes gazing down at her darkened with desire, she knew she was going to let him make love to her again.

It was not just because he was a superlative lover and knew how to make her feel gloriously alive. It was not even because he was so wondrously handsome. It was because she could not help herself. She knew in her heart he was the only man she would ever love and every second with him was to be treasured.

The room was lit by one small silver candelabra with three candles burning in it on a long table by the window. There was no fire in the fireplace but neither was aware of this as Simon laid Elizabeth gently down on the sofa before it. His warm

mouth covered hers again and Elizabeth gloried
in the feel of his lips against hers, — hard, masculine lips that stroked and caressed and devoured.
She felt his tongue invade her mouth and met it
with her own, slowly, delightfully, exploring.

His lips left hers to slide down the column of
her neck and she arched herself against the moist
heat as his fingers worked beneath her to loosen
her gown. He pushed the bodice down, releasing
her throbbing breasts, stroking the hardening
nipples with deft fingers, while his mouth became
harder and more demanding on hers.

Her fingers tangled in his hair, pressing his
head down to hers, deepening the fierce kiss. She
felt the weight of his hard body as he moved over
her and wished they dared remove their clothing.
She longed to feel his warm nakedness against
her own. She watched him fling off his cravat and
coat and slid her hands beneath his shirt, her
fingers moving slowly down his sides to his waist.

Bending his head, his lips closed over one pink-
tipped breast and then the other, and she felt her
need for him growing stronger, becoming a hungry ache. She longed to become one with him
again and experience the ecstasy she had known
before.

His hands were pushing up her gown, his fingers gently seeking the softness between her
thighs. She moaned aloud as he fondled and
explored, the hunger growing to a fevered pitch
within her. She wanted him so desperately, cared

about nothing but her need to become one with him again.

He sensed her urgency, yet he continued to arouse her with more and more delirious sensations until she could stand it no longer and surged against him, arching her body to his, offering herself eagerly, passionately, wholly, opening to his touch like a beautiful flower.

She felt the pressure of him bear down on her, felt the hot strength slip gently into her. He began to stroke slowly, languidly, trying to intensify her pleasure by holding himself back.

They moved as one, the soft warmth of her surrounding him, holding him sheathed deep within her. Waves of delight swept over her and her whole being came alive with pulsing joy. She strained against him, shuddering as he plunged even deeper. Her small teeth nipped his shoulder and she began to utter mindless little cries of rapture.

Concentrating on giving her pleasure, Simon found it was being returned in full. Her body twisted under him as she clung to him, rocked with him, lost in the incredible, sweet anguish that enveloped them both.

The frightening intensity rose and swelled and finally burst over them in a giant, engulfing wave of joy. Elizabeth trembled as the wave began to ebb, leaving her totally limp and exhausted in its wake.

"Dear God," Simon said huskily, "that was

worth waiting for."

"Oh, Simon . . . I love you so." Her voice was soft and her words a caress. Words she had been longing to say to him for so long. Words she would never say to him again. A lump formed in her throat.

He felt her lashes wet with tears and tenderly he kissed them away. When she had satisfied him that they were only tears of happiness, he made a move to withdraw from her, but she clasped him tight, reluctant to have him leave her.

"We must return," he murmured against her ear. "We will be missed."

He gave her a gentle kiss and then he was helping her to sit up, carefully arranging his breeches as she straightened her skirts.

"Turn about," he said, and skillfully began to relace her gown. "Is there no way I can come to you later?"

She shook her head.

"Then the sooner we are wed the better. I cannot bear being apart from you, my sweet.

"Nor I from you," Elizabeth kept her head away from his so he could not see the tears that stung her eyes.

"You go back first," she managed. " 'Twill give me time to repair any damage."

"As you will," he agreed, kissing the nape of her neck before getting to his feet.

Elizabeth watched him stride to the door, wanting him to come back to her, to make love to her again. She could not bear it all to end. She wanted Simon with her always. It wasn't fair! It wasn't fair!

Brushing at her tears and struggling to regain her poise, Elizabeth waited until the door closed behind him and then she rose and moved over to where a gilt framed mirror hung on the wall. Her hands shaking with emotion, she attempted to repair the wisps of hair that had become loosened during Simon's ardent lovemaking. When, at last, she was ready, she squared her slim shoulders, raised her chin, and putting on a mask of cool serenity, opened the door and left the room.

Within moments, Elizabeth had regained her cloak, slipped down the graceful staircase and flown out the door into the night.

"Where are we going?" Angela asked Lord Ramsden. She couldn't remember the corridor they were now traversing.

Whitehall was a bewildering labyrinth. Long corridors, all looking much the same with their portraits and gilded furniture and gigantic candelabras, intersecting unexpectedly, leading on and on.

"It's a shortcut," Ramsden said in a low voice. "We must hurry."

"But I do not understand. Why would the queen ask especially for me?"

Why indeed, Elizabeth, he thought to himself.

Aloud, he explained, "because you are one of her favorites, of course."

They turned a corner, crossed an empty gallery, and stopped before a doorway.

"Here we are," he said.

Angela looked surprised. "This isn't —" she began, but Lord Ramsden having quickly opened the door, shoved her inside, slamming, the portal behind them.

Angela gave a frightened exclamation as she realized she was standing in a man's dimly lit bedchamber. Whirling about, she saw Lord Ramsden leaning back against the door, a thin smile curling his lips.

"I only thought to finish what I started once before."

"What do you mean?" Angela demanded, a little desperate now. "You told me the queen wanted me. Why am I here?"

"You will find out very shortly," he said, walking across the room to yank on a gold-tassled bellpull.

A moment later there was a knock at the door and a servant entered bearing a tray with several wine glasses and a decanter. He placed it on a low table before the fireplace, which was flanked by two damask covered armchairs.

"Do sit down, my dear," Ramsden said to Angela. He whispered something to the servant and then dismissed him.

Angela, still standing in the middle of the

room, now made a little rush toward the door after the man, but Ramsden stepped in front of her, stopping her, and shot the bolt home.

"How dare you bring me here!" she cried. "Open the door this instant!"

"Can't you spare me a few minutes of your time, my dear? What I have to say to you is most important."

"But the queen ... "

"That was only a little ruse to get you here. She is quite well."

"You ... you lied to me?"

"It was necessary. Now, I pray you, sit down by the fire. I won't bite you."

Angela looked at him fearfully. She didn't believe his words for a minute. She would rather have trusted a snake. Oh, why had she been so foolish as to come with this man?

He indicated a chair by the fire and placing a firm hand on her arm, led her over to it. Seating himself across from her, he poured out two glasses of wine, handing one to her.

"We are waiting for someone," he told her.

She relaxed a little at his words. Surely with someone else coming, he wouldn't dare make advances toward her. She took a sip of the wine.

"Did you enjoy the ball?" Ramsden asked conversationally. He was quietly observing her over the rim of his glass, taking in every aspect of her, his glittering eyes watching the rise and fall of her full, young breasts beneath her modest gown.

258

Mentally, he was grabbing the neckline of that gown, ripping it savagely from shoulder to waist.

Angela felt a little shudder go through her as she glimpsed the lust in his eyes and would have attempted another rush at the door, but at that moment, there was a knock and Ramsden set down his glass and rose to answer it.

She followed him with her eyes as he moved to open the door, and as he slid back the bolt, he smiled back at her. Sensing the sensual cruelty of those lips, she nervously gulped down the rest of the wine.

Lady Quillby swept into the room with a great rustling of golden skirts and Lord Ramsden closed and bolted the door after her.

"Well?" he asked.

"She's the one," Hester nodded in Angela's direction. "I just spoke to the real Lady Angela in the gallery."

At her words, Angela straightened in her chair. "What do you mean?" she demanded. "What is this all about?"

"Just that we have found you out, my dear," Ramsden said smoothly. "Although I must admit you played your part very well indeed, Elizabeth."

"Elizabeth? My name is not Elizabeth." She struggled to her feet, but was forced to grasp the back of her chair, as a wave of dizziness swept over her.

"Don't worry, my dear," Hester Quillby said soothingly as she approached her. "I don't blame you for using my invitation. Do sit down, now, that's a good girl."

Angela had never felt so lightheaded. Was she drunk? She wondered. How in the world had one glass of wine affected her so much?

She heard that awful woman speaking to her again, calling her Elizabeth, when she, of all people, knew perfectly well that she was Angela.

"We may have quite a wait on our hands," Ramsden was saying. "Perhaps just a little taste ..." He took a step toward Angela.

"Patience, Ramsden, for God's sake," Hester snapped. "Do you want to ruin everything? Your servant will inform us when *he* is on his way. It may be hours yet."

Ramsden wet his lips. "I am not a patient man and I already have what I want."

Hester's eyes flashed dangerously at him. "Do not go back on our agreement, Ramsden, or I swear—"

The man nodded. "You have my word. I have a score to settle there."

"Good."

"If you do not wish to watch ..."

"I am no voyeur, Ramsden, but I intend to remain if only to make sure your lust does not get out of hand. My stake in this is too high."

"As you will. But first, shall we have some of this excellent wine?"

* * *

Although she had been delivered back to her room a half hour before, Elizabeth did not immediately go to bed. She still felt overexcited and knew that sleep was a long way away. Instead, she warmed some milk for herself and sat down in a chair by the fire to drink it.

Tonight she had reentered a lost world. It had been an evening that would remain with her for the rest of her life. The Palace, the dancing, the gaiety, but most of all . . . Simon. How much she loved him!

She began to relive every moment of magic that had passed between them. She recaptured every enthralling gesture, heard again every tender word. She pictured the two of them on the sofa in the small room and again felt the gentle touch of his lips and hands, saw his dark, tousled hair, his devastating smile as he lowered his head to her, as his broad shoulders blotted out the whole world.

When she entered, Elizabeth had built up the embers of the fire to warm her milk, and now she sat looking into the flames. The room about her was in semidarkness, the fire flickering shadows on the parlor walls. Trying to turn her thoughts from Simon, she wondered again about the girl who was most surely her twin. There could be no doubt of it. She had felt an affinity with her as soon as she had drawn near. Something that had nothing at all to do with her appearance, something much deeper.

261

How could she solve the puzzle? She knew there was no one now at Fairclough Manor who could help her. Her nurse had died three years before and although several of the servants had been there since her parent's time, none so far back as her birth. With the riddle still on her mind, she rose and was about to start back to her bedchamber, when suddenly she felt a queer, prickling shiver go down her spine. A strange feeling of unease swept over her. It was much like the time she had sensed something was not right with Marta.

She looked sharply around her. Nothing stirred. She was alone in the room. She shook her head. The uneasy feeling did not depart, in fact, it seemed to be growing. With it came the strong conviction that someone was in danger. It was not herself. Of that she was sure. But danger was threatening someone close to her.

Trembling, Elizabeth stood there trying desperately to regain her composure, but something inside her, something compelling and urgent pushed her towards the door.

Simon! Dear God, something must be happening to Simon!

"I must go to him," she cried. "I must!"

She rushed from the room into the hallway and finding Claridge's dark cloak hanging there, flung it about her shoulders to hide her ballgown and ran for the door.

The coach she had rented had long since departed and at this late hour, she realized, it would be difficult to find anything for hire. A damp drizzle had started, she found, as she reached the street, but pulling the hood of her cloak up over her head, she began to run.

Elizabeth took the direction the coach had followed and ran block after block through the almost deserted streets where she encountered only a few stray revellers. At that time of night, there weren't many abroad and she wisely stayed clear of those that were, allowing them to continue on their nocturnal and possibly nefarious pursuits.

When, at last, she reached the gates to Whitehall Palace, Elizabeth came to a stop holding her side, gasping for breath. She moved closer, when she had recovered enough to speak, and approached one of the yeomen.

"I have something important to impart to His Grace, the Duke of Claridge," she told him. "Can you direct me to his apartments?"

"How now, at this hour? I have no message from His Grace to expect a lady."

"He does not expect me. I bear a warning for him."

"A warning, is it?" the yeoman started to laugh, motioning to his colleague nearby. "Hear this likely tale, my friend. This wench wishes to see the Duke of Claridge. She wants to warn him."

The second yeoman, a big, heavyset man, stared down at Elizabeth and grinned. "There's many a wench who has urgent business with His Grace, I'll warrant. Doubtless ye want to warn him against any wench but thyself." He burst into a roar of laughter.

"I beg of you, let me by," Elizabeth pleaded. Oh, why hadn't she thought to bring her purse with her so she might bribe them?

"I let no one in who isn't expected," the first yeoman said to Elizabeth. "Away with ye, wench!"

"Pray listen to me. This is a matter of the greatest urgency." Elizabeth tried to calm her voice.

The other guard stopped laughing. "She speaks like a lady, she does. Do ye think . . . ?"

"Nay. Those actresses learn to speak like that. Ye didn't see her arrive in a coach or chair did ye? No real lady travels by foot."

"But I had dismissed my coach and—"

"Away wi' ye! Come back in the morning if it be so urgent. 'Tis only a few hours till daybreak," the yeoman added a little more kindly.

The Stone Gallery in Whitehall was accessible in the mornings to all, rich or poor, who wished to speak to the king or his courtiers.

Finding the two halberdiers could not be budged, Elizabeth, despite the frantic feelings that were surging through her, knew she could do nothing. She turned reluctantly away, vowing to return as soon as it was light.

Chapter Twenty

The lower hall leading to His Grace of Claridge's apartments was dimly illumined by a few wax tapers placed in two wall sconces which flanked a large arched window. The flickering light they threw failed to penetrate the dark corners of the large rectangular room.

At the side of the hall, opposite the window, was a stairway leading to a long open gallery above. As Claridge started across the hallway, he was surprised to hear someone call down to him.

"Is that you, Birch? Dammit, where have you been? We need more wine."

Claridge looked up to see an indistinct figure standing at the top of the stairway.

"You mistake my identity, sir. My name is Claridge."

"Claridge? I beg your pardon. I could see only your dim outline." The man began to descend the staircase and at that moment the moon chose to break through a cloud, revealing to Claridge the figure of Lord Ramsden.

His lordship was clad in only shirt and breeches. The lace-trimmed shirt hung wide open at the neck, its tail half protruding over his sword belt. His long, curled wig was slightly askew.

"I have not seen your servant," Claridge said, preparing to pass on across the hall.

"Again I beg pardon . . . I thought you to have retired, Your Grace." Lord Ramsden sounded strangely ill at ease.

"That is my intention," Claridge rejoined. "A goodnight to you, Rams—"

A feminine cry was heard above them.

Ramsden laughed lightly. "I must not keep the lady waiting," he said.

The laugh grated unpleasantly on Claridge's ears. "Then by all means return to your low pastimes."

"Low?" Ramsden lifted an eyebrow. "You, of all men, Your Grace, can hardly condemn—"

"Of all men? I find your manner insolent, my lord." Claridge's temper had grown short in the last hour while he searched futiley for the vanished Angela.

"Do you? I understand you and Lady Quillby—"

"You go too far naming names, Ramsden."

"Do I? Would you like another? I have learned that due to your close relationship with said lady, the Lady Angela is hardly overjoyed at becoming your wife."

"Where did you learn that?"

"From Lady Angela's own lips."

Claridge's eyes narrowed. "You know her then?"

"Quite intimately," Ramsden gave a knowing smile.

"Just what are you implying, my lord?"

"Only that the Snow Maid may not be quite as virtuous as she appears."

Claridge swung swiftly about to face the man who was now at the bottom of the staircase.

What was this swine implying about his own, sweet Angela? Angela, who only an hour ago had been in his arms, professing her love for him. Angela who had come to him so eagerly . . . so passionately . . . so . . . he shuddered at the thought . . . easily.

"Your words offend me, milord," he declared, his right hand moving to his sword hilt.

Ramsden gave a little bow of his head. "I am at your service, at any time, Your Grace."

Oh, he thought, it was delightful seeing the haughty Claridge cringe before his words. This man who had implied he was untrustworthy and ruined his plans with the king. Revenge was indeed sweet!

"I wish to defend the lady's honor NOW!" Claridge said, his eyes blazing in sudden rage as he drew his sword.

"But surely dawn would be soon enough to—"

"Are you also a coward, milord?"

267

He knew Ramsden to be unscrupulous and dishonest and he had heard from Musgrove that some of his sexual predilections had made the most popular madam in London ban him from her house. It was a pleasure, Claridge thought, to challenge the man.

"Damn you!" cried Ramsden, quickly unsheathing the sword that was buckled to his waist. "I want you to know this is not my doing, Claridge."

"Nay, 'tis mine. En garde!"

Ramsden had circled him before drawing his weapon, making sure his own back was towards the window and the flickering wall sconces, so that he could see his opponent in the best possible light. Claridge with the delicate white lace at his throat and the sparkling sapphire in its midst made a delightfully obvious target. He knew if he could keep this position, his own figure would appear only as a dark silhouette to His Grace.

Claridge, however, seemed unmindful of his disadvantage. Holding a sword again in his hand made him feel less the poor duped fool and more in command of the situation.

Had Ramsden only known, Claridge had been taught swordsmanship by the best teacher of the art, whether with poignard or rapier, Niccolo of Florence.

There was the customary brief salute and the next moment the swords rang together. The two antagonists played with one another at first, gauging the other's strength.

Ramsden soon saw that Claridge was an experienced and skillful swordsman. He was calm and cunning in his attack, slowly forcing Ramsden to give up his advantageous position, driving him, with the flashing brilliance of his wrist, away from the window and backward in the direction of the shadowy staircase.

Ramsden countered as well as he could, but he knew he was losing ground fast as he wearied before the vigorous attack. Steel rang against steel, together with the sounds of the men's heavy breathing.

Ruthlessly, Claridge's blade thrust at his opponent's broad expanse of chest. He was coming at Ramsden like a madman, lunging and thrusting so swiftly that only with the strength of despair did Ramsden's parrying help him escape imminent death.

His arm was aching now and his breath coming in great gasps, but Claridge's attacks seemed to be growing swifter and more violent. My God, this was something he had not planned on. What in the world had happened to . . .

Suddenly there was a piercing scream from the gallery above them.

"Stop!"

The two swords paused in midair and the heads of the antagonists shot up to see the source of the interruption.

The door that led from the gallery to Lord Ramsden's apartments stood open and the light from it illumined a figure by the gallery railing. A woman in dishabille, her long hair in a wild tanglement over her shoulders.

She made a little run toward the staircase, swaying and staggering as if intoxicated and grasping at the balustrade to keep herself from falling. As she reached the first landing, the full light of the moon washed over her and revealed to the men who stood below, her lush form, the lilac gown torn from her shoulders, baring the flawless white skin of her throat and one naked rose-tipped breast. The moonlight pale hair was a silver gilt snarl in the light.

Claridge gazed up at her with sick incredulity, his sword still poised in his hand.

It was Angela! His Angela. The same warm, sweet creature he had made such tender love to only a short time ago. He had kissed those now-dazed eyes, those love-bruised lips.

Seemingly surprised by her entrance, Ramsden looked only annoyed as she stumbled down the rest of the stairs, one arm stretched out in Claridge's direction.

"I met her in the gallery outside the Salon," Ramsden shrugged. "She, if I may say so, came with me quite eagerly." Almost swaggering, he strode over to her.

"Go back upstairs, Angela," he said curtly, roughly grasping her arm and turning her about. "You have had too much wine."

"But I want—" she slurred.

"We both know what you want," his words were suggestive as his fingers caressed one bare shoulder. "Go back, my dear. I will be with you shortly."

Claridge winced at Ramsden's words, his touch, his contemptuous attitude toward her. The whole scene was like a nightmare to him. What had happened to turn his love into this drunken hussy, flaunting her charms for all to see? Had he brought out a passion in her that no one man could appease? Was her desire now so great she would let a swine like Ramsden . . .

His eyes couldn't leave her. She seemed dazed and confused as she staggered back up the stairway, holding tight to the banister to keep her balance. At the landing, she again looked back at Claridge.

"Come," she cried, making a weak little beckoning gesture.

Ramsden broke into an ugly laugh. "It seems the chit wants l'amour à deux, Claridge."

Claridge's laugh was a mirthless sound of disillusionment as the girl stood there, swaying slightly, denying nothing. Never had he been forced into such a tawdry, degrading position before. He was filled with disgust for himself. How could he have been taken in by such a deceiving little baggage? From the first she had slipped easily from one role to another. Why hadn't he guessed she was a consummate actress? How could he have believed in her, trusted

271

her, loved her? Never before had he become involved in any of the slimy intrigues at court and now he found himself fighting for the favours of this little slut.

"The interruption was most opportune," Claridge snorted. "I cannot believe you and I, milord, crossed swords of *that*." He pointed his sword in Angela's direction and then he tossed it scornfully away.

The rapier flew through the air in a glittering arc, landing with a clatter against the staircase. Unknown to either man, the exquisitely carved hilt was caught firmly in the intricate wood carving between the rails, causing the blade to point upward at an odd and dangerous angle.

"I beg your pardon, milord," Claridge gave Ramsden a mocking bow, "for interfering in what no longer concerns me. The—er—lady is all yours."

He turned on his heel and strode proudly down the length of the hallway and out through the arched doorway at the end.

Angela was trying vainly to collect herself. Her head was whirling, as great waves of dizziness swept over her. That awful Quillby woman had forced her to drink more wine and then he . . . she shuddered at the memory . . . he had dragged her over to the bed and forced her back on it. He'd pinned her down and tore at her gown. His hands had been all over her, grasping, pinching, fondling. She had writhed frantically beneath him, pummelling at his shoulders with her fists, twisting and turning in an effort to escape from him.

She had cried out to the Quillby woman for help, but she had paid no mind, merely picked up her glass of wine and turned her back on her.

Angela had tried to scream, but Ramsden's slobbering lips had closed over hers, forcing her mouth to open, ramming his thick tongue within. A wave of revulsion had swept over her. This could not be happening! It could not! She thought she would go out of her mind if he continued.

His hot mouth had left her lips and covered one rose-colored breast, sucking at it noisily while his hands moved impatiently lower, pushing at her skirts.

She knew what he was trying to do. Very soon he would try to thrust himself into her. She couldn't bear the thought! She felt she was being dragged down to the very depths of degradation as Ramsden snorted and pawed at her and Lady Quillby did nothing to stop it.

Angela had felt her thighs being forced open, had felt him hard and swollen poking feverishly at her as he spread her legs wider.

And then it had come! That blessed knock at the door.

Reluctantly Ramsden had rearranged his breeches and risen from the bed. He had opened the door, said something to a person and then closed the door again.

Lady Quillby had got to her feet. "Hurry, Ramsden," she had urged. "That stupid Birch won't have given you much time."

"Just do your own job," he had grunted, quickly buckling on his sword and hurrying from the room.

Lady Quillby had calmly approached Angela and helped her to sit up. She had offered her more wine and excused her own inaction with a shrug. "I couldn't have stopped him. He had his mind made up."

Angela, however, had been hardly aware of what she said or what was going on about her. The drug she had received, the wine, and most of all the shock of Ramsden's near rape had all served to cloud her mind.

Hearing something outside the room, Hester Quillby had opened the door a crack. The sound of clashing arms could be heard from below. So it had come to that, Hester thought. She must move quickly. She had grasped Angela by the shoulders and half lifted, half pushed her forward, out of the room and over to the gallery railing.

"They're dueling over you," she had hissed, melting back into the shadows.

Looking down below her, Angela had caught sight of Ramsden in the moonlight, his sword flashing against that of . . . Simon! Her betrothed. He had come to save her and Ramsden seemed intent on killing him!

She had let out a piercing scream.

The rest she could barely remember: trying to get down the stairs to Claridge; being forced by Ramsden to go back; calling to Claridge to come after her; watching as he contemptuously threw his sword away and strode off.

Now Ramsden was climbing the stairs toward her and though she tried to get away from him she was too weak and too dizzy, and before she knew it he had roughly seized her wrist and was dragging her up the rest of the stairway.

"We have some unfinished business, my lady," he growled.

"No!" she cried, whirling suddenly around and bringing up her knee. Although it was an unconscious gesture on her part, it connected hard with his groin. The pain made him stumble and double over and before he could regain his footing, Angela shoved him away from her.

Ramsden went over backwards, tumbling down the stairs and falling hard against the railing where Claridge's sword was trapped. He let out a short, agonizing cry as the razor-sharp blade penetrated below his shoulders. The momentum of the fall turned him over, yanking the sword from its snare and taking it and him to the bottom of the stairs. He lay face down there, his legs sprawled above him, the rapier firmly embedded below his left shoulder.

Angela stood rigid on the landing, staring with terrified eyes at Ramsden's still form below her.

Claridge heard the slight commotion behind him after he left the hallway, but he tried to ignore the sounds. He wanted nothing more to do with the wanton little bitch who had made such a fool of him.

Yet, he had never trusted Ramsden. He remembered the ugly stories he had heard of Ramsden's mistreating women. What if he should hurt Angela physically, or force her, because of her intoxicated state to perform unspeakable ... Claridge came to a halt.

"Damn!" he exclaimed. "Why should I feel any chivalrous feelings toward the baggage?" Yet, he began to retrace his steps.

Coming to the archway that led into the hallway, he suddenly heard an agonizing cry and the sound of something falling.

Instantly alarmed, he sprinted along the dimly lit hallway, not daring to imagine what had happened.

He saw the body first, lying sprawled out at the foot of the stairs. He leaned over it. It was Ramsden! The man had been run threw with a sword! He bent over the body to determine if Ramsden were still breathing and it was then that he became aware that someone was watching him. He looked up the stairs.

She was standing rigid on the landing above. A ghostlike form in a torn gown, with a dazed, blank expression on her face.

Claridge caught the sound of approaching voices. He bridged the stairs in a few bounds.

"Get away from here," he hissed. "Get away, while there is still time!"

In that moment he did not see her as the wanton who had mocked him, but as his own sweet Beth, whom he had so dearly loved. At the thought of others seeing her half-naked and the worse for drink, his natural impulse was to protect her from shame and discovery. He felt only tenderness and pity for her as she saw that she had not moved at his words, but had remained rooted to the spot. The girl was in silent shock!

He pointed up the stairs to the gallery.

"Quick! Go!"

It was as if she had retreated to her own little world and could not hear him. Yet, he knew, there was not a moment to lose. Half dragging her up the rest of the stairs, he pointed her in the direction of the queen's wing.

"Flee, Angela! For God's sake, flee!"

Stumbling a little at first the girl finally began to move, heading off across the gallery, suddenly breaking into a wild run as if the devil himself were pursuing her.

Claridge was caught standing on the stairs when a group of people burst into the hallway below.

"What is it?"

"What is going on?"

There was a yeoman present amongst the courtiers and servants and he raised the torch he was carrying to see what was lying at the bottom of the stairs.

"Stop there!" he cried to Claridge, but he need not have worried, His Grace was already descending the stairway.

"Who is it?"

"Lord Ramsden," Birch said, as he leaned over the body of his master.

"Wounded?" someone asked.

"I'm afraid he is dead," His Grace said, quietly, and all eyes rose to where he stood just above Ramsden's body.

"But how?"

"Was there a duel?"

"How could there be a duel when his lordship's sword is still in its scabbard?" Birch asked, looking inquiringly up at Claridge.

One of the courtiers raised the candle he was carrying so that he could more closely see the sword embedded in Ramsden's back.

"Are these not Your Grace's arms on the hilt?" he asked.

There was a moment of expectant silence.

"Aye, 'tis my sword," Claridge admitted.

"But Your Grace can explain . . ." suggested another courtier.

Claridge was about to reply when one of the

servants interjected. "I'm sure I saw a woman fleeing across the gallery as we entered."

"I saw something too — a brief flash of light clothing," another remarked.

"Will Your Grace please tell us how this occurred?" asked an officer of the guard who had shouldered his way through the crowd.

"I'm afraid I can tell you nothing, Captain," Claridge said firmly.

"Nothing? Were you not here in the hallway?"

"Aye, I was here."

"Then, pray tell us if there was a woman involved."

"No," Claridge said clearly in his deep, rich voice. "I was alone with Lord Ramsden."

A shocked silence followed his words and then some of the group began to murmur. Surely, this could not be. His Grace of Claridge had been a brave soldier in the King's army. He would never kill a man without a fair fight. Why, to stab a man in the back ... it was unthinkable!

The officer of the guard stepped forward.

"I'm afraid I must ask you to come with me, Your Grace. I am placing you under arrest for the murder of Lord Ramsden."

Chapter Twenty-one

Having barely slept, Elizabeth rose with the first light and began to dress. She was filled with a terrible sense of despair. Whatever reason for the foreboding she had felt the night before, she now knew with certainty that the disaster had already occurred. Her warning would come too late.

Still, she felt she must retrace her steps to the Palace and as coral streaked the eastern sky, she arrived, by hackney coach, at the gates. She was surprised to see, as she descended to the street, a small crowd gathered there.

"What has happened?" she asked an old woman who had been chattering to another and appeared to know what was going on.

"A murder," the biddy cried. "There's been a 'orrible murder!"

"What!" Elizabeth exclaimed, her heart beginning to pound. "Can you tell me who was killed?"

"Some fine lord, they say. Got a sword straight through his back, he did."

"Oh, God in heaven!" Elizabeth swayed and would have fallen, except for an older man who quickly put out an arm to steady her.

"There now, lass. They say he was a bad sort, anyway. Got what he deserved."

"His—his name? Do you know his name?"

The older man shook his head, but another was eager to supply the information.

"Ramsden. Lord Ramsden," he answered. "That's what the guard told us."

"Ramsden!" Elizabeth murmured.

She could hardly believe it. Ramsden dead! The man from whom she had run away. The man who had assaulted her and robbed her of her home. He was dead! She could stop hiding now. She could reveal her true identity.

Elizabeth knew she should feel exulted at the news. Instead, the despair seemed only to deepen within her. Why? What was the matter with her?

"Here he comes now!" Someone in the crowd shouted.

"Here comes his coach!"

"What is happening?" Elizabeth asked, attempting to peer through the gate. "Who is coming?"

"Ramsen's murderer. They're taking him to the Tower."

"They caught him?"

"Aye, they caught him all right. 'Twas his sword

they found in his lordship's back."

"Who is he?" Elizabeth whispered, a feeling of dread slowly spreading through her.

"Why, His Grace, the Duke of Claridge, himself. Can you believe a fine gentleman like that would do such a dastardly thing?"

Hester Quillby had waited in the shadows of the gallery until she had heard Claridge's bitter laugh and derisive words, I cannot believe you and I, milord, crossed swords over *that!*' Happily assured that her plan had gone off successfully, Hester had then quietly returned to her own apartments.

She had rejoiced in her victory. The deed had been accomplished and she was proud of her part in driving a wedge between Simon and Angela. Hester doubted he would marry her now. He would find some way of quietly breaking the betrothal. She would be there to sympathize and Simon would naturally turn to her for solace. In no time their relationship would take up where it had left off.

Ramsden had fallen in with her plans so perfectly. She had been afraid that his overzealousness when he had finally got his hands on the girl might have jeopardized the whole venture and the chit might have run screaming to Claridge for protection. But, being Elizabeth Fairclough, she had never met Claridge before and for all she knew the man dueling with Ramsden might have been one of his cohorts. The several glasses of potent wine had done much to daze the girl, not to mention the drug Ramsden had administered earlier.

It had all gone off without a hitch, despite Ramsden being forced into a duel. Smiling with pleasure over an evening well spent, Hester had slipped easily off to sleep.

Now, she was awakened by a commotion outside her apartments. Angry at having her sleep disturbed, Hester sat up in bed and rang for her maid.

"What is all the screeching about outside?" she demanded when the girl quickly appeared. "How is a person supposed to sleep?"

" 'Tis all because of the murder, milady."

"Murder! What murder?"

"Lord Ramsden, milady. Got a sword in the back, he did!"

"What!"

"They found him at the bottom of the stairs leading up to his apartments."

"You're sure he is dead?"

"Quite sure, milady. They have arrested His Grace." Her eyes took on a dream-like stare. "So proud and handsome he looked even as they led him away."

Hester let out a little shriek. "His Grace of Claridge?" she managed.

"The same, milady. Can you fathom such a man

283

being a murderer?"

"Of course he's not a murderer, Betsy. There's been some mistake. Claridge would never . . ." Oh God, she thought. Had Ramsden taunted and humiliated Simon so much that he had lost his head? Turned on him and . . . No! Claridge would never have done something so shameful as stabbing a man in the back. It had to be a mistake. It had to be!

Hester threw back the bedcovers. "Get me something to wear," she screamed. "Immediately!"

As soon as Claridge's friend, Lord Musgrove, heard of the murder and arrest and the rumor that a woman was seen fleeing from the scene, he went immediately to see the lady Angela. He was convinced that, in some way, she was implicated. He had seen the two of them going off together after the dancing the night before.

Now, he learned from the Duchess of Benham that Angela was so deeply shocked by what had occurred, that she would see no one. Her father, it seemed, was even seeking the queen's permission to take her back to their home in Kent.

Feeling there was no time to lose, Musgrove then sought out the Earl of Westbury, begging him to question his daughter about what had happened the night before. Claridge's life, he explained, might very well be in her hands.

Westbury, looking as if he had not slept, had grown angry at Musgrove's implications.

"My daughter has absolutely nothing to do with this disgraceful affair," he bellowed. "I would call you out, my lord, for even thinking such a thing, but I realize you are distraught because of your friend."

With another door closed in his face, Musgrove then proceeded to request an audience with the king. This was granted sooner than he expected. The king, himself, was anxious to help Claridge.

Before Musgrove had even had a chance to bow before him, Charles was asking him if he knew anything that could clear his friend.

"I wish I did," Musgrove replied. "I saw little of him last night, Sire. My final glimpse of him, in fact, was when supper was announced and I saw him leading Lady Angela from the Salon."

"The whole affair is absolutely preposterous!" Charles said, pacing up and down. "Claridge, of all men, would never commit such an abominable act. The very accusation is ridiculous."

"Yet Claridge said before witnesses that he was the only one in the room with Ramsden."

"Why would he lie?"

"To shield a woman," Musgrove said quietly.

"What woman?"

"His betrothed, so it is whispered, Lady Angela Neville."

"Lady Angela! I can't believe she would have the physical strength to do such a deed."

"Nor can I, Sire. Besides, why would she need to? If Ramsden had not acted the gentleman with her, Claridge would have immediately come to her defense and challenged him."

"It makes no sense whatsoever."

"We can only pray more evidence will come to light before the trial. Has the date been set, Sire?"

"Aye, a month from now."

"Four weeks! Why so soon?"

"Claridge would have liked it even sooner. Because of his rank and position he requested a swift trial."

In a daze, Elizabeth stood by the Palace gates, watching Claridge's heavily guarded coach sweep through on its way to the Tower.

She could not understand how Simon, of all people, would be accused of murdering Ramsden. Someone must have stolen and purposely used his sword in order to implicate him. Surely that was what had happened. Before the day was over he would be released. The king would see to that. No one could possibly believe such a thing of His Grace of Claridge. She was sure there was no man in England as honorable or courageous as he. Never would he stoop so low as to stab a man in the back!

Elizabeth was about to return home, confident that all would be well, when she overheard someone discussing a woman who had been seen fleeing the hallway where the murdered Lord Ramsden had been found. It was thought she might have been His Grace's betrothed, the lady Angela Neville.

With this knowledge, Elizabeth's heart sank. Oh God, he was protecting her! She thought. Last night he had said he loved her and he truly believed *her* to be Angela! If Angela had been the one to kill Ramsden, he would, she knew, stand by her to the death!

Feeling an awful sense of desolation, Elizabeth began her weary way home. As she walked, she drew her cloak around her face and lowered her head against the cool, autumn wind that had blown up. She paid no attention to the elements, for her thoughts were on the murder. She tried to picture in her mind how it might have happened.

The last time she had seen Angela, she was being led off by someone in the direction away from the Salon. A thought sprang into her head. What if that someone had been Lord Ramsden? Elizabeth stopped in her tracks.

What if Lord Ramsden had mistaken Angela for herself, Elizabeth Fairclough? It was entirely possible. They had been dressed exactly alike. He might then have spirited her away, thinking she was the girl who had rejected and run away from him and desiring to seek his revenge on her. Elizabeth shivered at the thought. She remembered vividly how she had felt alone with Ramsden. If Angela had been forced into the same position, how terrified she would have been!

Could it have been Angela's fear she had felt when, after the ball, she had experienced that sudden, unaccountable feeling that someone was in danger? She had once heard that identical twins could sense when the other was injured or had died. And yet, she and Angela had not been raised together, so such a natural closeness had never been allowed to grow between them. On the other hand, there was her overwhelming love for Simon. It was far more likely she would have sensed the danger surrounding *him*.

Elizabeth started to walk on. Suppose Angela had cried out in her fright and Simon had heard her and come upon her and Ramsden struggling? It would have been second nature for him to have drawn his sword. Could the frenzied Angela have grabbed it from him and stabbed Ramsden in the back?

There were a dozen ways the murder might have occurred, but all were only conjecture without the testimony of those present. Elizabeth must see and talk with Angela herself — sister to sister. If Ramsden had mistaken her for Elizabeth, then Angela, seeing the resemblance between them, would understand and might even open up to her twin. There were so many things Elizabeth was anxious to know about her birth and her separation from her sister, but they would have to wait. The most important thing, at the moment, was to convince Angela that only her honest testimony would save Simon. Dear God, she *must* convince her! Tears filled Elizabeth's eyes, but she quickly checked them. She knew she must be strong for Simon, so that she could help him.

Back at her rooms, Elizabeth found her young assistant patiently waiting for her by the locked door. There would be no fortune telling that day, she told him, quietly dismissing him.

An hour later, dressed in her best gown and with a vizard covering her face, Elizabeth left for Whitehall in a sedan chair.

Arriving at the Palace, she sent word to the Lady Angela Neville that a close relative wished to see her. She was ushered into a small reception room to wait and a short time later a warder brought her the news that the lady Angela and her father, the Earl of Westbury, were no longer at Whitehall, having left for their country estate. Disappointed by this unexpected news, but not deterred, Elizabeth inquired as to its whereabouts. She would follow them to Kent, she quickly decided, and when she caught up to Angela, she would talk to her and convince her to come back and testify at Simon's trial.

Hester Quillby's was also contemplating how best she could save the life of His Grace of Claridge. Her greatest worry was how to go about it without implicating herself in the affair.

She, too, had heard the rumors that a woman had been seen fleeing across the gallery above the staircase where Ramsden's body had been found. Hester was sure it could be none other than the Fairclough woman. Obviously, she had been present at the time the crime had been committed, even if she had not been guilty of the actual stabbing. Hester found it hard to believe that a girl in Elizabeth's dazed and weak condition could have managed to strike a death blow, but she was forced to admit, the chit had had just cause. Ramsden had been pretty brutal with her. He had seemed to take joy in degrading her. The girl would likely bare the bruises and ugly marks of his abuse for some time to come. But for his servant's timely arrival, Ramsden would have indeed raped her.

Thank God that the servant had not seen *her* in Ramsden's apartments, Hester thought, for surely by now he had been questioned about the whole affair. All he would be able to tell was that Lord Ramsden had entertained a lady and wanted to be informed when His Grace would be entering the hall below. There was no possibility that she would be implicated. He knew naught of her or the rest of the plan.

Hester had not been surprised to learn, later in the day, of Angela Neville's departure. The frigid, solemn-eyed little bitch had never cared for Simon. That had been apparent from the start. She had only been obeying her father's wishes in agreeing to marry him.

She could imagine that Angela, upon hearing of the murder, and that another woman was rumored to be involved, might think that that woman was Hester. It was ironic. There was no way the lady Angela would stain her lily white hands to save Simon, and yet he would protect her with his life. What a fool he was! What a stupid, chivalrous fool to hold to a code of honor so utterly senseless.

The only way she could save him without implicating herself, Hester decided, was to find Elizabeth Fairclough. Yet, an hour later, when she arrived at the rooms of Divina The Soothsayer, it was to find the place locked and barred.

Elizabeth had already left London for Kent and Neville Hall.

Chapter Twenty-two

Imprisoned in the Tower, awaiting his trial, His Grace of Claridge had time to do a great deal of thinking. Looking about him at the cold, gray walls, he mulled over in his mind the deceitfulness of women and the end of a beautiful illusion.

Angela. He could not get her out of his mind. She haunted him like one of the many ghosts he had heard were supposed to walk the damp corridors of this Tower. He didn't have to close his eyes to see her as if she stood before him, her glorious moonlight hair, framing her lovely face. He remembered how her soft blue eyes had darkened in passion when he made love to her. She excited him as no other woman had ever succeeded in doing.

Yet, from the very first she had been elusive, had tortured and mystified him. She was always running away. Ever after he had saved her life and she had given herself to him, she had fled from him.

How she had mocked him with her many guises. First, as a gypsy, his "Beth," with her warm and loving ways, so strong one moment, so vulnerable and in need of his protection the next. Then Angela, the "Snow Maid," pretending they had never met before, acting so shy and hesitant of men. And finally she had assumed still another identity – that of a loose little wanton who had encouraged that swine, Ramsden, had let him have his way with her and then had turned on him in a rage, like a drunken street bawd, and run him through.

As the days of his imprisonment slowly passed, Claridge's face grew harder and his dark eyes took on a cold, angry glitter. Even his servant, who had been allowed to attend him, found it prudent to say no more than was necessary to him or risk a sharp reply.

The knowledge of Angela's perfidy sat like a stone in his stomach. If he had been free, Claridge might have taken out his disillusionment in many ways. Drink, perhaps, or wild living, accepting reckless wagers or dares, dueling at the slightest provocation. Instead, his form of self-destruction had been to accept the blame for a murder he had not committed.

And why? He wondered more than once. Why was he protecting a chit who had mocked and betrayed him? His grandfather had taught him honor and integrity, but she had turned out to be only a little slut who had staggered from Ramsden's bed, half naked, her cheeks still flushed from passion, her lips still bruised from kisses. The woman he loved had proved to be nothing but a liar and a whore.

If, when she had first appeared at the head of the stairs, Angela had run to him, had claimed Ramsden had assaulted her and begged for his protection, he would have believed her and given it gladly. But, instead, she had shown no shame, flaunting herself and her loose behavior before his eyes.

He had fallen in love with an illusion, and on that fatal night it had been rudely shattered forever. The cynical expression deepened in his face and together with the icy facade he had adopted, one might readily believe in looking at His Grace that he was indeed guilty of the murder for which he was charged.

Lord Musgrove ascended the staircase in the Tower of London, followed closely behind by the jailer.

" 'Tis the door on the left," the man said.

The jailer had eyed Musgrove with little friendliness when he had arrived. He had already turned away more than a dozen of His Grace's friends. But when Musgrove had handed him the document with the Royal Seal that granted permission to see the prisoner, he had hastily complied.

Now the man was turning the large key set in

the door and pushing it open, he announced, "Ye have a visitor, Your Grace."

"I wish to see no one. I thought I made that clear," Claridge growled.

He was seated at a table by the window, his large form silhouetted by the late afternoon sunshine.

"You'll see me or rue the day!" Musgrove told him as he strode purposefully into the room.

The heavy door was closed and locked noisily behind him.

"John?" Claridge leapt to his feet, dropping the quill with which he had been writing.

Musgrove grasped his shoulders in a strong grip. "Did you think your friends had deserted you?"

"Nay, but I know well there is naught they can do," Claridge said wearily, waving his friend to a chair before the hearth.

"I trust you are being well cared for," Musgrove said, looking about him as he seated himself.

"I want nothing," Claridge replied succinctly.

"Nothing?" his friend watched him closely as he sat down across from him.

Claridge seemed to have aged in the few days since he had seen him and there was a new uncompromising look about him. His mouth had hardened and the cynical twist at the corners had deepened. It was the face of a man who mocks at life because he has been sorely disillusioned by it.

"Boredom is the worst of it here," he said. "But

I'm being treated well."

"I'm going to come right to the point, Simon," Musgrove said. "We all know, from the king down, that you could not have done this odious thing. We only want your assurance that when you come before your judges and peers that you will refute the charge that has been brought against you."

"Refute it?" Claridge snorted. "How can I refute it when I have already made confession of the crime?"

"For God's sake, Simon. Enough of this farce! It is obvious to us all, you remain silent over this murder because of a chivalrous desire to shield a woman. A woman who was seen fleeing along the gallery after the murder was committed. A woman who some of those present are willing to swear was Angela Neville."

Claridge said nothing, and his face still retained its unrelenting expression.

"Angela, we have been told, was shocked to hear of the murder and your arrest. So shocked she could not be questioned. To make sure of this, her father has taken her away from court and back to his estate," Musgrove said bitterly. "Apparently thinking her reputation more important than your life."

"Angela had naught to do with this affair," Claridge said quietly. "I am protecting no one by confessing to this crime."

"And you expect me to believe that?" Musgrove

scoffed. "My God, I've known you most of your life. Fought for years at your side. I'm to believe you are so cowardly that you would stab a man in the back?"

"John—"

"Don't you realize this false confession will condemn you to death?"

" 'Tis not false, John. I killed Lord Ramsden."

"Well, there's not a sane man in this country, from the king down, who believes it," Musgrove cried, jumping to his feet. "And I am not going to see you die for a crime you didn't commit." *Even if I have to whip the truth out of that heartless little bitch to do it,* he vowed to himself.

Elizabeth would always remember her first sight of Neville Hall, as her rented coach swung slowly around the winding gravel driveway. Built in the fifteenth century, the great mansion of gray Kentish ragstone formed a broad sprawling H, with courtyards both in front and in back. It seemed to Elizabeth to have a forest of chimney tops, gables and finials. Due to its vast size, it was impressive and formidable, and for the first time, she began to feel a little nervous at the prospect of confronting the Earl of Westbury and his daughter.

The coach drew up before the front entrance and almost immediately the heavy carved doors opened and a footman in wine-colored livery appeared, followed by an elderly major domo.

The footman helped Elizabeth to alight from the coach. As she had pulled the hood of her cloak low over her face, her features were undiscernable.

"My name is Elizabeth Fairclough," she told the major domo. "I have come to see his lordship."

Ushered into the great hall, Elizabeth looked around her. A pair of broad, oak staircases ran up either side of the hall to a gallery above. The dark panelled walls were covered with faded tapestries and large dingy portraits of ancestors. The heavy dark furniture only added to the gloomy surroundings.

It was obvious to Elizabeth that Neville Hall was desperately in need of a caring hand. Nothing had apparently been changed here for decades.

Elizabeth was shown into the withdrawing room, another cheerless room filled with massive, ugly furniture in somber colors. When she was alone, she removed her cloak and sat down on the edge of a worn, straight-backed chair to wait for the appearance of the Earl.

He did not keep her waiting long. Entering the room rather quickly for such a big man, he carefully closed the heavy door behind him.

"Welcome to Neville Hall, Elizabeth," he said, his sad eyes observing the slim girl who sat with her hands folded nervously in her lap. "I've been expecting you."

Elizabeth looked up at him with surprise. "Expecting me?" she exclaimed. "But how could you —"

"For quite some time I've been trying to locate you."

He sat down in an armchair facing her and Elizabeth watched the cushioned seat sag beneath the weight of his heavy frame.

"I'm afraid I don't understand. I came here today to ask both you and your daughter for your help in saving Si —, His Grace of Claridge's life."

It was Westbury's turn to look surprised. "How is that? What do you know of Claridge?"

"I know he is not guilty of murdering Lord Ramsden and I believe Angela can —"

"Angela can tell you nothing," the Earl said firmly. "I told the same to Claridge's friend, Musgrove, when he followed me down here."

"That may well be true, but will you not allow me to speak with her? I will try not to upset her in any way."

Westbury stared at her. "I'm afraid your very appearance will upset her. You two are identical, did you know that?"

Elizabeth nodded. "I observed Angela at the Palace ball and was stunned, myself, by the resemblance."

"You attended the ball?"

"Yes. I'm afraid it's all rather a long story."

"I believe we both have much to tell one another," he said, his stern face softening. Elizabeth thought he had the saddest eyes she had ever seen.

"May I offer you a glass of wine while we proceed to enlighten one another?" He rose and moved to a bell cord.

When a footman had brought the wine, served it and departed, the Earl turned to Elizabeth. "If I may, I will begin first," he said. "For I must go back to the birth of you and your sister." He regarded her over the top of his glass as he took a long drink. "You must be aware by now that you and Angela are twin sisters," he began.

"I had thought we must be and yet ... I was brought up to believe I was a Fairclough."

"You were given to the Faircloughs when you were only hours old. I'm sure they looked upon you as their own daughter."

"Then I am really *your* daughter?"

Elizabeth caught the brief look of anguish that flared in his eyes before it was masked and Westbury said gruffly, "No. You are my wife's daughter. The result, I'm afraid, of her fleeting affair with a friend of mine, Sir Thomas Thynne."

Elizabeth was taken aback by his words and could only stare at him.

"I was away fighting at the time," the Earl explained, "and when I returned to this house, your mother showed me the child she claimed was mine ... Angela. Even then she looked so much like my beautiful Sarah that I never dreamed ..." He cleared his throat. "Thynne had been killed in the same battle in which I had fought, and your mother . . . well, each time I came home, I could see that she had faded a little more." He paused a moment and Elizabeth was sure she saw tears well up in his eyes. "When she died," he went on, "I sent Angela to a convent up north. I knew I would soon be forced to leave the country. It was only when I returned to England two years ago and brought Angela home from the convent, that I learned the truth."

He swallowed the rest of his wine in one gulp and set down his glass.

"The midwife who had helped deliver you and Angela came to see me a few months after I returned. She was very agitated. She had gone through the pension your mother had given her, she told me, and being too old for midwifery, was afraid she would be sent to the poorhouse.

"When I questioned her about the pension, the whole truth came out.

"She told me what she had kept secret for sixteen years. After the two of you were born that night, the nurse noticed that one of the babies bore a vivid birthmark on her left hand."

Elizabeth immediately opened her hand and showed it to him.

The Earl nodded. "This knowledge terrified your mother, as it was well known that such a feature ran in the Thynne family. She knew that if I should see it, I would instantly guess that she had been unfaithful to me with Thomas Thynne

301

and that he had fathered her twin daughters."

"And so she gave me away," Elizabeth whispered, over the lump forming in her throat.

"It was not done as coldheartedly as that. Sarah only allowed Mistress Bedloe to take you away when she learned that you would be given to a heartbroken mother who had just lost her newborn child and was unable to bear more. We now know that that mother was Lady Mary Fairclough, but all your mother was told was that you would be raised as a gentlewoman by a loving couple who shunned society and preferred the quiet country life. There would, therefore, be little chance that you and Angela would ever meet."

The Earl did not mention what had happened to himself after he had learned of his wife's infidelity. He had loved his beautiful Sarah more deeply than anyone had ever known and had mourned her death so greatly he had never remarried. He regretted so many things about their marriage—his inability to tell her how he felt about her, his rough clumsiness—he had never ben schooled in the art of making love and knew naught of gentlewomen. He had lost his own mother when only a child and been raised solely by men.

His grief at learning his wife's secret made him retreat into himself for awhile, ignore Angela who reminded him so much of Sarah, take to drink and assuage himself with any willing female at hand. Lately, he had been berating himself for those months of wild and thoughtless living. He had hardly been an example of gallant manhood to a young girl, fresh from ten years in a convent.

Suddenly the Earl reached over and patted Elizabeth's left hand. The hand that had changed so many lives, because of the mark on its palm.

"So you see, my dear," he said kindly, "you are really as much my daughter as Angela is and with the Faircloughs gone ... Yes, I learned about all that in my search to find you ... I would be happy to have you think of me as your father and make Neville Hall your home."

"Thank you," Elizabeth said quietly, giving him a little smile that reminded him so much of his Sarah he felt tears well up in his eyes. "But I have much to settle first. I beg you to let me see Angela."

Westbury sighed. "Angela is still in a state of extreme shock. I spoke with Frances Stewart, a young friend of hers who told me that it was she who had found her wandering aimlessly about the hulls outside the queen's apartments. Angela seemed to be in a dreamlike state, her face blank, her eyes shocked and staring, and she kept murmuring, 'I pushed him. I pushed him.'

"There were bruises on her body where her clothing had been torn away. It appeared that someone had made an attempt to ravish her." The Earl's eyes flared with anger. "Lady Frances took her back to her rooms, gave her some brandy and put her to bed. She hoped that after a good night's sleep, Angela would recover her senses, but in the morning, her mind still seemed deranged and she would talk to no one. That is why I brought her home."

"I feel I may be partly to blame," Elizabeth said, clearly upset by his words. "I fear that Lord Ramsden may have mistaken Angela for me."

"What!"

"I must tell you the reasons leading up to my running away from Fairclough Manor and eventually coming to London. Then you may judge for yourself."

The afternoon had drawn to a close and the Earl of Westbury had learned from Elizabeth all about her Uncle Matthew, Lord Ramsden, the gypsy Marta, her fortune telling, her meeting with Claridge and later his fortunate appearance in time to save her life. She, of course, had not gone into the intimate part of their relationship, but Westbury was not blind and he was well aware that each time Elizabeth mentioned His Grace, her lovely eyes softened and her face came alive.

That she thought herself in love with Claridge, the Earl had not the slightest doubt. He could even forgive her for her impersonation at the ball, guessing that it was more the opportunity of seeing Claridge again that had prompted it, than trying to deceive the girl who so resembled herself.

Resembled in appearance, he thought, but not in manner. Elizabeth had a lively mind and perhaps, through necessity, had developed strength and a definite tendency to think for herself. She was not intimidated by him as was Angela. Yet there was a soothing mildness and simplicity to Angela that Elizabeth lacked and recognizing a certain sensuality about her mouth, perhaps, he thought, she also lacked the innocence.

That Angela had been innocent—at least until that unfortunate incident with Ramsden—had been made quite obvious to him when he had confronted her about her meeting with Gerald Waybridge. Looking back, he now realized it was the first and only time she had ever contradicted him. She had thought Waybridge's lifestyle admirable. Had the girl, he wondered now, fancied herself in love with him? Perhaps that accounted for that sad-eyed look of hers, despite her quiet obedience to his wishes. She had shown little passion for Claridge, which was, in itself, remarkable considering how he effected most members of the opposite sex—Elizabeth, being one of them.

Westbury now rose and walked over to a window. "If Lord Ramsden mistook Angela for you," he said, "and tried to assault her, she might very easily have lost her senses. Angela is a shy, very gentle girl. She has never, in her life, disobeyed me. That is why she went with me to court, although I knew she hated to leave the country. I think now I was wrong. She was not used to the ways of the world. She believed the best of everyone and Whitehall is like a rotten egg. It looks good enough until you crack it open and smell what is inside."

"His Grace, the Duke of Claridge, was he not kind to her?" Elizabeth could not help but ask.

"He was reticent about meeting her, which angered me," the Earl admitted. "But when he did, I thought he succeeded in winning Angela over. She seemed almost happy after he had asked for her hand. And then . . ." he shook his head. "At their betrothal party I sensed she had withdrawn from him. It was as if he had done something to disillusion her."

"Perhaps she learned of Lady Quillby."

"Ah yes, his old mistress . . . Aye, that may have been it. Angela is idealistic, I'm afraid. Despite all that went on around her at court, she remained apart from it, quite innocent."

"Do you think that if someone like Lord Ramsden tried to rob her of that innocence she might be capable of murder?"

"Never!" the Earl exclaimed. "Even temporarily out of her head, Angela would never resort to violence. It would be completely against her nature. I believe Claridge came upon her struggling with Ramsden and in his anger killed the man."

"Striking him in the *back?*"

"Totally unlike the man, I admit, but what

306

other explanation is there?"

"I'm afraid only Angela can tell us."

"She is coming back, Elizabeth. Each day we notice a difference in her. She is talking a little now, but it is as if she has completely blocked out everything pertaining to London and the court."

"I would not wish to upset her or set her back," Elizabeth said, "but . . ."

"If you will make your home here at Neville Hall, my dear, perhaps . . . when she has recovered enough . . ."

"But don't you see, there is so little time. The trial—"

"Is still weeks away. You must be patient, child. Time heels all things and after a severe shock . . ."

It was therefore decided that Elizabeth would remain at Neville Hall. The Earl called most of the servants together in the downstairs hall and introduced Elizabeth to them as his long lost daughter who had finally returned home. Unable to hide their astonishment at her likeness to the lady Angela, they nevertheless welcomed her warmly.

It did not take Elizabeth long to ascertain the affection the servants at Neville Hall held for her sister. The elderly retainer who showed her to her large, old-fashioned bedchamber, the lady's maid who came to attend her, the housemaid who later slipped a warming pan between the sheets of her bed, all made mention of Lady Angela and her sweet, caring ways.

"Like an angel she be . . . So delicate and help-less . . . Never so much as a cross word . . ."

As they supped that evening in the dark pan-elled dining salon, Elizabeth told the Earl how much the servants cared for Angela.

"How fortunate she is to be surrounded by so much love. Surely that, in itself, will help in her recovery."

"You sound a little wistful, Elizabeth," he said, regarding her closely.

"I am not like my sister at all."

The Earl glanced down the table at the beauti-ful girl whose pale hair was haloed about her head in the soft candlelight.

"You are identical twins."

"I mean we are not alike in our natures."

"I'm aware of that. Angela is quiet and serious. In spite of her beauty, men are not instantly attracted to her. You, on the other hand, are quite different. You are spirited, vivacious. I don't doubt that many young men have been drawn to you."

Elizabeth found herself blushing at his words. "I'm afraid I'm more self-centered," she said.

"Self-reliant, yes. Self-centered, no," he smiled. "Come, I want you to see a portrait of your mother."

They stood below the painting in the library and Westbury watched Elizabeth's face as she gazed up at it.

"You and Angela are very like her, but Angela

308

has the same sense of innocence that Sarah retained until the day she died. I suppose that is why I never guessed ..."

"I'm so sorry," Elizabeth said, pressing the Earl's arm in sympathy.

"She never truly belonged to me," his voice was rough as he turned away from the portrait.

Chapter Twenty-three

Unable to see Devina the Soothsayer and learn of the whereabouts of Elizabeth Fairclough, a frustrated Hester Quillby returned to her apartments in the Palace.

Intent on finding some way to help Claridge, she decided to seek out Lord Musgrove, Simon's close friend. Perhaps between the two of them, they could come up with a plan.

Once again Hester found herself thwarted, for Musgrove, it seemed, had left for Kent in order to see the Earl of Westbury.

He hopes to bring Angela back, Hester thought to herself, but she knows nothing! she despaired. "It is Elizabeth we must find. Elizabeth who was drugged and assaulted by Ramsden and surely is behind his death. And Simon, foolish, chivalrous Simon, had thought she was his betrothed and was bent on protecting her fair name, even to the scaffold.

Could Elizabeth have gone back to her old home? With Ramsden dead, it was entirely possible. Perhaps she wished to see if she could retain the property. It was worth looking into. Hester made up her mind to dispatch a man on the morrow to the Fairclough estate.

The days passed and word finally came back to Lady Quillby that no one was in residence at Fairclough Manor but a few old retainers. She also heard that Lord Musgrove had returned to Whitehall alone. Hester did not waste any time in going to see him.

"Did you bring her back?" she asked Musgrove bluntly, as soon as she had been ushered into his apartments.

"You mean Angela?" He shook his head sadly. "No. Westbury would not let me see her. The knowledge that her betrothed has confessed to murdering Ramsden has greatly affected the girl. She is still in shock. Will speak to no one. Her nurse claims it may be months before she is herself again." He pounded the mantelpiece before which he stood. "Dear God, how are we to save him with no other witnesses?"

His usually pleasant face looked ravaged, Hester thought. He obviously cared deeply for Simon. I suppose, she decided, I am the only one who can help him now. If only I can do it without admitting my involvement with Ramsden . . .

"Perhaps I should have spoken up before," Hester said slowly. "I heard that a woman was seen

311

fleeing from the spot where the murder was committed, but no one is sure of her identity."

"That is correct." Musgrove stared at the bright haired beauty sitting on the sofa before him. Did she actually propose pretending that she was that woman? No one would possibly believe that Simon had killed Ramsden to protect the honor of a woman who was known to have slept with more than one man at court.

"I said nothing earlier," Hester went on, fussing as she spoke with the lace at her wrist, "because I – well, I was not sure . . ."

Musgrove's eyes suddenly narrowed. Did this woman know something about that evening that she had kept to herself until now. "Go on," he encouraged.

"I – er – attended a small party with some friends after the ball," Hester said, "and returned alone along the corridor leading to the gallery by Lord Ramsden's apartments. As I reached the gallery, I heard from below the sounds of a sword fight."

"Who was dueling?" Musgrove asked, instantly alert.

"I was about to head over to the railing and look down," Hester continued, "when I spied a girl standing in the shadows of the staircase landing. I could see that her gown had been torn from one shoulder and her hair was in disarray, but I could not make out her face.

"Not wanting to get involved in something that

was none of my affair, I hurried away across the gallery. Oh, how I wish now that I had stopped," she cried. "I'm almost positive it was Angela standing there. Could it not have been Claridge and Ramsden fighting below?"

Musgrove's face had come alive at her words "But don't you see, Hester, you saw enough to get him acquitted! All you have to do is speak up in court and repeat what you have just told me."

"But I did not actually see who was dueling," Hester protested.

Musgrove's voice lowered. "You could say that you did. Who is to know? Would you not do that to save him, Hester?"

"I would do anything to save him," she whispered. This would work out even better than the original plan, she thought. Simon would be forever grateful to her for saving his life. She might yet become the Duchess of Claridge!

Elizabeth could not help but enjoy her new status as the protected and cosseted Lady Elizabeth Neville, after the months of scorn and isolation she had experienced posing as a gypsy. Still, it was difficult for her to remain patient. For one thing it was not in her nature. For another, Simon was constantly in her thoughts and she could not bear to think of him imprisoned for a crime she was sure he had not committed.

She went for long walks about the estate. She

rode out over the surrounding countryside every day on a young mare she had chosen for herself from the Earl's excellent stable.

Every evening she supped with her new father at the long oaken table and heard the latest report on Angela's progress. To Elizabeth, things appeared to be moving much too slowly. Angela was conversing a little with the woman the Earl had brought down with them from London to nurse her, but she expressed no interest in anything outside her room.

Elizabeth kept asking if she might visit her sister, if only for a moment, but she was always told to wait just a little while longer. It was bound to be a shock to Angela to learn she had a twin sister. She still was not strong enough to withstand another shock.

How can she be strong enough constantly lying in her bed? Elizabeth thought. She should be made to get up and go about a little more each day. But the Earl insisted it was better to let Angela's nurse judge her condition. The woman had been highly recommended to him in London. She would soon tell Angela that she had a sister who no one had known about. Later, she would learn that that sister was her twin. Still later, that her sister was now at Neville Hall and anxious to see her. It must be taken in slow stages. Surely Elizabeth did not want to cause Angela to slip over the brink again.

Anxious and frustrated, Elizabeth stayed on at

Neville Hall hoping against hope her sister would soon recover. As the days passed, she began to know her new father better and found she rather liked this big, gruff man whose heart was obviously much softer than he allowed the world to see.

He told Elizabeth that Angela called him, "Papa" and asked her, rather shyly, if she would like to do the same. She agreed to his wish, impulsively giving him a hug and a kiss on the cheek.

The October days were beginning to cool and shorten. Elizabeth, starting out for an afternoon ride, shivered slightly as the sun disappeared behind some darkening clouds. She had rid herself of the well-meaning young groom, who continued to insist he must accompany her, by assuring him she would go no farther than the trees that bordered the south lawn. By now both of them knew she would not abide by that statement, but as he also knew if he did follow her she, being the superb horsewoman she was, would only lose him anyway, he shrugged and let her go.

Just the day before, she had chanced to see a track leading off the river road, and today she decided to explore it. So intent was she in searching for the narrow lane, that she did not see the heavy rain clouds building up overhead. At last she caught sight of the little used track off into the woods and slowed her horse from a canter to a walk. The lane she began to follow was more like an uneven cowtrack, bordered on two sides by the deep, quiet forest. As she rode along it, the clear, sharp smell of autumn slowly gave way to the dank, fertile odor of the deep woods. The spongy forest floor cushioned the hoofbeats of her horse and above her she heard the soft moan of the wind through the branches of the trees.

The road seemed to be gradually ascending, and up ahead Elizabeth saw an ancient stand of oaks, gnarled and massive. It was then that the heavens opened up and the rain began to pour down.

Elizabeth urged her horse on. There was no use turning back now. The only cover she had noticed was an old slate barn back several miles on the river road. Surely this lane must lead to some shelter.

All at once she sensed someone behind her. Over the pelting rain she had heard nothing, but now, looking over her shoulder, she saw through the gray curtain someone on horseback overtaking her. A horse nudged up beside her own on the narrow road and a man, hat pulled low over his forehead, shoulders hunched against the rain, motioned to her.

"Follow me," he cried. "There's shelter up on the hill."

He galloped on ahead of her, the wind belling out his dark cloak behind him and Elizabeth pressed her mare to greater speed in order to keep him in sight through the downpour.

The path broke through the trees at the spot of a burned-out monastery. Had Cromwell's troups destroyed even this remote structure? Elizabeth wondered. Stones and rubble lay all about, but one low side still bore a charred section of roof. The man pulled up and dismounted before this section and Elizabeth did the same.

Without speaking he secured both the horses under a jut-out of roof and led her inside, through a doorless archway. The room they entered was small and damp as what roof there was left leaked in several places. One wall was half open to the elements, the window frame having crumbled away. Over broken beams and around heaps of masonry they made their way to a back corner which appeared to be dry.

Elizabeth threw back the hood of her soaked riding cloak and removed it, draping it over a broken beam to dry. When she turned to face the man, who had also been divesting himself of his wet garments, she caught his look of surprise.

"You!" he cried, his eyes lighting up at the sight of her. "I never dreamed . . ."

All Elizabeth saw was sandy hair and soft brown eyes before an arm went about her waist and he was kissing her.

"I've missed you so," he murmured, releasing her. "But what are you doing out here alone? I heard you were not well."

At the kiss, Elizabeth's eyes had flown open wide and her hand had instinctively pushed against his chest. Now the anger and surprise quickly vanished as she saw the concern written on his face and the . . . it could only be love. Yes, love was apparent in those soft, kind eyes. Love, in the tender way he had held her as if she were made of exquisite porcelain that might easily break.

"You think I am Angela," she said quietly.

Shock darkened his eyes. "Has your illness affected your mind? Do you not remember me?" His arms reached for her again, but she pushed him gently but firmly away.

"Are you Angela's lover?" she questioned him, upset that under his touch she had felt a little surge of desire. This man was not Simon. Had her body, under his tutelage, grown so sensuous that any man could arouse it?

"We were never lovers," he said affronted. "We only professed our love for one another."

She held back a smile. "Who are you?" she asked.

"Gerald Waybridge." A look of anguish filled his eyes. "Does my name mean nothing to you?"

Elizabeth put him out of his misery. "I am not Angela Neville. I am her twin sister, Elizabeth."

"Her twin . . ." he looked astounded. "She never spoke of a sister."

"She is still unaware of my return. We are waiting for her health to improve before we tell her."

"How is it she became ill? Pray tell me what you can. I have been so very anxious about her."

"I think there is much for us to tell one another, Gerald Waybridge, but first . . . Do you think you might start a fire? The dampness has made me quite chilled."

Later, huddled beside a small, but warming blaze, they talked and talked. The rain lasted for nearly two hours, and in that time they learned much about each other and of Angela.

The knowledge that Angela loved this man and not her Simon made Elizabeth's heart soar. She could now understand her sister's cool reaction to the handsome Claridge. It was quite simple. She loved someone else. This man, this Gerald Waybridge, she soon realized, would be the perfect mate for her gentle and delicate sister.

He would never make any fierce demands of her. Their passion, she was sure, would never reach the heights of hers and Simon's. No heated couplings on royal sofas behind locked doors. They would have no conception of the urgent, uncontrollable desires that overcame all reason. It was not in their natures. But they would be happy — quietly, lovingly, happy — if only they were allowed to wed.

Angela had merely been honoring her father's pledge when she had consented to marry Claridge. If she had been in her place, Elizabeth knew, she would not have been as obedient a daughter. In many ways, she was learning, the two sisters were distinctly different. Perhaps nature divided certain qualities between twins, giving some to one and some to the other, she thought. Where Angela was meek and mild, she knew she was willful and determined. She needed a strong man like Claridge to keep her in line, but he would have clearly overpowered someone like Angela.

As Gerald accompanied her back to Neville Hall, a plan began to form in Elizabeth's mind. A plan in which she and Angela might help one another gain their heart's desires. She would find a way to convince their father that Gerald Waybridge was the man Angela should marry. Angela, in turn, would return with her to London to declare Simon's innocence.

It all sounded very simple, but Elizabeth knew this was not so. If Angela *had* killed Ramsden in self defense, would she be strong enough to stand up at the trial and in front of all those people recount the events of that terrifying night? Knowing what she did of her sister, Elizabeth was sure Angela would never, knowingly, let a man die on her account. Since arriving at Neville Hall, she had seen too many examples of Angela's unselfishness and compassion.

But they had all occurred before her shock. That was what frightened Elizabeth. Had the events that had happened in London changed her? She *must* see Angela for herself. She could not wait any longer. In the morning she would go to her.

Gerald Waybridge left Elizabeth at the border of trees below the south lawn of Neville Hall.

"I will send word to you of Angela's progress," Elizabeth assured him.

"Thank you," he smiled. "I feel much better having met you." Lifting his hat to her, he rode off through the trees.

Elizabeth was tired and cold and anxious to reach home — odd that she was beginning to think of Neville Hall as home. She put her mare into a canter and headed for the stables.

Her father was standing beside his big stallion, ready to mount, when she rode into the stable yard. He looked at her damp cloak and mud-stained skirt. Her hair was loose and hung down her back in damp tendrils.

"Where is your attendant?" he asked coldly.

"I didn't —" she began.

"Which of my grooms is so unhappy in my employ that he allowed you to ride out alone?"

Elizabeth was immediately remorseful. She did not want to cost anyone his job.

"It was my own fault, sir. No one saw me leave."

"You had us all very worried, Elizabeth," he chided her. "I was about to go looking for you myself."

This surprised Elizabeth. She did not know that, in the week she had been at Neville Hall, the Earl had grown very fond of her. In their long evening conversations, he had learned much about this new daughter of his and had grown to admire her strength and self reliance.

"I'm very sorry," she said to him now. "I promise never to worry you again."

"That I doubt," his lips curved into a smile. "Now go inside this minute and get out of those wet clothes before you catch a fever."

After a hot bath, Elizabeth went straight to bed, requesting her supper brought up to her on a tray. The Earl looked in on her as she finished it. He had come to say goodbye, he said, as he would be leaving first thing in the morning to visit his northern estates. This was all the encouragement Elizabeth needed. With her father away from the house, it seemed the perfect time to approach her sister.

Elizabeth rose early the next morning, determined not to wait a moment longer before seeing Angela. Simon's life was too precious for her to worry about her sister's reaction to her presence. She knew where Angela's bedchamber was located and after breakfasting, went along the corridor to the very end and stopped before a heavy oak door. She knocked gently and a moment later, a head in a mobcap poked out from behind the half-opened door and two steely eyes regarded her. They belonged to Mistress Logan, the nurse.

"Oh, 'tis you, milady," she said, her voice very low. She was examining Elizabeth carefully from head to toe.

"I wish to see my sister."

The nurse frowned. "I thought 'twas understood ... we must go about this very slowly."

"I've waited a full week. I must speak with my sister now."

The nurse stubbornly held her ground. "Does your father know you have come?"

"No, he does not. He has gone up north for a few days."

The nurse shrugged. "Well, then, I cannot—" she began, but Elizabeth put out a firm hand and pushed the door wider. Coolly she swept by the woman and entered the room.

For a moment Elizabeth stood still, regarding the bedchamber. It was a large, attractive room decorated in a shade of hyacinth blue that Elizabeth knew would compliment both Angela and herself, yet the heavy blue window hangings were drawn closer over the windows, making the whole room dark and somber.

"Why, 'tis a beautiful day!" she exclaimed, crossing to the windows and flinging back their covering, allowing the brilliant autumn sunshine into the room.

"We must keep them closed, milady," the nurse said, clearly angry at her intrusion. "This is a sickroom."

"And no wonder, if everything is kept so dark and dreary. We need some fresh air," Elizabeth cried, opening wide one of the casements.

"What is the matter?" a soft voice was heard

from the direction of the canopied bed.

"I'm sorry, Angela," Elizabeth said as she moved briskly across the room to where a fair head was visible on the pillows. "I could not countenance you staying closed up in this stuffy room one more day."

"Pray come closer," Angela said, her eyes squinting in the unaccustomed light. "Who are you?"

"I am your sister, Elizabeth, and I thought it time we became acquainted."

"My — my what?" Angela had pushed herself up on her pillows. Her dull eyes were staring.

"Your twin sister, Elizabeth." She drew closer to the bed.

Angela let out a muffled scream. One slender hand covering her mouth, while the blue eyes above grew wide in terror.

"See what you've done, you wicked girl!" the nurse cried, pushing rudely past Elizabeth to get to her charge.

"You must let me touch her," Elizabeth insisted. "Let her see that I am real, that I am not a figment of her imagination."

"Go!" shrieked the woman, over her shoulder, as she firmly pressed Angela's shoulders back against the pillows.

"No!" Angela wailed, somehow summoning the strength to roll free of her, her eyes striving to see past the woman's square frame.

Quickly Elizabeth rounded the bed to the other

side. "I'm here, Angela," she said, as calmly as she could. She reached out to take the other's hand in her own and holding it sat down on the blue coverlet before her sister.

"You *are* real," Angela whispered in awe. "But you look—"

"Exactly like you. We are identical twins, Angela, who have been separated all our lives, but now, dear sister, we've finally found one another." Elizabeth's voice broke a little as she smiled down at Angela.

The nurse stood red-faced with anger staring at the two of them. Elizabeth reached for the soft pillows with her left hand and fluffed them up behind Angela's back. Her right hand stayed clasping her sister's. Slowly Angela's eyes clouded as she gazed into Elizabeth's face. One by one the tears spilled over and began to run in rivulets down her pale cheeks. Her lips trembled.

"Elizabeth," she murmured. "My sister . . ."

Elizabeth could not hold herself back any longer. She opened her arms and gently enfolded her sister, tears filling her own eyes. For a full moment they stayed clasped together, embracing one another. Elizabeth finally sat back, still holding Angela's hands.

"You're all right?" she asked anxiously. "I've been waiting a week to see you. I couldn't wait any longer."

"I'm glad," Angela sniffed. "But I—I just don't understand. Why were we ever parted? Where have you been?"

"There are a lot of questions to be answered," Elizabeth said quietly, "but I don't want to tire you now."

"Tire me! But this is the most wonderful day of my life!"

Still Elizabeth could see that Angela's pale cheeks had grown unnaturally flushed and her dark eyes seemed over-bright.

"You must rest now. I will return this afternoon and we will talk some more. We have much to tell one another, you and I."

Elizabeth nodded at the nurse. "Keep the window open if the weather is fair outside and only close the curtains when she wishes to sleep. My sister is no longer an invalid."

Chapter Twenty-four

In the days that followed, Elizabeth visited Angela in her room at least twice a day. Angela was anxious to learn all she could about her twin, but was reluctant to volunteer much about her own past life. She mentioned her years in the convent and her work with the children, but touched on very little of her life after returning to Neville Hall and naught of her months at court.

Angela was shocked to learn from Elizabeth that their real father had been Thomas Thynne and not the man she had always thought to be her Papa. She stared at the birthmark on Elizabeth's hand, finding it difficult to accept the fact that the quiet little mother she remembered had been an unfaithful wife. Nevertheless, she understood better than Elizabeth the abject fear that had forced their mother to give her babe away, having always been cowed herself by her Papa's overbearing presence and gruff manner.

She told Elizabeth about her Nana and how she had been with her the day she died. It was as she spoke of it that she remembered the last words her Nana had said to her about a babe . . . an identical twin.

"I don't know why I didn't guess her meaning at the time," Angela murmured. "I've often felt a strange loneliness . . . as if I were missing someone."

"I, too," agreed Elizabeth. "Old Marta mentioned twins to me when she read my hand, but I didn't put much credence . . ."

" 'Twas God's will we should find each other," Angela gave her sister a radiant smile. "How happy you have made me. I now have someone to whom I can speak my thoughts and confide."

"I do hope you *will* confide in me," Elizabeth said, her hopes rising. "Perhaps you'll start by telling me what happened after your Nana died?" Gerald Waybridge had told her how he and Angela had met and Elizabeth was hoping to draw her sister out about him, first of all, but Angela answered her question with one of her own.

"Why did you leave Fairclough Manor, Elizabeth?"

Her sister regarded her closely. It was obvious her task was not going to be easy. Angela had, perhaps quite unconsciously, built a wall around her emotions. She felt it best not to pursue the matter right then and instead told her sister about her uncle and the day she had been forced to run away, not wishing to marry the man he had chosen for her. She was careful not to mention

Ramsden by name.

Angela was fascinated by Elizabeth's account of meeting the gypsy, Marta, and her months travelling with her in the caravan. She was clearly amazed that her twin had had the courage to make her own living telling fortunes after Marta's death. She listened wide-eyed and enthralled as Elizabeth sat by her bed and recounted her soothsaying days, careful never to bring up Claridge or his part in her life. All this, she knew, would have to be told in time, but she did not want to force Angela to remember anything. She wanted things to come back to her sister gradually, so she would be better able to accept them.

On the day of the Earl's expected return, Elizabeth encouraged Angela to come downstairs with her and sit in the sunshine of the morning room. Elizabeth considered it to be the most cheerful room in the Hall, and was not surprised to learn from her sister that it had also been their mother's favorite.

Angela lay on a sofa before one of the bow windows, the bright autumn sunshine making her features seem even paler and more delicate.

Taking a sip of the herbal tea the nurse had just brought her, Angela looked apprehensive as she asked Elizabeth.

"Papa . . . when is he expected back?"

Mistress Logan had not been pleased when Elizabeth had insisted upon bringing her patient downstairs, and now as she prepared to withdraw from the room she gave her a withering look.

Elizabeth ignored it and the woman's departure. "Later today, I believe," she answered her sister. Then, seeing Angela's instant reaction, added. "You must not be afraid of him, Angela. He loves you dearly."

"But he is so big and powerful. You—you have never seen him when he gets angry," she said, trembling a little.

"He hasn't . . . He's never laid a hand on you, has he?" Elizabeth was suddenly concerned.

"Oh no, but he has shouted at me and when he has had too much to drink . . ." She gave a shiver, spilling some of her tea into its saucer.

"I've never seen him thus," Elizabeth admitted. "From the time I came until he went away we spent every evening together. We discussed books and politics and I asked him much about the war and his time on the Continent. We never seemed to run out of things to say to one another."

"Were you not offended by his crude manners and vulgar speech?"

"I learned from him that he was brought up almost solely by men. He has lived a good part of his life as a soldier and seen much violence and very little of delicate etiquette and gentle ways."

She went on to tell Angela how much he had worshipped their mother and how it had nearly killed him to discover, some months after his return, that his wife had not been true to him. That, Elizabeth explained, might account for him

330

trying to drown his sorrow in drink.

"Sometimes," Angela said, "I feel it hurts him to look at me."

"I've noticed that. 'Tis because we both resemble our mother so much."

"Our faithless, immoral mother," Angela said quietly.

"Oh, Angela, do not pass judgment on her."

"How can I not? She hurt so many people by her actions. Papa and you —"

"And herself . . . herself most of all, I think. She must have loved Thomas Thynne beyond all reason to have done what she did. Can you imagine her fear when she found she was with child? The pain and desolation when she learned of his death?"

"Or the guilt when she had to give you up. The guilt whenever she looked at Papa. Always the guilt . . ."

Angela said nothing more. Her eyes had again taken on the blank look that Elizabeth had grown to recognize. The look that meant she had retreated back behind her wall of silence and oblivion.

Her reaction frightened Elizabeth. It seemed to happen when Angela remembered something she was trying desperately to forget.

Sleep was elusive to Elizabeth that night. She lay awake trying to think of a solution to her problem. If she forced Angela to remember the events of that terrible night at Whitehall, she was

331

certain it would harm her immeasurably. And yet
... how was she to save Simon? The time was
drawing closer and closer to the date of his trial.

Oh Simon, my love, she despaired. What a
coward you must think of your betrothed for not
coming forth and absolving you. You think I am
she and I wish with all my heart that I were. I
would know then what to say of that night to set
you free. Instead, you remain imprisoned in that
dreadful tower which has seen the last days of so
many brave men and women. She felt a sense of
panic. What was she to do?

When sleep finally claimed her, she dreamed.
She was again in the ruined monastery on the
hill, but this time the man with her was Simon
and not Gerald Waybridge. Simon. Dear, dear,
Simon ...

He led her out through the opening in the stone
wall and suddenly all was beautiful around them.
Under a clear blue sky was a wide, sun-baked
slope of grass with a spectacular view below it of
lush meadows and a winding stream. Simon had
brought a picnic basket with him which he
opened and spread its contents out on the warm
grass — chicken and a loaf of fresh bread, cheese
and wine. She watched him remove each item
from the basket, but neither attempted to eat
when he was through. Instead, they gazed for a
long time at one another and then, as if in slow
motion, he drew her toward him.

The intensity in Simon's eyes made her tremble

but when his fingers began unfastening the buttons at her neck, she put out a hand to stop him, feeling a bold eagerness, wanting to undress him first. The breeze caught his coat and then his shirt and blew them from her hands. She paused to kiss him then, her lips moving against his broad expanse of chest, slowly, savoring every warm inch of him, feeling the passion rise within her, murmuring with pleasure as his hands slid beneath her bodice to cup her naked breasts. She fell back with him on the warm grass and he was rearing over her, huge, magnificent, and her eager hands were pulling him down to her, down . . . down . . .

The sound of horses in the courtyard below her open window caused her to awaken. Abruptly. Hearing the commotion, she knew that it was her father returning. For a moment she lay there, her heart racing, her body eager . . . aching from her dream. She wanted to cry aloud her frustrated need.

Had her mother once felt a like need for her Thomas? "Our faithless, immoral mother," Angela had said. Angela, who was sweet and loving, but seemed, by all accounts, to be passionless. Would she be shocked to learn of her sister's two passionate encounters with Simon? Would she ever understand such uncontrollable emotions? How could they both be identical twins if they possessed such different characteristics? Was one twin robbed of an attribute in order to give the other the major share?

Elizabeth knew she would never be as good and trusting a person as her sister. Only that morning Angela had said to her that Mistress Logan did not mean to be sullen and ill-tempered. It was simply that she was afraid that as soon as Angela recovered, she would be dismissed.

It was hopeless to point out to Angela that the woman might have kept her in a darkened room for years if she had not lost patience and insisted upon seeing her sister.

Angela, Elizabeth decided, was a sentimentalist and she was a realist. That was another of their differences. How strange it was that two who so closely resembled each other physically, could look at life in such dissimilar ways.

Elizabeth was wise enough to approach her father the next morning before Mistress Logan had a chance to air her grievances. With no apology, she explained to him what she had done in his absence and begged him to see Angela for himself. He did as she asked and was soon convinced that no harm had been done and, in fact, Angela seemed much improved. She told him how happy she was that Elizabeth had come and hoped they would stay together at Neville Hall always.

Encouraged by her appearance, her father was nevertheless concerned by her words, for he knew that Elizabeth's main purpose in remaining was her hope to clear Claridge's name.

Elizabeth was in the morning room the next afternoon, waiting for Angela to join her, when it happened.

Descending the staircase with her nurse, Angela caught sight of two people waiting in the great hall downstairs. A footman, crossing to the library to inform His Lordship of their arrival, stopped in his tracks when he heard her cry.

"Auntie Maude! Willie!"

The two looked up as Angela come flying down the rest of the stairs toward them, her face alight with pleasure, her arms outstretched. She greeted the two warmly, stooping to embrace the young lad.

It was at that precise moment that the Earl threw open the door of the library, brushing aside the footman to see what was causing the commotion in the hall. He frowned darkly at the woman who had come to see him. The woman whose admissions had caused him so much pain. He had given her a goodly sum at the time of her last visit. Was she thinking to get more from him? And why had she brought a child with her?

Seeing her father glowering at them in the doorway to the library, the color left Angela's face, but she spoke up bravely, "Papa, these are my friends," she said to him.

The Earl made an impatient gesture toward the three of them. "All of you . . . come into the library," he ordered, turning on his heel and striding back into the room.

Later, sitting imperiously behind his massive desk, His Lordship learned something that had long been kept secret from him. An orphanage had been set up in the Manor House that bordered his property. Auntie Maude explained that she had obtained permission to house the children in the then empty house from his wife, the Countess, as he had been absent fighting for his king at the time.

The Earl stared at the woman he knew as Mistress Bedloe, the mid-wife who had attended his Sarah. He could think of nothing to say.

The woman apologized for not being honest with him the previous time she had called. "You see, Your Lordship," she said, not meeting his eyes, "it was not a pension for myself I was really needing, but funds for the children's needs. I was afraid to tell you this in case you accused me of trespassing on another's land and made us vacate the Squire's empty house."

"But 'tis no longer empty," the Earl looked perplexed. "Sir Gerald Waybridge inherited the land and Manor House from his uncle."

"Sir Gerald has kindly allowed us to remain, Your Lordship." Which was why she now felt braver in approaching the Earl. Still, just in case, she had brought along the sweet-faced, curly-haired Willie, who had been known to beguile food and clothing from the stingiest of shopkeepers.

His Lordship now looked to his daughter for an explanation as to how she had become acquainted with these people and Angela revealed to him, with some trepidation, the story of her accident with the dog cart.

When she hesitated, Auntie Maude quickly stepped in to tell the Earl how kind his daughter had been in sending gifts to them afterwards, even finding a woman to help out, for the orphanage was short staffed and—

His Lordship rudely cut her off. "Pray get to the point, woman. What, may I ask, is the purpose of *this* visit?"

"Well, you see ..." Mistress Bedloe herself looked nervous now. "The rainstorm we had several days ago was accompanied by high winds. Many slates were dislodged from the roof over the west wing where the orphanage is housed. Most of them broke in their fall and the roof is now leaking badly."

"May I ask why you have not approached your Squire to repair it?"

"Sir Gerald cannot afford the expense until his crops are sold and then there are other things more pressing he must first consider ..."

"If Waybridge had not increased the wages of his farm laborers," the Earl growled, "he—"

"Might have had some of his ricks fired as yours were, Your Lordship," interrupted a voice from the doorway. "Isn't that why you have been visiting your northern estates?"

Gerald Waybridge stood very still, regarding Angela who had grown quite pale at the sight of him and now clutched a table for support. He had ridden over as quickly as he could when he had learned of Auntie Maude's mission.

The Earl rose from his chair. He looked very big and overpowering standing there. "I do not tolerate the destruction of my property, Waybridge. The men responsible are now in prison."

"Did you not attempt to discover why they were so discontented?" Gerald asked, walking toward him. It was clear that he was not intimidated by the big man.

Westbury glared at the young squire. "I believe that is solely my concern."

"Of course, Your Lordship. And I consider the roof of my house solely *my* concern. I do not require your assistance."

"You are both stubborn and bullheaded," Elizabeth announced entering the room. She had grown tired of waiting for Angela in the morning room and had come looking for her.

Auntie Maude and Willie both stared at her in amazement. They had not been told of Angela's twin.

"Papa," Elizabeth went on, "you won't admit that you were forced to raise your laborer's wages to what Gerald is already paying, and you, Gerald, appear to be taking the orphanage's problems as your own. If they were not occupying

338

that wing of the manor house, would you not simply vacate it until you could afford to repair the roof?"

Looking a little sheepish, Waybridge slowly nodded.

"Then the solution is very simple. Papa, will you give the orphanage funds to reslate their roof?"

The Earl's anger had melted with Elizabeth's appearance. Now his mouth twitched at the corners as he regarded her conciliatory stance.

He nodded. "I will do so."

"Good." She turned to the others. "Then the matter is settled."

"Now wait—" Waybridge began.

"Would your pride stand in the way of this child having a roof over his head?" Elizabeth asked, pointing a finger in Willie's direction.

"Of course it wouldn't," Angela said quietly, smiling shyly at Gerald.

"Of course it wouldn't," he murmured, his eyes never leaving Angela's sweet face.

Elizabeth saw that her father was looking from one to the other, a frown appearing between his eyes.

"I do believe, Papa," she said, "when Angela feels a little better, it would do her much good to spend some time with the children at the orphanage."

Westbury was about to say something when he caught Angela's expression. Her delicate face had come alive with happiness at Elizabeth's suggestion and now her eyes were turned pleadingly toward him.

"Papa, could I?" she managed. "I do so miss the children at the convent. It gave me so much pleasure—"

"We will see," he said, but Elizabeth gave her sister an encouraging nod.

Sitting before the window in her bedchamber, Elizabeth looked out at the moonswept lawn below. After the others had left that afternoon, she had taken Angela into the morning room. She hoped that seeing Auntie Maude and Gerald Waybridge would have opened the door of her sister's memory a little wider.

She found that this was so, up to a point. Angela told her all that had happened the day of the accident, but when Elizabeth ventured to suggest that she had met Gerald afterwards and they had fallen in love, Angela immediately grew silent and retreated into herself.

Elizabeth was now sure in her mind that it would take some time before Angela would be able to face what she had hidden away. Because a man's very life was involved, should she attempt to force her sister to remember? Elizabeth shook her head. Despite her love for Simon, she hadn't the right to destroy Angela in the process. What then was she to do? If Angela did not speak out, how could she save the life of the man she loved?

If only it had happened to me and not to Angela, Elizabeth thought, cupping her face in her hands as she rested her elbows on the windowsill. If only I had been the woman seen fleeing along the gallery above the staircase where the murder took place.

At that moment she caught the reflection of her drawn face in the dark window. How similar her features were to Angela's. How . . . In a flash it came to her what she must do. Why hadn't it occurred to her before? No one else had been present who could dispute her words . . .

She searched the room for writing materials and sat down at a table to write a note to her father.

In the early dawn, Elizabeth crept out of the house carrying only a small bag. She made for the stable where she saddled her mare and was soon riding off in the direction of London.

Chapter Twenty-five

The trial of His Grace of Claridge on a charge of murder was to be held in the Great Hall of Westminister. The Lord High Steward, the judges and an assembly of His Grace's peers, who were to try him, would all be gathered at the appointed hour.

People from all walks of life would come to view the trial. A trial which, seeing that the accused had confessed to the crime, would not take long. In an hour, at most, judgment would be pronounced against His Grace of Claridge, ending in a sentence of death.

The gray October morning dawned. Inside the Great Hall the jostling crowd was noisy – shouting and calling to each other, sharing jokes, quarreling, cajoling, threatening. Suddenly silenced, they gaped as they watched the scarlet and ermine cloaked nobles enter in a grand, yet solemn procession, followed by the judges and the Lord

High Steward.

The Clerk of the Crown was the first to speak as he rose and read the indictment, "Whereas Simon Edward Blair, fourth Duke of Claridge did on the night of the twenty fourth of September of this year of our Lord, one thousand, six hundred and sixty three, unlawfully kill Cecil Raymond, Lord Ramsden..."

The voice of the clerk droned on, describing the dastardly crime performed by a man who had once been held in high esteem by his king and country and had now sunk to the low degree of a coward and a murderer. The form and severity of punishment of this man was all that was to be decided that day, for Simon Edward Blair, fourth Duke of Claridge had already confessed to the heinous crime.

The indictment having been read, there was a general turning of heads to observe the prisoner who was now entering the Great Hall.

Claridge was marched in after the armed guards of the Tower of London, between the Lieutenant of the Tower and a peer of equal station. He was dressed all in gray and his face looked pale and hard as he crossed the hall and was led up some steps to stand facing the assembly.

Tall and erect, the prisoner at the bar seemed calm and indifferent to the whispers and stares directed his way.

The Clark of the Crown again stood up and

called upon the accused to hold up his right hand.

The prisoner at the bar having done so, the King's Sergeant, opened the contents of the indictment:

"Whereas it is said that on the twenty fourth day of September, thou, Simon Edward Blair, the fourth Duke of Claridge didst unlawfully kill Cecil Raymond, Lord Ramsden, thou art therefore to make answer to this charge of murder. I therefore charge thee once again before this company ... Art thou guilty of this crime where of thou art indicted, yea or nay?"

"I am guilty," Claridge said stiffly, "and I have confessed."

A groan went up from the assembled crowd.

"By whom wilt thou be tried?"

"By God and by my peers."

"And was Your Grace's confession given willingly and freely without extortion or unfair means to obtain it?"

"I made my confession freely, and it is all true."

"The Clerk of the Crown will now read that confession," said the King's Sergeant.

The Clark began, "The voluntary confession of Simon Edward Blair, fourth Duke of Claridge, now a prisoner in the Tower, and accused of murder and felony and made at the Tower of London on the twenty fifth day of September, one thousand, six hundred and sixty three.

"I hereby acknowledge and confess that on the

twenty fourth day of September, I did unlawfully
kill Cecil Raymond, Lord Ramsden, by thrusting
my sword into his back. For this murder I plead
neither excuse nor justification and submit myself to a trail by my peers and to the justice of
this realm. So help me God."

The Duke of Claridge had a great many friends
in the crowded hall and not one present believed
that the confession they had just heard was the
truth. From his peers to the judges and attor-
neys, even the Clerk of the Crown, all thought
that His Grace was sheltering someone and there
was more of a mystery to the matter than was
apparent in Claridge's straightforward confession.

"Deny it, Claridge!" someone cried out from the
rear of the hall.

"Deny it!" a chorus of voices joined in before
silence was demanded.

Claridge said nothing, although his hard gaze
seemed to soften for an instant at the cries.

Having restored silence, the King's Sergeant
continued. "My lords, this man hath been indicted and arraigned of a most heinous crime and
hath confessed it before you, which is of record.
Wherefore there resteth no more to be done but
for the court to pronounce judgement accord-
ingly."

The Lord High Steward, with a look of deep
sorrow at the prisoner, rose and said, "Simon

Edward Blair, Duke of Claridge, what have you to say why I may not proceed to judgment?"

There was a hushed silence in the huge hall that was suddenly broken by a woman's voice, clear and distinct.

"I hereby bear witness that the Duke of Claridge is innocent of the charge brought against him."

A female, clad in a dark cloak, stepped forward and throwing back the hood, raised her head to meet the eyes of the Lord High Steward.

Lord Musgrove gave a gasp of surprise when he saw her face.

"Who are you?" the Lord High Steward asked.

"I am Angela Neville," she replied, "daughter of the Earl of Westbury and the betrothed of His Grace of Claridge, the prisoner at the bar."

Claridge had started at the sound of her voice and the knuckles of his hands that were gripping the wooden bar turned white. Before she could continue, he broke in.

"I pray your lordship to disregard this interruption. I desire no witnesses on my behalf."

He stared at her standing there before the august assembly and was suddenly terrified by what she might say or do. She looked almost as she had when he had seen her tied to the stake before a wild mob bent on burning her alive. Frightened, but determined not to show it. Graceful and proud—every inch the lady. That other part of her that he had viewed and scorned, that faithless slut who had openly mocked him and then committed the murder for which he stood self-convicted, had vanished, leaving only this beautiful creature looking imploringly up at the Lord High Steward.

She did not turn towards him when he spoke, but he saw her sway slightly and then steady herself. He longed to go to her and put his arms about her. This was the sweet, vulnerable Beth who had told him how much she loved him.

"How say you, my lords?" the Lord High Steward turned to those who flanked him. "Ought we to hear this lady or no?"

"Aye! Aye!" shouted the assembly.

"I protest," Claridge's deep voice was drowned out.

"We will hear the lady," exclaimed the Lord High Steward, "for God has seen fit at this eleventh hour to move her to speak that which she knows. Let her step forward and be made to swear the truth of her assertions."

Elizabeth moved closer.

"You are the Lady Angela Neville, daughter of the Earl of Westbury, maid of honor to her Majesty Queen Catherine?"

"I am."

"Then I do charge thee to speak the truth, the whole truth, and naught but the truth, so help you God."

347

"My lords," protested Claridge, "I beg you not to—"

"My lord of Claridge," demanded the Lord High Steward, "in the name of justice and for the dignity of this court, I charge you to be silent."

He turned back to Elizabeth. "Speak, my lady. This court will listen."

She waited until all was quiet and then she began in a voice that trembled a little at first and then became stronger and more resolute as she continued.

"It was late on the twenty fourth day of September, after the ball in Whitehall Palace honoring Prince Rupert's return. I was in the company of Lord Ramsden . . ." She paused, her whirling brain trying to choose the right words that would convince those present that she had indeed been at the scene of the murder.

"My lords," Claridge spoke up again. She was going to confess it all before this whole assembly, he was sure. She was going to shame and disgrace herself to save him and he could not endure that. Whatever had got into her that night—passion, drink, whatever had crazed her mind—appeared to be gone now and she was standing there as warm and lovely as when he had first held her in his arms.

"I entreat you," he went on. "In the name of justice, do not hear this lady; she is overwrought and does not know what she is saying. I have

348

confessed to the crime; there is nothing—"

"Prisoner at the bar," commanded the Lord High Steward. "I charge you again to be silent. Lady Angela, pray continue."

Elizabeth took a deep breath and again began, "I was in the company of Lord Ramsden, who, I had thought, was escorting me to join my father and His Grace of Claridge. Instead he—he forced his attentions on me. He—he seized me and would not let me go, despite how much I struggled. He tried ... I beg pardon, my lords. Pray bear with me. This—this is not easy for me ..." Her voice broke a little. She was remembering only too clearly how Ramsden had been all over her that night at Fairclough Manor. She was reenacting in her mind the horrible moments she had spent trying to free herself.

"It was then that His Grace of Claridge came upon us and seeing me thus abused—I, who was his betrothed—to save my honor, he struck Lord Ramsden down."

When Elizabeth finished speaking a dead silence fell over the Great Hall. Claridge who had been staring unbelievingly at her suddenly gave a short, bitter laugh.

He had actually thought Angela was about to tell the truth, to admit to the crime she had committed. He might have known she would not admit to the blood being on her *own* hands. The lie was well concocted. And what was another

349

falsehood after all the others she had told him. Apparently, she liked him well enough not to wish to see him hanged, but not enough to admit the truth and clear his name completely. It made him laugh at his own gullibility. To be taken in again by that chit? What a damn fool he was!

He listened with disbelieving ears as she was questioned and cross-questioned by the judges and never once did she waver from her original story. Nevertheless, she did not dare look at him.

"Lady Angela Neville," said the Lord High Steward at last, "do you swear upon your honor that you have spoken the truth?"

"I swear upon mine honor," she replied.

What honor? Claridge snorted to himself.

" 'Tis false from beginning to end," he protested in a loud voice.

Gazing up at him for the first time, Elizabeth was taken aback by the utter contempt in his eyes as he stared back at her.

For his sake she had lied and spoken a false oath before God and all these people. Not only was Claridge ungrateful to her for this, he clearly despised her for what she had done. Elizabeth looked quickly away, her eyes filling with tears.

"My lords," the Lord High Steward was saying, "you have heard the evidence of this lady, and Simon, Duke of Claridge, having put himself upon the trial of God and you his peers, I charge you to consider if it appeareth that he is guilty of this murder or whether he had justification."

There was no deliberation amongst his peers. The lords who were trying him with almost one voice, quickly and joyously exclaimed, "Not guilty!"

A cheer went up from the crowd in the Great Hall. And over the noise and enthusiasm that ensued, the King's Sergeant could hardly be heard dissolving the commission and charging all persons to depart in God's peace.

Claridge stood still, watching Angela being escorted out through a side door. An acquittal was not what he had expected this day. Especially an acquittal based on a lie. A lie he could not refute without branding her as a murderess or worse. He felt he had been forced to barter his honor and his pride in order to save his own worthless hide. At least if he had gone to the scaffold, he would have suffered an honorable death.

He only half listened to the Lord High Steward's concluding speech, absolving him of the crime of murder.

"My lord Duke," the man's voice at last drew his attention, "what the lady has told us was guessed at by all your friends. We cannot but thank heaven that Lady Angela's heart was touched at the eleventh hour and that you were not allowed to sacrifice your honor and your life in so worthless a cause. Your Grace leaves the Court this day with the respect and admiration of all

Englishmen, with unsullied honor and with stainless name."

Cheered by the crowds, Claridge left Westminster Hall a free man, but many of those watching him wondered why he did not look more exultant.

Perhaps, some thought, he would always feel guilt for taking a life, despite the justification. He was, after all, a most honorable gentleman.

Chapter Twenty-six

Musgrove had wished to talk with Claridge, but by the time he had pushed his way through the crowd, His Grace was climbing into his coach. He gave Musgrove a smile, but it was a strange, unfathomable smile and even after the coach had departed, his friend stood where he was, staring after it.

"Well, that *was* a surprise," said a husky feminine voice and Musgrove turned to see Hester Quillby standing beside him. "Here I am wearing my best gown and my new sable cape and wholly prepared to speak up and save him when out of no where *she* steps forward."

"I was just as surprised as you," Musgrove said, looking back at the departing coach. "I thought from what her father said she was unable to see anyone. Still in shock."

"She still might be," was Hester's enigmatic reply, but when Musgrove swung back to her, she had melted into the crowd.

Elizabeth was escorted back to Whitehall Palace by the Lord Chief Justice himself. Being an old friend of Claridge's late father, he was jubilant at His Grace's release, and did not seem to notice the fact that Elizabeth spoke little on the way.

She felt dead inside. She had willingly lied for him and sacrificed her dignity and honor before a crowd of strangers. Not only had he disdainfully rejected what she had done, he had scorned her for doing it. Her heart ached, remembering the cold contempt she had read in his eyes. He had known she had lied, but didn't he realize it was because she loved him and wanted to save him, that had made her swear to such falsehoods? Why should he blame her for that? He had saved her life. Had she no right to return the favor?

Elizabeth closed her eyes. How many nights since Simon had been taken off to the Tower had she lain awake reliving the memories of their love and wanting him desperately, aching for his touch. He had said he loved her. She knew he loved her. And yet, her heart cried, if this were truly so would he have looked at her so scornfully in court?

Back at the Palace, she refused to allow the Lord Chief Justice to lead her back to the apartments which had belonged to her sister. Instead, she told him that she wished a little time to herself. She would walk for awhile in the Privy Garden.

A brief rain shower while they were gathered in the Hall of Westminster had sweetened the air and a gentle breeze rustled the trees as the two halberdiers who stood by the entrance, stepped aside and let her enter.

Walking slowly along the gravel path, Elizabeth soon became aware that someone was overtaking her. She turned her head and stopped, allowing Lord Musgrove to catch up to her. He had claimed a dance with her at the ball and she knew him to be a close friend of Simon's.

Reaching her side, Musgrove said, "On behalf of all of Simon's friends, I wish to thank you for saving him today." He took a step backward and surveyed her. "Just who are you?"

Elizabeth looked bewildered by his words.

"I know you are not Angela Neville," he went on. "I journeyed to Neville Hall and His Lordship told me his daughter was still in shock and could see no one."

"Perhaps she recovered and returned to London."

"I think not. Simon once confided in me that the girl to whom he was betrothed seemed to him to be two different people. He had fallen in love with warm little Beth and yet she kept turning into the Snow Maid, Angela Neville."

"He said that?"

Musgrove nodded. "You *are* Beth, aren't you?"

355

She looked away from him, her lips trembling, "Aye," she whispered.

"The fortune teller. The one he searched for so long and thought he had found in Angela."

Elizabeth turned back to him and he could see that her eyes were luminous with tears. "Angela and I are twin sisters," she explained. "We were separated at birth and it was only recently that I learned of her existence. Unexpectedly, I was given the opportunity of attending the Palace ball. With the thought of seeing not only Simon, but the twin I had never known, I could not resist dressing to resemble her and using the invitation I had acquired."

"Did you manage to see Angela?"

"Aye. I saw her going off in the opposite direction to the Salon, but I did not see whom she was with. I think now it must have been Lord Ramsden."

"So it was she who was present at the murder and not you."

"I believe that to be so. I had left the Palace long before. When I heard that a woman had been seen fleeing from the scene, I felt it must be Angela, and so I, too, went to Neville Hall to bring her back. Finding her suffering from shock, I was afraid to force her to recall what had happened. It may come back to her slowly, but it will take time and ... there was no time."

"Do you think she killed Lord Ramsden?"

"I don't know. I understand she was found that

night wandering about the halls half crazed and muttering, 'I pushed him!', 'I pushed him!' "

"She might have meant that she had pushed Ramsden down the stairs."

"Quite possibly."

"But was it she who stabbed him in the back with Simon's sword?"

"I'm sure you believe as I do that Simon would never strike another man in the back. He obviously confessed to the crime in order to shield Angela. I could not allow him to go to the gallows for something he didn't do. I had to pretend I was Angela today and try and save him."

"Which you did magnificently."

She gave a sad little smile. "No. Simon regarded me as if I were beneath contempt."

"But he did not know what you have just told me. He had no idea of any sacrifices on your part. Perhaps he witnessed the murder and expected you—Angela—to confess to it today. When you did not, and still let the blame rest on him, he must have thought what you had done merely a weak attempt to save his life."

"He despises me." Tears again welled up in her lovely eyes.

Musgrove looked down at her, his face full of concern. "You love him very much, don't you?"

"I do," she whispered. "For all the good it does me now." Suddenly she placed a hand on his arm. "Would you do one small thing for me?" she asked softly.

"Certainly," he replied. "I'm at your command."

"I would like to speak with Simon for a moment this afternoon. Could you arrange that?"

"I will try."

"Tell him I will be here, in the Privy Garden, at three o'clock."

Musgrove was puzzled as he went in search of Claridge. In his mind he was carefully reviewing the murder and everything he knew concerning it. There were several things that did not make sense to him.

If what Hester Quillby had told him was true, Claridge and Ramsden had fought a duel. Therefore, Claridge had not come upon Ramsden assaulting Angela and in anger thrust his sword into his back. Instead, he had challenged him to a duel. Why then was Ramsden's sword in its sheath when his body was found and Claridge's was not?

Perhaps Angela had grabbed it away from him and stabbed it into Ramsden's back. It was possible, and yet . . . Musgrove shook his head. Somehow, an important part of the puzzle was still eluding him.

Hester Quillby was happy. Things had gone off better than she had planned and she could not help but rejoice when she remembered the way

Simon had looked at the woman who had saved his life. Elizabeth Fairclough. For, of course, it was Elizabeth who had come forward at the eleventh hour and saved his life. Remembering so little, she had had to concoct an explanation for the events of that night. Fortunately, the court had believed her.

Now the murder could be forgotten and Simon would come back to her. Angela would not soon return to Whitehall and Elizabeth was no threat. Even if Simon thought her to be his betrothed, he would never marry her now. He would never make a woman he thought to be a wanton and a murderess the Duchess of Claridge. Hester laughed aloud at her triumph.

Elizabeth returned to her rented rooms and removed the dark clothing she had worn to the trial. She was about to dress in a simple blue gown for her proposed meeting with Simon, when she changed her mind. It would probably be the last time she would see him. She would wear the original gypsy costume she had worn when they had met and when he had saved her life and conceal it under the cloak he had lent her.

She arrived at the Privy Garden at half past two. At a quarter to three Lord Musgrove appeared and approached her. He took her cold hands in his and smiled at her.

"Will he come?" she asked, her blue eyes searching his face.

"He'll come. He owes you his life."

"Did you tell him anything?"

He shook his head. "No. We had no time alone. He had a long audience with the king and I only managed a word with him in the anteroom afterwards."

"Then he still thinks . . ." an anxious expression crossed her face.

"Aye. It will be up to you to enlighten him."

"If he will but listen."

Firm footsteps were heard coming along the path and both of them turned to meet a solemn-faced Duke of Claridge.

Musgrove greeted him and then quietly withdrew, leaving Simon and Elizabeth standing alone in the garden.

Seeing him up close, the first thing Elizabeth noticed was how much older he looked. The cynical lines seemed to have deepened about his mouth, but he still projected that powerful magnetism. He stood before her, tall and broad-shouldered, and she felt her heart begin to race within her. She wanted to run into his arms, kiss those tightly pressed lips, bring back the brightness to those cold, remote eyes.

A gust of wind caught the corner of her cloak and he recognized the bright gypsy costume she wore beneath. He frowned. Was she not also wearing his cloak as well? Why had she dressed herself in these clothes? Did she want him to remember the way things had been between them that glorious night in Bridgetown? She looked up at him with her wide, expressive eyes and for a moment he thought he saw tears glistening on the long dark lashes.

He felt an urge to take her in his arms, to murmur reassuring words to her, to kiss those soft, trembling lips. He couldn't tear his eyes away from her. The sweet perfume of violets penetrated his nostrils and every nerve in his body reached out to her, longing for her, remembering the joy they had shared, the all-encompassing passion. He felt an instant surge of desire, but reality, stark, cruel reality chased away the tender memories and brought back to him that same face and form, dishevelled, half naked, stumbling drunkenly from Ramsden's bed.

Elizabeth saw the cold, contemptuous look return to the gray eyes which for a short moment had seemed to soften. The color left her face as he swept her a little bow.

"I am entirely at your service, my lady. What may I do for you?"

She had wanted to see him to tell him that she was Beth, not Angela. To tell him why she had lied. To explain so much. Now, his coldness chilled her and the words she would have spoken were lost to her.

"That is all you can say?" she returned, in as cold and haughty a voice as he had used.

"Nay, I should thank you for saving my life,

shouldn't I?" he sneered. "Although it was hardly worth saving."

"You sound so bitter."

"Bitter!" he scoffed. "Why should I be bitter? I have only been ridiculed and deceived and lied to by the one woman I had learned to love above all others and thought loved me."

She gave a little gasp. "There is an explanation."

"Oh, I'm sure there is. You are very good at concocting explanations. The one told before the court today was a masterpiece. Honor threatened indeed," he laughed disdainfully. "My timely interference . . . And I thought for a moment you would make a full confession."

"I could not . . . You do not understand."

"On the contrary, I understand very well, my dear. What difference did it make, you thought, if the stigma of murder remained with me, so long as I was saved from the gallows? Well, you saved me and I am grateful, does that satisfy you?"

She said nothing. She could only stare at him.

"Now what do you desire of me? My name and protection are at your service. I am quite ready to fulfill the marriage contract if that is what is worrying you."

She could hardly speak. The color that had earlier left her cheeks returned to stain them crimson. "You—you thought I was afraid you wouldn't honor—"

"At least be honest about *that*. We both know

your reputation is bound to have suffered today with your story of Ramsden's near ravishment. Near ..." he gave a short harsh laugh. "But I suppose only poor Ramsden himself would enjoy that joke. I think, under the circumstances, the sooner we become man and wife the better."

He wanted to hurt her, wanted to destroy her pride and self-respect as she had destroyed his life and honor.

"You would marry me," she gulped, "thinking I lied ... thinking the worst ... Are you mad, Simon?"

"Aye," he cried, "I'm mad. Despite everything I saw that night ..., despite your deception and your faithlessness ... I can't stop loving you."

He reached out for her, pulling her roughly against him and although her body began to tremble at his nearness, the blue eyes blazed up at him.

"Let me go!"

He paid no attention to her demand, crushing her closer to him, devouring her lips with his own. She would *not* give in to the sensations that were making her blood race through her veins, that were making a longing surge of desire grow and swell within her. She had wanted him to hold her for so many long nights. He had said he could not stop loving her. Well, no matter what he said to her, no matter what he did, she could not stop loving *him*.

She struggled to pull away from him, beating

with her fists at his chest. But it was useless. His kiss only deepened and she felt herself giving in to the demands of his mouth, opening her lips to his, allowing his hands to slide slowly over her body.

His breathing was deeper now, as his kisses covered her eyelids, her cheeks, and moved from the pulse in her throat to where the neckline of her gown dipped above the swelling of her breasts. His hands had moved down to the gentle curves of her hips and now they were firmly, urgently pushing her closer against him.

Her arms slid about his neck and her heart pounded wildly within her. With a will of its own, she felt her body move in response against his and as it did he raised his head and she caught a glimpse of his eyes. No desire rested in their smokey depths, only icy cold contempt!

"Slut!" he growled, pushing her away from him. "Always ready and willing, aren't you?"

Stunned, she gave a little moan. "I love you . . ."

"And did you love Ramsden, too? And God knows how many others while I was in prison?"

She slapped him hard across the cheek. She was well aware that he had been as aroused as she. How could he accuse her . . .

His eyes glittered angrily down at her. "The typical indignant reaction. You've learned quickly, Angela. You'll fit in beautifully with Castlemaine and Quillby and all the other little whores here in this rotten cesspool of a court."

It took all her strength to draw herself up proudly. "Since you care to believe the worst of me, I don't think there is any more for us to say to one another, is there? Good day, Your Grace."

She started to brush past him, but he grasped her arm, stopping her.

"You'll not run away from me, Angela," he said tightly. "I fully intend to honor my commitment. I'll marry you as soon as the arrangements can be made."

"You—you can't mean that?" she gasped.

"Oh, I mean every word. I may henceforth be regarded as slime for killing a man when his back was turned, but no one can say the Duke of Claridge breaks his promises."

He stood before her, his face strong and proud, a muscle working in his jaw and Elizabeth fought a battle between flinging the truth in his arrogant face or letting him continue to believe the lies.

She threw up her head and looked at him defiantly. "I would not marry you if you got down on your knees and begged me to."

"You can be assured I would never do that," he snorted.

"Then so be it," she declared. "The betrothal is broken. Now, if you will release my arm—"

But he was looking down at it. She had opened her hand and for the first time he noticed the vivid birthmark on her palm. He stared at it. He had kissed that palm when Angela had agreed to marry him and he could have sworn there had been no mark on it.

Elizabeth saw the look of surprise in his eyes and managed to disengage her arm. She tossed her head. "Solve the riddle yourself," she said, and removing his cloak from about her shoulders, she flung it at him and lifting her skirts, ran back down the path.

Chapter Twenty-seven

In the hansom coach on the way back to her rooms, Elizabeth seethed with anger. How could Simon have accused her and treated her the way he had when she had risked everything to save his life? He had never given her the least chance to explain. He had seemed bent on nothing but hurting her and crushing her pride. Why had she ever thought he loved her? If he *had* felt affection for her, it had long since disappeared when he had decided to believe the worst about her. Yet it had *not* been her he had seen that night with Ramsden, but Angela. And knowing Ramsden, Elizabeth could not believe Angela had gone willingly to his arms. Why had Simon believed it?

But what did it matter now? She gave a little sob. She would never see him again anyway. A sudden sense of desolation filled her and tears stung her eyes. The rest of the way home she alternated between weeping for Simon and raging at his lack of faith. Neither brought her comfort.

When the coach reached her rooms, Elizabeth sat still for a long moment numbly staring at the sign that hung above the door. What was she going to do now? It did not take Devina, the Soothsayer, to tell her that in the past weeks her bag of coins had been sadly depleted. Should she go back to telling fortunes or return to Neville Hall? Simon was in her past now. She had no time to mourn him. Perhaps she should go far away. It had once been her plan to travel to the colonies. Perhaps there she would be able to escape the vivid memories of a tall, broad-shouldered giant with a lazy grin.

Claridge strode into his own apartments and slammed the door behind him. He tossed his cloak onto a chair and headed for a side table in front of the windows where there was a tray containing a crystal decanter and some goblets. Pouring himself a goodly portion of brandy, he swallowed deeply.

How had he allowed the little wanton to get such a hold on him? He wondered. Damn the wench! She had nearly driven him mad this afternoon. Mad with desire. Mad with longing. Yet his pride had made him strike out at her. Wanting to hurt her as he had been hurt. He would never forget how stricken she had looked when he had pushed her away from him. He drained his glass.

"Calmer now?" asked a familiar voice and Claridge spun quickly around to see his friend, Musgrove, leaning back in a chair and watching him.

"How the devil . . ."

Musgrove shrugged. "Told your man you were expecting me."

"I'm in no mood for company, John."

"I gather you were your usual autocratic self and didn't give the poor lass a chance to explain."

"Damn it, John! What do you know about all this?"

"Only a little, I'm afraid. Only what Elizabeth could tell me."

"Elizabeth?"

"Aye, your little Beth. The lass you just met in the Privy Garden. The lass who saved your miserable hide this morning."

"You know I'm not the most patient man, Musgrove. Either you tell me what you know, or so help me, I'll . . ."

As Claridge took a few angry steps in his friend's direction, Musgrove threw up his hands in mock surrender.

"I fully intend to, if you will only calm down," he said, as Claridge stood menacingly before him. " 'Tis all very simple when you realize that Elizabeth and Angela are identical twins."

"Twins!" Claridge exclaimed and then, remembering the birthmark, he murmured to himself, "I should have known."

He threw himself into an armchair across from Musgrove as his friend went on.

"Elizabeth was apparently given away to the Faircloughs at birth, and only recently learned of Angela's existence. The little gypsy, Beth, whom you encountered at the fair and fell in love with, was in reality, Elizabeth. The sad-eyed Snow Maid you asked to marry you was Angela. Although they look identical, their natures are so different that that should have been an indication to you."

"I *did* notice a difference," Claridge groaned. "I told you that. I could not understand why Angela seemed so distant. I thought she had decided to play a game. Pretend we were only meeting for the first time. Then, on the day of our betrothal party, I found her even more distant. I put it down to the fact that Hester had been to see her."

"Both twins attended the ball. Elizabeth had, by this time, learned she had a twin sister. Somehow she obtained an invitation and came to the ball dressed in a like gown to Angela's. It was only natural that she would be curious to see her sister and she must have hoped to see you as well," he added with a smile.

Claridge frowned. "The two were dressed indentically?"

"So I believe."

"How could Beth have managed that?"

"I've no notion, but I remember thinking how different Angela was at the ball that night. You see, I had danced with her before. At your betrothal party. Now gone was the shy, remote little Snow Maid, replaced by an animated beauty who was having the time of her life. Elizabeth, of course, had replaced Angela, but none of us was aware of it."

"*I* should have been," Claridge murmured. He was thinking that it had been Beth he had taken into the little Privy Chamber that night and made love to. It had always been Beth who had come so willingly into his arms. Beth whom he had loved from the very beginning.

"I cannot tell you much more, except that Elizabeth left the ball before the murder."

"You're sure of that?" Claridge's voice was sharp.

"Perfectly sure. Why else would she think, as I did, that it must be Angela you were protecting? We both discovered Westbury had taken her home to Kent and each made the journey there to try and plead with Angela to come back and tell what she knew.

I arrived first and learned that Angela was still in shock and would see no one. I was at my wit's end to try and think of a way to save you, but Elizabeth, after trying to get through to her sister, made up her mind what to do."

"She decided to get up in court and pretend she

was her sister," Claridge said. An expression of revelation crossed his face as he realized what she had done for him. No one, until Beth, had ever loved him that much.

"In court today, she told what she thought must have happened that night. She perjured herself to save you, Simon."

"And I thought she lied to save herself."

"She wasn't even in the Palace when it happened. But someone else was at the scene. Someone, I discovered, who was prepared to come forward at the eleventh hour if need be."

Simon looked surprised. "Who was that?"

"Hester Quillby."

"Hester! What had she to do with it?"

"She claimed she was returning along the gallery that night and overheard a sword fight below. Before she could see who was dueling, she noticed Angela on the landing, looking dazed and dishevelled. However, not wanting to get involved in something that was none of her business, she discreetly slipped away."

Claridge looked incredulous. "And you believed that? Good lord, John, there's no worse gossip in all of Whitehall than Hester. She would die rather than *not* know what was going on and who was involved. And what the devil," he frowned, "was she doing around Ramsden's apartments at that hour?"

"A rendezvous with someone else, perhaps? You *had* been ignoring her, Simon. Yet," Musgrove rubbed a thumb and finger along his jaw, "I did have the feeling she wasn't telling me everything."

"Hester delights in being devious."

"She is also very jealous. Why else would she go to see Angela before the betrothal party and brag to her about your relationship? She probably hoped it would make her want to call everything off."

"I suppose I should have confronted Hester when I heard about that. I was angry enough. But," Claridge shrugged, "I simply decided, henceforth, to stay as far away from her as possible."

"Which made her resolve more than ever to get you back."

"You think that?" Claridge frowned.

"I think you owe it to me to tell me exactly what occurred that night."

Claridge sighed. "I'll tell you, but I see little to be gained. It's all over now."

"Not quite. There is always the possibility we can completely clear your name."

Claridge proceeded to tell his friend what had happened from the time he had entered the hall on his way to his apartments to the conclusion of the duel when he had flung his sword away in disgust at the appearance of Angela.

"Stop there," Musgrove commanded. "Just *where* did you fling your sword?"

"I have no idea. Toward the stairs, I believe."

"You believe?"

"My eyes didn't follow it."

"Did you not hear it crash down? Perhaps bounce or roll down the stairs?"

"Not that I can remember."

"Odd," Musgrove frowned. "And you say Angela's gown was torn from one shoulder and she appeared dazed with drink. Don't you think that pretty much out of character for your Snow Maid?"

"Very much so, but you see . . . I thought . . ."

"What *did* you think?"

"How can I explain? She—Elizabeth that is—possesses a very . . . passionate nature."

"Devil take it, because of this you equate her with the other loose wenches at court? Believe she would go straight from your arms to Ramsden's? You sell not only Elizabeth, but yourself pretty short, my friend."

"I didn't want to think it was so, but there she stood before me looking as though she had just tumbled from that bastard's bed."

"But your Beth had already left the Palace. That was poor Angela you saw on the stairs. Only God knows what he'd put her through. She was dazed and half out of her head by then."

"I see it all now, dammit! I escorted Angela to the ball and at the first opportunity, she sent me off to fetch her a glass of wine and conveniently disappeared."

"We now know she was never seen again, for

374

Beth appeared to take her place. But where then did Angela go? Did Ramsden abduct her? It is crucial we find that out."

"At the moment, John, all I care about is finding Elizabeth. I must beg her forgiveness." Claridge got to his feet.

"You know where she lives?"

Claridge had started to cross the room, now he stopped and turned back to his friend. "My God, John! Where *do* I find her?"

Musgrove shook his head. "I only saw her here . . . in the Privy Garden."

"Damn the luck! Where do I look? In the past few months, I've spent half my time searching for her."

Musgrove grinned. "You could start with the halberdiers outside the gates. Perhaps they could tell you which way she was headed when she left the garden."

One of the guards remembered the girl in the garish costume. He had stopped a hansom coach for her. The one Old Bert drove, he explained to Claridge. Old Bert was a fixture, it appeared, in the area of King Street. He—but there was no need to say more. That was his coach now, coming along the drive.

Hester Quillby had been joyous to see the

contempt on Simon's face when Elizabeth spoke up at the trial. She was quite sure the chit would never be a threat to her again.

But early that afternoon, a friend brought a message to her. He had overheard a conversation between Musgrove and Claridge in the anteroom adjoining the King's private chambers. It seemed Claridge had an appointment at three o'clock in the Privy Garden to meet the lady who had saved his life. The friend thought Lady Quillby might be interested in the information. Lady Quillby was indeed.

She did not directly observe the meeting between Elizabeth and Simon, but instead waited in the shadows of the Stone Gallery, where she could view the entrance to the Privy Garden. Unobserved, she saw the three enter the garden individually. It was when Musgrove departed soon afterward, a smug expression on his face, that Hester became apprehensive. What if Simon were attracted to the girl? He had obviously been attracted to Angela, who was her very image. Hester's mind whirled. She must put a stop to this before it was too late!

Elizabeth wiped away the traces of tears from her face as the hansom driver opened the coach door for her. She alighted quickly, noticing as she paid her fare that another coach had pulled up behind them.

As her own vehicle disappeared around the corner of the street, a huge man in the livery of a footman descended from the newly arrived coach and intercepted her before she reached her door.

"Elizabeth Fairclough?" he asked.

"I am she," Elizabeth said, without thinking. She was anxious to get inside. Without a cloak, the cool autumn air was chilling her.

"I have someone in my coach who would like to see you," he told her, indicating the vehicle.

Without hesitating, Elizabeth walked back to it and bent to look inside the open door. The window blinds had been lowered and she narrowed her eyes to see in the dimness. Caught off guard, she was given a hard push from behind and sent tumbling into the back seat. The big man jumped in after her and slammed the door. Immediately the horses started forward.

Elizabeth could hardly credit what had happened. It had all occurred so quickly. She had fallen forward on the seat, but before she could move, a thick cloth was tied about her head, blindfolding her completely.

She struggled with all her strength as her hands were forced behind her back and roughly tied. When the man attempted to secure her ankles, she kicked out at him and he cursed and hit her hard on the side of the head. Overcome with dizziness, Elizabeth was afraid she would faint, but he yanked her up into a sitting position beside him.

"Sit still and don't move or oi'll give ye more o'that," he growled.

Her head reeling with pain, Elizabeth did as she was told.

The man did not speak again, but she heard a movement across from her and realized that there was someone else in the coach with them. A woman, she thought, catching the scent of her perfume. It was musky and heavy.

Beside her the man took the object he had been handed by the woman and put it up to Elizabeth's mouth.

"Drink!" he ordered.

She caught the smell of rum as the flask was thrust between her lips and tilted back.

Elizabeth tried to writhe away, sputtering and choking, as the burning liquid was poured down her throat. The rum ran from her mouth, trickling down her chin and she began to gag.

The flask was removed and she tried desperately to get her breath, before it was shoved into her mouth again. Forced to swallow more of the rum, or risk choking to death, she gulped as much as she could. Her chin and throat became wet with the liquid that spilled from her mouth and she felt it running down her neck and between her breasts.

Grabbing one of her shoulders with a hard hand, the man jammed a cloth into her mouth with the other. "That'll keep ye quiet," he said harshly.

Elizabeth could do nothing. Only once before had she felt so helpless. That had been when she had been accused of witchcraft and dragged by an ugly mob to be tied at the stake.

Simon had saved her then, but this time there was no one to save her. She was totally on her own.

Her mind was spinning with the effects of the strong rum she had been forced to swallow. She could not seem to think coherently. Who could have planned this kidnapping? She wondered. And why? She had no money. What was the purpose? And more important, what was to be done with her?

She felt like a small insect caught in a spider's web, and every instinct told her that the spider, itself, was sitting across from her, relishing every moment of her discomfort. She could almost feel the hatred in the air. Dear God, what woman hated her so much?

Hester Quillby, said a voice inside her. Aye, it had to be Hester Quillby. The woman must have thought Angela was behind all that had happened to Claridge and hated her for it. Hated her enough to try and ... But what *did* the woman plan to do with her?

She couldn't think straight. Nothing made any sense. There was something else ... something that was there just below the surface and she couldn't seem to recall.

Then it came to her! If Hester had really

thought she was Angela, why had she come to Elizabeth's rooms? She must know that Elizabeth had posed as Angela today. But how could that be possible?

Her brain was too fuzzy. She couldn't seem to think any more. And besides it took an effort to keep her eyes open behind the blindfold. She would just doze a little. Perhaps when she woke up everything would be clearer.

Questioning Bert, the hansom coach driver, Claridge learned where he had taken Elizabeth and promptly directed him to return there. When they arrived before the rooms of Devina the Soothsayer, he bade the driver wait, but after knocking several times at the door, and receiving no answer, he was forced to head back to the coach.

"Did you see the lady enter?" he asked the driver.

Bert shook his head. "Another coach pulled up behind mine as the gypsy was payin' me. A footman from it was approachin' her as I drove away.

"Did she get into the other coach?"

"I did not see, milord," Bert said, wondering why a simple gypsy woman would interest such a grand gentleman.

"I did," piped up a small voice.

Claridge looked down to see a ragged urchin of

six or seven emerge from a darkened doorway nearby. He reached into his pocket and held a coin up before the lad's face.

"Just what did you see?" he asked.

The boy's hand snaked out in a quick grab for the coin, but Claridge was too fast for him.

"Nay," he said, "I'll pay you gladly, lad, but first, tell me what you saw."

"The last time I speaks first the cove went off without payin' me a penny."

"I'll pay you if what you tell me is true."

" 'Tis true. I'll swear to that." The boy looked closely at Claridge and deciding to trust him started in.

"As soon as 'e drives off," he nodded at Bert, the big cove from the coach goes over to the gypsy lady and says somethin' to 'er. She walks back wi' him to the open door o' the coach and looks in. Wi' that, the big cove gives 'er a shove inside, jumps in after 'er slammin' the door and the coach takes off."

"Good lord! She was abducted!" Claridge exclaimed. He turned to the boy, trying to keep his voice calm as he asked: "Think, lad. Have you any idea where the coach could have been headed?"

"I might 'ave."

Claridge produced another coin.

"If 'twas me, milord. I'd try down by the docks," the boy grinned.

The two gold coins gleamed as they were spun through the air and deftly caught.

With a nod to Bert, Claridge jumped back into the coach and they were soon off down the street. The young lad stood gazing at his open palm. "Two golden guineas!" he murmured in awe.

Chapter Twenty-eight

Elizabeth awoke when the coach stopped. In the distance she could hear the sound of a ship's bell. They must be down by the waterfront, she thought.

The man beside her hissed in her ear, "don't ye dare to move 'till I gets back or I swear I'll 'it ye twice as 'ard!"

With that she heard the coach door open and felt the vehicle dip to the side as the big man stepped down. His heavy footsteps echoed over rough cobbles as he walked away.

A moment later she heard him hail someone. "Ho, ye there, Captain!"

She heard no more from outside the coach. Inside, the woman sitting across from her cleared her throat. Elizabeth wished she would speak so that she could be sure it was Hester Quillby who was behind her kidnapping.

Several minutes passed before the man returned and opening the door of the coach, said to the woman, " 'e'll take 'er. 'Tis a tradin' ship bound for the Guinea coasts with a load o' trade goods. Then," he gave a harsh laugh, "over to Jamaica with its "human cargo."

"Perfect," was all the woman said, but Elizabeth was almost certain of Hester Quillby's deep tone.

A bag of coins must have been passed to the man, for now Elizabeth heard the dull clink of them.

"The Cap'n should be 'appy wi' that," the man chuckled. " 'e'll see a duel profit with 'er. There are black kings in Guinea who will pay well for such a one. No wonder 'e's so glad to oblige." He laughed again, a short, cruel laugh that made Elizabeth's blood run cold.

She was to be transported away on a ship sailing for Africa—sold as a slave for barbarians to use for their pleasure! She shuddered at the thought. She had to find a way to escape from the ship before it weighed anchor!

Again Elizabeth was roughly seized and this time a mantle was cast over her head and firmly wrapped around her. She felt herself lifted off the seat of the coach and the next moment slung over one of the big man's shoulders, head down.

She bounced uncomfortably as the man strode off along the quay. Even with the covering over her head, a foul smell came to Elizabeth's nostrils as they approached the ship, a smell that reminded her of the stench of animals in a pen.

Elizabeth's head dropped lower as the big man ascended a gangway and reaching the deck of the ship stopped.

A deep voice close by demanded, "Give it here!"

Elizabeth felt herself being shifted a little and again heard the sound of coins clinking together as the bag was passed over.

"Thank 'ee, friend," the other sounded pleased. "Now get her down below fast."

The big man's steps rang hollowly on the wooden deck as he carried his burden over to what must have been an open hatch, for he began to descend a ladder. It must lead down to the hold of the ship, Elizabeth thought. When he reached firm footing again he walked a few steps and then dumped Elizabeth down hard onto the wooden planking.

The mantle was roughly yanked from around her and in so doing her blindfold was dislodged from her eyes. It was so dark, Elizabeth could barely see the big man's outline as he retreated up the ladder. She heard him slide back the hatch and then she began to struggle to sit up.

She almost retched from the putrid smell all around her. Slowly, things came into focus in the dim light of a single lantern, hanging from a ceiling beam.

Cargo was stacked in barrels, kegs, and bails all

around her. Along each side of the ship, halfway between the deck and the low ceiling, stretched a wooden shelf about six feet deep. Chains and manacles hung down from these shelves and fastened in intervals to the deck were dozens more.

"A slave ship!" Elizabeth shuddered. That was the human cargo of whom the big man had spoken. The stench that permeated the ship was not animal, but human! The blacks that were taken out of Africa, must be chained and manacled and stowed in layers, some on the deck, some on the shelves above. They were treated more like beasts than human beings!

Elizabeth knew nothing about Africans and had heard little about the African trade, but the horror of these poor people who were brought and sold and brutalized in this way, was suddenly brought home to her.

She was going to be sold in much the same way! Dear God in heaven, how was she to get away from here before the ship sailed? Her head pounded from the rum and the blow she had received.

Nothing had ever been easy for her since the day she'd been born. Over and over again she had been cast aside, forced to flee, obliged to rely on her own resources. And over and over again she had survived. She would survive this. But she must not panic. She must use her head.

She looked up at a square grating in the low

ceiling and saw that it was still daylight, but being autumn the sun would be setting early and soon it would be dark.

Darting around the crowded hold, Elizabeth's eyes came to rest on the bulkhead. There was an empty iron hook jutting out of the heavy wood in a position just above her head. She must get over to it!

Because her ankles were tied, she was forced to squirm across the rough wooden planking in a sitting position thankful for the bulky skirts of her gypsy costume to protect her flesh from splinters.

When she reached the bulkhead, she struggled onto one elbow and pushing herself up, managed to gain her knees. The hook was now right beside her mouth. Reaching over, she moved her lips against it, pressing it into the folds of the kerchief that had been used to gag her, then pulling her head back. The hook became entangled in the cloth and with a quick jerk of her head, Elizabeth dislodged it.

She spat out what remained of the kerchief and it fell to the deck below her. Her tongue felt dry as she ran it over her lips and the roof of her mouth hurt where the cloth had been tightly jammed between her teeth. Her throat was so parched and dry, she would have given anything in that moment for a cool drink of water.

But she knew she must work quickly. She had

no time to lose. The cargo was loaded, so the ship might weigh anchor at any time!

Again she used the bulkhead to her advantage. She sat down again rather heavily, forcing her back against the heavy wooden support. Raising her knees so that her feet were on the floor, she worked her buttocks slowly up the side of the bulkhead, bringing her tied ankles in close until she was standing. The hook was now just above her tied hands.

Lifting her hands behind her back, she began to work the heavy metal hook into the knot of the rope, pulling gently, releasing, pulling some more.

Suddenly, Elizabeth heard the creaking of timbers above her head and a shiver of fear ran through her. She tried to hurry and only succeeded in scraping her wrist with the sharp hook. She felt a warm trickle of blood run across her hand.

"Who be in the hold?" she heard a harsh voice above her ask.

She ceased her exertions and remained poised, listening.

"Only a rum-sodden wench, I'm told. Let's hope she be young enough to pleasure us all on the long trip to Guinea."

An ugly laugh broke out. "What's t' stop us now?"

"Would ye be givin' up yer last evenin' ashore for *that*, Josh? There's plenty o' young, willin' wenches at the Crown and Anchor."

"None wot smiles at an ugly bloke like me. Besides, the tide turns at eleven and we must catch the ebb."

"We'll be back in plenty o' time. The wench below'll keep."

Their laughter drifted back to Elizabeth as they moved away.

Knowledge of this new horror made the terror she had striven so hard to control overwhelm Elizabeth completely. Nausea rose in her throat at the thought of what the rough crew on this ship might do to her. You must not think of it. She told herself. You must concentrate wholly on getting free.

Trying to calm herself, she was reminded that there were still several hours before the ship sailed. A lot could be accomplished in several hours.

Again she worked the knot over the hook, pulling, releasing, pulling. Her wrists were rubbed raw by the coarse rope, but she would not give up. She gritted her teeth and worked on.

Claridge was convinced that Elizabeth had been spirited aboard a ship. He searched up and down the waterfront until he had narrowed it down to a three-masted, square-rigged vessel berthed alongside a wharf just east of the Tower of London. The Sally Jane's prow faced downstream and she was lying low in the water as if fully laden. Her sails, he noticed, were loosened, but not unfurled. It seemed obvious to him that she was planning to sail shortly. He instructed Bert, the coach driver, to take him immediately back to Whitehall. Alone, his sword would be as good as useless against the whole ship's crew. Yet, it would take time to find the ship's owner and rouse the proper authorities. Instead, he would seek the support of Musgrove and some of his more adventuresome friends. A show of strength would indeed be needed if he wished to board and search the Sally Jane.

At long last, Elizabeth managed to free her hands and now she worked at the rope about her ankles. It was growing darker outside, she noticed, with a glance upward at the grating. The time had grown short. Soon the sailors on shore would be returning and they would be setting sail. At last her trembling fingers unfastened the rope and she was free. She stamped her feet as quietly as she could on the wooden floor of the hold, hoping to restore a normal coursing of blood through her veins. After a few moments she began to move about.

This was going to be her greatest task. She must find a way to get off the ship without being observed. She headed for the ladder.

Hope springs eternal in the human breast, and having released herself from her bonds, she felt quite optimistic about getting free of the ship. If only the man who had kidnapped her had been careless enough or confident enough to leave the hatch above unfastened. She could then open it a crack to see how many were keeping watch on deck and her best means of escape.

Elizabeth climbed the ladder until she could reach above her head with her hands. She tried to move the hatch. She had heard the big man slide it closed. She attempted to move it sideways. She tried to lift it. She pushed it this way and that. It would not budge! It must, she thought with a sinking heart, be fastened on the other side!

What could she do? She felt like banging on the hatch and screaming. She felt like bursting into tears. Her fingers were bloody and her nails torn from attempting to lift the rough wooden cover. Wearily, she climbed back down the ladder.

There was one more option open to her. She could try to maneuver one of the barrels over to the place below the grating, where she could climb up and see if she could loosen the screen. It was her last chance!

The closest barrel was about six feet away from the opening. Putting her shoulder to the heavy barrel, she pushed with all her might. It moved only a few inches. She tried again. Again it barely moved.

Her long fair hair was getting in her eyes, so Elizabeth went back to the bulkhead and retrieved the kerchief she had dropped there. She tied it about her head in gypsy fashion, completely covering her hair, and went back to where the barrel stood.

The light from the lantern illuminated the cover on it as she approached, and Elizabeth noticed that there was a slight split in the wooden top. Perhaps if she could pry it open and remove some of the goods inside, she might be able to push it more easily into position below the grating.

Working her bloody fingertips into the crack in the wood, Elizabeth managed with a little effort to pull off the top of the barrel. There must be something heavy in the bottom, she decided, for on top there were only bolts of brightly printed cotton and some colorful fringed shawls.

She was struggling to remove one of the bolts, when she heard the sound of heavy footsteps above her head. Someone was walking towards the hatch! The footsteps stopped and Elizabeth held her breath. There was a scraping sound as the hatch door was opened. Someone was coming down into the hold!

Elizabeth's mind raced. Should she pretend to tie herself up again? No! She had a better idea. Marta had once told her that seamen were a very superstitious lot. She desperately hoped this was true! Grabbing one of the shawls from the barrel, she ducked into the recess behind the ladder.

Holding a lantern in one hand and peering cautiously about him, a sailor slowly descended the ladder. When he reached the bottom, he turned, so that the light illumined his face. It was heavy jowled, with a nose that had been broken so often it now lay almost flat against his pock-marked face. The man was not tall, but heavily built. To Elizabeth, he did not look like someone who would be very easily intimidated.

"Where the devil . . . ?" he said thickly, looking about him, and then he spied the pile of rope before the bulkhead. He started over to it, with a slightly uneven gait. He had just come from the Crown and Anchor where he had been imbibing pretty freely. Where was the wench? He wondered. Had she escaped?

"I'm here," Elizabeth said in her hoarse, gypsy voice as she stepped out from behind the ladder.

The sailor whirled about, a knife suddenly appearing in his hand.

"No need for that," she said quietly.

The sailor stared at her, his eyes almost bulging as she came into the light of his lantern.

A gypsy! The wench was a gypsy! There she stood in her bright gown and shawl and the eyes that stared at him from her dark face seemed to pierce right through him. A cold finger of fear ran down his spine.

Elizabeth had managed to rub dirt from the floor beneath the ladder over her already dusty face and hands. Unblinkingly she continued to regard him.

"Your name is Josh, isn't it?" she asked him.

He nodded mutely, his eyes as wide as saucers.

"You see, Jose, no bonds can hold me," she told him. "Do you know why?"

Speechless, he could only shake his head.

"Because I am in league with the devil," she hissed between her teeth.

The sailor started and took a frightened step backwards.

"Look," she said, her eyes glittering in the dim light. "See this mark on the palm of my hand? Do you know what it means?"

Again he shook his head. His hands were trembling so hard, he set down the lantern.

"Look closely. Do you see the cloven hoof? 'Tis the devil's mark. Through him I can administer evil."

The seaman's eyes were enormous now in his pale face.

"Wh–what would ye have me do? he stuttered.

"Lead my way off this ship," she said quietly. "But you must make very sure we are not seen. If we should be stopped . . . , if I should be taken prisoner again . . . , I would put a terrible curse on you. A curse that would haunt you and not give you a moment's peace for the rest of your miserable life." She said each word slowly, menacingly.

"I — I'll get ye off safely," the sailor managed.

"Then see to it."

"We must wait for the lookout to pass."

They waited in silence until they heard footsteps over their heads and a hoarse voice calling out, "All quiet!"

Several voices answered faintly from other areas of the ship. "All quiet!" . . . "All quiet!"

The footsteps receded.

Elizabeth nodded to the seaman. "You go first," she said, indicating the ladder.

He began to scale it and Elizabeth climbed quickly after him. At the top, he peered out of the hatch and then made a motion for her to follow him.

All was darkness on deck, except for a lantern shining in the rigging above which swayed in the light breeze coming off the river. Dancing beams from it shone across the empty deck.

Moving stealthily, the two made their way to the wharfside of the ship.

"Climb over," the sailor muttered. "The gangway will be watched."

Elizabeth looked down to see that the quay lay only a few feet below the deck of the laden ship. She didn't hesitate, but went quickly over the side, hanging for a moment by her fingers before dropping to the hard wooden landing below.

She never looked back. Taking to her heels, Elizabeth raced down the quay and across the rough cobbles beyond, melting into the shadows of the waterside buildings.

She hoped she was headed in the right direction, but as she sprinted around a corner, a huge form suddenly loomed up out of the darkness and seized her!

Chapter Twenty-nine

"Not so fast!" a deep voice demanded. "Did you come off the Sally Jane?"

The wild struggling ceased.

"Simon!" Elizabeth gave an anguished cry of relief.

"Beth?" he asked incredulously, forcing her to step out into the light from a nearby window. "It *is* you," he exclaimed, pulling the kerchief from her head. Her long, silky hair fell in silvery disarray about her shoulders.

What was the matter with her? Elizabeth thought. Why was she so glad to see him when he had treated her so badly? Why did the sight of him make her feel so safe and secure? Her head went up. She wasn't about to let him know how she felt.

"Let me go!" she cried, fighting the weakness she always felt when he was near.

He ignored her protests and her renewed struggle to be free of his grasp.

"How the devil did you manage to escape?" he growled. He had never been so relieved in his life as to have her unharmed and safe in his arms. "I was afraid I wouldn't find you in time," he added in a more gentle tone.

"Were you? I would have thought you'd be happy to be rid of me."

"You thought wrong." He brought his lips down hard on hers and drew her closer to him. He could feel her body straining against his, straining to be free. He merely tightened the grip as she began to fight him, pounding at his shoulders with her fists, kicking wildly at his shins. His mouth pressed down more fiercely, moving until the lips beneath his gave at last.

She no longer had the strength to fight him. All her anger, her hurt, evaporated as the warmth of his nearness thawed the chill of bitter reproaches and cruel accusations.

"Damn you, Simon!" Humiliated by her reaction to him, she started to cry He held her close as she buried her face against his broad shoulder and sobbed. He rocked her gently and murmured words of endearment to her which made her cry even more, feeling that lean body pressed against hers, those strong arms so tenderly cradling her. It had been so long. So very long, since he had held her so lovingly.

Musgrove and the other men appeared before Claridge, having become worried that he—out to scout the strength on board the Sally Jane — had not returned. Seeing Beth firmly clasped in his arms they grinned and at a sign from Claridge behind Beth's back, quietly retraced their steps. A few minutes later, the sound of horses hooves could be heard moving off down the cobblestone street.

"You escaped just in time," Simon murmured. "The ship sails on the tide."

"I know," she said, trembling at the thought of what could have happened to her if she had not escaped. At the little hiccuping sob she made, he lifted her chin from his shoulder, his heart turning over as he saw her grimy, tear-streaked face.

"Hush, my sweet. Hush. 'Tis all over now," he whispered, gently wiping her cheeks with his handkerchief.

"Why did you come?" she asked.

"I think you know. Musgrove told me everything. I had to find you. Apologize for my loutish behavior . . . the despicable things I said to you."

"You want my forgiveness?"

"I want you. I'll never let you go again, Beth. Never!"

Her arms crept around him and he felt her clasp him tight, surrendering at last to his strength after the many hours she had been forced to rely on her own.

He bent his head and kissed her tear drenched cheeks and lips. Kissed her again and again.

"Every hour of every day I spent in the Tower

you were with me. I alternated between cursing you and longing for you. You have no idea what agony and despair you put me through."

"Oh, Simon," she whispered.

So intoxicating were his kisses that she soon forgot where she was, overcome with longing as he crushed her to him.

"This is no place for loving," he grunted, as a door slammed and angry, raucous voices were heard arguing close by.

With a strong arm about her waist he hurried her back along a dark alleyway to where Satan waited in the shadows.

"I never remember to bring a white horse, do I?" he grinned.

She managed her first smile as he lifted her onto the saddle and swung easily up behind her, wrapping his warm cloak about them both.

"Where are to taking me?" she asked, as he spurred Satan away from the wharves.

"To my apartments. I believe a hot bath is in order." He chuckled. "You smell like a rum-soaked sailor."

" 'Tis no wonder. I almost drowned in what was poured down my throat. I suppose they wanted me dazed when I was carried aboard ship."

"You must tell me everything later. At the moment, 'tis enough to hold you close to me again." His lips brushed her forehead as Elizabeth settled back against his broad chest.

She tried to reassure herself that she was not

dreaming as they rode through the dark streets in the direction of Whitehall Palace. Every now and then she glanced back at Simon, a surge of joy sweeping through her veins when he smiled at her.

Claridge's living quarters at Whitehall were large and well furnished. At first glance his man-servant regarded Elizabeth's gaudy gypsy attire with some consternation, but looking closer he recognized her with some surprise as his master's betrothed, the Lady Angela. This lady had saved His Grace's life and he bowed low before her.

"I will send for a maid to attend you, milady."

"Not tonight, Fielding. Set up a bath for milady in the west chamber and in the meantime bring us some brandy."

He ushered Elizabeth into the sitting room where a fire was burning brightly, and soon they stood before it, facing each other.

There was so much they had to say to one another and yet as they stood silently gazing at each other, neither spoke a word. Words, at that moment, seemed a poor expression of all that filled their hearts. Smiling, Simon at last held his arms out to her and Elizabeth moved naturally into them.

They had been so near, so very near to being wrested apart forever. The magic of their reunion engulfed them both as they clung to each other.

"My sweet Beth," he whispered, "I never did stop loving you." He bent his head to kiss her but was stopped by a knock at the door and Fielding's announcement that milady's bath was ready.

Her long hair pinned to the top of her head, Elizabeth luxuriated in the warm, scented water. She gave a blissful sigh of pleasure as the heat spread deliciously over her bruised body. Picking up a cake of fragrant soap, she had just begun scrubbing herself and was struggling to reach her back, when the door beside her opened.

Simon stood there, his big frame almost filling the doorway. He was dressed in a wine colored dressing robe and was holding a brandy goblet in his hand.

"May I be of assistance?" he asked, grinning in the way that Elizabeth found so devastating.

He set down his glass and taking the soap from Elizabeth's hands, leaned over the tub. Soapy fingers trailed lazily over her shoulders as he began to lather her neck and she felt her skin warming and glowing beneath his touch. His sensitive hands began to massage the tired muscles of her back and with a long sigh, she relaxed and let him gently kneed them.

When he was through, Simon held out a large soft towel and Elizabeth felt no embarrassment as she slipped from the water and let him envelop her in it. Gently he rubbed her down, until her skin was flushed and tingling.

"You make a perfect lady's maid," she smiled at him as he swung her up into his arms and carried her through to the bedchamber. Tenderly, he deposited her on a thick fur rug before the fire, where a fresh log burned brightly, filling the room with cozy warmth.

"I want to see you," he said, huskily. "Every inch of you. You've always been hidden from me before."

He removed the towel, and she lay before him naked in the firelight, the flames illuminating her breathtaking beauty. The breath caught in his throat as he gazed down at her and she saw the pupils darken in his eyes as they viewed the full, high breasts that emphasized the smallness of her waist, the gently rounded hips, the long shapely legs, the silver triangle.

"No one could be more lovely," he said in awe, his voice deep with love and desire. His mouth covered hers and he kissed her almost roughly before nestling his face in her neck, nibbling the softness of her white shoulders.

She looked up at him from under her thick, dark lashes with a glance that was ingenuously seductive, as the longing pulsated through her body for this dark, handsome man who could raise her to such heights of ecstasy.

She watched as he stripped off his robe, curiosity mingling with desire as his hard, muscular body was revealed to her. How magnificent he was! Perfectly proportioned from his wide shoulders and broad chest to his lean hips and long, firmly muscled thighs. The reality of his masculinity made her shiver slightly.

He knelt for a moment looking down at her, the fire reflecting in dark eyes now burning with a fire of their own.

Delightful tremors ran through her body as his hands continued to explore the soft curves and hollows more and more intimately. Feeling a desperate need of him, she arched herself like a sensuous cat, writhing against him as he rained kisses in a hot trail down her twisting body. She moaned at the touch of his lips and his hands, crying out for him to hurry.

His flesh burned against her as his hands folded her under him. Blind to everything but her need, Elizabeth urgently directed one who needed no direction.

Locked together before the roaring fire, they moved in joyous harmony, doubt and suspicion lovingly laid to rest between them. The passion that stirred them grew greater, wilder, until it entirely encompassed them both, taking them to a world of their own where they gave everything to each other, holding nothing back.

Afterwards, they lay entwined, drowsy, warm, and sated on the hearth rug.

Elizabeth gave a contented sigh, thinking how wonderfully happy she was.

Simon, looking down at her thought she had never looked more beautiful. A radiance seemed to light up her whole face.

"Happy?" he asked.

"Gloriously," she answered. "I feel as if I've finally come home . . . as if everything is going to be all right from now on."

"It will." He pulled her closer to him, curling his strong body around hers.

She felt her heart overflowing with love for him and buried her face against his warm chest. If they could only stay like this forever, she thought.

Later, much later, they sat before the same fireplace contentedly devouring the last of the supper Fielding had brought them.

Elizabeth was now clad in a deep blue velvet robe of Simon's, the long sleeves rolled up. The soft candlelight illuminated her face as she smiled at him from across the little table.

"Now you must tell me something that has been troubling me. How did you find me tonight?"

"One of the halberdiers at the gate pointed out to me the hansom driver who had taken you home. I hired him to repeat the journey and he drove me to the rooms of Devina the Soothsayer — which I decided must be your latest identity — only to find you gone. Fortunately, a young lad had witnessed your abduction. He thought the coach had headed off in the direction of the docks. Carefully searching the waterfront, I then discovered the Sally Jane ready to sail. If one wished to be rid of someone, a ship about to weigh anchor seemed the logical choice."

"So when I ran into you you were about to come on board and play the knight errant again, rescuing the damsel in distress."

"Not alone. I had Musgrove and some friends to back me up, but you outsmarted us all." He looked at her proudly. "How *did* you manage to escape?"

"I was left bound and gagged in the hold," she told him. "I tried not to panic, to keep my head and I finally managed to untie myself only to have a sailor come down into the hold and discover me. I was forced to use all my gypsy wiles to make him think I was a witch and would put a curse on him if he didn't help me escape."

"A clever and resourceful witch, if I may say so," he said. "But do you know who abducted you? And why?"

"A big, powerful man did the actual deed, but Hester Quillby was the one behind it."

"What! Not that bitch again!"

"It was she who originally discovered the similarity between Angela and me. She paid Devina the Soothsayer a visit and accidently caught sight of me without my veil. She left behind an invitation to the king's ball, hoping I would be curious enough about Angela to use it."

"She must have had more than that in mind."

"A plan in which she included Lord Ramsden. I believe he must have told her of Angela's resemblance to Elizabeth Fairclough, and Hester Quillby decided I must be she."

Simon looked surprised. "You knew Ramsden before?"

"My uncle unfortunately arranged my marriage to him. I was horrified, and when Ramsden tried to force himself upon me, I ran away from home."

"So that's what happened. You masqueraded as a gypsy to hide from Ramsden. You should have told me before, Beth."

"There was much I should have told you, but my pride was hurt when, although you professed to care for me, you wanted me only as your mistress. That is why I left you at the inn."

"I was a fool," Claridge shook his head, reaching across the table to take her hand. "A stupid, bloody fool."

"You were forced into a corner by your father's pledge," she said, "and there was so much that was kept from you."

"But Ramsden—"

"With Lady Quillby devised a plot in the hope that I would take the bait and come to the Palace ball. She wanted to discredit Angela in your eyes so you would return to her, and he wanted to seek his revenge on me for spurning him."

"They both thought they were using you for their own ends that night, but in truth it was Angela that they used."

"Exactly. Poor Angela. She went into shock. Even now she still remembers naught of that night."

Claridge shook his head. "I still wonder how I could ever have thought for a moment that you and Angela were one and the same person. You cannot know how devastated I felt that night when I saw who I thought was you, half naked, staggering from Ramsden's rooms."

"Poor Simon," she whispered, putting a hand to his cheek.

"That dazed, wanton creature has haunted me waking and sleeping ever since. I did not want to believe it of you, and yet my pride was shattered. It wasn't until I spoke to Musgrove this afternoon that I learned the truth." His eyes met hers. "Will you ever forgive me, Beth?" He rose and came around the table to her side.

"I will always forgive you," she said softly. "I love you."

He reached for her then, kissing her as he lifted her up into his arms. Heading for the big four poster bed, he pulled back the coverlet and laid her down, tenderly tucking the covers about her.

He could not believe that after everything that had happened, she could still love him. There was a world of forgiveness in loving, he thought, forgiveness for all the things said and left unsaid. He vowed he would spend the rest of his life trying to make it up to her.

Blowing out the candle on the nightstand, he lay down beside her, bending to kiss her again. But in the space of that moment, her eyes had closed and her breathing had become deep and regular. Exhausted by all that had happened that day, sleep had finally overtaken her.

In the dim light from the fire, Simon could see Elizabeth's moonlight pale hair fanned out about her on the pillow. There was a faint smile on her lips. With featherlike softness, Simon kissed those sweet lips and drew her sleeping body gently against his side.

Chapter Thirty

When Elizabeth opened her eyes in the morning, bright rays of sunlight were already streaming in through the uncovered windows of the bedchamber.

It must be quite late, she thought, sitting up sleepily and gracefully stretching her arms above her head. Looking toward the door, she was startled to see a maid standing in the opening, holding a breakfast tray in her hands.

"Good morning, milady," the girl said, approaching her.

"Good morning," Elizabeth replied, her eyes darting to the bed beside her. She had awakened once in the night to find Simon's warm body close against her own. Now, he was gone, leaving only an indentation in the pillow as evidence that he had slept there.

The maid set the tray down on the nightstand in order to fluff up the pillows behind Elizabeth's shoulders.

"Your belongings have just arrived, milady. Do you wish me to brush your hair?"

Elizabeth nodded, whereupon the maid produced a hairbrush from one of the pockets of her apron and proceeded, with long, rhythmic strokes to remove the tangles from Elizabeth's hair.

The maid had made her departure and Elizabeth was half through her breakfast, when there was a knock at the door. Without waiting for an answer, Simon strode in.

"I see you have been looked after," he smiled, as he sat down on the end of the bed.

"It was kind of you to send for my things."

"I understand a young man named Jimmy was most helpful."

"He's a good lad. I asked him to keep an eye on my rooms while I was away."

"Perhaps you can still keep him in your service."

"I would like that." She took a sip of her chocolate. "Have you been up long?"

"For hours, my slug-a-bed," he grinned. "I've had a busy morning. An early audience with the king, followed by an official visit to Lady Quillby."

"You saw her?"

"I did indeed. You will be glad to hear that she is not only dismissed from court for her actions, but banished from England as well. I told her that if ever she was tempted to return, I would make it my business to see that she is charged with fraud, abduction, and whatever else is needed to put her in Newgate Prison for the rest of her days. I can assure you, you need never worry about her again."

There was a time that Elizabeth might have felt sorry for Hester Quillby. They had, after all, both suffered from the same malady—loving Simon. Each of them had been willing to go to any lengths for him. The difference had been that Elizabeth had not hurt anyone by her lie to save his life, while Angela was still suffering from the plan Hester had concocted, Ramsden was dead, and she, herself, would have suffered a fate too horrible to contemplate, if she had not managed to escape from the Sally Jane.

"I have more to tell you," Simon was saying. "I met Musgrove in the corridor. Something you mentioned to him yesterday stuck in his craw and he couldn't forget it. I had told him that after my duel with Ramsden I had thrown my sword aside and in disgust left him with Angela.

What if, Musgrove considered, Ramsden had then mounted the stairs to where Angela was standing on the landing. Remember, you mentioned to him that she had murmured something about pushing someone. Suppose, he thought, that that someone was Ramsden. Suppose she pushed him backwards down the stairs."

"I've thought of that, but it doesn't explain the sword—"

"Let me finish. Musgrove rose this morning intent on making a careful examination of that staircase. Halfway down, he told me, he found that the intricate wood carving between the stair rails had been damaged. A piece had been broken out.

"Now, think on this. Suppose when I threw my sword, the handle became lodged in the wood carving with the blade pointed upward. Could it not be possible that Ramsden, falling backward down those stairs, was impaled on the rapier? The weight of his body could then have jerked out the blade and part of the carving from the stairway might have come with it."

"If that were true," Elizabeth said, "then the piece of carving must have been found."

Claridge gave a smug smile. "It was. Musgrove inquired of the servants. It was found on the floor beside the staircase the next morning. It has yet to be repaired, as the carpenter who is experienced in such work has been ill."

Elizabeth frowned. "But could the blade have penetrated His Lordship's back deeply enough to kill him . . . just by *falling* against it?" She shuddered at the thought.

"I was a soldier, Beth. My rapier is more sharply honed than most."

" 'Tis horrible to think about — even to a man so loathsome."

"I can only thank God he never got his hands on you again."

413

"Yet my poor sister suffered in my place," Elizabeth said, compassionately. "First to be assaulted by Ramsden and then thinking she had murdered him . . . 'Tis little wonder she was so badly affected."

"Hester must have been present when Angela struggled with Ramsden, for she swears she was not raped."

Elizabeth's eyes flared. "Does she, indeed! If she were witness to it, then why did she not try to stop it?"

"Because, being Hester, she was only concerned with her own interests in the matter. I think you and I must go to Neville Hall, Beth, and strive to impart all that we have learned to Angela."

"She must be made to realize that she is not guilty. Perhaps Gerald can help her."

"Gerald?" Simon looked puzzled. "Who is Gerald?"

"The man Angela loves."

"I seem to have learned a great many things in the space of a morning," Simon said. "No wonder I sensed Angela's unhappiness when I met her, and her reticence. Why did she not tell me she loved another? I would have released her from her pledge."

"Angela has always been conscious of her duty and would never disobey our father. I was only getting to know her, Simon, when I had to leave. In my haste, I didn't even stop to say goodbye."

"You are worried about her, aren't you?"

"I am." She reached for his hand. "I cannot bear to leave you now that we have found each other again, and yet ..."

"You must go to her," he said. "I will settle things here as quickly as I can and join you. Then, I swear to you Beth, we will never be parted again."

Learning of Elizabeth's departure from Neville Hall, Angela had been quite distraught, and so, that very day, to take her mind from it, His Lordship allowed her to make a short visit to the orphanage.

Nan, the lady's maid Angela had acquired at court and who had accompanied her back to Neville Hall, drove over to the Manor House with her young mistress after being carefully instructed by His Lordship not to let her remain for more than an hour.

Warmly welcomed by Auntie Maude and the children, Angela enjoyed every minute of her visit. She found herself particularly attracted to the younger children. She had brought baskets of fruit with her from the estate and the little ones sat in a circle about her and joyously munched on peaches and apples as she told them stories.

Too soon the hour was up and Angela was forced to take her leave, the children holding onto her skirts and begging her to stay "only a little while longer."

She was stepping out the front door when she caught sight of Gerald Waybridge crossing the courtyard toward her. His eyes lit up at the sight of her.

"You *did* come," he smiled, meeting her at the bottom of the steps. "I hoped you would."

They stood gazing at each other for a long moment until Gerald broke the spell. "The children must have been delighted to see you," he managed.

"Auntie Maude told me everyone is so busy here there is no one to spend time with them alone."

"That is what they need," he said eagerly. "Someone like yourself to make them feel that they matter in the world, that they are wanted."

"Perhaps we all need that," Angela said, a little sadly.

"Oh, my dear," his voice lowered, "you know I long to—"

She stopped him, taking a step back from him, "I am pledged to another, Gerald."

Another who is imprisoned in the Tower for murder, he wanted to say to her, but he dared not upset her. Elizabeth had warned him.

"Just remember that I am always here if you should ever need me, Angela," he reminded her. "I love you."

"Pray don't—" she began, her eyes filling with tears. "I will not be able to come here unless we both . . ."

"Forgive me," he said, his eyes imploring. He held out his arm to her. "May I help you to your coach?"

Angela dined with her father that evening and he was delighted to find her more animated than he had ever seen her before. She talked about the children and the orphanage and all she wished to do to help. Did he think the older children might be taught to read and to cipher? It would surely serve to improve their lot later in life.

His Lordship smiled indulgently at his daughter and patiently listened to all she had to say. He agreed to add his financial assistance where improvements were warranted, but warned her that she must be careful not to spoil the children.

"Love never spoiled anyone," Angela murmured and then her lips began to tremble. "I miss Elizabeth already. Did she say when she would return?"

"She should not be away for long," he assured her. "Now, I think it time for you to seek your bed. 'Tis been a long day and you still are not very strong."

His Lordship was wakened in the middle of the night by an ear-splitting scream. He jumped from his bed, realizing that the sound had come from the direction of Angela's bedchamber.

Bursting into the room, Westbury found Mistress Logan striving to pinion Angela's flailing arms to her sides and get her back to bed. The girl's face was contorted, her eyes glazed and staring.

"I pushed him! I pushed him!" she cried. "He was evil and vile and I killed him! I killed him!"

Between the two of them, the nurse and His Lordship managed to get Angela back into bed, but she was trembling all over now, cowering back against the headboard.

"Milady should never have gone out today," Mistress Logan said reprovingly. "It has made her much worse."

"She has had a bad dream, mistress, nothing more."

"She had that same dream often in the beginning, but she was getting better. Surely, milord, you saw that for yourself."

"The Lady Elizabeth did much to help her."

"Aye, until she insisted my lady leave her room. The poor lamb wasn't ready, milord."

The Earl nodded sadly. Angela had seemed so much better today. What had happened to make her regress?

Angela did not leave her room the next day or the day after and each night her nightmares seemed to return. When His Lordship visited her she hardly seemed to recognize him. She lay in the shadowed room with blank, staring eyes, not seeming to care about anything or anyone around her. Only Mistress Logan appeared able to communicate with her.

Gerald Waybridge rode over on the third day to inquire after Angela. The children had been so disappointed that she hadn't returned, he told His Lordship.

"The visit to the orphanage was too much for her," the Earl said coldly. "I don't know what happened, Waybridge, but she grew much worse afterwards." He shook his head. "That damned orphanage! I wish she had never heard of it."

Waybridge looked puzzled. "But I don't see how her visit . . . Could I not . . . Could I not see her, Your Lordship, just for a moment?"

"See her!" the Earl exploded. "Haven't you done enough harm? Get out of here, Waybridge and don't come back. I don't want to see you or that Bedloe woman around Neville Hall again!"

Elizabeth arrived home in the late afternoon. His Lordship, hearing the noise in the courtyard, rushed out to meet her himself. He took Elizabeth's hands in his and searched her face.

"Claridge is not . . . ?"

"Nay, Papa. He will be joining us in a few days. He was released on my evidence."

"Your evidence?" He looked astonished.

"I will tell you about it over supper, but — " She frowned, seeing how weary and anxious he looked. "Is it Angela? Has something happened to her?"

Entering the house, the Earl told Elizabeth in as few words as possible what had happened in her absence.

" 'Tis my fault, isn't it? Angela was upset by my leaving so precipitantly."

"She was naturally upset, but I assured her you would return soon. I did not tell her, but I supposed your trip to London had something to do with Claridge. Did you not trust me to let you go?"

"I did not know if you would understand what I had to do."

He smiled at her. "I am not unaware of your impulsiveness."

"But I sincerely regret it if it has harmed Angela."

"Nay, 'twas not that so much as her visit to the orphanage."

"You let her go?" Elizabeth looked pleased.

"It was a mistake," he said tightly. "She was much worse afterwards."

Surprise showed on Elizabeth's face. "I was so sure being with the children would help her."

"She has had nightmares every night since."

"How very strange . . ."

"Mistress Logan says it may take months before she is back to where she was before. It was a mistake. A grievous mistake to let her leave her room and this house."

* * *

Elizabeth was shown to her old room and after changing from her travelling clothes and freshening herself, she joined her father for supper in the dining hall.

As the meal progressed, His Lordship learned from Elizabeth all that had happened at the trial and how she had impersonated her sister in order to free Claridge. She went on to tell him of Lady Quillby and Lord Ramsden's plan and what Lord Musgrove had discovered about the murder, but she did not tell him of her abduction. She did not wish to upset him when he was so clearly concerned about Angela.

"So Angela inadvertantly *did* commit the crime," he affirmed.

"It was an accident, Papa, and not her fault. Ramsden was a dreadful man and she was only protecting herself from his advances by pushing him away from her. Still," Elizabeth said, "I believe in Angela's mind she is totally convinced she is to blame for his death. The guilt weighs heavily upon her."

He nodded. "She is having dreadful nightmares. Waking in the night screaming aloud about pushing and killing him."

"She must be told what really happened," Elizabeth said firmly. "Only when she learns the truth will she become well again."

" 'Twill not be easy. She barely knows me these days. Just lies there in the dark room and — "

Elizabeth interrupted him. "Has Mistress Logan closed up the windows again? Made Angela remain in bed?"

"How could she not do so? Since the day she went to the orphanage, Angela has completely regressed."

"Most strange . . ." Elizabeth pondered. "Did you inquire from Mistress Bedloe if anything occurred while she was there?"

"I had no need to." The Earl's face darkened. "Waybridge had the gall to come here himself to inquire after her when she did not visit them again. I told him I blamed the orphanage and demanded he not set foot in Neville Hall again."

"That was hardly fair, Papa. Why, you said yourself earlier that Angela had dined with you that night and seemed happy and filled with ideas to help the children."

"She clearly exhausted herself. The excitement and the planning and the many things she need do to complete those plans . . . it was simply too much for her."

"I can't believe that. It makes no sense at all."

"Believe it, Elizabeth," her father said sternly. "You have not known your sister very long. Her constitution is very delicate and she has been through a great deal."

Elizabeth's eyes went to her father. She longed to say, "And I have not?", but she felt ashamed to be thinking of herself when she was so fortunate to be well and have Simon's love.

* * *

That night Elizabeth was awakened by a scream — a terrible, shrill sound in the quiet night. She started up, horror dawning on her as she realized it must have come from Angela's room.

A few minutes later she was before the door to her sister's bedchamber. Angela's maid stood outside, wringing her hands together. Elizabeth went past her and opened the door.

The room was lit by a candelabra that stood on the table by the canopied bed. In its light, Elizabeth could see that Mistress Logan was forcing her sister back against the pillows.

Suddenly Angela's struggling ceased and she lay still, wild-eyed, breathing heavily. She caught sight of Elizabeth approaching the bed.

"Who's that?" she hissed, pointing a trembling finger in her sister's direction.

"Don't you recognize me, Angela. I'm Elizabeth."

Angela's face immediately changed, recognition struggling with something else. "Don't come near me," she cried. "I'm evil! I'm a murderess!" There was anguish in the look she turned on her sister.

"You killed no one," Elizabeth said quietly. "You must believe that." She came closer to the bed and began to talk to her to reassure her. Her words seemed to calm Angela a little, until she said, " 'Tis going to be a lovely, sunny day tomorrow. Perhaps you and I could ride over to the orphanage and see the children."

"No!" Angela stiffened. "No! No!" she shrieked. "I must not see the children. I might harm them. I am evil! Can't you see that I am evil? Go away! Go away!"

"You'd best leave, milady," Mistress Logan said tightly. "Your coming has only upset her more."

"But, I only tried—"

"You must go," the woman said, rudely pushing Elizabeth toward the door.

With her hand on the latch, Elizabeth looked back and caught the smug smile Mistress Logan had not been able to suppress.

Chapter Thirty-one

Elizabeth confronted her father at his desk in the library the next morning.

"Papa, I must talk with you. I've been awake most of the night thinking on this."

"What is it, Elizabeth?" Westbury asked impatiently. He hated to be interrupted when he was going over his estate records.

"I believe the medication Mistress Logan is giving Angela is far too strong for her."

"What do you mean?" the Earl frowned. "All she is given is a posset at night to make her sleep."

"Which it does not seem to do, does it?"

"She sleeps, but when the nightmare comes, it forces her to wake. Afterwards, she sleeps the clock around."

"And don't you think that strange? I saw her last night. She was reliving the murder. Flailing out at things only she could see. Her eyes were so wild."

"Oh, my dear," her father set down his quill. "I tried to tell you last evening how she was. I don't even go to her room now when she cries out with her nightmares. Only Mistress Logan is able to handle her at such times. That woman is a God-send."

"Is she, Papa? I can't help but wonder . . ."

"You do not understand, Elizabeth," he sighed. "You haven't been here to see."

"Nevertheless, I've had a feeling about Mistress Logan from the very first. She seemed to be trying to keep Angela an invalid, so that she might remain here to nurse her. 'Tis a comfortable position, Papa."

"Comfortable! That poor woman is up every night with Angela and her wild dreams."

"But then, as you say, Angela sleeps the clock around. With the hours of sleep before she wakens in the middle of the night, I would judge Angela slumbers at least sixteen hours a day! Mistress Logan has, therefore, much time to herself, a good roof over her head and three meals a day. 'Tis a very comfortable position, Papa!"

His Lordship stared hard at his daughter. "How can you think such a thing? I cannot believe this of you, Elizabeth. I realize because of unfortunate circumstances in your life you have come in contact with unscrupulous people, but—"

"The gypsy I lived with taught me a great deal about healing herbs and plants," Elizabeth went on, ignoring his outburst. "She also warned me of other plants. Plants that are poison or if ingested can affect the mind in strange ways."

"A witch! That's what the woman was. I will not have you speaking of such things in this house, Elizabeth. You must forget that part of your life. 'Tis all over now." His voice softened. "You seemed to help Angela before. Perhaps you can again. But remember, others are trying to help her, too, and I believe Mistress Logan most of all. For your sister's sake, try to work with her, not against her, to make Angela well."

Elizabeth could not agree with her father. All her instincts told her otherwise. Later that morning, anxious to see her sister when Mistress Logan was not about, she waited behind a half open door until she saw the nurse leave Angela's bedchamber for her noon meal. As the woman disappeared in the direction of the servant's stairway, Elizabeth stepped out into the corridor and opened the door to her sister's room.

Angela, she found, was not alone. Nan, her maid, was sitting beside her bed.

"Good morning," Elizabeth said pleasantly as she entered the room. "Is my sister still asleep?"

"Aye," the girl said. "She never wakes before two o'clock. I sit with her while Mistress Logan has her meal."

"I will sit with her today," Elizabeth smiled at

her. "I'm sure there are things you would like to do."

"Oh, would ye?" the maid's eyes lit up. "I would love to get out in the open air. I haven't been outside for so long."

"Of course. 'Tis a lovely day. Go ahead."

"You don't think Mistress Logan would object?"

"We won't tell her," Elizabeth smiled conspiratorally. "She won't spy you if you walk behind the yew hedge."

The maid was gone in a moment and Elizabeth moved over to the windows and drew back the hangings, letting in the noon sunshine. She returned to the bed and sat down in the chair which Nan had vacated.

A beam of sunlight shone on Angela's pillow and as Elizabeth watched, she moved her head slightly, the sunlight bathing her pale face. Angela's eyes opened and she blinked them, covering them quickly with one hand.

" 'Tis so bright," she murmured.

"A lovely autumn day," Elizabeth said, closing the curtains a little around the bed.

Angela again opened her eyes and this time regarded her sister. No sign of recognition crossed her face.

"I would like to go out in the dog cart today," she said, in the voice of a mistress to her servant.

"That would be nice," Elizabeth agreed. "The leaves are so pretty just now, every shade of red and gold and—"

"We will go along the river road to the place where we stopped before." Suddenly Angela appeared agitated. "But you must not tell Papa. Promise me, Jenny, you won't tell my father."

"Of course I won't."

Angela seemed to relax a little. "Gerald will be there to meet me." A sweet smile came to her lips, but the blue eyes seemed blank, unseeing.

Elizabeth's heart turned over. It appeared that Angela had slipped back to a happier time in her life.

"Gerald loves me," she murmured. Her hands fluttered slightly, as if trying to grasp something and Elizabeth leaned over and took them in her own.

"Aye, he loves you very much," she said.

"Gerald said he would ask Papa for my hand if I were not promised to another."

Elizabeth held her hands more tightly. "Look at me, Angela. Turn your head and look at me."

"Who are you?"

"Your sister, Elizabeth."

"I have no sister. I only have Papa."

"But what of Gerald?"

"I cannot wed him. I am pledged to His Grace of Claridge, yet I have never met him."

"*I* have met him, Angela, and I have fallen in love with him," Elizabeth said. "Will you let me marry him in your stead? Then you would be free to marry your Gerald."

Angela shook her head. "Papa would never allow you to marry him, Jenny."

"Oh, my dear," Elizabeth's eyes filled with tears. "I am not Jenny. I am Elizabeth."

But Angela had closed her eyes again.

When Nan returned, Elizabeth conferred with her a moment and then went back to her room and changed into her riding clothes.

She was soon on the back of the mare she had brought back with her from London and heading off toward the Manor House.

Told that Gerald Waybridge was out somewhere in his fields, she rode out in search of him.

The fields Elizabeth passed were filled with golden sheaves of grain and men were loading them onto carts to take back to the barns. She picked out Gerald Waybridge on horseback directing some of the loading and drew her horse up beside him.

"You seem to have harvested a good crop," she said.

"Elizabeth?" he exclaimed, his tanned face breaking into a smile. "When did you return?"

"Just yesterday. I think we must talk, Gerald."

He led her over to some shade trees that bordered the field. "What has happened to Angela?" his voice was anxious. "Your father would not let me see her and I've been beside myself with worry."

Elizabeth told him about Angela's worsening condition. "I do not believe for a moment that visiting the orphanage caused her to regress," she said. "Papa, himself, told me that Angela was so happy afterwards, planning what she could do to help the children."

"Then, what could have happened?"

"I know nothing for sure, Gerald, but I must tell you that I've never trusted Mistress Logan, Angela's nurse. I think that seeing her patient well on the road to recovery upset her greatly. Soon her services would no longer be required. Her position at Neville Hall is a good one. She didn't want to leave," Elizabeth's eyes flashed, "so out of desperation she decided to make sure that that would not happen."

Gerald grasped her arm. "Are you saying that she is doing something to Angela?"

"As I said, I have no evidence, only a hunch. Mistress Logan was already making up a posset to help Angela sleep. Could she not have obtained other substances — ones to make her confused and bring back her nightmares?"

"But Elizabeth, it seems so monstrous . . ."

"I have inquired of the servants. Mistress Logan makes her sleeping potions in a small stillroom in the cellar. I went there, hoping I might find some proof to support my suspicions, but the door was locked and apparently Mistress Logan has the only key."

"Have you spoken of this to your father?"

Elizabeth sighed. "He refused to believe me."

"There must be some way we can prove . . ."

"I have turned it over and over in my mind. There *is* a way, but I will need your help."

"You have it, of course."

"Come to the Hall this evening. I will instruct my maid to let you in at the north door about nine o'clock. That door is seldom used and from there you can make your way upstairs by a back staircase."

"And then?"

Elizabeth told him the rest of her plan and he smiled in agreement.

"It just may work."

"It *has* to work, Gerald. It has to."

The plan went off well, despite the necessity of involving not only Elizabeth's maid, Maggie, but Angela's Nan, to help them.

Elizabeth, feigning a headache, retired early to her bedchamber. At a little after nine o'clock, Maggie slipped Gerald into her room. He remained with her until ten o'clock when, as was Mistress Logan's habit, she went downstairs to the kitchen for her evening cup of chocolate.

Nan, left in charge, quickly undressed the sleeping Angela, putting her in another nightdress. When Gerald entered moments later with Elizabeth, he gently picked up the sleeping girl and carried her back to Elizabeth's room to bed.

Elizabeth, after closing the door behind him, slipped into Angela's discarded nightdress and climbed into the empty bed. Nan mussed up her hair to resemble Angela's tangled locks and even added a little rice powder to her cheeks to make them appear more palid. Then she sat down by the bed to await Mistress Logan's return.

An hour later, with a sign from Nan, Elizabeth closed her eyes. She heard someone enter the room and felt Nan's hand squeeze hers as the maid left her side.

Elizabeth lay absolutely still, feigning sleep, her breathing as even as she could make it. It was not easy. She was desperately afraid that with her eyes closed, she might really fall asleep and she knew it was essential to her plan that she remain awake and alert.

The time seemed to crawl by. Elizabeth could hear the click of Mistress Logan's needles as she sat knitting by the bed. It must be close to midnight, she thought. It had been about two o'clock in the morning when she had been wakened the night before by Angela's screams. How long before that had Mistress Logan administered the mind-affecting dose?

She heard a noise beside her, as a chair scraped back and then she sensed the woman bending over her.

"Not a movement yet and not a word," the woman muttered. "You sleep well tonight, milady."

The chair creaked as she sat down again.

"You showed that prying sister of yours last night, you did. Scared her out of her wits," the nurse chuckled. "Me thinks there'll be no more trouble there."

Safe in Elizabeth's bed, Angela let out a moan. Gerald drew his chair closer, reaching out to take her hand.

" 'Tis all right, Angela. I'm here. I won't leave your side," he soothed, talking to her softly, repeating words of comfort and affection to her.

It was a little after midnight when she awoke.

"Gerald," she breathed, as her eyes focused on him. "I'm so glad 'tis a nice dream this time."

"I'm no dream, my dear. I'm quite real. Elizabeth asked me to come."

Angela raised her head from the pillows and looked around her. "This is not my room," she said agitatedly, her eyes darting about.

"Hush now! Don't be alarmed. You are in Elizabeth's bed."

"Elizabeth? Has she come back?"

"Aye, last night."

Angela let out a sigh of relief. "I'm so glad. Everything has been so confused since she left and so . . ." she trembled, ". . . so frightening. I've seen such terrible things. Were they real, Gerald? Were they real?"

"No, my dear. You have been suffering from

visions. That is all over now."

"Over," she repeated. "All over." She collapsed back against her pillows. "Could I have something to drink, Gerald. I feel so very thirsty."

Elizabeth's maid, Maggie, poured out a glass of water for her from a jug on the nightstand and handed it to Gerald. He lifted Angela's head and she was able to swallow a little.

"I want you to go back to sleep now," he said. "I'll still be here when you awaken."

"But I do not feel at all sleepy."

"Then we will talk. There is much to tell you, but tonight, I think, we will only talk of ourselves."

"I love you very much, Gerald," Angela whispered.

He swallowed over the lump in his throat. She looked so frail and defenseless.

"And I love you. Everything is going to be all right from now on. You will never again have to do anything you do not wish to do. I will see to that."

Elizabeth felt someone shaking her by the shoulder. Had she dozed off? She fluttered open her eyes to see Mistress Logan staring down at her, her steel-gray eyes seeming to pierce right through her.

"Are you awake, Missy?"

"Y—yes," she managed in a weak voice.

"You have slept longer than usual."

"Have I?" Elizabeth was unsure of how she should be acting. Should she be dazed or wide awake?

"It be time for your tonic," the nurse said, bringing out a small, corked bottle from the pocket of her apron.

"I don't want it," Elizabeth turned her head away.

"Nonsense," Mistress Logan frowned. "You know you fancy the peppermint taste."

"Not tonight. Take it away."

"Now. Now. It be only a wee dose you need." The nurse poured a small amount from the bottle into a glass and set the bottle down on the table by the bed, holding the glass out to Elizabeth.

"Drink it down like a good girl."

"No!" Suddenly Elizabeth thrust out her hand and sent the glass sailing across the room.

"Why, you little—" Mistress Logan gave a sharp retort as she grasped Elizabeth's hand and gave her wrist a painful twist.

"You'll take what I give you or you'll be sorry."

"I think not, mistress," Elizabeth said, but her words were unnecessary. The nurse was staring open-mouthed at Elizabeth's palm, seeing the vivid birthmark, realizing the significance of it.

"You . . ." she began, fear flaring up in her eyes as she dropped Elizabeth's hand on the coverlet.

"Aye, I am not Angela. I am her sister." Elizabeth reached across the bed and grabbed the

436

bottle from the nightstand. "I think this will be sufficient evidence of what you have been doing."

Mistress Logan seemed to crumple before Elizabeth's eyes. She began to sob.

"I only wanted to stay here. I was so weary of nursing the old and dying. She was young. She would have lived a long time."

"As a madwoman!" You were driving her out of her mind with your concoctions!" Elizabeth accused her, feeling no sympathy for the woman who had almost destroyed her sister's life.

She rose to her feet beside the sobbing form of the nurse. "Didn't you care for her at all? Didn't you feel the least guilt at what you were doing?"

The sobbing only increased in volume.

Elizabeth could still hear it behind her as she opened the door and walked down the corridor in the direction of her father's apartments.

Epilogue

Elizabeth and Simon strolled along the secluded path that led through the gardens behind Neville Hall. On one side was a high hedge that prevented them from being seen from the house, on the other, the fragrant, well-designed gardens.

Simon stopped a moment, his arm about Elizabeth's waist as he surveyed the pleasant scene before them.

"I've been so involved with the rebuilding of Claridge House, I completely forgot that new gardens must be laid out."

"Would you allow me to help with their design?" Elizabeth asked. "My mother taught me much about growing things, and when I was with Marta, I learned more about rare plants and herbs. You may laugh at me," she looked up at him from beneath her long lashes, "but ever since I was small, I've dreamed of obtaining plants and seeds from botanists all over the world and trying to grow them in English soil."

"That is nothing to ridicule. I hereby grant you free reign to do with my gardens as you will," he said solemnly, though his eyes gazed fondly down at her.

"Then you wish me to go with you to Claridge House?" He still had said nothing of marriage, although, she had to admit, he had arrived only a few hours before.

"I already have a surprise waiting for you there," he smiled, thinking of the chestnut filly he'd sent on from London.

"You have? I love surprises." She looked like a child as she returned his smile.

"And parties. I remember how much you enjoyed the king's ball. I must warn you that life at Claridge House is very quiet just now. The house is not yet ready for entertaining, so do not expect a very social life."

"You think that matters to me? Sometimes I don't believe you know me very well, Simon."

"I've had very little time to do so," he admonished.

They walked on a little further to where a marble bench stood against the garden wall, in the shade of an ancient cedar of Lebanon. The tree was scarred and broken by the centuries, but still vigorous and throwing wide its branches of clustering spikes as it had done for the previous five hundred years.

Noticing Simon viewing it, Elizabeth said, "The seed was probably brought from Syria by one of the returning Crusaders."

They sat down on the bench beneath it and for a moment did not speak, caught up in the beauty all around them. Then, Elizabeth sat forward.

"Look at them," she said quietly, pointing through a hole in the hedge where Angela and Gerald could be seen walking hand and hand across the lawn below them.

"Is your father allowing Waybridge to court her?"

Elizabeth smiled. "He has said nothing, but at least he is not opposing it. He seems more kindly disposed to Gerald since he has helped Angela so much. I believe he may be mellowing. He even apologized to me for doubting my suspicions about Mistress Logan. Under all that bluster, Simon, he truly loves us both and wants us to be happy."

"I spoke with Angela after I arrived. She seemed to understand much that had happened."

"That is solely Gerald's doing. He is so patient and loving with her. He is hoping she will soon overcome her guilt and accept what happened to Ramsden, but he is not rushing her. He only answers her questions as she asks them. He is a fine man."

"And will make her a good husband. You

should know that I released Angela from our betrothal. Your father was present at the time and afterwards, I asked his permission to speak to you."

"How correct of you," she said, suppressing a smile.

"I suppose to do it properly," he went on, "I must go down on one knee, so."

She stared at him dumbfounded, remembering how he had vowed in the Privy Garden never to do such a thing. Never, in her wildest dreams had she thought to bring the arrogant Duke of Claridge to his knees before her.

"I'm not very good at poetry, so I will simply say that I love you and have loved you since first we met," he said, gazing up at her. "I adore you for your courage, your beauty, your selflessness and I want only to protect and cherish you for the rest of my life. Will you marry me, Beth?"

"I would love to marry you," she whispered, her heart beating so wildly she thought it might burst from her breast, "but . . . Oh, Simon, I must warn you that I will not be as complacent a wife as my sister. I am not someone you can mold, if that is what you are wanting. You cannot train me like a recruit in the army to go weak in the knees every time you appear."

Claridge laughed aloud. "I am well aware of that, my love. But speaking of going weak in the knees . . ."

"Do get up," she laughed, giving him her hand.

"Beth, I know you have been forced to be self-reliant for a long time," he said, seating himself beside her again. "But a wife who clung to my every word and obeyed my every wish would only bore me. What I need is a true wife and helpmate. Someone to challenge my decisions, if she disagrees with them. Someone to work by my side, not sit meekly in the drawing room and expect to be pampered and spoiled like one of His Majesty's spaniels."

"Needlework and flower arranging would never be enough for me."

"I'm quite aware of that," he grinned. "Still, I must have your promise that you will not run away from me again. I'm decidedly weary of that."

"I promise never to leave your side," she whispered.

His thumb caressed her cheek. "We will have to return to court from time to time."

"I know that and it will be difficult for me to hold my peace. I've seen too many wrongs that need to be righted. Tiny urchins begging for food in the streets, disease-bearing filth and squalid slums. Slave ships ... Oh, Simon, how can men make fortunes selling human beings?"

"A filthy business," he agreed. "England would be well rid of it and yet even the king himself has chartered a slaving company for the trade in blacks."

"Then I will speak to him myself," Elizabeth

said resolutely. She searched his face. "If you think my tongue will hurt you at court, you'd best not marry me."

He grinned down at her. "Surely you know by now that I don't care that—" he snapped his fingers, "—for the court."

"Still, there are many who look up to you. I saw that at the trial."

"Then, perhaps, you and I can influence some of them. We may not be able to cure all the wrongs of the world, my sweet, but we'll do what we can together."

"Together," she repeated, smiling up at him. "What a lovely word."

There were more things Elizabeth wished to say to him, more questions she wished to ask. But suddenly they ceased to matter. It was only the man at her side who mattered.

Simon was gazing down at her with the brooding look that desire always brought to his face, his smokey eyes making love to her.

"You look so incredibly beautiful with the last rays of the sun forming a glow about you. During those long weeks in prison, I dreamed of being with you like this, dreamed I made love to you again and again."

"Come," she said simply, slipping her small hand into his big one. She led him to a small pavilion at the end of the garden, quite hidden by climbing vines. "You need dream of it no longer, Simon," she murmured, her arms going about his neck.

In the green-scented beauty of this private spot, they reaffirmed their love for one another. A love that had overcome every obstacle to bring them together forever.

MORE BLAZING ROMANCES
From Zebra Books

FRONTIER FLAME   (1965, $3.95)
by Rochelle Wayne

When her cousin deserted the army, spirited Suzanne Donovan knew that she had to go and get him back. But once the luscious blonde confronted towering Major Blade Landon, she wished she'd never left home. The lean, muscled officer seemed as wild as the land — and made her think only of the rapture his touch could bring!

ARIZONA TEMPTRESS   (1785, $3.95)
by Bobbi Smith

Rick Peralta found the freedom he craved only in his disguise as El Cazador. Then he saw the alluring Jennie mcCaine among his compadres and swore she'd belong just to him. When he left his lawless life, he'd leave the enticing captive behind . . . but until then the hot-blooded Rick would have all of his needs fulfilled by his provocative ARIZONA TEMPTRESS.

PRAIRIE EMBRACE   (2035, $3.95)
by F. Rosanne Bittner

Katie Russell was shocked by her passionate reaction to her bronze-skinned, jet-haired Indian captor. The gorgeous pioneer reminded herself that he was a savage heathen and beneath her regard, but deep inside she knew she longed to yield to the ecstasy of his PRAIRIE EMBRACE.

PIRATE'S CONQUEST   (2036, $3.95)
by Mary Martin

Starlin Cambridge always scoffed that the ruthless pirate Scorpio would never capture her sleek, treasure-laden ship. But one day, the notorious outlaw overtook her vessel—and kidnapped its raven-haired owner. Furious that the muscular marauder has taken her freedom, Starlin is shocked when she longs for him to take her innocence as well!

MEMENTO   (2037, $3.95)
by Eleanora Brownleigh

Just one chance encounter with the compelling Gregory West settles Katherine's mind: she knows he is the man for her, even if it means forsaking her rich and comfortable New York City home to travel across the uncivilized continent,. And though the dark secrets of the past ruled out marriage for Gregory, nothing could stop him from savoring Katherine's whole body for a brief, intense fling that would forever be this most cherished MEMENTO.

Available wherever paperbacks are sold, or order direct from the Publisher. Send cover price plus 50¢ per copy for mailing and handling to Zebra Books, Dept. 2150, 475 Park Avenue South, New York, N.Y. 10016. Residents of New York, New Jersey and Pennsylvania must include sales tax. DO NOT SEND CASH.

Now you can get more of HEARTFIRE right at home and $ave.

Preview
Four Brand New
ZEBRA
Heartfire
Romance Novels...

FREE for 10 days.

No Obligation and No Strings Attached!

Enjoy all of the passion and fiery romance as you soar back through history, right in the comfort of your own home.

Now that you have read a Zebra HEARTFIRE Romance novel, we're sure you'll agree that HEARTFIRE sets new standards of excellence for historical romantic fiction. Each Zebra HEARTFIRE novel is the ultimate blend of intimate romance and grand adventure and each takes place in the kinds of historical settings you want most...the American Revolution, the Old West, Civil War and more.

<u>FREE</u> Preview Each Month and $ave

Zebra has made arrangements for you to preview 4 brand new HEARTFIRE novels each month…FREE for 10 days. You'll get them as soon as they are published. If you are not delighted with any of them, just return them with no questions asked. But if you decide these are everything we said they are, you'll pay just $3.25 each— a total of $13.00 (a $15.00 value). **That's a $2.00 saving each month off the regular price.** Plus there is NO shipping or handling charge. These are delivered right to your door absolutely free! There is no obligation and there is no minimum number of books to buy.

TO GET YOUR FIRST MONTH'S PREVIEW… Mail the Coupon Below!